Dr. Nicole Légende and Dr. Drew Tower.

They both had pasts shadowed by painful memories
of lost love. But now in India during the smallpox
epidemic, they found each other—and love—as
they struggled to save the lives of others, in a place
of constant medical crises . . . and as they
surrendered with explosive passion to the long
dormant hungers within them

Theirs was a love that would be tested by time and
distance. for each had a destiny they were
determined to achieve—destinies they could only
achieve alone.

But in between past and future, in a world of danger
and intrigue, Nicole and Drew had each other—as
they lived a lifetime's worth of dreams and desires
for the moment. . . .

CATCH THE WIND

"A colorful, first-rate saga . . . a dramatic, affecting
love story." —*Deltona Enterprise*

CATCH the WIND

HARRIET SEGAL

A SIGNET BOOK

NEW AMERICAN LIBRARY

SIGNET TRADEMARK REG. U.S. PAT. OFF. AND FOREIGN COUNTRIES
REGISTERED TRADEMARK—MARCA REGISTRADA
HECHO EN CHICAGO, U.S.A.

SIGNET, SIGNET CLASSIC, MENTOR, ONYX, PLUME, MERIDIAN
and NAL BOOKS are published by NAL PENGUIN INC.,
1633 Broadway, New York, New York 10019

First Signet Printing, February, 1988

1 2 3 4 5 6 7 8 9

PRINTED IN THE UNITED STATES OF AMERICA

For Amy, Jennifer, and Laura
and always, for Sheldon . . .
my flowers of the wind

H.S.

Contents

Author's Note

This is a story and all of its characters are products of the imagination. They are not based on, nor meant to represent, any actual person.

Certain international events and personalities referred to are real and matters of public record. The global eradication of smallpox, a landmark achievement in the field of world health, is one of the most exciting chapters in medical history, occurring within the past decade in October 1977. Similarly, the political upheavals in Peru from 1968 to 1980 are recorded fact, part of the continuing unrest in that troubled nation. In using these as background for this tale, every attempt has been made to maintain historical accuracy. For purposes of fiction, places and episodes have been invented.

I am indebted to many individuals and institutions who assisted me in gathering information for this novel. I was graciously received and helped in my research by staff members at the Centers for Disease Control in Atlanta, Georgia, and at the headquarters of the World Health Organization in Geneva, Switzerland. The Press and Information Service of the French Embassy and the Peruvian Tourist Office, both in New York, furnished me with valuable material, as did a number of other organizations and people who wish to remain anonymous. In all cases, they have my gratitude.

I am grateful to my Doubleday editor, Carolyn Blakemore, for her professional guidance and encouragement.

Most of all, I wish to thank my husband, Sheldon, for the inspiration only he can provide, and for his belief and understanding.

Harriet Segal

November 1986

PROLOGUE

On a moonless summer night in December 1939 a Portuguese freighter steamed north in the Pacific Ocean off the coast of Peru. The *Bianca*'s last port of call, Callao, lay 150 miles to the south.

Suddenly the vessel veered sharply to starboard, running on an easterly course, until it came within a mile of the shoreline, an uninhabited stretch of desert as desolate and cratered as the moon.

Her engines brought to idle speed, the ship remained in position while a small boat was lowered and rowed to shore. When the bow scraped rocky sand, three men jumped into the surf and waded to the beach. They waved as the lifeboat disappeared in the darkness and kept watch until the lights of the *Bianca* had been swallowed by the night.

With the ship went their last link to everything they had ever known . . . families, homes, France.

Windswept and barren, the coastal wasteland offered no shelter to the three travelers. Daniel's companions looked to him for guidance, as they had throughout the long, discouraging voyage from Lisbon to the Azores, and across the Atlantic to South America.

They were the doves sent out by their families in search of a haven from the Nazis. A dangerous mission, but one that had been repeated by their people many times, for had the Jews not been searching for refuge throughout their long history?

After bribing their way across borders, they had reached Lisbon to find it crowded with the displaced. Long lines at the embassies of the American nations were filled with desperate men and women. Leaving his two friends at the consular office of Canada, Daniel roamed the docks, and there found the *Bianca,* bound for South America.

1

The captain had not deceived them. Without visas he could not guarantee that any country would admit them. Yes, other ships had carried refugees to Ecuador, to Chile, and to Colombia, but he had no such personal experience. How it was done without the proper papers, he could not say. He was willing to take them as passengers on the *Bianca*, but he would not deviate from his schedule by even one port of call, and they must understand that.

Daniel thought the captain was honest. At least he was not making any false promises. Benjamin and Marcel, Daniel's friends from the small town of La Prée, agreed that if he was willing to trust the captain, so were they. They paid their passage, boarded the *Bianca*, and stowed their few belongings in the cabin they would share for the next six weeks.

Port after port refused them entry. Port-of-Spain, Georgetown, Cayenne. Recife, Salvador, Rio. At Montevideo they had some hope when their case was referred to a higher official, but in the end it was the same. Without visas, they could not be given landing permits.

The *Bianca* sailed through the Strait of Magellan and up the long coast of Chile, discharging and taking on cargo. Finally they docked at Callao, the port of Lima, depositing the last of their European cargo.

The Peruvian officials were polite, attentive to their request for asylum, even encouraging. The captain delayed his departure waiting for the permissions, but after hours of hope they were turned away. Only the approved quota of fleeing Europeans may enter Peru, they were told. There were long waiting lists in all the capitals of Europe. For these three, the door was closed.

"It's such a big continent, you would think a few more people wouldn't matter to them," said Daniel.

The captain shrugged. "These countries don't want to be flooded with refugees. They're afraid to anger the Germans." He showed no emotion, yet Daniel sensed he was sympathetic. Just taking them on as passengers had been an act of compassion.

Daniel returned to the cabin to report the bad news.

"What about Panama?" asked Marcel.

"Not a chance," replied Daniel. "We only stop to refuel there and it will be under the eyes of the American military. They're not letting that many Jews into the United States, so it's doubtful they would give us landing papers in the Canal Zone. I'm afraid it's back to Europe." They gazed at one another in despair.

They left Callao near dusk, sailing within sight of the shore. It was already dark when the captain came to them with a plan.

"Your best hope is to cross the desert at night," the captain told them, spreading a chart on the table. "Once you get into the mountains, you can probably stay for a while in one of the market towns. The Indians are harmless and not too curious."

Daniel studied the weathered face as the captain turned the map. He had been right about this man.

They headed inland across the coastal desert, guided by the stars. In the first hour they covered a fair distance but soon began losing the spurt of energy fueled by sudden exertion after so many weeks of inactivity.

The captain had been generous in supplying them from the ship's stores, but they were limited by the amount a man could carry. Each had a blanket, tins of sardines and biscuits, a water bottle, matches, and selected clothing from his luggage.

In the pre-dawn light they could see the mist-shrouded foothills on the horizon. Before the sun was high, they found a cluster of boulders surrounded by scrub. Here they made the first rest stop, shading themselves and sleeping through the hottest hours of the day. It was late afternoon when they set out toward the mountains, turned a deep mauve by the slanting rays of the setting sun.

They walked south in search of one of the rivers that flow toward the ocean from high in the Andes. Soon they came to the stream whose course would be their path through the coastal range. As the trail grew steeper, the river ran with greater force. They bathed, standing on a rocky ledge under a foamy waterfall, drinking the glacial water in great gulps, not minding its metallic taste.

Now that they were in the mountains, they would walk by day and sleep at night.

On the fifth day their troubles began.

Marcel became ill with fever, chills, and dysentery. He

had continued to drink the river water after Daniel maintained they should first boil it.

Their food supply was dwindling. Daniel and Benjamin foraged for edible plants, but the mountains were almost as arid and infertile as the desert. Except for some berries growing at the river's edge, they found little to sustain them. Daniel cut a branch and began sharpening the point to make a spear. There were fish in the stream, birds and small animals. That night they ate wild hare.

By the afternoon of the seventh day, Benjamin was sick. As Daniel tried to help his friends, he felt the first cramping pains in his own intestines and the nausea that sapped his strength.

On the ninth day, Marcel died. With Benjamin too ill to help bury him, Daniel attempted to dig a grave, but after three hours he had succeeded in scooping out only a shallow hole in the unyielding rocky soil.

This was how the four *campesinos* from Huaranca found them. In their makeshift camp on the harsh mountainous terrain, with Marcel's body wrapped in a blanket shroud and Benjamin staring wordlessly, awaiting death.

Daniel rose unsteadily to his feet as the four peasants in woolen ponchos rode up on donkeys. He spoke to them in fragments of the Spanish he remembered from his school days, his voice hoarse and weak. Where had they come from, the *campesinos* asked. From the sea, he waved a vague hand to the west. Where were they going? To a place where they could find shelter.

The *campesinos* shared food and water with the sick men. They dug a grave for Marcel. When one of them fashioned a cross out of sticks, Daniel stopped him and drew a diagram in the dirt, a six-pointed star, explaining that they were Jews and for them the cross was not holy. To the Indians it made no difference, for Christianity was largely a ceremonial veneer superimposed on their true beliefs, which had more to do with the old mountain gods and animal spirits than the formal religion of the Church.

The Indians put Benjamin in a sling tied to their pack animal. For a while Daniel was able to ride, but soon he swayed and would have fallen from the donkey if they had not caught him.

They spent the night in a village of nine adobe huts

where they found a shaman who exorcised the evil spirits from the sick men. By early light, Benjamin was also dead.

Again the *campesinos* dug a grave, and this time they lashed together some sticks in the form of a six-pointed star, explaining to the villagers, with the sense of importance men gain from newly-acquired knowledge, that these were not Christians, but Hebrews, of whom the padre sometimes spoke.

No longer lucid, Daniel was unaware that his friend had died. The *campesinos* preferred to leave him there, but the people in the village feared the evil of the death spirits and wanted him gone. They tied him to the burro's back and continued on their way.

When they reached the gorge, Daniel had lost consciousness. He had no impression of the sharp descent from the rocky ridge to the deep sheltered valley, no sense of the green hills as they approached the village of Huaranca, no memory of passing under the old wrought iron gateway of the hacienda whose name was lost among the ornate vines of swirled metal . . . Flor del Viento.

BOOK I

Nicole

Chapter 1

Late on a Friday afternoon in July 1972, a battered taxicab halted at the emergency entrance of San Martín University Hospital.

The driver hurried to assist the two women passengers. The younger woman sagged in the arms of her companion and would have fallen if the driver had not caught her. Together they helped her to the door of the Emergencia.

The two women made their way directly to the reception desk, ignoring the waiting line. "Please, you must help her! She's bleeding. A heavy flow, a hemorrhage," the older woman said, her arms still supporting the patient, whose face was ashen and beaded with sweat.

When the receptionist did not look up, the woman pleaded, "She's too heavy for me. Can't you bring a litter? She must see a doctor immediately."

A stern-faced nurse who had been making an assessment of the crowded waiting room came to the desk. "You pushed ahead of the line," she accused the women. "Go wait your turn."

"But my sister is very ill. She's lost much blood. She'll die! *Please* get a doctor."

There was a sudden exclamation from the sick woman as a gush of blood ran down her legs, pooling on the floor. The people standing near her hurriedly moved aside.

"Out of here!" shouted the nurse, raising her hand in a threatening gesture. "How dare you bring us that . . . that *whore?*"

"No, no," protested the bleeding woman, her voice weak, eyes rolling in fear.

"Where is your mercy, señorita? Have God's mercy! She is a mother with seven children. She's a good woman."

9

The nurse put her hand to the sick woman's face. "She's burning with fever. *She's had an abortion!* Take her back to the abortionist."

The patient fell to the floor in a faint, her weight too much for her sister.

"Pick her up," said the nurse. "Take her away, I tell you. We don't admit evil women here."

A woman's voice, strong and authoritative, silenced her. "We admit *all* women, Nurse Ramos. And we don't make judgments about their characters."

The nurse turned to face Nicole Légende.

"But, *doctora,* this woman has committed a sin against God." Her eyes blazed at Nicole in self-righteous indignation.

"What difference does that make?" Nicole snapped. Her gold-flecked emerald eyes were unwavering under the arch of dark brows. Only the flaring of the delicate nostrils showed the effort she made to control her temper.

"Bring a stretcher," she ordered an attendant, moving toward the prostrate woman.

Everyone in the congested waiting room was watching intently as Nicole knelt beside the woman, feeling for her pulse. She raised the closed eyelids, noting the hot flesh.

Two orderlies lifted the patient onto a gurney. The angry nurse, having retreated to her office next to the waiting room, muttered under her breath as Nicole followed the stretcher down the corridor.

Despite her youth, the tall, slender woman doctor was a commanding presence. Jet black hair glistened in a severe knot at the nape of her neck. Her creamy skin and classic profile gave her an elegance that was not diminished by the mannish cut of her white hospital coat.

"Raise her feet," Nicole instructed the nurses, once they were in a treatment room. "We need a cross-match for blood transfusion."

She had difficulty drawing blood. "I can't get a vein! I'll have to do a cutdown. Hurry! We're going to lose her. . . ."

There was no time to call a surgeon. They rushed the patient into the emergency operating room. A young nun joined them. "You don't have to, Sister," Nicole told her, knowing it would be offensive to her.

"It's all right, Dr. Légende. I'll stay."

Nicole smiled gratefully. "Thank you. I really do need you."

For the next hour Nicole worked frantically to save the woman's life. By cutting into a vein deep in the leg, they were able to give her blood. It was necessary to perform a curettage to stop the uterine bleeding. How Nicole wished for the modern facilities of the hospital in Paris where she had been trained—for all the instruments and medicines, the laboratory and stored blood she had taken for granted when she was a medical student. At least we have penicillin here at San Martín, she thought, as she selected a curette from a tray of instruments.

Seven children! What would I do if I had seven children and found myself pregnant? How desperate the woman must have been, living in the *barriada,* that hideous slum. Whoever had performed this butchery had left part of the placenta in situ. No wonder she was bleeding out! A few more minutes and she would have died.

Nicole pulled off the surgical gloves and mask. She felt drained of energy as she watched the anesthetized woman being wheeled away.

An hour later, Nicole hurried out of the clinic. As she passed the administration office, she saw Mona Ramos at her desk. She paused and entered the room, closing the door behind her.

The head nurse looked up, a hostile light in her eyes. Her unpleasant manner and appearance were forbidding. For a moment, Nicole's resolve faltered. She sensed that this woman had not liked her from the first day she arrived at San Martín as an intern four years ago, but she was determined not to let it interfere with their working together.

Women often came to the hospital with complications from illegal abortions. The staff seemed to have a sixth sense about them. They were routinely ignored by the elevator operators, nurses, and sometimes even by doctors, so although it was true that Nurse Ramos was a fanatically religious woman, her attitude was not unusual. It had infuriated Nicole, however, and her quick reaction had caused the supervisor to lose face in front of

the watching staff and the people in the reception area
who were witnesses. Having handled it badly, she now
tried to make amends.

"I would have expected humaneness from you of all
people, Señorita Ramos. That woman has a pelvic infection. She would have bled to death without an immediate
transfusion and curettage, and left her seven living children motherless."

"That would be God's punishment," replied the nurse,
unbending.

Nicole shook her head. "Then I must believe that God
is more forgiving than you do," she retorted. "An emergency clinic is for the purpose of saving lives, not examining souls. We'll leave that to the priests."

She left the hospital without further conversation.

Behind the steering wheel of her Renault, Nicole realized
the encounter with the nurse had affected her more than
she cared to admit. It had always been difficult for her to
throw off the agitation she felt after an argument. It
would be best to put this behind her, to forget about it.
But she would have to deal with the clinic administrator
in the future—and Mona Ramos was known to bear a
grudge.

It was important to Nicole to get along well with all of
the hospital staff. As the youngest medical doctor and
the only woman ever to have been appointed a clinical
fellow under Professor Jorge Alvares, the Director of
Maternal and Child Health at San Martín University Hospital, she was conscious of the jealousies her role had
engendered.

As a rule, she took great pains to treat the other
residents and clinic workers with consideration and courtesy. She knew they believed Professor Alvares favored
her because of her family's influence, that her father's
money and power had secured her position in the department. They assumed that Alvares, who was himself a
member of one of Peru's leading families, had chosen her
not for her excellent training and ability, but because she
was the daughter of Daniel Légende.

To be honest, she had arranged the initial interview
with Professor Alvares through her father. But it was her

first-rate medical education at the University of Paris and the recommendation of her professor of pediatrics at Hôpital Necker des Enfants Malades that had prompted Alvares to grant her an internship at San Martín Hospital.

And it was her professional dedication, her long hours of extra work, and his belief in her ability that had caused Jorge Alvares to recommend her for a fellowship in the United States at the Center for Disease Control, the institution recognized around the world as the leader in epidemiology and public health. A year ago, when she had completed the training program in Atlanta and returned to Lima, Professor Alvares had made her his clinical fellow.

Nicole eased her way through the congestion of downtown Lima's late afternoon traffic. She had to visit a patient on her way home. That meant she was going to be late again for her date with Manuel.

He had been specific about the time for this evening. "Remember, Nicole, when the French ambassador invites us for nine o'clock, he doesn't mean midnight," he had told her in his chiding way.

Manuel Caldeiro-León never became angry with her, even if she kept him waiting for hours when she was delayed at the hospital. *Perhaps if he lost his temper once in a while, I'd find him more exciting!* Sometimes she had an urge to do or say something outrageous, just to see what his reaction would be.

Manuel wanted to marry her. He was so persistent in his attentions . . . even coming to Atlanta often during the two years she had studied in the States. He had been a constant presence in her life ever since they first met in Paris, four years ago, in the Place Vendôme headquarters of Légende et Cie, her father's international corporation. At the time, Manuel had recently joined the Légende board of directors as its youngest member and had come to Paris from Lima for his first meeting. It had been Nicole's final year of medical school then, and her father invited her to sit in on some of the board's deliberations. She was his only heir and it was his hope that she would begin to take an active interest in the empire he had created.

Manuel had lingered in France longer than intended,

courting her, encouraged by her father's obvious approval. Approval, because Manuel was one of Peru's most respected young lawyers and economists. Daniel thought Caldeiro had character and a brilliant future.

That had been only a year after her love affair with Erik. She had already begun to weave a cocoon around herself, a protective shield that would ensure she would never again depend on love. By exerting an iron will, she had managed to drive Erik from her thoughts, but now her mind wouldn't obey.

Nicole imagined once more, in a flash of renewed pain, the golden flesh she had loved as her own. . . . *Bone of my bones, and flesh of my flesh.* That was from Genesis, one of the few Biblical verses she remembered. Erik had always been astonished at how little she knew the Bible. He, who was an atheist, had grown up reading the Scriptures, while Nicole, with her years of education in a Catholic convent school, could quote no more than a few passages.

Finally, after all this time, she could think of him without panic, without fear of the years left alone. How different her life could have been. By now they would have been married for three years, perhaps had a child. Erik would have continued with his research at the Institut Pasteur, and no doubt she would have been working with the woman she admired at the Hôpital Necker, the professor of pediatrics she had hoped to emulate.

A clamor of horns interrupted Nicole's reverie. Traffic was at a standstill. Her hands gripped the steering wheel and, to relieve her tension, she observed the crowded Avenida Arequipa with its double row of stately palm trees. Wherever her eyes fell, people seemed to be in pairs. In the car ahead a young couple kissed while waiting for traffic to move. The boy was dependable-looking, the girl small on the seat next to him, her hair reflecting the fading winter light. He nuzzled her playfully, running his hand twice over her head in a fond, intimate gesture that sent a pang of remembered passion through Nicole.

Why am I doing this? I mustn't allow myself to think this way! Her protective guard had taken so long to form. If she permitted a chink in her armor, it would be eroded bit by bit.

The traffic flowed ahead. Nicole engaged the gears, shooting into the next lane, crossing over Avenida Ricardo Palma to República. When she reached Barranca, she followed Avenida Panama beyond the army schools and turned into a side street, carefully steering the Renault along the rutted road leading to one of Lima's *pueblos jóvenes,* young towns, the euphemistic name given to the new neighborhoods—little more than shantytowns— that had sprung up on the fringe of the city since the influx of more people from the countryside.

Father would have fits if he knew I was coming here! He doesn't even like me to drive to the hospital alone.

Poor Papá. He deserved a daughter who would marry someone like Manuel, have lots of grandchildren for him to cuddle, and grow fat and contented like a good *peruana* wife.

No, that wasn't fair to Daniel. Hadn't he been the one to take her to live in Paris after her mother's death? He had engaged Mademoiselle to tutor her, to help her perfect her French so she would not continue to speak with his provincial accent but would sound like a Parisienne. It was he who had encouraged her at age sixteen to finish her *baccalauréat* and go on to the University of Paris as a medical student.

Daniel had always been pleased with her scholarship, proud of her honors. And when she had fallen in love with Erik, he had been willing for them to marry as soon as she graduated. But things never turned out the way you expected, and here they were back in Lima . . . and Daniel would absolutely disapprove of her paying a house call in Chorrillos as the sun was going down!

Nicole turned into an unpaved alley at the edge of the slum. An urchin dashed across the lane, inches in front of her automobile. She jammed her foot on the brake, stalling the engine. As she worked the starter, children clamored around the sedan, begging for money. Nicole opened the window to distribute coins into the small, grimy, outstretched hands. They did not fight each other for the *soles.* They knew the *doctora* on this side of the *barriada.* Even the smallest would have theirs, for she would give something to each of them.

Nicole walked up the steep incline toward the hut

made from old shipping crates and tar paper, where
Estriana lived with her three older children, her man
when he was there, and the newborn infant. This neighborhood was not in a district ordinarily serviced by San
Martín Hospital, but the mother had been brought to the
Emergencia in premature labor. Nicole was particularly
proud of this case and was including it in a paper she was
submitting to the *Journal of Pediatric Medicine*. The difficult breech delivery had been further complicated by the
mother's anemia and poor general health, and the baby
boy had been jaundiced, needing resuscitation and a
blood transfusion. This would be the final post-natal visit
to check his progress.

Nicole steeled herself against the stench of the slum.
The hillside was crowded with hovels patched with rush
mats or corrugated cardboard, and caulked with dried
mud. Rotting garbage and excrement lay in piles around
the houses. There was an overpowering odor of urine
and sex from the open doorways of the insubstantial
dwellings. The only factor that prevented complete decay
and disintegration was the lack of rain in Lima. Each
time Nicole came to one of these neighborhoods, she
wondered how people could survive here year after year.

Estriana was making soup, holding the baby to her
breast while she stirred the pot. *You would never know
she's only twenty-five—my age!* The careworn woman
greeted Nicole with a smile, pulling an upturned produce
box from a corner for her to use as a chair.

"How is the baby?" Nicole asked, peering at the infant, who had fallen asleep.

"Good, *doctora*. I have sufficient milk this time, so he
is content."

"It's important that he be weighed regularly, Estriana,
to be sure he's gaining weight." Nicole opened her bag
and took out her stethoscope and light. "I'll try not to
wake him, but I should examine him."

As she checked the baby's heart and lungs and gently
palpated his abdomen, he stirred and opened his eyes.
He did seem contented for a baby who lived in such
dismal surroundings. *Sweet little thing*, she thought. Now
you can be happy, for all you need is your mother's
breast and for her to love you and hold you in her arms.

But the older children—they were the ones who tore at her heart! The most difficult thing for her was to harden herself, not to let her emotions get the upper hand. To see them, their bellies large with malnutrition, their skin depigmented with disease, those large, round eyes, like bottomless wells of need . . . if she gave in to her pity, she would become incapable of helping them.

Estriana watched anxiously as Nicole examined her son. Her last child had died of dysentery because she was unable to nurse it. It was impossible to keep feeding bottles or their contents sterile in a house without running water or refrigeration. Diseases spread like wildfire in the *barriada*.

"The baby is wonderful, Estriana! I'm very pleased. Will you bring him to the clinic once a month? And what about the other children?"

"They go to school, *doctora*, There they are given breakfast and lunch, so they are healthy."

"Yes, but even well-fed children should be checked and receive vaccinations, Estriana."

The woman looked frightened. "I have no money for vaccinations."

"There isn't a charge at the clinic, Estriana. You weren't charged for the delivery, remember?"

"Yes, *doctora*. thank you."

"So, you will come?" Eager to follow this baby's growth, she was unable to extract a promise from the woman. "Is there some other reason why you don't want to come to the clinic, Estriana?"

"It is far to go alone, the busses are too crowded. And I can't miss my work."

"I see. It's important, Estriana. He should be examined by a doctor in *some* clinic, even if it isn't mine. Try to ask a friend to go with you on the days when you don't work. I won't be able to visit you again. I can take care of many patients in the time I use to come here." But Estriana seemed disinclined to travel even to a hospital clinic closer to the *barriada*.

Nicole left feeling discouraged. This is exactly why we must have mobile clinics in the *barriadas,* she reminded herself. She doubted that she would ever see the woman again.

*   *   *

Whenever she entered her home after having been in a *barriada,* Nicole felt ashamed of her relief. The contrast between her life and that of a woman like Estriana was startling.

She wondered what Estriana would think if she could have driven with her through the great iron gates of Casa Loma, along the curving driveway, past the formal gardens to the courtyard of the huge Spanish colonial mansion with its red tiled roof and splashing fountain.

The house had a commanding view of the Pacific Ocean in one direction and the distant Andes in the other. Daniel Légende had moved his family to Miraflores from the older district of Lima preferred by many of the established families because Tina, his wife, had missed the sunshine of her mountain home. The mist of winter, the *garua,* did not seem as penetrating here in the garden reserve above the Pacific.

She was met at the door by Vera, the head maid, who whispered, "Señor Caldeiro is here, Señorita Nicole. He is with your father in his study."

Nicole made a face of mock guilt and together they laughed. "Thanks, Vera. I guess I'm in trouble again."

She walked through the patterned marble entrance foyer to the gallery that led to her father's private retreat. The broad corridor, forming a quadrangle, was hung with colorful antique Paracas tapestries and framed Chancay and Chimu fabric panels from Daniel Légende's collection. Two massive refectory tables, holding Chinese porcelain vases filled with loose arrangements of fresh flowers, stood on either side of paned glass doors opening to a central patio, which was tiled with prized *azulejos.*

Daniel had furnished each of his three homes in harmony with their settings. This house in Lima was in the style of a colonial palacio, containing rich, carved, hand-rubbed woods, creamy stucco walls, and accents of vibrant color; while in the Paris apartment on the Avenue Foch, pale Aubusson carpets and elegant pastel fabrics complemented the Impressionist and Cubist oil paintings and modern sculptures. But it was the villa at Huaranca, nestled in a little-known valley of the Andes, that always remained Nicole's favorite. With the mellowness of age and the charm of the traditional plantation manor house,

Hacienda Flor del Viento would always seem more like home to Nicole than any place on earth.

At the open door of the study, Nicole paused. She heard the polished tones of Manuel's voice and then the deep rumble of her father asking a question. They laughed, and taking that as her cue, Nicole rapped on the door frame and entered.

"I'm home, Father." She crossed the room to kiss him as both men rose to their feet.

Turning to Manuel, she extended her hands with an apologetic gesture. "I'm dreadfully sorry, Manuel. We had a terrible day at the clinic."

He bent to kiss her cheek, smiling in that way she had come to recognize as partly indulgent and partly something else that said she wasn't fooling him for a minute. As always, he was dressed with meticulous care, in formal dinner clothes this evening, as was Daniel, because they were going to a reception for Lima's diplomatic corps at the French Embassy.

Manuel Caldeiro-León was considered handsome. Tall for a Peruvian, with a lean, compact body, his full, wavy, dark hair swept back from his aristocratic forehead. His face was long, with aquiline features and drawn-in cheeks. Light eyes, *"ojos del gato,"* gray-blue, meant that he was not completely Latin, a much noticed characteristic in Lima, where to be European, or non-Indian, in appearance carried cachet.

When Nicole first met Manuel in Paris she had dubbed him "the patent leather man" to her friend Françoise Bercy. As she had learned since, there was substance beneath his groomed exterior. Manuel was certainly brilliant. The surprising thing was that he was kind.

Daniel said, "I won't offer you a cocktail, Nicole, because Manuel has been waiting. I wouldn't want to delay you any longer." It was spoken with good humor, but she understood it as a gentle reproof.

"All right . . . I'm running! I'll be ready in twenty minutes, Manuel, you'll see," she called back over her shoulder as she hurried from the room.

Vera was waiting for her upstairs. She had hung the Balmain gown, an ombre flame chiffon, in the dressing room and was laying out lingerie on a settee.

"Vera, do you really think that's the right dress for tonight?"

"It's a lovely dress, and it will make you look beautiful," the maid answered.

"I didn't think I would be quite that formal. Oh, all right. I'd better hurry or he'll leave without me." She shrugged out of her skirt, kicked off her shoes and stockings, and headed for the bathroom, where Vera had filled the tub.

The warm water felt wonderful. She was tempted to lie back and close her eyes for a moment, but she washed hastily, opened the drain and, standing, rinsed herself with the hand shower. After she had dried and powdered her body, she put on the silk underwear and stockings and sat at the dressing table.

"Shall I comb your hair, señorita?" Vera had returned.

"I was just going to twist it up in my usual way."

"I think tonight we could do something a little special."

Nicole sat quietly and allowed the woman, who had once been personal maid to a fashionable Lima hostess, to brush out the silky black hair that fell to her waist. It had never been cut more than an inch because all during her younger years her father had wanted it kept long. She had almost decided to have a shorter hairstyle when she met Erik, but he had loved her long hair. . . .

Why had she been thinking of Erik so often lately? Why had she been dwelling on *love?* She did not want to remember, to dream. Her life had no room for that kind of love, ever again.

"All finished, Señorita Nicole. How do you like it?" Vera stood back, smiling into the mirror.

The maid had created an elaborate chignon edged with a braid high on the crown of her head. "It's spectacular, Vera. Thank you."

Nicole leaned forward and lightly applied eyeshadow and mascara. She seldom used makeup, but tonight she looked pale. Touching her ears and wrists with the stopper from a Lalique flacon of Nicole, the perfume her father had named for her, she glanced at the clock.

"My twenty minutes are up! Will you help me with the dress, please, Vera?"

Nicole fastened the diamond and pearl eardrops and

matching bracelet her father had given her for her twenty-fourth birthday. With a last glance in the mirror, she hurried from the room to the pillared Moorish hallway and down the broad stairs.

Manuel was standing below in the foyer. His eyes swept over her appreciatively. "It was worth waiting for," he said, offering his arm. "Your father went on ahead. He said he would see us there."

Chapter 2

The headlights of the long line of automobiles at the entrance to the Embassy of France were hazy in the mist. Manuel's chauffeur pulled the Bentley behind a large Chrysler limousine with CD plates.

"That's the American ambassador," Manuel remarked. "I wondered whether he would be here."

The relationship between Peru and the United States had deteriorated in the four years since the leftist military regime, a week after it took office, had seized the property of IPC, International Petroleum Company, a subsidiary of Standard Oil and a symbol of all that was wrong in Peru.

"Well," he laughed, "it's France that's giving the party, so of course he would come!"

"We can't be too late if all these people are just arriving."

"We're not late, Nicole." He took her hand. "Your father is always afraid you're offending me. He doesn't realize how thick-skinned I am." He smiled at her. "You're especially beautiful tonight. I like your hair that way."

She squeezed Manuel's hand in response. "Thank you, señor. You're looking quite handsome yourself."

She was feeling happy suddenly. The lights of the embassy, the glitter of women in jewels and silk gowns being helped out of sedans by their distinguished escorts, the strains of music from the open doors, gave her a fleeting sense of girlish anticipation. It has been too long since I felt excited about going to a party, she thought.

They came to the receiving line. The chargé announced, "Mademoiselle le docteur Nicole Légende Iglesias, Monsieur Manuel Caldeiro-León."

They were greeted by the French ambassador and his wife, a chic woman who had acquired a reputation as a remarkable hostess in each of her husband's diplomatic posts. Tonight was a special occasion, Le Quatorze Juillet, the national holiday of France. The entire *corps diplomatique* would be here, as well as the leading citizens of Lima. And the generals, the Peruvian junta.

Nicole's father had almost decided to decline the invitation because General Juan Velasco Alvarado and other members of the military would be present. Nicole had convinced him that he had an obligation to accept, since he held French as well as Peruvian citizenship.

Daniel did not like the men who ruled Peru. He thought they were ruining the economy with their "socialist revolution," chasing capital investment from the country. Beside that, he had a basic distrust of all military governments.

"If you educate a man to fight wars, then he thinks he's a failure unless he has the chance to practice his profession," Daniel said. "In Peru, we're not going to make big wars on foreign powers. So, who will they make war against? The people!"

Manuel guided Nicole from the receiving hall into the ballroom, ablaze with light. He took two champagnes from a waiter's tray, handing one to Nicole and raising his glass.

"Salud. . . y amor, querida." Their eyes met and his flickered with emotion, then lowered as he sipped.

Nicole surveyed the room. Many of the diplomats were in full dress with their decorations hanging on colorful ribbons. Her father wore the rosette of the *Légion d'Honneur* in his lapel. She spied him across the room, speaking to the Minister of Economics, who had the good grace not to attend tonight's affair in uniform.

She studied Daniel. He was the quintessential Frenchman, she thought fondly, despite his having lived half his life in Peru. He stood tall and substantial, slightly stoop-shouldered with his head thrust forward. She took her height from her father, who had been slim and wiry as a young man.

Daniel had put on weight after Tina died. French food and wine. In Paris he had become close to Isabelle Somme, a soft, pretty woman who loved to eat. Nicole supposed that Isabelle and her father were still lovers, since he often went to Paris to see her. Despite the allure of the

high fashion models and actresses who appeared in
Légende advertisements, he had not formed a liaison
with any of them. Daniel preferred women who were
feminine and rounded. He was a man who liked comfortable relationships. But no one had ever taken her mother's place. Although he had never said so, Nicole knew
her father would not marry again.

Several others had joined the group around Daniel.
People were drawn to him. Nicole thought he looked
weary tonight. She watched his heavy-lidded eyes and
expressive mouth suggesting wry wit or mock dismay. He
talked with his shoulders and eyebrows. Someone had
once remarked that you could decipher Daniel Légende's
conversation from across a room. He was admired and
envied in Lima, but she was not at all certain that he was
liked.

In Huaranca, Daniel was revered by the *campesinos*.
He had brought prosperity to the forgotten little Andes
village where the people had eked out a living by plant-
ing corn, wheat, and barley on the hacienda, taking their
share in food—until Daniel had developed the thriving
industry that had changed all their fortunes.

Now the workers were shareholders in the hacienda.
Long before the junta had instituted land reforms, Daniel Légende had created his own collective community,
building houses, a school, and a clinic for the families
who lived on the lands of the hacienda. By the time the
junta had begun breaking up large land holdings, there
was nothing to take over at Flor del Viento.

Manuel, with Nicole at his side, moved through the
crowded ballroom easily, nodding to acquaintances. He
was known by everyone in Lima society and government
circles. For years he had been considered one of the
capital's most eligible bachelors. His influence had not
faded with the bloodless coup d'etat of October 3,
1968—shortly after Nicole had come back from Paris to
live in Lima. If anything, Manuel was consulted even
more frequently as an economic advisor by the new military government than he had been by the previous civilian administration of Fernando Belaúnde Terry.

Manuel was one of those men who sail with the winds
of change. "You have to be suicidal to be anti-government
in South America!" he often joked.

They overheard some guests discussing a bomb that had been thrown near the American Embassy earlier that week. They were saying the military police had apprehended three suspects, members of a radical left association. Manuel purposefully steered her away from the group.

Nicole still felt the lightness of the mood that had come over her in the automobile. Manuel's hand was warm on her arm as they stopped to speak to friends. The women eyed her speculatively, uncertain at the simplicity of her dress. Heavily made up, with stiff, teased hair, they were gowned in satins and brocades, wearing ornate jewelry. Some carried showy mink wraps, reluctant to leave them in the cloakroom. They stood apart from the men, admiring each other's attire.

Clothes were an obsession for wealthy Lima women. Bored, leading indolent lives, they filled their idle time by visiting dressmakers and boutiques, while their husbands sought new conquests in the rites of machismo. If she had continued her education in Lima instead of going to Paris, would she have been among them, Nicole wondered.

"Good evening, counselor," a tall, svelte woman in black addressed Manuel. She spoke in an arch, almost mocking manner, her lips pursed in a wry smile.

"Well, well . . . Lucy! You're looking much too glamorous. What would your clients think?"

"They'd never believe it," she laughed. Extending her hand to Nicole, she said, "I'm Lucy Monaco. You must be Dr. Légende."

"Forgive me," Manuel apologized. "I should have realized you hadn't met. Lucy is one of my most formidable colleagues at the bar. Luckily, I'm not a prosecutor. I'd hate to have to face her in court!"

"You flatter me, Manuel." She turned to Nicole, saying in a rich husky voice, "I've heard about your work in the *barriadas*, Dr. Légende."

"Please call me Nicole. If you're interested, I'd be happy to take you around with me sometime." Nicole instantly liked Señora Monaco. She was direct and projected intense energy. And it was a pleasure to meet a woman who was as tall as she was.

Lucy reached into her handbag. "My card."

Nicole smiled. "Sorry, I didn't bring mine. I'll call you."

"Who is she?" Nicole asked, as they continued across the room.

"Lucy is a one-woman crusade. She defends the downtrodden and disaffected. Leftist students, criminals, malcontents. Fortunately, she has money, because her clients can't afford to pay her."

"I'd like to know her."

Manuel gave her an amused look. "I have a feeling you may get your wish."

Her father was still engaged in conversation with the Minister of Economics when they reached his side. "General, you know my daughter, Nicole, and Señor Caldeiro."

The minister bowed over Nicole's hand. "A great pleasure, señorita."

To Manuel he said, "I was interested in your speech on foreign debt at the Bankers' Club."

The minister's wife, a strong-looking woman, joined them when she saw Nicole. Daniel introduced them. "I understand you're a medical doctor, Señorita Légende. Do you have a private practice?"

"No, señora, I'm at San Martín University. I have a full-time clinical fellowship and I teach pediatrics and maternal health."

"Excellent! We need more women to serve the people."

There was a sudden hush.

The crowd turned and parted as President Juan Velasco Alvarado entered the ballroom, resplendent in the full dress uniform of a general. He supported himself with a cane because of a circulatory disease of his leg. Followed by members of his cabinet and bodyguard, all *mestizos,* like most of the military, he allowed the French Ambassador to escort him as he made the rounds of the assembled diplomats.

Nicole noticed the immediate change in atmosphere. It was as if someone had super-charged the gathering with an electric current. Being near the center of power had that effect on people.

Well, not on *everyone,* she smiled to herself. Daniel Légende continued to sip champagne, calmly chatting with an old friend, the owner of a leading newspaper and radio station. Her father's friend was no admirer of

Velasco, certainly. The editors of his publication had been intimidated, while the government was threatening to expropriate his newspaper and take over his radio station.

Many people in this room were members of the traditional elite, the white *criollos* who had long ruled Peru. They were the citizens who had lost money and power, an entire way of life, under this government. The junta had seized their industries, broken up their land holdings, closed the exclusive social clubs from which they had run the country outside the electoral process. That they had attended the reception tonight surprised Nicole. They considered the military men their social inferiors. Those who did not move to another room pointedly snubbed the presidential party.

"I have no appetite for politics," Nicole told Manuel later that evening when they were alone in the library of her home. "No matter who's in office, the poor suffer, and the politicians get richer."

Her father had retired after having raked over every government official attending the reception. Daniel had always believed in socialist government, but he hated the leftist junta, except for the Minister of Economics. "He won't last. Too sensible and too honest."

After he left the room, Nicole said, "Father looks awfully tired, doesn't he, Manuel?"

Manuel came to sit on the couch next to her. "I didn't notice. Your father is in remarkable condition for a man his age, Nicole."

"He's only fifty-three, Manuel. That's not old."

"No, it isn't old. . . ." Manuel's mind was not on Daniel.

He put his arms around her and she let him. His hands softly caressed her bare shoulders and back. She laid her head against his chest, inhaling the spicy masculine odor of his cologne. This had not happened for so long, this warm lassitude. She felt the need to be closer to him, to his maleness.

When he kissed her, it was gentle, yet passionate, and she knew it wasn't fair to him because she could never be what he wanted. But she could not help responding to him.

"Oh . . . Nicole!" His lips were on her throat, the soft skin above her breasts. "I've wanted to do this all evening," he breathed.

Nicole closed her eyes, letting the melting sensation flow over her. She had been alone so long, and although she had sworn she would never marry, she knew she did not want to spend the rest of her life not ever going to bed with a man. How easy it would be to marry Manuel. She was as attracted to him as she would even be to anyone.

His hands were moving, touching her breasts through the gown, sliding down to her hips and thighs, as his kisses became more insistent. They were both aroused, but she knew she had to stop him. This was not something you let a man do in Peru, unless you *were* going to marry him! Gently she disengaged herself.

He took her face between his hands, his eyes filled with longing. "I'm in love with you, Nicole."

She nodded, looking down. "I know," she whispered.

At the door, he started to speak, then sighed and left her.

The chauffeur had fallen asleep in the front seat. Poor man had been waiting around most of the night. Lima was a nighttime city. Most evenings did not end for Manuel until the early hours of the morning.

His mood was pensive as they drove along the ocean toward San Isidro. He was still sexually aroused. Nicole excited him as no other woman ever had.

Why? Because she was elusive? Perhaps. He enjoyed a challenge. She was beautiful; he liked beautiful women. And he admired her; so many women he knew had no substance.

He remembered the first time he met her in her father's executive offices. How serious she was, that tall, coltish medical student, wearing somber tweeds and an Austrian loden coat. He had taken her off to the Ritz for tea and it had become a challenge to get her to smile.

Even in repose, her lovely face with its delicate nose, high cheekbones, and soft-molded mouth had captured him. When she finally laughed, the flash in the green-gold eyes matched the lights in her shining black hair, and he saw for an instant the ghosts of royal Inca and

Spanish *conquistador* that surely were combined with the heritage of her father.

From that day, he had been determined to make her his wife, no matter how long it took to woo her. No need to explain it to himself. He loved her . . . as simple as that. And he would do *anything* to possess her!

Women had always been easy for him. The nice ones were subtle, the others blatant. Back in the days when he had been a graduate student at the Harvard Business School, they used to come to his Cambridge apartment looking for him.

In Peru, women from good families did not have affairs. It was unthinkable! Manuel used to agree with the conventions, but the years he had spent in the States had changed his opinions.

Elena had changed him, too.

Elena. His best friend's widow. She had been in love with Manuel but had married Héctor. An ill-considered and impetuous decision. Manuel had lost out because his code of honor had prevented him from courting a woman his friend loved. By the time she was free again, he had already met Nicole.

Héctor loved Elena . . . Elena loved Manuel. . . Manuel loved Nicole. Why couldn't it get properly sorted out?

He *had* to have a woman tonight! Should he tell his driver to go there? No, they were almost at his house. He would call her first, then drive himself.

Changed into a soft shirt and comfortable slacks, Manuel dialed her number. It rang seven times. He was about to hang up when she answered.

"I knew it would be you," she said.

She had a throaty voice. It always stirred him.

"May I come over?"

There was a long silence. "I should say no. . . ."

"Please say yes."

She sighed. "You knew I couldn't say anything else, didn't you? Come on, then."

She was waiting for him at the door of her house, watching through the sidelight when he turned in through the gates.

Her luxuriant auburn hair, always a little wild when loose, fell in waves around her shoulders. Wearing a burgundy velvet robe with a deep V at the neck, she looked faintly disreputable. *She has done that on purpose!*

He put his hands on her shoulders and she looked at him without expression. Then, closing her eyes, she threw herself against him, pulling his mouth down to hers with ferocious greed. Moments later they were feverishly removing each other's clothes, falling in bed, locked together in desperate urgency. It was always like this with Elena.

"Again!" she commanded. "Only slowly this time. Make it last."

He closed his eyes and made believe she was Nicole.

Chapter 3

Nicole shut the bedroom window against the cool mist. She had read for a while after Manuel left, still feeling the sexual tension he had aroused. Although it was late, she could not seem to fall asleep.

Returning to bed, she stretched restlessly under the smooth sheets, rolling onto her stomach and reaching for a pillow. *He probably has a mistress waiting for him somewhere. How unfair.*

Women in France and the States were free to take lovers. They didn't even bother to be discreet these days. When she had been in Atlanta for her fellowship, she had met perfectly respectable unmarried couples who openly lived together. No one seemed to think anything of it.

That could never happen in Lima. Unless, of course, a woman was as independent as Lucy Monaco. Nicole had been interested in the woman attorney and asked Manuel about her again on the drive home from the reception.

"How old would you say she is?"

"Lucy's over thirty by now. She has a son who must be at least five, and she was in her late twenties when he was born."

"What's her husband like?"

He had drawn in his cheeks and regarded her with a sly smile. "She doesn't have a husband. I think she did at one time, but he's not the father of her child."

Nicole had stared at him.

"Are you shocked, Nicole?" He seemed to enjoy the idea that he might have discomfited her.

"Not really, Manuel. Surprised, perhaps. You have to admit that's unusual in Lima—at least in our circles."

He nodded in agreement. "But then Lucy is a most unusual woman. It's rumored she had an affair with Horacio Salamanca and that the child is his."

31

"The dissident writer? But, how extraordinary!" Horacio Salamanca Rosenn was one of Peru's most famous and controversial authors, and an irritant to the military government.

Well, maybe Lucy Monaco didn't have to play by the rules, but Nicole couldn't see herself living that way, especially under the eyes of her father. After what Manuel had told her, she became even more intrigued with the idea of getting to know Lucy.

Still restless, she got out of bed and opened the window again. Leaning out the casement, she let the mist blow against her face. The *garua*. She understood why her mother had hated it. Tina had always wished they could spend the winters in Huaranca where it was warm and sunny, but Nicole's school was in Lima, and Daniel had offices in the city.

There was a light in her father's room across the court, in the opposite wing. That was surprising. Daniel usually slept soundly all night. Was he worried about business, or the junta?

He *had* been looking tired lately. Manuel wouldn't notice something like that, but she did because she was Daniel's daughter. She was also a doctor, and she thought he didn't look well. Maybe he needed a rest. Perhaps they should go up to Huaranca for a few days. It had been ages since they'd spent any time at Flor del Viento. She didn't have to work next weekend, and Friday was her twenty-fifth birthday. They could be there in only five hours if they drove the Jaguar. It had a gasoline permit for Fridays. Ironically enough, in a country which had recently discovered and begun exporting its own oil, there was alternate day rationing to conserve fuel. The Jaguar sports model was Daniel's toy. He liked to drive fast cars. It seemed uncharacteristic, but it was a streak of the adventurer in him.

Lying in bed, she thought it was an excellent idea. A good tearing gallop across the hacienda would shake her out of this peculiar frame of mind. She would speak to her father first thing in the morning.

On Monday when Nicole entered the clinic, Mona Ramos averted her eyes. Nicole went out of her way to be pleasant to the head nurse, but it was obvious that the woman was not going to forgive her so easily.

In the afternoon, Nicole gave an epidemiology lecture to the third year medical students. When she returned to the department, the secretary told her that Señora Monaco had called and left her number. And the chief, Professor Jorge Alvares, wanted to see her in his office. Since the department head had someone with him, she returned Lucy Monaco's call at once.

"I thought I might talk you into inviting me over there someday," said Lucy in her husky voice. "I'd like to see what you're up to!"

Nicole laughed. "I'm glad you called."

They made a date and Nicole put a reminder on her calendar. "I'll try to arrange something interesting," she said.

"Now *that's* a statement that makes me nervous! How does a doctor 'arrange' to have an interesting case on hand?" Nicole had a feeling that she and Lucy were going to be great friends.

The chief was ready to see her, so Nicole hurried to his office. Alvares was a short man with a round, sympathetic face. He cultivated an exuberant mustache, perhaps to compensate for the scant growth of hair on his head. Nicole had become fond of the affable doctor while working under his direction in the Department of Maternal and Child Health. Beneath his fatherly attitude and courtly manners was a tremendous energy and a quick, incisive mind. He commanded the respect and allegiance of his entire staff.

The professor was smiling broadly. "I have good news, Nicole! The department has received the grant from the Cartwright Foundation for the mobile clinics."

"That *is* good news, Dr. Alvares. When may we begin?"

"Just as soon as you can get organized."

"I've been ready for months. I have several excellent volunteers lined up from among the students who helped with the pilot clinics we ran."

The mobile clinics would use vans to rotate among the *barriadas*, bringing health care within easy reach of the poor. This was Nicole's idea, a project she had planned during the two years she had spent in Atlanta. With all she had learned about the prevention and control of disease at the CDC, she was eager to put that knowledge to use.

When she returned to Peru, Nicole concentrated on improving health services for poor mothers and their children. At first, she organized classes in newborn infant care in the slums. Since San Martín was close to one of the oldest and most congested slum neighborhoods, some of the patients they received were the poorest of the poor. It had not taken Nicole long to see that when a mother was ill herself, or had to go to work, it was impossible for her to come to the hospital during clinic hours. The present system did not accommodate these women, and Nicole thought mobile clinics were a solution.

A tragic accident had spurred her to action. A woman had brought her two older children to the hospital, leaving the others locked in their hut. Somehow the shack caught fire. When the mother returned home, four of her children had died in the flames. Nicole had learned about the disaster the next day. Immediately, she made plans for holding clinics one day a week in the more distant *barriadas*. She enlisted the help of some medical students and young doctors who were sympathetic to the plight of Lima's poor. The clinics were a success, but they came to a halt because it had been difficult getting the funds for their support allocated from the Health Ministry. Thus, she was elated to hear this good news.

As she was leaving his office, Professor Alvares said, with a twinkle in his eyes, "By the way, I understand you had a little problem in the emergency clinic on Friday."

Nicole was embarrassed. "I'm afraid I really blew up." She related what had happened when she crossed wills with the head nurse over the admission of the abortion patient. "But I just couldn't *believe* she was going to let that patient go! The woman would have been in shock any minute, the way she was hemorrhaging."

Alvares was understanding. In his kindly way, though, he gave her some advice. "I'd be a little careful of Nurse Ramos, Nicole. I know she can be difficult, but she's not a person you would want to antagonize."

On Friday afternoon, Nicole and Daniel drove to Huaranca. They headed for the Callejón de Huaylas, the long, narrow, heavily populated corridor of fertile land that runs between the two principle ranges of the Andes. On the Callejón's western periphery stands the arid coastal range, the Cordillera Negra, bare of snows. To the east rises the magnificent snow-capped Cordillera Blanca, peerless in its splendor. Together they form a continuous wall along the entire length of Peru from Ecuador to Chile.

In a deep, hidden valley off the southern end of the Callejón, sheltered from the harsh weather of the sierra, lies Huaranca, the pueblo where Nicole's mother had grown up on her family's hacienda. Both Nicole and Daniel believed it was the most beautiful spot on earth.

"Are you certain that's what you want to do for your birthday?" Daniel had asked when she proposed the trip.

"Nothing would please me more."

He had looked at her skeptically. "What about a party at home? I'm sure Manuel Caldeiro will be disappointed not to spend the evening with you."

"I told him I would see him the night before," she replied.

"You could invite him along," he suggested, trying to keep his tone casual.

She laughed. "*No*, Papá! You're not very subtle, you know." And then she had bent over his chair to kiss him. "I really do prefer just to be with you at the hacienda."

Before they left Lima, Daniel gave her his birthday present—the most exquisite antique Moorish jewelry. It was fashioned of carnelian set in open-work gold and edged with seed pearls. The necklace hung on a long, heavy, intricate chain of filigreed gold and, with the matching bracelet and earrings, must once have graced the bride of a grandee.

"Father! How magnificent! You know how I love old jewelry. Wherever did you flnd it?"

Pleased at her delight, he said, "In Marrakech, when I was there in February. There's a very special dealer. He has pieces like no one else in the world." That was characteristic of her father's thoughtful, generous nature, the way he had of finding rare and beautiful objects to please someone he loved.

It was dark when they arrived at the hacienda. The rambling manor house looked inviting in the glow of lanterns and candlelight.

Rosa and Tomás greeted them. Rosa, who had been

Nicole's nurse when she was a baby, threw her arms
around Nicole and kissed her. Face flushing and eyes
tearing with emotion, she wished her a happy birthday,
saying, "To think you were my little *huahua*," as she
looked up at Nicole, who was at least a foot taller than she.

Rosa had filled the rooms with fragrant boughs of
eucalyptus and winter greens. For dinner, she had prepared Daniel's favorite *shakwi*, a bean soup, followed by
calabaza soufflé and grilled beef with a spicy creole sauce,
and for dessert there was a coconut creme in a meringue
pastry, called *canasta de coco*.

They tried their best to do justice to the meal, but no
matter how much they ate, Rosa was never satisfied.
Accustomed to cooking for Tomás and her sons, who
worked hard on the hacienda, she could not believe that
Nicole's small appetite would sustain life.

After dinner they sat talking with Rosa and Tomás.
And then, because it was her birthday, the men from the
hacienda serenaded Nicole, accompanying themselves on
guitars. When they were finished, Daniel called for *chicha*,
the fermented corn liquor of the sierra, serving it to the
men, and the celebration continued far into the night.

In the old carved wooden bed that had been hers since
girlhood, nestled under a plump feather comforter, Nicole breathed in the cold, pure mountain air. She was
relieved to be here.

She remembered lying in this room when she was very
young, watching the shadows from a candle lamp dance
across the ceiling. An aura would surround her . . . the
walls and ceiling seemed to move away, the room en-
large, until she was as small as her dolls. Sometimes it
was she who grew large, dwarfing everything else. It was
a frightening phenomenon, and she used to call for her
father, who came in the night, soothing her fears with his
strong, gentle touch, holding her in his arms as he pointed
through the window to the mountain peaks flooded with
moonlight. As long as he was there, she had known no
harm could come to her.

Such were the simple truths of childhood.

Sunny winter mornings on the hacienda made the blood
race. Nicole cantered across the plantation on Flame III,
taking pleasure from the wind in her face and the stag-

gering sight of snowy peaks sparkling in the distance against a sky of intense, deep blue. When she reached the brook Nicole walked her horse until they came to a vast sloping meadow. At its far edge in a sweeping arc, stood the thorny, winter-bare stalks of the flamesword plants.

Nicole remounted and turned the horse, making slow traverses back and forth until she neared the place where the valley narrows before it heads down to the gorge. Dismounting again, she hitched Flame's bridle to a tree, then lounged against a boulder, not minding the coolness of the earth. Winter days were mild in this deep, protected valley, although the nights were cold.

Far in the distance, high over the Cordillera, a condor glided in wide circles, swooping down and hanging motionless on spread wings. As Nicole watched, it soared upward, then plunged toward the mountain, disappearing from view. Part of her detached itself and floated aloft, joining the condor in the flight to its rocky lair. A sense of well-being came over her, a rare contentment. It always seemed to await her in the valley of the flamesword. Here at the hacienda that elusive, aching tension, the fear that haunted her, did not seem as threatening. The fear of being alone.

Nicole loved the story of how her father had been brought to Flor del Viento as a young man.

Found by some men from her grandfather's hacienda, he had been deathly ill. His two friends died in the mountains, but Daniel clung to life. Don Juan Carlos Iglesias y Alba took Daniel into the main house, putting him in the care of Rosa's mother, Jacinta, who ran the household and watched over his daughter, María Christina.

Daniel lay in delirium for many days. They thought he would die. Then one evening he opened his eyes and there was the exquisite María Christina at his bedside, dressed in white, bathing his face.

"I thought I was in heaven and she was an angel," he used to tell Nicole when she was younger. Tina, lying on a chaise, pale and weak from a heart condition, would smile, and a look would pass between her parents that made Nicole feel she had wandered into a moment of intimacy.

By the time Daniel recovered, Tina had fallen hope-

lessly in love with the gentle boy who often gazed into
the distance, as he thought of his family in France at the
mercy of the Nazis.

On Don Juan Carlos's short wave radio, Daniel heard
about the fall of France, the Pétain government in Vichy,
the rounding up and deporting of Jews. What did it mean
for his family in the little town of La Prée? Perhaps they
could still escape . . . they were 250 kilometers south of
Paris.

Daniel insisted he had to get to Lima, to a government
office. He had to try to send for them.

Juan Carlos Iglesias gave him clothes and money and a
letter of introduction to a Jewish merchant, Miguel Cohen. He sent one of his men to accompany him because
he feared Daniel would attract too much attention alone.

Cohen told Daniel it was impossible to obtain visas for
his family, even with a bribe. They would never be able
to get out of France because the borders were closed.

"The safest place for you, Daniel, is with Don Juan
Carlos in Huaranca," Miguel Cohen told him. "If you
stay in Lima without immigration papers and someone
should report you, you could be sent back to France."

Daniel returned to Huaranca. Tina was overjoyed to
see him. She was fifteen and he was twenty, and when
she reached her seventeenth birthday, they were married
by the padre in the small church of the pueblo. To
himself, Daniel recited the only Hebrew prayer for happy
occasions he could remember: *"Boruch Atoh Adonai
Elohaino Melech Ho'olom, shehecheyonu, v'kiy'monu,
v'higionu, lazman hazzeh.* Praised art Thou, O Lord our
God, King of the universe, who hast kept us alive and
sustained us, and enabled us to reach this season."

It was November 1942 and the Germans had occupied
southern France.

Daniel was curious about the herbal medicines he had
been given when he was sick. There was one in particular, a bitter potion that Jacinta had forced him to swallow. Too weak to protest, he had sipped the liquid through
a straw. There was immediate relief from the paralyzing
stomach cramps and diarrhea.

The medicine was made from a plant that grew wild in
the lee of the valley, Juan Carlos told him. It was called

espada del fuego, flamesword, because its thick fibrous branches were blade-shaped, with sharp edges that could cut into a man's palm, and in summer it bloomed with a multitude of blossoms that matured to a bright flame color. Only the hardiest survived because the seeds were sown by the wind and the young shoots were eaten by animals.

Daniel gathered some of the seedlings and experimented with cultivation. He had studied pharmacy at the university in Clermont-Ferrand. With Juan Carlos's permission, he set up a makeshift laboratory in a shed. Taking pulp from the mature plants, after many months he succeeded in making a stable, pasteurized syrup more palatable than the mixture the Indians concocted.

One day a worker on the hacienda was severely burned. Don Juan Carlos came rushing into Daniel's laboratory and asked for some *ungüento* from the flamesword. Daniel watched his father-in-law soak a bandage in the substance and apply the dressing to the *campesino*'s arm. The man was in considerable pain, so Juan Carlos gave him coca leaves to chew. All the people in the sierra chewed coca, but Juan Carlos had discouraged his workers from this habit because he knew how it drained them and made them dependent on its narcotic effects.

When Daniel remarked on the skill with which Don Juan Carlos attended the worker, his father-in-law said, "There's not a *médico* within fifty miles of Huaranca. That's why you were fortunate to be brought here when you were ill, Daniel. In the hands of the shamans, you would have died."

By the next day Daniel was surprised to see the *campesino*'s burns had not blistered. Soon new skin began to form, but most remarkable of all, the wounds did not become infected.

After that, Daniel worked far into the night to develop an ointment. Tina gave him reproachful looks when he came to their bed. She had a considerable appetite for lovemaking, as Daniel had discovered in the months after their marriage. Soon she was pregnant.

Their son was born at the end of 1943. Don Juan Carlos's joy matched Daniel's, but it also reminded him of his own parents, whose fate was unknown.

Daniel had written to them, telling them what had

happened to him and about the deaths of the other two
boys from La Prée. He sent the letters through Señor
Cohen in Lima, who had a way of getting mail to Jews in
occupied countries.

Only once had Daniel received a reply, early in 1941.
The letter had been written in September and smuggled
out through Spain. His father was circumspect, but mentioned that the family was "making plans." Daniel prayed
those plans had been realized in an escape. His father's
letter ended with a plea:

> Please stay there in the mountains, Daniel. Be safe,
> survive! If you should perish, our family line would
> come to an end. You are the only male Légende left.

When his son was born, Daniel experienced a longing
such as he had never known to see his parents and his
sisters, to have his father hold his grandson in his arms
just as Don Juan Carlos Iglesias y Alba now held him.

By 1945, when the war came to an end, Daniel was
traveling regularly to Lima to sell his bottles of tonic for
maladies of the stomach and pots of salve for burns and
irritations of the skin to Miguel Cohen. At the immigration office, Daniel learned that he was eligible for citizenship, since he was married to a *peruana*.

He told Tina he had to go to France to find his family.
Tina understood, but in her heart she feared he might
never return to her. María Christina Iglesias de Légende
realized that her husband was an educated man from
Europe who had been deposited at the Hacienda Flor del
Viento by the winds of fate, just as the seeds of the
flamesword plant were cast by the winds. Their love,
their marriage itself, was a *flor del viento,* a flower of the
wind. Only their little boy, Benjamin, was a tangible
bond that might bring him back to her.

Daniel reached La Prée, the village in the Loire Valley
where his family had lived. His father's pharmacy was
now a bakery. Their house was being repaired to make
way for new owners. None of the workers could tell him
what had happened to the family who had once lived
there.

In a daze, Daniel wandered through the town looking
for familiar faces. He went to the Hôtel de Ville to

consult the village records and there he ran into a former schoolmate, Claude Montagne, who had always been called Petit Claude in the town, even after he grew to an enormous height.

"Daniel!" Petit Claude cried, his eyes full of tears. "Where have you been? I thought you were dead, like the others!"

"What others? Do you know where my family is, Claude?"

Claude told him that in 1943 the *Maquis* had killed a German officer who was especially brutal in the rounding up and shipping east of Jewish children left behind when their parents were deported by the Vichy government.

"In retribution for the assassination, the Germans arrested the mayor and the village council and had them shot. Then . . . all the Jews of La Prée were sent to a concentration camp in Poland . . ." Daniel knew what Claude was going to say. ". . . and most of them did not come back."

Daniel's entire family—his father, his mother, his two sisters—were dead. Claude put his hand on Daniel's shoulder. "I'm so sorry, Daniel."

Daniel remained at Claude's home for two weeks. His friend allowed him to mourn in solitude, sensing he did not want to be comforted. Claude himself was half Jewish. He had gone underground with the Maquis.

Since he was a lawyer, Claude offered to reclaim the Légende property in Daniel's name.

"They certainly were in a hurry to dispose of it," said Daniel bitterly.

Claude nodded. "Yes. There are opportunists here—all over Europe—grabbing up houses and businesses that were owned by Jews."

"I have no heart to come back, Claude. I have a wife and son in Peru. Tina wouldn't like it here." They were sitting in a café. He looked around. "I feel like a stranger myself."

"What do you do for a living, Daniel? You were going to be a pharmacist, weren't you?"

"Yes. I'm still a pharmacist, in a way." When they were back at the house, Daniel gave Claude some samples of his tonic and healing ointment. He could see the lawyer's immediate interest.

"You know, Daniel," Montagne said thoughtfully, "France will recover economically. All of Europe will come back. Anyone who has a good idea, a product worth marketing, and a little money to get him started, will make a success. If you furnish the product, we'll recover the value of your father's property, and I'll pool my money with yours! I can handle all the legal technicalities here. What do you say? Shall we be partners?"

That was the beginning of Légende et Cie, the renowned French line of beauty and health products, whose magazine advertisements feature photographs of famous and beautiful women with the caption, "The legend that is LÉGENDE . . ."

Additional heartbreak awaited Daniel in Huaranca. He returned to find his beloved Tina desperately ill with typhoid fever and two-year-old Benjamin dead. Juan Carlos had sent for a doctor in Huaráz, to no avail. The child had died two days before Daniel's arrival. Tina had lost all desire to live in her grief at the boy's death.

Daniel did not have time to mourn his son. He spent every moment nursing Tina until he was at the point of collapse. She was all he had left in the world! He had never felt so bereft, so abandoned, as he did when he sat at her bedside.

Tina's improvement was slow, so Daniel took her to a specialist in Lima. Soon she recovered, and the following year their daughter was born.

When Nicole was three, Daniel rented a house in the capital, and from then on they lived there. But they returned to Huaranca whenever possible. And always in April . . . in time to see the wind flowers.

Chapter 4

Daniel arrived before the final mass of wind flowers. It was an amazing sight, unique in nature, and no matter how many times he had seen it, he always felt he was watching for the first time.

He took Nicole with him to the meadow. High above loomed Huascarán, mightiest of all the mountains in the Andes, its 22,000-foot summit sparkling white in the bright sunlight, dominating the horizon.

Daniel watched his four-year-old daughter fly across the field. Running recklessly, with the grace and freedom of an untamed creature, she threw back her head, shouting with glee.

Nicole was attracted by the violent splashes of color on the far slope of the field. These were the blossoms that nurtured the fortune of Daniel Légende, the flowers of the flamesword plants that had dried to a deep, lush crimson. At the end of the rainy season, the seed pods became puffy and brittle. The sacs, with their scarlet flowers, were then carried on the breezes high across the meadow and down into the gorge, where they were deposited in the humus of a eucalyptus forest.

Nicole ran in circles in the grass while Daniel sat on a boulder. He had not long to wait. As if on cue, a gust of wind stirred the stalks of the flameswords. A few flowers detached themselves and were carried along with the breeze, swirling in circles with a peculiar weightlessness.

Nicole stopped playing and raised her head, as if she had heard a voice in the wind.

Suddenly a mass of blossoms rose and the air was filled with flying flowers. Like thousands of brilliant scarlet hummingbirds, they swirled and darted until the wind swept over the meadow, carrying them in a cloud of crimson to the floor of the valley.

Nicole watched, spellbound, lifting her arms in joy. She turned to her father, an enraptured smile on her face. But then, as he gazed at her, enchanted with her beauty, her face crumpled and she began to cry.

"What is it, *chérie?*" he asked, picking her up and holding her close to comfort her.

She pointed to the edge of the field, to the barren stalks of the flameswords, jagged and forbidding. All of the brilliant color had fled, blown away by the wind.

Her father stroked her arm. "The flowers aren't gone forever, *ma chère*. Every year they'll bloom again and be beautiful for a short time, and then the wind will carry them down to the forest where they'll make new little plants. That's why they're called wind flowers, *flores del viento.*"

"Like the hacienda!"

"Yes, Nicole. Like the hacienda. . . . Do you know what the *campesinos* call it when something unexpected happens, something fateful and wonderful?"

"Like a surprise?"

"Umm . . . yes, like a surprise." She shook her head. "They call it a *flor del viento.*"

Nicole was too young to fully understand what her father told her about the wind flowers. But as she grew older, she came to believe that Daniel Légende himself was a flower of the wind, whose destiny it had been to be brought to this remote, hidden valley in the Andes, a region of majestic beauty.

The person Nicole loved most at the hacienda was her grandfather, Don Juan Carlos. He was a romantic figure to the little girl. She followed him around the plantation, listening to his tales of how he had come there from Trujillo to manage his family's property when he was a young man. He grew to love the mountains and the valley, and he stayed.

When he was forty, Juan Carlos married a beautiful Indian girl much younger than he. "The first time I saw your grandmother was in the church," he told Nicole. "She looked like a madonna."

Juan Carlos's wife had died giving birth to Nicole's mother, María Christina.

The *campesinos* became accustomed to the sight of

their *patrón* riding on his horse with his granddaughter perched in front of him on the withers. His thick shock of silver hair flying, his eyes narrowed against the wind, he galloped across the hacienda holding her in the protective circle of his arm.

For her fifth birthday, Don Juan Carlos gave Nicole a pony. She named him Flame. After that, they rode together side by side.

Nicole always wished for a baby brother.

Despite repeated miscarriages, Tina had tried again and again to have another child. Each time she became pregnant there was a sense of joy and hope in the household. Tina would appear especially radiant, and Daniel became even more solicitous than usual. Rosa, who had come from Huaranca to Lima as Nicole's nurse, would tell the little girl her mother was expecting a baby.

"Soon you will have a baby brother, Nicole. A fat baby brother!" Finally, Daniel had to instruct Rosa to say nothing because each time Tina miscarried, it was too painful to have to explain to Nicole why she would not have a baby brother after all.

Daniel wondered about keeping Rosa with the family in Lima. They had been living at the hacienda when Nicole was born, and Rosa, who was the daughter of the housekeeper Jacinta, was given the job of nursemaid. Nicole loved Rosa and Tina trusted her, but Daniel had misgivings.

Rosa was a child of the Andes, a *mestiza* whose speech was a mixture of Quechua and Spanish. Sweet-tempered and loyal, she retained all the superstitions of the high sierra. Rosa believed in the mountain gods, the *apus*, and although she prayed to Jesus, she depended as much on the old pre-Columbian beliefs of her people as she did on the religion of the padres.

By the time Nicole was five years old, Daniel realized that her speech had the intonations of a *campesina*, and she was picking up expressions and mannerisms from Rosa. It was Daniel's intention that his daughter, already showing signs of extraordinary beauty, would enter Lima society one day. To do this, she could not be encumbered with a *chola* accent. Her mixed blood would be handicap enough.

Among the old *criollo* families in Peru there were few without some Indian ancestry, no matter how they might pride themselves on their purity of blood, their *limpieza de sangre*. In Peru wealth had a bleaching effect on skin tone. No, it was not her Indian grandmother who would prevent Nicole from advancing in Lima society. More likely, it would be her Jewish father! This could be a considerable hindrance in a country where every national holiday and public institution, including the government, had a connection to the Church. To compound that disadvantage with a lack of social graces would be foolhardy.

Nicole was unusually bright. In addition to the Spanish and Quechua she had spoken since infancy, Daniel had taught her French, which they often spoke together. She had a wonderful mind, and now her father thought it was time to expand her knowledge.

Rosa was sent back to Huaranca, where a good marriage with Tomás, one of the plantation overseers, was arranged for her. In her place, Daniel hired an English woman who had been governess to the British Ambassador's children before they were sent home to boarding school.

The new governess was sensitive enough to understand that Nicole would miss her nurse, so she did not throw away the little dolls and charms Nicole kept as mementos from Rosa. Instead, she endeared herself to the child by finding a velvet-lined box of papier maché to hold the treasures. Nicole's favorite item from among this trove was the little cloth bag containing herbs and pebbles that had been fashioned to look like a female doll. Certainly the English woman could not have known this was a fertility charm.

Nicole was six when her mother finally gave birth to a healthy baby boy. There was much rejoicing in the Légende family and among the workers and house staff at Huaranca. Nicole was certain that Rosa's fertility doll had succeeded where nature had failed in the past.

The new baby was named André Emile Légende Iglesias. Nicole was his godmother. This meant that she would always be André's protector, her mother told her. She held the baby during the christening ceremony, and as she looked into his peaceful face, she felt the strength of her love for him. There would always be a special bond between them, she promised herself.

Nicole had been an only child for so long that it would not have been surprising if she resented the birth of the baby. But she had hungered for a brother or sister. All of her classmates at the exclusive convent school she attended had siblings. Sometimes in her daydreams she had pretended that one of them was hers.

Now she had André. She adored the little boy, assuming her role as his protector with great seriousness. When she heard there was an epidemic of spinal meningitis, she watched over the baby while he played, not allowing anyone except his nurse to approach him. When the nurse wheeled him through the gardens in his perambulator, Nicole accompanied them. No one knew she did this so that no harm would befall him. She had taken her mother's words literally, believing nothing evil could touch the baby as long as she watched over him.

Nicole had to leave André when it was time for her to go to school again. One day the little boy became ill with scarlet fever. To keep Nicole away from him, her parents sent her to Huaranca to stay with her grandfather.

André died while Nicole was away in the valley of the flamesword. Don Juan Carlos was the one who had to tell her. The child was inconsolable, believing her brother had died because she had not stayed with him. It was her responsibility as his godmother to remain at his side, and she had left him. The magic shield of her presence had been removed.

They brought the tiny coffin to Huaranca, where André was buried next to the firstborn son of Daniel and Tina, the brother she had never known. Nicole stared at the small grave with a stony face, unable to cry and unwilling to reconcile herself to the loss of André. She could take no comfort when her mother told her that he was with God in heaven. If God was so good and kind, she thought, he would have permitted the baby brother she loved to remain on earth with her.

Nicole's mother, who had nursed her son while he was ill, had contracted his strep infection. Shortly after the boy's death, she developed rheumatic fever. Tina had to remain in bed for many months, and her heart was permanently damaged.

Meanwhile, Nicole's parents were worried about her.
She continued to mourn silently for her brother, becoming thin and listless. It seemed unnatural to the family for
a girl of eight to grieve for so long a period. Daniel
remembered the joyful sprite who had cantered across
the meadow at Huaranca the previous summer. That was
the place where Nicole always seemed to be happiest.
The sooner the child returned there, he thought, the
faster she would regain her normal good health.

Jacinta bustled around the kitchen of the big house,
muttering to herself, trying to contain her annoyance at
Don Juan Carlos.
The heavy trestle table was laid for the midday meal,
the pot of *estofado de carne* simmered on the great iron
stove, and she had made *dulce de leche* for Nicole because the child liked the sweet caramel sauce spread on
pancakes. The old tiles of the floor had been swept clean,
the baskets of flowers replenished on the broad ledges of
the windows. Everything was in readiness. Where were
they?
How many times had she told Don Juan Carlos not to
be late for meals? Nicole needed her nourishment. The
child had been thin as a stray dog when she came to the
hacienda last month! On Jacinta's cooking, she was getting fatter and healthier by the day, *gracias a Dios*. They
had better get here soon. They were already an hour
late.
When another hour had passed, Jacinta went to find
Rosa's husband, Tomás. It was siesta and nothing stirred
in the courtyard of the plantation house. A thin film of
dust lay on the veranda, which was shaded by heavy
bougainvillea vines.
Jacinta hurried across the tiled court, through the rose
trellis of the back gardens, to the stucco house where
Rosa and Tomás lived. She hesitated a moment, thinking
she should not disturb them if they were in bed, then
knocked.
Rosa came to the door looking sleepy. "What is it,
Mamá?"
"I want to talk to Tomás. *El Patrón* has not returned
for his meal. The child is with him."

*   *   *

Don Juan Carlos led the way along the narrow ledge overlooking the gorge. It was a steep drop, but the horses were sure-footed and Nicole was a fine rider.

He stopped to point to a waterfall on the mountain across the gap. "That's where we're going to put in a hydroelectric station, Nicole. The water will give us the energy for electric power."

"We studied that in school, Grandpapa."

"Good! I'm glad the nuns are teaching you something besides sewing."

The child looked at him quizzically. "Girls are supposed to learn to sew, aren't they?"

"No harm will come from knowing how to sew. But whatever a boy learns, a girl should be taught as well."

"That's what my father says, but my governess says I must learn to be a lady."

"You can do both, Nicole. Many ladies are well educated."

Juan Carlos had recently told his daughter that Nicole should be taken out of the academy run by Dominican nuns and placed in a more modern institution. "She's old enough to be challenged, Tina," he had said. "If you leave her there, her brain will stop developing." Of course, that was before the baby's death and Tina's illness. Her parents didn't want to send the child to a new school now because there were already too many changes in Nicole's life.

The trail became steeper as they continued. "Let's go down here a little further. Stay behind me and keep the horse's head turned away from the ravine," the silver-haired *patrón* instructed her.

Nicole was frightened, but she did as her grandfather said. Sometimes he seemed to be testing her. She knew that he wanted her to be as brave as a boy.

The trail narrowed as it ran along the edge of the gulley. It was used as a footpath by the Indians when they went to one of the market towns in the Callejón de Huaylas, because it was miles shorter than the main road. Nicole made sure her horse's head was leading toward the left side of the track. Just looking into the sheer drop gave her a queasy feeling. She hoped they were not going over the bridge. It had rope rails and wooden slats, and you could see through to the chasm below.

When they reached the end of the ledge, Juan Carlos turned away from the bridge, taking the road leading toward the eucalyptus grove. The roadway was broad here and the ravine not as deep.

They were riding abreast. Juan Carlos kept to the outside, to Nicole's right. "That was real courage, Nicole. I wasn't sure you would do it without me taking your bridle. And you didn't even ask not to go on the bridge!" He smiled proudly at her.

She let out a shaky breath. "I was scared, but I didn't want to say so."

He nodded in approval. "That's good. When you pretend not to be frightened, it helps to overcome fear."

Grandpapa always taught her lessons like that. Little challenges, he called them.

She was beginning to feel better. Last month, when Papá brought her to Flor del Viento, she was angry and hurt that he would leave her here without anyone from home. She loved her grandfather, though, and soon his good humor and interesting stories dissolved her anger. Before long, she had stopped mourning for André. She still took flowers to his grave and left stones there where she had begun a little shrine, an *apacheta*, for him—but she no longer thought of dying herself.

She had purposely not eaten after André died. If she didn't eat, she thought, she would get sick and die too. It wasn't exactly that she wanted to die, but something had compelled her to push her plate away at dinner. Soon, she really had no appetite. Since coming to Huaranca, though, she was always hungry, eagerly waiting for Jacinta to prepare the next meal.

Flame stopped to nibble at some bushes on the side of the path. Nicole squinted at the sky, shading her eyes with her hand. The sun was high overhead. It was almost time for the midday meal.

She saw the edge of rock break off under the hooves of Juan Carlos's horse before she heard her grandfather's cry. Her mount shied and reared, as the great stallion whinnied in terror, desperately striving for a foothold. Frozen with horror, Nicole watched the slow, headlong tumble of horse and rider into the ravine.

"Grandpapa! Grandpapa!" she screamed.

But there was no sound except the soughing of the wind through the eucalyptus forest.

They found them near the bottom of the canyon. Nicole was sitting on the ground. Don Juan Carlos was dead. His head was resting in her lap and she stroked his forehead while she stared at nothing.

How Nicole had climbed down there no one could imagine. She had tied her horse to a tree, and that was how the men from the hacienda were able to find them.

It was a double tragedy, the loss of Don Juan Carlos Iglesias y Alba and the emotional trauma suffered by his young granddaughter. Tomás punished himself, feeling he was to blame for having let the *patrón* ride off alone with the girl. Daniel arrived at the hacienda, grief stricken and fearful about how the awful experience would affect Nicole.

He found his daughter dry-eyed and remote, unwilling to discuss the accident. She stood in the cemetery when they buried her grandfather, not crying, not sharing her grief with anyone. It wasn't normal for a child to react like this, thought Daniel. He knew Nicole well enough to realize all of her feelings were purposely held within.

Overnight Nicole seemed to have grown up. Her governess told her parents she was exemplary in every way. Her English was almost perfect. The nuns at school found her a bright and cooperative pupil. The only problem was she no longer acted like a child. Although she was only eight, she behaved like someone years older. Only Daniel knew something was wrong. He tried to talk to Nicole but was unsuccessful.

"I'd like to know what you're thinking, chérie, what's going on inside. I want to know the inner you."

She looked at him innocently. "There is no inner me," she replied.

Nicole was eleven when she came to Daniel's study.

"Papá? Are you Jewish?"

"Yes I am, Nicole. You know that. You've seen when I go to the synagogue."

"Did you kill Jesus?"

Daniel gasped. "Did I *what?* Where did you hear such a thing?"

"Sister says the Jews killed Jesus. Does that mean *all* the Jews, or just some of them?"

"It means . . . it means . . . that *Sister Constanza is a wicked woman, a lying bigot* . . . to tell such things to children. . . ." Daniel completely lost control.

He and Tina agreed that Nicole should be removed at once from the academy and placed in the English school attended by the foreign diplomats' children. Daniel castigated himself for not having taken this step earlier. In his determination that she be given all the advantages of the children of Lima's first families, he had sent her to school with their daughters. Nicole was almost past childhood. What harm had been done?

He lay in the big bed in Tina's room. They had stopped sleeping together when the doctor advised that sexual relations would be harmful to her weak heart. But there were times when he could not stand to spend the night apart from her, when he needed the comfort of just being able to touch her, like now.

He thought she had fallen asleep.

"Take her to the synagogue," she said.

"What did you say, my dearest?"

"I said I want you to take Nicole to the synagogue with you."

He drew her into his arms. "I think it's too late for that, Tina. It will confuse her."

"She's been a Catholic all these years because we thought it had to be that way, Daniel. We thought it would be best for her. For now, the Church has failed her. Let her learn something about her father's religion, and then she'll be free to choose."

With his face pressed against her breast, he let the tears come. "I didn't know it would mean so much to me," he told her. He could hear the beating of her heart, that fragile organ on which her life depended.

It was a new kind of fear, the dread of a new school. The first time, walking into a classroom filled with strange, curious faces. And *boys!*

No uniforms here. She was the only one wearing oxfords and dark blue knee socks, the only one with braids going down her back to her waist.

She had forgotten how to smile. *They hate me. I know they all hate me.* Expressionlessly, she endured the morning classes, conducted entirely in English, until recess, when everyone filed out to the playground.

Nicole sat on a bench watching the groups form for games.

"Hello! I'm Françoise Bercy. What's your name?" She looked up to see a short, fine-boned girl with dark springy curls and mischievous brown eyes. Her English was French-accented and her smile infectious.

By the end of recess, Nicole had made a new friend.

In the summer after Nicole's fourteenth birthday, her mother died of heart failure.

The silver-gray Rolls Royce followed the hearse north along the Panamericana and inland through the river valley to the mountains. In eight hours they reached Huaranca, where Tina was buried in the hacienda's cemetery, near her parents and next to the small graves of André and Benjamin.

Nicole could scarcely remember a time when her mother had not been ill. Whenever she imagined Tina, it was as a beautiful and delicate, spiritual presence, all peaceful and good. Sometimes she tried to picture Tina before André had died, when she had been active and able to run and play with her, but something prevented the image from forming. It was as if a curtain had been drawn over a segment of Nicole's childhood.

She had watched her father as he sat at his dying wife's bedside, holding her hand and stroking her cheek. How devoted they had been. Most rich Lima businessmen tired of their wives, Nicole knew. Especially when the husband was an urbane European and the wife a *mestiza* from the sierra. But Daniel was one of those constant men. He had treasured Tina's love and nurtured her intellect. She was wise, despite her lack of education, and he had relied on her advice in all the facets of his life.

Nicole clung to her grieving father. One by one the members of her family were dying. He would be next! Who would be there for her if her father should die?

She returned to the cemetery alone the day after her

mother's funeral, bringing a bouquet of wildflowers. The freshly turned earth was soft in the summer heat. With her finger, she traced the carving on the stone marker:

María Christina Iglesias de Légende
January 19, 1925–February 12, 1960

The gravestone was warmed by the sun. Nicole remembered how her mother had longed for the sun of Huaranca when the pervasive fog of Lima's winter cast its pall on the city.

"I hope you're warm now, Mamá. I hope you're not in pain any longer," she whispered.

She had thought she could not cry, but she wept now, sobbing convulsively, shedding tears for all the sorrows she had known in the past and held inside. Her tears fell on the soil of her mother's Inca ancestors, as she thought of the strange destiny that had brought her parents together. That twist of fate that was responsible for the unlikely meeting of Daniel and Tina had left her a legacy.

She, too, was a flower of the wind.

Chapter 5

We're going to Paris, Nicole!'' Daniel burst into the music room. He swooped her up, swinging her around in circles, while she laughed helplessly.

"Papá!" She was almost as tall as he . . . he hadn't done this since she was a little girl. It was the first time she'd seen him so animated or happy in the three months since Tina had died.

"Did you hear what I said, my sweet? I'm taking you to Paris!"

"On a trip, Papá?"

"Not on a trip, Nicole. For a long stay . . . maybe permanently."

It meant saying good-bye to her governess, to Rosa and Tomás and Jacinta, to all of her friends in Lima except Françoise Bercy, whose family was French and who would be returning to Paris soon to finish her education.

Daniel held a party for all the workers at Flor del Viento. There were *anticuchos,* skewered and barbecued meat; *cazuelado,* roasted guinea pig and potatoes; and much drinking of *chicha,* the fermented corn brew.

As Daniel sat laughing and trading jokes with the workers, he overheard some *campesinos* saying, "We have a good *patrón!*"

With a chill, he realized they meant him.

Daniel's last act before leaving the country was to divest himself of the working lands of the hacienda and to transfer the plantation house and its gardens to the ownership of Nicole Légende.

They sailed to England from Panama. At the House of Lords, Daniel said, "Jews could be elected to Parliament in 1858, but they weren't given full citizenship until 1890.

Can you imagine that? But on the whole, the English have been good to their Jews."

From there they proceeded to Amsterdam, where Daniel had business. At the Rijksmuseum he said, "The Dutch have been good to their Jews. They tried to shield them from the Nazis. Jews have had full citizenship in Holland since 1796."

Finally, they reached Paris. They stayed at Le Bristol until Daniel found the apartment on the Avenue Foch which became their home in France.

He spent the first month taking her on excursions. They visited La Prée, the village where he had been born. He showed her the small synagogue he had rebuilt in memory of his parents and sisters and the other Holocaust victims of the town.

"The French were . . ."

"Don't tell me," she cut him off, laughing. "I know! They were good to their Jews."

He smiled self-consciously. "To tell you the truth, Nicole, the French haven't been so good to the Jews . . . but they were the first European country to give them full citizenship—under Napoleon. The best thing Napoleon ever did was to free the ghettos of Europe."

"Father," she asked, "why is it that every country we visit you judge according to how they treat their Jews? Why does everything have to be measured by that?"

He looked at her sternly. "There is no other measure, Nicole. That is *my yardstick!* If a country has persecuted the Jews, I have little regard for anything else it may have accomplished."

"You never used to speak like this, Father. I don't recall you often talking about being Jewish when I was younger."

"That was my mistake."

Another new school with different faces and customs. Nicole was advanced a grade because of her languages and the private tutoring she had been given in science and math. It was not easy to make friends. The French were difficult to know, and her classmates were older.

Nicole was delighted when Françoise arrived for the second semester and was enrolled in the same lycée with her. The two girls became inseparable. When Daniel had to travel for business, Nicole was invited to stay at the Bercy residence. Françoise always came along when they spent weekends at the house Nicole's father bought in Normandy. Daniel's business partner and best friend, Claude Montagne, was usually there, and often the charming Isabelle Somme would join them.

"Does your father sleep with her?" asked Françoise, who was a year older and had always been more worldly and knowledgeable than Nicole.

"Of course not!" Nicole answered. But after that, despite Daniel's discretion, she came to believe he did.

On weekends in Paris Uncle Claude, who was a bachelor, sometimes took her to the ballet or the opera. Her father told her the woman Claude once loved had been killed in the war. They met when they were resistance fighters in the Maquis. She was caught by the Gestapo, tortured, and died rather than betray her friends. Nicole thought it terribly romantic that Claude had remained true to her memory. She wondered whether she would be able to withstand the pain of torture like Uncle Claude's brave fiancée.

The following summer they returned to Peru for July and August, the South American winter. Daniel had business to conduct in Lima, but the city was dreary for Nicole, so she stayed at Flor del Viento, and her father came up at the end of each week.

Daniel noticed how joyful Nicole was at the hacienda. He congratulated himself. It had been the right decision to take her to Paris when Tina died. Before they left Peru, the Andean valley had become a place of sorrow for them, a pilgrimage to graves. By going away, Nicole had forgotten the unhappiness and retained her love for the people and the land. Now, she was able to enjoy Huaranca.

They rode together and as he watched Nicole gallop across the plantation on Flame II, he was filled with nostalgia. She was on the brink of maturity, he realized, not yet aware of herself, still clinging to girlhood. What a beautiful woman she promised to become.

At the Paris apartment, Nicole was accustomed to being with Daniel's contemporaries. She began to act as her father's hostess when he gave parties. Her facility

with languages was an asset with his business associates
from other countries.

"Don't you find it a *bore?*" Françoise groaned. The
lively gamin had been invited for one of these occasions
and found it less than diverting.

"Sometimes," Nicole admitted. "But Papá always tries
to seat someone interesting next to me."

The two girls were in their nightgowns, lying on the
bed in Nicole's room. Françoise studied Nicole. "It's
strange. You're so mature in some ways . . . and yet *look*
at you, with your hair in braids! Why don't you cut it?"

"Papá wouldn't like it."

"That was when you were a child. You're almost sixteen! Well, *at least* let me show you how to wear it so the
boys will notice you."

Françoise strove to help her acquire sophistication, but
Nicole told her friend it was hopeless. "You're built to be
stylish, but I'm too tall. I'll always be gawky."

In the fall of 1962 Nicole began the six-year course of
study at the University of Paris that would lead to a
medical degree. Françoise, for lack of another interest,
decided to join her. In the French system, it was easy to
register for medical studies and postpone the day of
reckoning until final examinations. At the end of the first
year, Nicole passed with high marks and, thanks to her
help, Françoise managed to get through without failing.

They had finished the fourth year at the Faculté de
Médecine by June of 1966. Nicole and her father would
soon be leaving for their annual visit to Peru. Françoise
insisted Nicole come to a Scandinavian students' party
aboard an excursion boat on the River Seine. Nicole was
reluctant to join her because this was a group she did not
know.

"Nicole, you *never* go to parties! How will you meet
anyone if you spend all your time with your father and
his friends?"

When the boat pulled away from the landing, Nicole
stayed close to Françoise as the petite brunette pushed
her way through the crowded cabin. Everyone seemed to
know her, especially the boys, who shouted greetings.
Nicole admired her friend's savoir faire with these tall
Swedes and Danes, whose fair coloring was such a con-

trast to Françoise's dark chic. The Scandinavians in their nautical student caps reminded her of turn-of-the-century photographs of the Russian Czar and his family on royal outings.

In the rear of the cabin an impromptu band played campy American dance tunes from the forties. The woodwinds were good; the brass . . . well, brassy. The tempo dragged, despite the drummer's efforts to carry the beat along.

She followed Françoise out to the rear deck, where it was quieter and less crowded. From the river, Paris had the softness of a painting in the rosy light of the lingering sunset. The celebrated bridges and stone buildings were tinged with umbers and vermilions. Nicole regretted that the lighthearted essence of Paris had eluded her. Her life with her father, privileged and formal, was such a contrast to the way these students lived. She wondered, with a tinge of envy, what it was like to be one of them.

Girls in Peru were carefully chaperoned. She enjoyed more freedom here than she would in Lima, of course, but although her father was French and not as strict as most Peruvian parents, she had never gone out alone with a boy.

Nicole turned from the passing city and leaned back against the railing. She glanced inside, where the band was playing sing-alongs. The drummer still held the group together, his foot keeping rhythm on the bass drum. He played with loose-jointed nonchalance, his shoulders hunching a little with the beat, his head nodding under the cap, worn at a rakish angle. He was blond, with lean, regular Nordic features and a flashing smile. She became absorbed in watching him, fascinated by his understated way with the music.

"That's Erik," said Françoise. "Good-looking, isn't he? He's a great favorite with women. I think he's sexy!"

Embarrassed to have been caught watching the drummer, Nicole pretended to study him for the first time. She turned away. "He's not my type."

Françoise laughed. "I would be interested to know who *is* your type, Nicole. Tell me!"

She tossed her head. "I haven't met him yet. When I do, I'll let you know."

The boat returned upstream under a full moon. When

the band played again, Nicole leaned sideways against the rail in order to have a view of the drummer.

A few days later she flew to Lima with her father.

Back in Paris in the autumn, Nicole resumed her medical studies. The program had advanced well into clinical and therapeutical work, requiring an intensive schedule of mornings in the hospital and afternoon labs at the Rue des Sts. Pères. As the work became more demanding, she often begged out of the dinners her father planned, explaining that the clinics took too much of her time now. She found it a challenge to keep up with her lab reports and reading assignments, often studying in the medical library, where it was quiet and reference materials were at hand.

On the day that she met him, Nicole was still working in the library at five o'clock. Returning from the stacks with a book, she was chagrined to find a man sitting in her place at the table, perusing her texts, riffling through her notebook. She was about to confront him, when he turned his head.

It was the drummer.

"I . . . you . . . that was my seat," she stammered. "You're sitting in my chair."

"How else was I going to get you to notice me . . . Nicole?" He grinned, and her irritation melted away. She felt a rush of warm affection and a kind of longing she did not recognize.

"You were on the *bateau* last summer. I noticed you then."

"Yes," he answered, as he gathered her books together and placed them in her knapsack. "You watched me all evening long."

What effrontery! she thought. But she allowed him to take her arm and steer her through the hallway, past the grand staircase and the amphitheater, and out to the Rue de L'Université.

All that time he had not said a word. He turned, smiling at her, and her heartbeat quickened. "Well, Nicole, shall we go eat *cassoulet* at the Brasserie St. Louis? My name is Erik . . . Erik Sonnenborg."

So it began.

For all of that lingering autumn, throughout the damp

and dreary winter and on into the promise-filled beauty of Paris spring, they were together. She discovered a Paris she had suspected but never known, an intoxicating Paris of beauty and life and laughter.

They wandered through the winding streets of the Latin Quarter, peering into dusty shops, stopping to embrace in the shadow of a doorway. Standing on the Pont Royal, leaning over the railing to toss bread crumbs to the ducks, they waved at tourists on the *bateaux mouches*.

The aroma of roasting lamb in the Algerian section, the hurdy gurdy of street minstrels, the slickness of rain-puddled pavements—everything took on a new enchantment and meaning. Seen through Erik's eyes, Paris became the most enthralling city in the world because it was their city.

He taught her how to cook. Wine and food were important because they were shared with Erik. . . . And flowers! Everywhere, flowers from the stalls, which he bought in great bunches until there was no space left in her room for another vase.

Each night she closed her eyes, eager for the next day to begin because it meant she would be with him again.

He attracted people more than anyone she had ever known. Erik's friends! They gave concerts, recitals, and art openings. They held *salons* in small cramped apartments where students mingled with painters and musicians, scientists and political theorists. They wanted to meet her because if she was with Erik, then of course she must be interesting.

There were quiet times alone, when she could share her confusion. For Erik, like Nicole, was a product of crossed cultures, but he was secure in his identity, drawing strength from his mixed background.

Erik was born in Copenhagen. His parents had been a respected Jewish physician and a Finnish concert pianist of some renown. When the Germans invaded Denmark in 1940, Dr. Nils Sonnenborg was no more apprehensive than other Danes. His patients included members of the royal family, and his Christian wife was the toast of the concert circuit. Besides, the Danes demonstrated how they would defy the German edicts regarding Jews. Every Dane, including the King, appeared in public wearing the six-pointed Star of David.

In 1943 the Germans put the King and his ministers under house arrest and began rounding up Jews. The Danish people hid almost all of their seven thousand Jewish compatriots, and under cover of darkness smuggled them in fishing boats across the Oresund to Sweden. Active in this rescue operation were Erik's parents. The doctor insisted that Anikka, his wife, take their infant with the last boatload to Malmö. Once in Sweden, she arranged for Erik to go to Palestine with the Youth Aliyah. Intending to return to her husband in Copenhagen, Anikka learned that Nils had been arrested by the Gestapo. She was warned that she, too, faced arrest if she went back to Denmark.

Anikka fled to her native Finland where she stayed with her family, waiting for Nils to be freed. By the time she heard he had been executed, the Russians had invaded that part of Finland, closing the borders. For the rest of the war years, and for ten years after that, Anikka was unable to leave the town where she had been born because it was now part of the Soviet Union.

Meanwhile, Erik had grown tall, strong, and confident in Palestine. He had witnessed the birth of the new State of Israel. Living on a kibbutz, he expected to spend the rest of his life there. He knew his father had died, and his mother was missing, presumed dead. There was every reason to think he would never return to Denmark, the country of the parents he could not remember.

In 1955 the Jewish Agency heard from Anikka Sonnenborg, requesting their help in locating her son. The Russians were permitting a few citizens of Finnish birth who lived in the captured territories to leave in order to join their families. Reunited, Anikka and thirteen-year-old Erik went to Copenhagen, where she recovered whatever could be salvaged of the Sonnenborg wealth.

Erik had finished high school in Denmark and entered the university as a medical student when his mother died. At the end of his medical training, he went to Israel to rediscover the country that had shaped him. There, at the Weizmann Institute in Rehovot, he met a professor from Paris—a man who was experimenting with ovum transfer for the breeding of domestic animals. So excited was Erik with this work that in 1965 he came to Paris to do post-graduate research in the laboratory of the professor.

Soon the word got around among his friends that Erik had a new girl friend.

Françoise, who thought Nicole naive, warned her about him. "Be careful! He's always taking up with girls and dropping them. Don't get hurt, Nicole."

The first time he kissed her they were at his apartment on the Rue du Bac. He bent his head to hers and slowly, tantalizingly, his lips caressed hers until she swayed toward him, wanting more and more of him. Never before had she experienced the longing his kisses aroused in her. Never had she thought she could feel such passionate desire. Drunk on the wine of his kisses, she dreamed of making love to him.

Theirs was an afternoon romance because her father seemed to think that nothing untoward could happen before sunset. They became lovers on a rainy Sunday afternoon in April. In later years, whenever Nicole remembered making love with Erik, she thought of that first time, how happy she had felt lying in his arms, daylight dappling their bodies through the blinds of the rain-washed bedroom windows.

"Is it always like this?" she had asked.

He had looked down at her, gently smoothing her cheek with his hand. "No," he replied, his voice soft and husky with spent desire. "Never has it been like this before. . . ."

Daniel Légende liked Erik. He approved of his Danish good manners, his command of languages, and his intelligence. Erik, too, had a Jewish father, which was oddly reassuring to Daniel. If Nicole and he were to marry next year when she finished medical school, they would live in Paris, or perhaps Copenhagen. Daniel's code would permit his daughter to live in Denmark. The Danes were good to their Jews.

That summer of 1967 was meant to be theirs, for the two of them to be together. They had made wonderful plans.

The professor of pediatric medicine had asked Nicole to work in the clinic at Hôpital Necker des Enfants

Malades, and her father had agreed. Daniel had decided not to spend the vacation in Peru that year because of the political unrest. From each of his recent trips to Lima, he had returned to Paris alarmed at the growing threat to the weak constitutional government of President Fernando Belaúnde Terry. He reported that life in the Peruvian capital was full of inconveniences because of riots and workers' strikes.

Daniel was going on an extended business trip to the United States, before joining Isabelle Somme in Monaco. From Orly, where she had bid farewell to her father, Nicole went directly to Erik's apartment.

It was Monday, the 5th of June. They were celebrating the anniversary of their encounter aboard the excursion boat, a year ago, a year in which Erik had become the most important person in the world to her, even more important than her father. Erik was everything that a father could not be—her best friend, the confidant with whom she was able to share her most intimate thoughts . . . and her lover.

At Erik's apartment house, she squeezed into the lift, a baguette protruding from the overstuffed shopping bag, nearly getting caught in the door. The apartment was empty, but a lamp was lit and there was a note propped up against it. "Chérie—I had to go out. Will return in time for dinner. I love you. E."

Nicole opened the refrigerator to begin preparing the food. There was a bottle of champagne chilling. They *were* going to celebrate!

She finished cutting the asparagus and was whisking egg whites for the sauce when she heard the apartment door open and close quietly. "Is that you, chéri?" she called.

Erik walked slowly into the room, his face sober.

Nicole set down the bowl and went to him. She put her arms around his neck and kissed him. "Erik! You should be smiling. This is a celebration, remember?" He held her against him, his arms tightening. "Erik? What is it? Something has happened."

"Israel," was all he said. Then, "The war has begun."

Nicole knew how concerned he had been over the past month. Since early May, the Israeli army had been on alert. The Arab forces were poised on Israel's borders.

After demanding that the UN peace-keeping forces leave Gaza and Sinai, Egypt closed off the Gulf of Aqaba, blocking Israel's only southern outlet to the sea. Erik had told her there would almost certainly be another war. But it had been going on for so many weeks that she had begun to doubt there would actually be fighting.

"What's happening? When did it begin?"

"This morning. I've been at the embassy to see my friends. Israel is so *small* compared to the Arabs . . . so vastly outnumbered." His eyes would not meet hers.

She held her breath. "What are you trying to tell me?"

He took her face in his hands. "I must go there, darling. They need everyone."

"*No!* Why must *you* go? You're a Dane! You don't belong to Israel."

He shook his head. "Yes, I'm a Dane. But I *do* belong to Israel. I owe my life to Israel. It was the only place in the world I could go when I needed a home. And now I can't turn my back on them when they need me."

She argued with him, terrified that he would be killed or injured, but soon realized it was futile. To assuage her fears, he said, "I won't be a combatant, Nicole. I'm a doctor and they'll use me for medical work, so I won't be in danger."

Fighting back tears, Nicole said, "Dinner will be ready soon. Will you open the wine?"

But he shook his head. "I'm not hungry for food." He turned her to face him. "I'm hungry for you."

He was gone within two hours. Nicole stayed at his apartment, wanting to be where he had been, touching the pillow where his head had lain, the desk where his books and papers were piled, his covered drums in a corner of the living room. If she could maintain a physical link with him, she thought, he would be safe. The old superstitions of her childhood persisted against all reason. Through the remainder of that night she kept a watch, falling asleep at last as dawn rose.

She was glad for the distraction of the Clinique des Enfants, spending extra long hours and then staying even later to record the day's work. Each night she would rush to the newsstand near the Metro stop at Montparnasse to

buy *Paris-Soire* and the *Herald Tribune,* reading everything she could find about the war in Israel.

The Israelis had occupied the Gaza Strip . . . the Sinai
Peninsula . . . Jordanian territory west of the Jordan
River. All of Jerusalem was in Israeli hands. By the end
of the week, five days after the war began, fighting was
concentrated in the north on the Syrian border, at the
Golan Heights. Nicole remembered Erik telling her that
his kibbutz, the place where he had lived as a young boy,
was in the north near the Golan.

On Saturday, June 10, Françoise came to dinner.
They had not been together often since Nicole had begun
seeing Erik. After dinner, Nicole carried the open bottle
of Pinot Chardonnay to the library.

Françoise had just launched into an amusing tale about
her summer internship on the men's urological ward when
the maid announced that there was an overseas call for
Nicole. She assumed it would be her father.

It was Erik. The connection was terrible, full of static
and interrupted regularly by an operator speaking Hebrew. But she understood what he was saying, his voice
excited and confident. "It's over, Nicole! They've called
a cease-fire. We've *won!*"

She was laughing and crying at once. "When will you
be home?" she shouted into the telephone. "I miss you,
darling."

"In a few days. I'll send you a cable. I love you,
Nicole!"

"I love you, Erik . . . I love you more than life. . . ."

"We'll have our anniversary dinner, after all. Soon."
Then they were cut off.

Nicole returned to Françoise and they both got high on
the wine, drinking to Erik, to Israel, to love.

Erik cabled at the end of the following week. Nicole
rushed around, buying ingredients for the same menu she
had thrown away two weeks before. Full of anticipation,
she smiled at the champagne, still resting on its side in
Erik's refrigerator. She filled the apartment with bunches
of flowers, the way Erik had the first time he had taken
her there.

By six o'clock the asparagus was ready for steaming,
the veal scallops pounded thin and seasoned. Nicole sat
on the couch with a book but found she could not con-

centrate. Excited and nervous, she listened to records, turned on the radio, then switched it off, glancing at her watch every fifteen minutes.

Erik's cable had said "ARRIVING DINNER LATE MONDAY/ KEEP EVERYTHING WARM/ LOVE ERIK." She had no idea how he was traveling—whether by military transport or commercial airline. Although regular service had not been reestablished, there were El Al flights coming out of Lod Airport.

She called one of his friends at the Israeli embassy to ask if Erik was on the manifest of an El Al flight, and he promised to let her know if he was able to get any information. "He'll probably arrive in Paris before I hear anything." Nicole told him she would be waiting for Erik at his apartment.

At half past eleven the doorbell rang. Nicole had dozed off. She sat up with a start as the bell rang a second time. With a cry of joy, she crossed the room and threw open the door. "Erik . . . !"

But it wasn't Erik.

First came denial. *It has to be a mistake! The war is over. His cable said he was coming home.*

No, it wasn't a mistake. Erik had been on his way to the airfield. He had been shot by a sniper when he stopped to help an old Arab who had fallen on the side of the road.

Next came anger. *Erik was a doctor! He wore the medical armband clearly identifying him as a non-combatant.*

Terrorists don't respect symbols or non-combatants. Chances are the old Arab was a decoy.

Then came despair. How would she go on? She had no desire to live without him. "I love you more than life. . . ." she had said, and she meant it.

In the first weeks, she was paralyzed by her grief. Then she returned to the hospital and began working frantically, as if something dreadful would happen if she stopped.

Françoise tried to console her. "Time will help, Nicole. I know you don't believe it now, but you'll eventually forget your sorrow."

"I don't want to forget."

"But you will! Everyone does. You'll want to be loved again. Someday you'll marry . . ."

"No!" Her vehemence shocked Françoise. She breathed deeply, "I will never marry anyone."

"Erik wouldn't want you to be bitter."

"I'm not bitter," she replied. "Only realistic. *I'll never take that chance.*"

"Sometimes it's worth it to take chances. Think about the happiness you might find."

"I don't want to think about it!"

Until Erik, she had been alone. Now she would always be alone.

Daniel had immediately flown back to Paris from New York to be with Nicole. After the initial shock, he found her increasingly unresponsive, continuing with her work at the hospital, unwilling to discuss Erik or his death. It was like a replay of her reaction as a child when André and her grandfather had died.

As time passed, he feared Nicole would suffer a deep depression if she did not grieve, did not allow her sorrow to come to the surface. He thought he understood something and that there was a solution. Nicole could not grieve because she did not *believe* in Erik's death. If she saw his grave, if she had visible proof that he no longer walked the earth, she would acknowledge it, go through a period of mourning, and then recover. They flew to Israel together, traveled to Galilee to the kibbutz where Erik had spent his youth and where he now lay in the ground among the fresh graves of so many other young people.

Nicole achieved a strange release there at Erik's graveside. Daniel could not have perceived what really happened to her as she stood with bowed head, eyes dry, staring at the simple inscription:

Erik Sonnenborg, 1942–1967
He returned in our hour of need.

Everyone I love dies, she thought. The only one left is my father. All the others are gone. My mother, my grandfather, my baby brother, and now Erik. He took the place of all of them. I loved him more than I've ever loved anyone, more than I thought it was possible to love.

If love makes you so vulnerable, then to love someone is to open yourself to heartbreak. It's self-destructive to love, to become dependent on another person for your happiness. *Never again will I permit myself to fall in love!*

Paris held only poignant memories for Nicole. Immersed in her final year of medical school, she avoided all social contacts except for Françoise. In the spring of 1968, the university was closed because of a nationwide student strike. With no classes for Nicole to attend, Daniel took the opportunity to invite her to the meeting of the Board of Directors of Légende et Cie . . . and it was there that she was introduced to Manuel Caldeiro-León.

She and Daniel traveled to Lima that summer, the first time Nicole had been home in over two years. She was startled at the sights in the Peruvian capital. Perhaps she had been blind in the past to the terrible living conditions of the poor in the *barriadas,* the permanent slums that staggered up the hillsides surrounding the city. When she was young, she had not questioned the vast inequities in living standards. Her careful upbringing had shielded her from the unpleasantness that existed around her.

The political and economic situation had become even more volatile in Peru during the past year. Daniel, the witness of history, waited for an eruption. The mood among all but the wealthy who depended on foreign capital, was anti-American. The leftists blamed American interests for all of Peru's ills.

"They speak as if the *campesinos* had a wonderful life before International Petroleum!" scoffed Daniel.

It was his view that, because of its violent history as a Spanish colony, it was Peru's destiny to be ruled by a succession of "conquistadors," foreign and domestic. Oppression and militarism seemed to have been bred into her people. President Belaúnde, who had come into office promising agrarian reforms, raising hopes for the success of a representative, republican government, had been unable to carry out the promises of his party. It was only a matter of time until he would be forced out.

It was Nicole's idea that she work as a summer intern

in one of Lima's hospitals. She had always spent the
vacations in Peru relaxing and amusing herself in Lima or
at the hacienda. But no more. In June she visited Professor Jorge Alvares at the San Martín University Hospital.

She would never forget the shock of her first sight of
the outpatient clinic. The sick filled every available space
in the waiting area, sitting and lying on the floor, spilling
over into the hallways. Victims of heart attacks, puncture
wounds, broken bones, domestic quarrels, and venereal
disease waited alongside nursing mothers who suckled
their sickly babies while older children clung to their
knees, crying with pain and fright.

In a corner, slumped against a wall, a heavyset man lay
dying. His head and neck were swathed in a makeshift
bandage darkened with congealed blood. A distraught
woman knelt at his side. No one paid the slightest attention to them.

Diseased, malnourished, and dirty, they repelled her.
She was certain she could not work with such patients.
Just to touch them would be distasteful, but to examine
them, to probe mouths studded with rotting teeth, to
press her fingers into matted hair full of vermin, or to
give a pelvic or rectal examination to women who had no
understanding of personal hygiene—she could imagine
the diseases they would have—no, she could not possibly
bring herself to do it!

Following Dr. Alvares, the chief of the Department of
Maternal and Child Health, through the maternity ward
where there were two patients to a bed and mattresses on
the floor besides, she thought about the order and efficiency of the Hôpital Necker in Paris. She had been
trained to use the latest medical and scientific equipment,
the most modern facilities and diagnostic procedures. What
good would that training do her here? She would just
become frustrated—the way she had always heard students from the Third World did when they returned to
their own countries after training in the modern hospitals
and laboratories of the United States and Europe.

Nicole cleared her throat. "Professor Alvares . . . where
are . . . uh . . . private patients admitted if they should
come to the University Hospital?"

Alvares sighed, indicating his disappointment. "The
private hospital is also part of San Martín, Dr. Légende.

It's in the Garden Annex near the Government Palace. You haven't ever been to the Odría Pavilion?"

"No, I haven't. You see, I've been living in Paris since I was fourteen." She knew it sounded inadequate.

"I had hoped . . ." he began, but smiled and said, "Of course, we're happy to have you in any case. I'm sure it can be arranged."

By this time they had reached the children's ward. They stopped at the foot of a crib where a listless two-year-old lay sucking her thumb. Nicole assumed that the intravenous fluid infusion attached to the little girl's arm meant she was being treated for dehydration, probably from dysentery. She paused to read the chart hanging from the crib.

"Professor Alvares, this baby has been diagnosed as having a salt-losing adrenal insufficiency. She should be on aldosterone . . . but I don't see it ordered for her."

The professor's smile was sad. "Sometimes we must do the best we can, when modern drugs aren't available," was his gentle reply.

Nicole looked down at the small girl, who had not yet noticed her. There was an unfathomable sadness in the wide, staring eyes. Nicole moved to the side of the crib. The vacant look changed when the child saw her. She removed her finger from her mouth and struggled to rise, holding out her thin arms to Nicole and giving her the smile of an angel.

Nicole felt the prick of tears behind her eyes and was flooded with a sense of shame. How selfish I am, she thought. I have never known what it is to lie ill in an iron hospital crib without someone to love me or care what happens to me.

She bent to pick up the child, holding it close, lowering her head so the professor would not see how emotional she had become. The little girl put her free arm around Nicole's neck, laying her head on her shoulder.

What would happen to such children if every well-trained physician rejected hospitals like San Martín with its limited resources? She knew what she wanted to do.

"I'd like to work *here*, Professor Alvares. I would like to work with the children, and the mothers."

Nicole could hardly function in her first days at San

Martín Hospital. After the highly organized structure of
the Hôpital Necker, San Martín was chaotic. By the end
of the second week she had learned to practice a selec-
tion process, quickly deciding which patients needed immediate attention and which could wait. The kindly Dr.
Alvares observed her closely and gradually gave her more
and more responsibility in the Maternal and Child Health
clinic.

It was a happy summer for Nicole, despite the frustra-
tions of working in a poorly equipped hospital. For the
first time, she felt truly needed by her patients. It put her
own problems in perspective. She realized how fortunate
she was when she saw the misery of the women and
children who came to San Martín.

With one exception, she got along well with the staff.
After an initial reserve, they accepted her, realizing that
she would work hard and expected no special privileges.
Only Mona Ramos, superintendent of the outpatient clinics, remained unfriendly to her, but Nicole was certain
that with time she would gain the woman's respect. Alvares
ran his own show at San Martín, which caused some
friction and jealousies. Mona Ramos was one of those
who occasionally obstructed the work of the autonomous
Maternal and Child clinic.

As the end of the summer approached and Daniel
began to speak of returning to Paris, Nicole went to the
private office of Jorge Alvares.

"Well, Nicole," he said, dropping the formality of the
clinic. "Soon you'll be leaving us. I'll miss you."

She leaned forward. "Professor Alvares, I don't want
to leave San Martín. I want to stay here for the rest of
my internship instead of returning to Paris. Do you think
that would be possible?"

Alvares could not contain his pleasure, nor his surprise. "My dear Nicole! I would consider it a privilege to
act as your sponsor."

He clasped his hands together, smiling. Nodding his
head in approval, he said, "Yes, Nicole, this is right for
you. You and I, we understand these things. When much
has been given to you, it is necessary to return the debt."

Daniel had never expected this. His plans for Nicole,
even before she met Erik, had been for her to remain in

Paris after medical school, to pursue her career as a pediatrician or as a researcher at one of the elite laboratories. Légende was an important name in France and many doors would be open to her. Certainly he had not envisioned her spending the rest of her days in Lima.

Peru was not a country where a woman could lead a rewarding life unless she was content to remain within the heart of her family. The Légende family . . . what was it? Nicole and Daniel.

Daniel was often depressed thinking about this. How broad were his dreams when he was young! Once there had been two little sons. If only they had lived, Nicole would have two brothers to protect her when he was gone. Now there was no one until Nicole married.

She would be far better off in Paris, where women were respected and able to go out in the streets alone. It worried Daniel when Nicole drove to the hospital. She wouldn't agree to have the chauffeur take her. The ideas she had about not wanting the staff or medical students to see a display of her father's wealth! Daniel shook his head in exasperation.

She was a *wonderful* daughter, a beauty, and smarter than most men he knew. But she had become too independent since the death of Erik Sonnenborg. When Erik died, he had taken the essence of Nicole's carefree spirit and joyousness with him. The Nicole who went to San Martín Hospital each day was a far different person from the girl who had lived in Paris. This Nicole seldom laughed, never sang for sheer joy, no longer teased him or called him *papi*.

She was a strong woman, with serious aims, and a desperate drive to work, work, work.

Chapter 6

T he Day of the Generals," Daniel called it. . . . October 3, 1968, when President Belaúnde was toppled and exiled, and a military junta took over the government of Peru.

It was a bloodless coup. The Peruvian people were too disenchanted with government to protest at the loss of the elected administration.

"We should have stayed in France," Daniel told Nicole that night over dinner.

"It doesn't seem ominous, Papá. From what they say, the changes will be mostly economic. You've been telling me for years that Peru needs land reforms. In fact, haven't you already conducted your own personal redistribution? I don't think this will affect our lives."

Daniel disagreed. "You mark my words, the changes will be far-reaching. Land reform is only the beginning. By the time they're finished, they'll rearrange the whole country."

Daniel was right. The junta's first dramatic action was to expropriate IPC, the American oil company. They intended to break the dependence of Peru on foreign interests. Next, they turned to the land holdings of the elite Forty-five Families, the traditional owners of the country's resources. The large plantations—sugar, coffee, and cotton-producing enterprises—were nationalized and redistributed to the *campesinos* who worked the land.

The social and economic fabric of Peru would never be the same. A number of wealthy people made plans to leave the country. If they had Swiss bank accounts, the time had come to use them. With a military government, it was never certain where the lines would be drawn.

When Nicole arrived at the hospital the next morning, there were military guards posted at the entrances. Governments may come and go, but sickness pays no heed. The work went on as usual in the clinic and the wards. Nicole had a rotating internship, but she spent more time in Maternal and Child Health than other departments because she had elected pediatrics as her specialty.

Jorge Alvares suggested she apply for a fellowship in epidemiology at the Center for Disease Control in Atlanta, Georgia, for the following year. He said it would enhance her academic standing at San Martín and give her international recognition.

"My old friend, Henry Campion, from the University of Pennsylvania Medical School, is one of the organizers of the fellowship program. Wonderful man. He was at the CDC for years, heading the Division of Viral Diseases."

On the day that Professor Alvares announced that her fellowship had been awarded, Nicole went home in a daze. What would her father say? He had moved back to Lima because of *her,* and now she was about to tell him she would be going to the United States for two years!

Daniel would always surprise her. Not only did he not object, but he was enthusiastic about the plan. "It's a wonderful opportunity, Nicole. I've never been to Atlanta, but I suppose I'll be visiting there often now."

It occurred to Nicole then that her father must always have been reluctant to leave her alone in Lima when he went away on his business trips. He seemed to take advantage of every chance to go to Paris, where Isabelle Somme eagerly awaited his visits. Could it be that he wanted to marry Isabelle but hesitated because he thought Nicole might not approve?

Before leaving for the States, she broached the subject with him. "Papá . . . ? Wouldn't you like to marry again? I mean . . . Isabelle is lovely . . . I know you're very fond of her. And so am I."

He was extremely touched and told her so. Each time they met in Atlanta or New York over the next two years, Nicole was prepared for him to announce that he would marry Isabelle. But somehow he never did.

Dr. Henry Campion, who seemed years younger than Jorge Alvares, came to the CDC from the University of Pennsylvania to give a summer seminar on immunization.

Nicole met him at a wine and cheese party. A stocky man bearing the healthy appearance she associated with Americans from the Middle West, he had sandy hair and mild blue eyes behind horn-rimmed glasses.

"So, you're the one from Jorge's department at San Martín," he said when he was introduced to her. "He's a great friend of mine. We were at Hopkins together."

Nicole instantly liked Henry Campion. He was warm and interested in all the trainees, and he did not insist on the formalities between senior and junior staff, as they did in South America and Europe. "May I call you Nicole?" he asked immediately.

"Of course." But she could not bring herself to call him Henry, even though he suggested it.

"Tell me about your work," he urged.

Nicole described the department at San Martín. She talked about health services in Peru and her ideas on establishing a reach-out program for maternal and child health in the *barriadas*.

"What would you do?" he asked.

"The most important thing would be an immunization program for the children. And I would combine it with family planning. No one knows how many abortions are performed each year . . . any more than they know the incidence of communicable diseases. There *aren't* any reliable statistics. Preventive health care could make such a difference in those communities! Many of the mothers don't realize they don't have to pay for inoculations or smallpox vaccinations. . . ."

"Soon smallpox will be a thing of the past," said Campion. "The WHO smallpox eradication program is moving along."

"But there are still epidemics in Africa and Asia. Do you really believe it will happen *soon?*"

"There are some problems, but the end result is inevitable. Their goal is to bring an end to smallpox by 1976. If they succeed, *it will be the first time in history that a disease has been eradicated*. And what a disease! The worst scourge on the face of the earth. Have you ever seen an active case of smallpox, Nicole?"

"No," she answered. "But I've seen many people who had it during their childhood. Complete eradication seems unrealistic, Dr. Campion. They can't possibly vaccinate everyone in the world!"

"That won't be necessary," he replied. "The United States and Europe have been free of smallpox since the 1940s. Unlike diseases like malaria, plague, and yellow fever, which have insect hosts, there is no reservoir for smallpox other than humans. Since that means the virus can only pass directly from one person to another, mass vaccination in affected areas will work because it will break the chain of infection. If the virus has no place to go, it will die out."

Near the end of her stay at the CDC, Nicole was in the live virus lab, a maximum-containment facility where scientists worked on Class IV organisms, the most dangerous. It was difficult for her to become accustomed to spending the entire day indoors in the artificial environment. Sometimes she joined Gail McPherson, a fellow trainee on leave from Northwestern University, in the garden during their lunch break. But when she was in a secure lab like this, she often went without lunch because it was too much trouble to shower and change, using the elaborate prophylactic measures necessary to prevent the escape of potentially lethal viruses into the outer world.

At first it had been an unnerving experience, knowing a careless moment—forgetting to clean under the fingernails, for example—could theoretically unleash a dangerous epidemic. It soon became a habit, and it was this familiarity that they had been warned against. When a precaution becomes so routine that you no longer attach significance to it, lapses will occur. There were signs all over the CDC reminding personnel to practice contamination-containment measures.

Late one afternoon Nicole looked up from her microscope to see Henry Campion entering through the pressure-lock in the hall, which could be seen through the glass windows of her lab. Campion was followed by a younger man, both of them wearing the sterile suits, cap and mask required in the controlled areas.

Campion pointed at Nicole's unit, nodding at her when he saw her watching him over her mask. His companion looked in her direction. Nicole noted his penetrating eyes, deep blue under dark brows, all of him that she could see.

There was anger and hurt in those eyes.

The next morning, she and Gail were on their way to a virology lecture, when Dr. Campion came walking rapidly in their direction across the compound. A tall, dark, arrestingly handsome young man wearing a blazer and tan slacks kept pace with Campion, the two of them deep in conversation.

As they passed, the man looked up. Their glances met and Nicole realized it was the same person she had seen with Campion in the live virus lab. She was struck by the troubled look of bewilderment in his eyes, as she had been the first time she had seen him.

"Who was that with Dr. Campion?" she asked Gail, who had taken her medical degree at Penn and knew Campion well.

Gail regarded Nicole for a moment before replying. She thought she detected more than idle curiosity in her question. Gail could not recall Nicole ever expressing an interest in a particular man before. But then, this was no ordinary man!

"That's the guest lecturer. His name is Andrew Tower . . . a virologist from Penn. He's sort of a protégé of Campion's."

"Is he going to be here for the rest of the course?"

"No," said Gail. "He came down to learn a new tissue culture technique and to give this talk. He's leaving today." Then she added, "I hear his wife is ill. She's in the University of Pennsylvania Hospital, so he has to get back to Philadelphia." She watched Nicole from under lowered lids, but her beautiful friend's face was, as usual, unreadable.

Dr. Tower's lecture was excellent. Nicole listened with great interest as the tall, striking young man described his research in the virology lab at Penn. He spoke well, with an easy confidence, seldom referring to notes. His speech was more cultivated than most Americans. He used the broad *a*, as the British did. Perhaps he came from New England.

Nicole found herself wondering about Andrew Tower. She liked his looks. He was ruggedly handsome, with a broad-shouldered, athletic body. She thought there was no question that American men were more attractive than Europeans!

The lights were turned down for Tower to show his slides. When the room was illuminated, the lecture came to an end. Nicole would have gone down to the front of the auditorium to meet the speaker, as she generally did at these lectures, but he had apologized beforehand to the audience for not being able to take questions, explaining he had to rush to the airport to catch a plane.

In July 1971, Nicole returned to Lima. Professor Alvares welcomed her back to the department, securing her joint appointment to the university medical school as a teaching assistant and making her his clinical fellow.

Alvares had received a letter from Henry Campion while Nicole was in Atlanta, telling him how satisfied he was with her participation in his seminar:

> . . . I'm building a network of young investigators from leading medical schools around the world, Jorge. . . . You and I have often talked of the need for good people trained in epidemiology and immunology to attack health problems in the developing nations. . . . Technology alone won't do the job where cultural patterns intervene or delivery of health services is hampered by primitive conditions. Good personnel and technical assistance are vital.
>
> With your permission, I would like to add Nicole Légende to my list of those I may call upon in the future. I won't say more now, but you know me well enough to be able to guess I have a plan brewing!

The American went on to tell Professor Alvares that he would be coming to Peru during the next year and hoped to visit the Department of Maternal and Child Health at San Martín University.

Alvares replied, inviting Dr. Campion to give a lecture at the medical school when he visited Lima. "Nicole Légende is the best resident I've ever had in all my years of teaching," he wrote. "I told you that when I first requested a place in the epidemiology course for her. I'm glad you recognize her ability, Henry. Of course, I'm delighted to have her included in your mysterious network! You've stirred up my curiosity. I hope you'll have more details to divulge when you come to Lima."

*   *   *

Back in Peru, Nicole found the atmosphere around San Martín University and the hospital much more politically charged than before her two-year absence. Many students at San Martín belonged to leftist organizations. University students had long played an important role in Peruvian politics, particularly in espousing the cause of the poor. All the universities in Peru were under the jurisdiction of the military government. Although the regulations had been eased somewhat recently, political activities on campus were still restricted.

Pepe and Carlos were two medical students whom Nicole found especially likeable. When she asked for volunteers to work in her new pilot project, the mobile clinics that would rotate among the different slums of Lima, Pepe and Carlos had been the first to offer their time. They quickly became the mainstays of the operation. With the two students helping her, Nicole found she could run a clinic for two hundred people.

Both were from the department, or state, of Ayacucho in the southeastern Andes. They seemed to do everything together, including sharing an apartment. Nicole never thought of them individually. *Pepe and Carlos*. They were like alter egos. Among the more idealistic of the students, they were always talking about how they wanted to go back to the sierra and serve the peasants. She thought they were sweet and rather naive.

Nicole achieved a new inner contentment. She had lost the anger and bitterness she felt in the years immediately after Erik's death. She had developed her protective shell and learned how to direct her energies into productive channels.

Since her return from the States, Professor Alvares had entrusted her with the major responsibility for the Maternal and Child clinic. It was a completely separate operation from the running of the other outpatient services, which continued under the direct supervision of the nurse Mona Ramos.

Nicole's work was her major interest. If she occasionally wished there was something else in her life, the evenings she spent with Manuel were a reasonable substitute for a more meaningful relationship.

As she wrote to Françoise Bercy, who was doing research in Paris on male infertility and had just become engaged to a urologist:

> I'll always miss the intellectual stimulation of Paris. I found it again briefly during the two years I spent at the CDC, so now I've had to make the adjustment a second time. But the rewards of working in a place where you can really make a *difference* are compensation enough.
>
> As for Manuel, I wouldn't like to think I'll end by marrying him just because I don't want to be lonely for the rest of my life! I really don't expect that I'll ever marry anyone.

Chapter 7

Nicole used a piece of *chuta*, the peasant yeast bread, to soak up the sauce from her barbecued chicken. They were having dinner at a popular inn that specialized in the spicy cuisine of the Andes.

"Would you like me to order more chicken, Nicole?" asked Manuel, registering faint disapproval at the mopping operation.

Nicole shook her head. "No, thanks." She swallowed. "I *do* love peppers. It must be my *indio* blood." She could almost see him wince.

"What would you like to do?" he asked. "There's a native song and dance festival at the Municipal Theatre. I have tickets." He was clearly catering to her tastes. Like most *criollos*, Manuel had little appreciation of Peru's Indian culture.

"Umm . . . I don't know. I'm not in a patient mood tonight, Manuel. I'd fall asleep." She swirled her coffee in the cup. "How would you like to go to a party?"

He looked surprised. "A party? Who's giving a party?"

She laughed. "No one you know! Some of the medical students who work in the mobile clinics. They're honoring their old professor who's visiting from Ayacucho. I think it might be fun."

He knew she was challenging him. "All right," he said. "Let's go." He followed her out of the restaurant.

The apartment was in a fringe area, a lower class neighborhood on the edge of respectability.

"This doesn't look right, Nicole. Are you sure you have the correct address?" Manuel pulled his red Ferrari Daytona off the road under the light of the single street lamp.

"This is the right address. I've been here before," she

answered. "It'll do you good to go slumming, Manuelito," she teased him, running a finger down his cheek.

He took heart from the gesture of affection, although it did not improve his view of their surroundings.

The apartment was on the second floor, above a machine shop. It was crowded with students, young men in shirt sleeves and blue jeans, some of the women wearing jeans too. A record player blared American disco music. Couples danced in close contact, using it as an excuse to touch. Manuel detected the distinct odor of marijuana.

Nicole threaded her way through the crush of bodies, making a trail for Manuel to follow. She greeted several people who eyed Manuel with speculation.

A short, baby-faced young man gave a shout when he saw her. "Welcome, Nicole! I didn't think you'd show." Noticing Manuel, he extended his hand and smiled. "You've brought your friend. Hello, I'm Pepe."

"This is Manuel, Pepe. He's never been to the apartment of a medical student before." Nicole tossed it off with a careless air.

Manuel did not like her high-handed, flip manner. She was at ease here and he was not.

"Maestro Gordo's in the other room with Carlos and some of the others," said Pepe. "Get a beer and come back."

In a rear bedroom, young men and women sat in a circle on the floor, their attention on a wiry, energetic middle-aged man with an untrimmed mustache and a full head of shaggy dark brown hair, streaked with gray. His food-spotted shirt was open at the neck. So thin and ascetic was his appearance that the name Gordo could only have been an irony.

Nicole noticed Carlos across the room. She took a seat on the floor, and Manuel leaned against the wall, arms folded, his face in shadow.

The maestro gesticulated wildly as he lectured the rapt students. ". . . The masses are lulled by this socialist government. They've been led to believe they can achieve their goals without taking up arms. The people will always choose the peaceful way to bring about change until they're forced to resort to violence. . . ." He ranted on for half an hour, his speech peppered with revolutionary jargon.

When Gordo had finished, Pepe introduced Nicole to his teacher. The maestro's eyes rested on her with an electric intensity. "Pepe has told me about your clinics, Señorita Légende. You are well-motivated," he said, with a benevolent smile.

He's patronizing me, she thought, with a prick of irritation. "Maestro, I'm a doctor, not a political person . . . but in my opinion, education for the poor, free medical care, and redistribution of land will be of far more benefit to the people than trying to incite them to armed rebellion."

As all eyes turned in her direction, Nicole felt her face grow warm. These students were not accustomed to hearing their professor challenged.

His piercing black eyes bored into her. Aware of Manuel standing in the dimness behind her, she sensed his tension. *Why did I say anything?*

"Ahh . . ." said the Maestro. "It is the daughter of the reformer of Huaranca district who speaks! You believe in your family that all problems can be solved by the benevolence of the *patrón,* don't you, señorita?" She resented his biting sarcasm.

"Certainly not! But what good will it do the peasants to fight and die, when there's nothing left to salvage? It's far better to bring about peaceful change without destroying the farms and institutions that are necessary for a society."

"Spoken like a true daughter of the wealthy class! Do *you* know what it is to go without the necessities of life, señorita?" He sipped abstemiously from a cup.

"You see, my dear señorita," he continued, more gently. "Not every landholder is a Daniel Légende. It is the landowner of goodwill who is the *hidden* enemy . . . and it is the junta, with its half-way measures of agrarian reform, that is the *greatest* enemy of the revolution, for they would make fat and contented landholders of the peasants!"

As they left the apartment, Pepe said in a low voice, "I hope you weren't worried about your automobile, Manuel. We've kept an eye on it." Manuel thanked Pepe, and went outside with an uncharacteristically reserved Nicole.

They had reached the suburbs, with their walled mansions, when Manuel said, "Nicole, I advise you not to go to such parties in the future. It could be . . . dangerous."

"Dangerous? How could it be dangerous?"

"Do you realize who Maestro Gordo is?" When she did not reply, he said, "He's an avowed Maoist and a follower of José Lorca, the guerrilla leader. Lorca's imprisoned at El Frontón, in case that has escaped your attention. Gordo's real name is Diego Pérez and he's a marked man."

Nicole let out a sharp breath. "A *marked man?* At a student party in Lima? I doubt it, Manuel. Someone might turn him in."

"I don't mean he would be arrested if the police knew he was there. They haven't been able to get any evidence on him. But he's watched wherever he goes . . . and the people who associate with him are also kept under surveillance. That's what I meant by danger, Nicole. It's risky for you to be seen at a party like that. One of the guests is almost certain to have been a police informer."

They had reached her home. The watchman unlocked the gates after making sure who was in the car. Manuel drove up the sloping driveway, swinging around to the far side of the fountain.

"What you mean is, it's risky for *you,* don't you, Manuel? It's bad for your career to be seen in the wrong places, with the wrong people." She saw his facial muscles contract, with anger or hurt—she could not tell which.

"No, that isn't what I meant," he said quietly. *"I* didn't call attention to myself by speaking out about things I have no knowledge of. You shouldn't have done that. Everyone there knows who you are now . . . a doctor at San Martín, the daughter of Daniel Légende. That puts you in a vulnerable position."

"Ohh, Manuel!" she was exasperated.

"Nicole . . . I don't want to argue with you. I'm only concerned because I *care* so much about you." He reached for her hand and brought it to his lips. Nicole was rigid in the seat next to him. He slid an arm around her shoulders. "You know I'm in love with you. I want you to marry me so that I can watch over you. You need a husband, darling."

Nicole withdrew her hand from his, crossing her arms

and holding her elbows. "Please, Manuel . . . please don't." Her voice was muffled as she bent her head.

"Why not, Nicole? Is it such a terrible thing for you to contemplate marriage with me? Do you feel offended because I love you?"

"No! No, of course I don't feel offended, Manuel. I feel . . . honored. But, I just can't marry you."

"Why not?"

"Because I'm not in love with you . . . why else not?"

Manuel closed his eyes briefly, turning his head away from her. "Are you in love with someone else?"

"No. There's no one else. No one at all."

"Then *marry me!* You'll grow to love me in time. I can *make* you love me."

He put his arms around her and before she could pull away, he was kissing her, a hard, desperate kiss at first, covering her mouth with his. Then his lips softened and in spite of herself, she responded.

"You see," he whispered, "I can melt the ice maiden. I can make you so happy, Nicole . . . Tell me you don't like this." His hand caressed her. She pushed it away.

"You're a very attractive man, Manuel. But that doesn't mean I'm in love with you. Surely you can understand that. You must have been drawn to women you didn't love."

"That's different, Nicole. I'm a man . . ."

"Not so different!"

He kissed her again, but this time his kiss left her unmoved. She was contained within herself, waiting for it to come to an end. And when at last he released her, she sat staring straight ahead until Manuel opened the door and got out of the car.

The following week, Nicole invited Lucy Monaco to dinner at Casa Loma. Daniel was in New York on a business trip and it seemed a perfect time to get to know her better.

Lucy took a long drag through her onyx and silver cigarette holder and blew out the smoke. Looking around the patio where they were having drinks, she said, "Yes, this is the perfect setting for you, Nicole. Palatial and exotic."

Nicole was embarrassed. She looked down as she spread

caviar on toast points and offered them to her guest. "Oh, Lucy, I was hoping we could get beyond all this," she gestured with one hand.

"I don't hold it against you, if that's what you're thinking. Truthfully, I meant it as a compliment. You're the most exotically beautiful woman I've ever known, and you *belong* in these surroundings." She chewed on a canapé, allowing Nicole to struggle with her discomfort. "You deserve a hell of a lot of credit for the work you're doing."

"I imagine a psychiatrist would say that's why I'm working at a place like San Martín. To purge myself of guilt."

"*Do* you feel guilty?" Lucy leaned forward, resting her chin in her hand.

Nicole did not answer immediately. She thought about Lucy's question. "No," she answered, as if surprised at herself. "I can't help the fact that I was born into a wealthy family. My father didn't inherit his money. He worked hard to earn it, and he was lucky."

"Yes, and he spends his money wisely, from what I've heard. He's done a lot of good things in this country."

It pleased Nicole to hear Lucy speak about her father in admiring terms. It reminded her of the evening at Pepe and Carlos's apartment, and the maestro.

"Lucy, have you ever heard of a man named Diego Pérez? He's a political science professor from Ayacucho. I met him the other night."

Lucy almost choked on her *pisco capitán*. "*Diego Pérez!* How in the world did you ever meet *him?*"

"He taught some of my med students before they came to Lima. They call him Maestro Gordo." She told Lucy about the party at the students' apartment and how Manuel had warned her not to go to such gatherings.

Lucy thought Manuel might have overreacted. She did not see anything sinister in the party Nicole had attended. However, she knew about Gordo and she did not like him.

"I think he uses impressionable young people to feed his own ego. He has never gone to jail for his principles, but he gets a lot of mileage out of his association with José Lorca. He's become a guru to his students, and someday he'll get them in trouble."

Lucy was active on the Lima Bar Association's committee to advocate the upholding of guaranteed rights in Peru. Nicole was shocked to hear that some of the political prisoners Lucy had defended had been tortured. "I have to *dash* whenever a client is arrested," Lucy told her. "The police can get pretty rough."

It was long after midnight when Lucy reluctantly left. Nicole planned to invite her soon again. By comparison to the woman attorney, she thought herself frivolous. *How coddled I am.* Lucy walked alone, fearless. She didn't need a man to act as her protector.

Chapter 8

Dr. Henry Campion arrived in Lima in the third week of September, the end of the southern hemisphere's winter. Jorge Alvares acted as Campion's official host at San Martín, arranging with colleagues at rival institutions for him to visit the medical school of San Marcos University . . . *and* the Military Hospital.

"It's the diplomatic thing to do, my dear," he told Nicole, a twinkle in his eye.

Campion was on a tour of Latin American universities. Professor Alvares planned a large official reception in his honor at the University, a departmental dinner following the lecture Dr. Campion would give at the medical school, and a banquet for the entire faculty on his last night in Lima. In addition, Nicole was invited to a private dinner Jorge Alvares was giving at his home for his old friend and classmate.

Nicole was delighted to see Henry again. "I'd like to spend a few hours with you, Nicole," he told her. "There's something I want to talk about. They have me so scheduled this week, I don't know when we'll find the time."

"Will you come to my home for dinner, Dr. Campion? My father would enjoy seeing you again. He's been in New York for three weeks, but he returns tomorrow."

Henry had met Daniel when he visited Nicole in Atlanta. The dinner was arranged for two nights later. At Campion's suggestion, Nicole included Jorge Alvares and his wife in the invitation.

Several people in the lobby of the Harkness Pavilion at Columbia-Presbyterian Medical Center glanced curiously at the courtly gentleman who checked out on a sunny Indian summer day in September. He was a person you would notice—tall, imposing, well-dressed, with an air of self-confidence that comes with possessing money and power.

An attendant carried his luggage to the waiting limousine. With a nod to the uniformed chauffeur, Daniel Légende settled into the deeply upholstered rear seat.

The trip to John F. Kennedy International Airport was pleasant on this rare, bright-skied day. Traffic was light, and Daniel enjoyed the sharpness of the New York skyline, appreciating the clarity of shape and color.

I wonder how much I've missed by not being more observant? he thought. Not much! *You've lived well in the years allotted to you, Daniel.*

Two hours later, he was seated in the first class section of the Braniff flight to Lima by way of Miami, enjoying a glass of Dom Perignon Brut, pleased that the seat next to him was empty. This was not a time to make conversation with a stranger.

He would be happy to reach home. Nicole would be waiting for him at the airport.

Nicole . . . my lovely Nicole. . . . I can't hide it from you any longer, my sweet. You've noticed something. I've seen you watching me when you didn't think I was looking.

She was so tender, when you knew what she was like underneath her aloof exterior. Daniel understood her. He knew the hurts she had suffered. He remembered a remark she had made once during childhood. . . . "There is no inner me," she had told him, and he had never forgotten it. He was sure what she had meant by that was that she had buried her feelings, buried them deep, in order to protect herself from being hurt again.

What would become of her? He could not die leaving her alone. All the money in the world could not make up for the loneliness of having no one. He had lived the last twelve years with his memories . . . and with the understanding and devotion of Isabelle . . . but Nicole was too young to be satisfied with memories.

He had hoped something would come of her friendship with Manuel Caldeiro-León. Although Manuel was ten years older than Nicole, Daniel thought that was in his favor. She needed someone strong and mature, someone who would command her respect.

Daniel had known Manuel's father and considered him a fine gentleman. He had seen young Caldeiro's transition from Harvard graduate, to student of the law, to a distinguished member of the legal profession and advisor to government ministers. Manuel served on the boards of several international corporations and a major bank—and most important, was a director of Légende et Cie.

Manuel was certainly in love with Nicole, if Daniel could be a judge of that. He called her daily, sent flowers, escorted her to concerts and dinners. . . . But Nicole treated him in such an offhand manner! Her indifference only seemed to fuel Manuel's ardor.

Just before Daniel had left for New York, Manuel had come to call for Nicole one evening. As usual, she was late getting home. "Come sit with me and have a drink," Daniel had invited him. "Is that daughter of mine late again?"

Manuel had shrugged it off with gallantry. "But such a charming daughter, Daniel."

Daniel had felt a sympathetic warmth for Manuel. He liked the man . . . he *really liked* him. He had come close to telling him why he was going to New York, but then thought better of it.

Instead he had said, "I apologize for Nicole, Manuel. When she gets to that hospital, she forgets time . . . she forgets *everything.*"

Henry Campion thought it was the most elegant house he had ever visited. These wealthy South Americans certainly did know how to live! Casa Loma was even more impressive than the Alvares mansion. Instead of being crammed full of ornate furniture and elaborate silver curios, though, it was furnished with restrained elegance. Daniel Légende's fine collection of pre-Columbian artifacts rivaled those he had seen in Lima's museums.

Nicole's modesty had left him unprepared for the opulence of her family estate. Beth would say that anyone except a spaced-out professor would have recognized the name Légende, and *realized*. He probably should have suspected. There had always been something about Nicole that set her apart from other women—her carriage, her social presence, and that way she had of commanding attention when she entered a room.

The dinner was superb, the best food he had eaten since coming to Lima. Daniel had a French chef and kept an excellent cellar. Légende was a charming host. What an unusual life he had led. The man did not look well, though. He had a pallor under his suntan and a look of pain in the eyes that Dr. Campion associated with serious illness. Nicole hadn't said anything about her father being sick, so he wouldn't mention it.

They went into the library after dinner for coffee and cordials, and Henry took the opportunity to draw Nicole aside for a private talk, while Daniel entertained Jorge Alvares and his wife.

Nicole listened with growing excitement as Dr. Campion described the new international organization he was forming. How thrilling it would be to take part in such an endeavor!

Of course, he cautioned her, it had not yet been approved or funded. It would take time, at least six months. But he had the unofficial go-ahead from a representative of the WHO, the World Health Organization. This was a necessity, since his new group would come under the auspices of the health agency of the United Nations.

"There will be ten members from different countries," Henry explained to Nicole. "Each one of you has been selected for your work in a specialized area of medicine or epidemiology and your interest in the problems of the developing world. Underprivileged nations have special health problems, compounded by climate, lack of pure water, poor communications, inadequate housing and education—and, of course, lack of money."

Nicole nodded. Her own experiences in the *barriadas* of Lima proved everything he said to be true.

"Well, Nicole, what do you say? It will mean being away from Peru for months at a time. It will mean working hard in the field under the most difficult conditions. And there won't be much glory in it, except for the sense of satisfaction you'll get from doing an important job. But I can tell you, if you join us, it will be the *grand adventure of a hundred lifetimes.*"

She was so carried away that she grabbed his hands, holding onto them and saying "Yes!" with such fervor that the three others sitting across the room, stopped their conversation.

Professor Alvares congratulated her. "We're proud to

have a member of our department involved in this important work," he told her father.

Daniel's reaction was strangely subdued, Nicole thought. He seemed so sober tonight. In fact, she thought he was not looking at all well since his return from New York. He said he had intestinal problems in the States, caused by foreign organisms. That seemed a little unlikely, but she supposed it was possible. She had been so busy this week with Henry's visit that she had neglected her father. She must talk to him and insist he go to a doctor and have a complete check-up.

Vera opened the door the next evening to find Manuel Caldeiro standing on the doorstep. "The señorita *doctora* is not at home, Señor Caldeiro."

"It isn't the señorita I've come to see, Vera," he chided her. "Señor Légende is expecting me."

"I beg your pardon, señor. Please follow me." Vera conducted him to the study, where Daniel awaited him.

"Welcome home, Daniel. How was your trip to New York?" Manuel was shocked at Légende's appearance. In the month since Manuel had seen him, Daniel had lost weight. His heavy-lidded eyes seemed to have sunk into his face, and there were dark bluish circles around them.

"Thank you, Manuel." He threw his arms around the younger man in the traditional *abrazo*. "I'll tell you all about the trip. Come sit with me and have a brandy. Nicole will be along later. She's attending a reception at the University."

"I *hope* that's where she is, and not in the *barriadas* . . ." He stopped short, seeing Daniel's expression. "Forgive me, Daniel, I thought you knew. Of course, she wouldn't go there at night . . . I wasn't being serious."

Daniel sighed. "I worry about her, Manuel. She's headstrong and fearless. It's almost as if she's daring something to happen at times." He shook his head. "I worry about what she'll do when I'm. . . ." He changed the subject abruptly. "New York is very pleasant this time of year."

"Did you meet with the directors of the American subsidiary?" Légende et Cie had recently formed a separate American company. Manuel, as a member of the board of the parent company, had wondered why Daniel had not discussed his trip to the States with him before leaving.

Daniel poured two brandies. "No. I didn't go to New York on business . . . at least, not on company business." He handed Manuel the liqueur and seated himself opposite on a burgundy leather club chair.

"I went to the Columbia-Presbyterian Medical Center to see some doctors."

Manuel studied Daniel's face with concern. "Are you ill, my friend?"

Daniel sighed. "Yes. I seem to be. It has been going on for some time. At first the doctors here thought it was pernicious anemia, and they were treating me with liver extracts. But now, there's no doubt. The diagnosis has been confirmed . . . acute leukemia." He sipped his brandy and laid his head against the back of the chair.

"Damn! I am *so sorry,* Daniel. But, can they be certain?"

"I'm afraid so. I went to the most famous hematologist at Columbia University. Unfortunately, this isn't the type of leukemia that responds well to treatment, and it progresses rapidly, I'm told." He smiled wryly. "I'm rather glad it won't be a drawn-out affair, truthfully." He fiddled with a silver box on the table. "The specialist says six months to a year."

Manuel's eyes filled with tears. "Daniel . . . is there . . .? You *know* I'll do anything to help you. I'm still . . . I can't believe . . ." He lowered his head, overcome with emotion.

Daniel walked over and put his hand on Manuel's shoulder. "I would like to think you will be a friend to my daughter, Manuel. She will need someone to lean on."

Manuel raised his head. "*I swear it!* On my honor." He stood and embraced the older man. "You must know how I feel about Nicole, Daniel. I'd give anything if she would marry me . . . but she tells me she doesn't plan to marry at all!"

"Childish words from a woman. Give her time, Manuel. She'll change her mind. I could die with a happy heart if I thought she would be with you."

Manuel was still feeling the shock of what Daniel had told him. "Does Nicole know?"

Daniel threw up his hand. "Ohh . . . no! You can imagine what a time I've had deceiving her. After all, she's a doctor. She suspects something, though. She was concerned at my appearance when I returned. I told her I had *la turista* in New York. She's so busy with the visit of Professor Campion from the States that she hasn't given me her full attention yet. We had him here for dinner last night. He has an interesting project in mind. He wants to involve Nicole . . . but I'll let her tell you about that. It won't materialize for a while."

They heard Nicole's voice calling from the hall, and a minute later she appeared in the doorway.

"Father, I'm glad you're still awake." She was surprised when she saw Manuel. "Manuel!" She looked from one to the other. "I didn't know you would be here."

Daniel rose to kiss her. "I asked him to come over tonight. I wanted to talk about New York." That was technically true, he told himself.

"What a day! I never stopped for a minute. I have to run upstairs to see if I have an address in Chile for Dr. Campion. He's going there next." As she rushed out, she called in English, "I'll be back in two shakes. . . ."

"What is 'two shakes'?" asked Daniel.

"That's American slang; 'two shakes of a lamb's tail' is the full expression. It means *pronto*."

"Is that what you learned at the Harvard Business School? American slang?"

"Among other things." Manuel smiled, and the two men locked eyes for some moments.

Daniel relaxed. There was an understanding between them.

Chapter 9

Was anyone ever prepared to become an orphan, Nicole wondered as she sat at her father's bedside, watching the uneven rise and fall of the massive chest. His gaunt face, the cheeks sunken into the skull, bore little resemblance to that of the dynamic force that had been Daniel Légende.

The hand she held in her own gave no answering pressure. She continued stroking it to bring him comfort, in case he had some awareness in his coma. His mouth opened with each breath, gasping for air, the eyebrows rising with the strain of his struggle.

"Let go, Papá," she whispered. "Rest, please . . . find peace." She spoke in French, their language, his and hers.

She wanted to cry, but the tears would not come. There would be time for tears.

It was impossible to imagine life without him. For all of her years he had dominated everyone around him. Daniel Légende. The legend. *The legend that is Légende. . . .*

A nurse entered the room, one of the religious from San Martín Convent who looked after private patients at the Odría Pavilion. Adjusting the blankets, she checked the tubes, moved a tray of medicines, trying to show that, although it was hopeless, someone cared, something was being done. Then she stopped, realizing that Nicole was herself a physician, making pretenses unnecessary.

"Shall I bring some food, Doctor Légende?" she asked.

"No, thank you, Sister," Nicole replied.

"Some coffee, then. You've been here for so long."

Nicole smiled. "Perhaps later."

Alone again with her father, Nicole laid her cheek against his hand. "How I shall miss you! There's no one else."

For eight months she had known he would die. At first she had insisted he should seek other opinions, have chemotherapy, immunotherapy, anything that might offer a glimmer of hope.

"No, my sweet. I don't want to spend the last year of my life running from one doctor to another, having my veins filled with chemicals that will make me feel dead while I'm still alive. At the most, what could that do? Prolong my life by a few months? No. I don't want that."

"But, Papá, you can't just give up! *Please!*"

"Nicole. You're a doctor. If you can honestly tell me there is some treatment that will prolong my life by a year, two years, with decent quality—then I will do it."

But of course, that was a promise she could not make.

She remained at his side, holding his hand against her face, until she sensed something had changed. Slowly she lifted her head. She felt the panic rising in her throat. There had been no sound, no telltale movement. . . .

Daniel Légende was gone. The legend had come to an end.

Nicole rose, tall and severe in her starched white hospital coat, the glistening blue-black coil of her hair a sharp contrast to the creamy complexion. She leaned over to kiss her father's cheek while it was still warm.

"I love you, Papá. *Adieu.* . . ."

Gazing down at his quiet countenance, she felt a presence in the room. Manuel stood just inside the door, taking in the scene, pain and compassion on his handsome features. He held out his arms and she went to him, holding onto him because he was a rock in the storm-tossed sea.

And now the tears came.

She moved from one gravestone to another, pausing for a moment at each: *María de la Luz Rosado de Iglesias, Juan Carlos Iglesias y Alba. . . Benjamin Marcel Légende Iglesias, André Emile Légende Iglesias . . . María Christina Iglesias de Légende . . .* and now . . . *Daniel Légende.*

The milestones of my life. One day I, too, shall lie here, another *flor del viento.* This was the fear she had lived with since childhood, to be the only one left.

She wept silent tears, for her father and her mother,

for her little brother and her grandfather. For Erik . . . and for Nicole.

It was a clear summer night, the kind Nicole had always loved at Huaranca. They stayed on at the hacienda after Daniel's burial. Rosa had prepared the house and cooked food for them. Nicole stood in her dressing gown at the open paned-glass doors of her bedroom, looking to the east, where the snow-capped peaks of the Cordillera Blanca loomed above the valley, silent and ghostly in the light of the moon.

She saw the glow of a cigarette at the other end of the covered gallery that ran along the second story of the house. *Manuel.* He couldn't sleep either. Since when had he smoked? Unaware of her presence, he sat on the banister, leaning against a post. His white shirt was open at the throat, revealing his neck and chest. In the bright moonlight she could see him clearly, his face sad, the lock of hair that fell on his forehead making him look young and romantic.

Nicole was glad he was there. How strange that Manuel was closer to her than any living person. Suddenly she wanted to be near him.

Slowly he turned his head as she moved toward him. He came to meet her, taking her into his arms and bringing her close against his body. Through the thin fabric of the gown, she could feel his strength and the warm throbbing of his growing desire. There was an aching in her throat and loins, a rush of warmth spreading through her. She pressed herself against him. Let him do whatever he would. Half of her wanted him to make love to her, wanted him to drive away the abandoned feeling, the knowledge that there was no longer someone to love her . . . or to be loved.

With one hand he caressed the length of her back, while his other tangled itself in her hair. They were clever hands, knowing and sure, promising ecstasy. She looked up, certain what she would find, his clear eyes, not gray, not blue, waiting for an answer. As he bent his head to kiss her, she knew her body would betray her.

Manuel carried her to the bed. He laid her down

gently, pulling the covers up and smoothing them over her. Bending over, he kissed her forehead.

"Go to sleep, little one," he said softly. "I'm here." He sat on the edge of the bed, holding her hand and stroking her arm until her eyes closed.

He had never wanted anyone so much in all his life. He knew he could have her at that moment. But, he had promised Daniel to look after her. Would it not be breaking his word if he took her now, this way?

He had been obsessed with her ever since the first time he saw her in Paris, five years ago. Every night he dreamed of making love to her. Every time he was with a woman, he wished she were Nicole. And now, when she would give herself to him, he hesitated, because of a promise he had made to a man . . . a man who was no longer alive.

For a long time he stood in the doorway, listening to the peaceful sounds of the night. Sighing, he moved back to the bed. Nicole had not changed position. She seemed to be asleep. He lay on top of the covers next to her, eyes open, watching the shadows on the ceiling. Nicole's breathing was gentle and even, a whisper in the night. He could smell the light feminine fragrance of her. Turning his head, he saw the curving outline of her body in the stream of moonlight. He was overwhelmed with longing. Every part of him ached with desire for her.

He had only to reach out, to touch her shoulder, to stroke her back, to run his fingers through the long, silky hair. To touch the loveliness of her face, to caress and kiss the softness of her breasts, to press himself against the length of her smooth young body. To drink deeply the sweetness of her mouth, to plunge himself into her with all the urgency and fervor and passion of his need for her, for her only. For she was and always would be the true love of his life . . . and nothing, no one would ever be able to change that.

Rising from the bed, he left the room, quietly closing the doors behind him.

He was a sergeant in the Peruvian Investigative Police. It was a dull job. When he enlisted, he thought it would bring him security and adventure. The salary did not even cover his living expenses in Lima. He was constantly in debt, and his wife hated the city.

By nature, he was a peaceful man. He would never harm so much as an alley cat—but the pay increase was substantial if he went to the training course for the control of subversives, so he had signed up for it. The school for interrogation would come later, the captain told him. First, he must learn to be an investigator by going out on routine assignments.

He looked once more at the slip of paper, memorizing the name. It still felt strange to be out of uniform on a working day.

"Yes?" The receptionist at the emergency clinic of San Martín Hospital was annoyed. What was this husky *cholo* doing here at this hour? It was closing time.

"I would like to see Señorita Mona Ramos."

"She is busy. We are closing now."

He withdrew an envelope from his pocket. "Give her this."

It was not long until he was ushered into the clinic administrator's office. "I don't wish to be disturbed," the head nurse told the receptionist. "Have the guards lock the clinic."

The two of them remained closeted in the room for over an hour. Except in prayer, Nurse Ramos had never before experienced this exalted feeling.

As the squat, muscular man left her office, he said, "You have the gratitude of your country, señorita. *Hasta la vista.*"

"Go with God," she replied.

Nicole stopped at the mobile clinic to distribute some vaccines that had arrived from the World Health Organization. Carlos was there alone.

"Where's Pepe today?" she asked.

Carlos busied himself unloading the cartons of sera from her car and storing them in the van. "Pepe's sick." Carlos was behaving strangely, not looking at her.

"That's too bad. What's wrong with him?"

Carlos shrugged. "Just the flu. Nothing serious."

"He should see a doctor, Carlos. He could have picked up something working in the *barriada*." Many more serious diseases began with flu-like symptoms.

"Okay. I'll tell him. Only, I've already examined him and I think it's the flu."

Nicole let it go. She did not want to offend Carlos, but his skills as a diagnostician were not his strong point.

She left the hospital early that afternoon. Pepe was on her mind. She had to be certain he had not contracted something infectious. There were all sorts of diseases in the rat-infested slums. She decided to go to his apartment to make sure it was not serious.

A vagrant eyed her as she left her parked automobile and entered the building where Pepe lived. The stairway smelled of fumes from the machine shop. She knocked on the apartment door, but there was no answer. Something was wrong. Carlos would not lie about Pepe—and Pepe was far too conscientious to pretend to be sick just to get out of working in the clinic. She knocked again, louder, and called his name. "Pepe! Pepe! It's Nicole. Are you there?"

She heard something on the other side of the door, a movement. "Pepe? Is someone there? Please open the door."

"Nicole?" It was said softly, just above a whisper.

"Yes, Pepe. It's me. I came to see how you are."

"I'm fine, Nicole. Please go away." He sounded awful.

"Pepe—I've come all this way just to see you. Why won't you let me in?" After a minute she heard the lock turn, and the door opened slowly.

"*My God!* What *happened* to you?" One arm was in a sling. An eye was swollen shut, his upper lip was twice its normal size, and his face was covered with cuts and bruises.

"You shouldn't have come here, Nicole. You'll only cause trouble for yourself."

"Pepe, what are you talking about? Who did this to you?"

"It's a personal matter. Two people jumped me and beat me up. I'll be all right." He winced as he walked over to a chair.

"You don't look all right to me. Is that the worst of it?"

"Yes. No broken bones. Just a good old-fashioned beating."

"You're not going to tell me anything? Who they were? They should be prosecuted, you know. I can have the medical school look into it."

"No! Promise me you won't say anything about this to anyone at San Martín! Please, Nicole. You don't understand. *You don't know, and you don't want to know.* Just promise me."

"All right. I promise. But, before I go, let me take a look at you to be sure they haven't done any serious damage to that eye."

Nicole left the apartment, greatly agitated. When she reached her car, she was at first horrified and then furious to find that someone had smeared her windshield with excrement. Was it a random act of vandalism, or was it directed against her? It seemed unlikely that anyone would know who she was. She looked around the shabby streets of the neighborhood, largely warehouses and factories, but saw no one loitering nearby. Taking some papers from her briefcase, she attempted to clean the window, but it only made it worse. She shuddered, revolted by the filth.

Pepe did not return to the clinic for two weeks. The yellow marks of fading bruises were evident around his eye. He never spoke of the beating to Nicole, and she soon forgot about it, busy as she was with her work and the complicated legal procedures related to her father's estate.

She disliked living alone, finding the dinner hour especially depressing. Most evenings she asked Vera to serve a tray in the study. It was a warm, comfortable room, full of the things that had been Daniel's, and she felt better when she sat in there.

The settlement of the estate would take months, perhaps years. Daniel had made Nicole the co-executor of his estate with Manuel Caldeiro, designating Claude Montagne as executor-trustee in France. Nicole thought her father had made a wise decision to include Manuel, who had been at once a close personal friend, a business associate, and a lawyer. Probating this will was a complicated procedure, and to add to that, the Peruvian government was suspicious of all personal wealth.

Daniel had kept relatively few assets in Peru. Légende et Cie was a French corporation with subsidiaries in a number of countries, including Peru. Years ago, he had transferred most of his stocks to France, to a trust in Nicole's name. Eventually, she would have to go to Paris to sign papers and to attend the board meetings of the company he had founded. Now that Daniel was gone, it was essential that she take a place at the directors' table.

Daniel had forgotten no one. All of the servants and caretakers at his houses had been remembered in his will. He had established a fund for Jewish education that was to be under the trusteeship of his old friend, Miguel Cohen, the first person, and the first Jew, he had known in Lima. Cohen told Nicole with tears in his eyes that he had never expected to outlive her father.

Daniel had made a bequest to Isabelle Somme. One day, when he began to fail, he said, "Isabelle has been . . . important to me, Nicole. I know you're able to understand that."

"Of course, Papá! You know I always hoped you would marry her."

He had looked off for a moment. "Perhaps I should have. I love her, but my heart was half in the sierra, and she understood that." And then he had said something she would always remember. "Some relationships thrive on separations."

Daniel's will even provided an annuity for Nicole's former governess, "for her years of loyal friendship and companionship to my daughter." When Daniel took Nicole to live in Paris, the English woman had retired to Surrey, where she shared a cottage with her sister.

All the dangling ends of his life neatly tied, Nicole thought. *All except me. I am still dangling.*

Manuel wanted to be with her every evening, but she tried not to see him more than twice a week. He had become extremely possessive, almost paternal, acting as if he had the right to know everything that was going on in her life.

"This house is too large for you alone," he said one night.

"It's too soon for me to think of leaving here," she replied.

He smiled. "I didn't necessarily mean you should leave it!"

He would do that frequently, not exactly putting pressure on her, but letting her know he had not changed. He still wanted to marry her.

To be a woman alone in Latin society was difficult.

Only to herself would she admit it. If she married Manuel, it would not be for love. But in a way she *did* love him. Their relationship had been subtly altered since her father's death. After that night in Huaranca, she felt as if she were in Manuel's debt. She had invited him into her bed, and he had refused. *Honor.* It was as much a part of machismo as conquest.

Nicole wondered whether she had the temperament to be married to a Latino.

Manuel studied Elena as she carried a tray of drinks and *conchitas a la criolla* to the tiled courtyard, placing it on a table next to the round goldfish pool. She had made a pitcher of iced *chilcano*, a *pisco* punch, to go with the spicy grilled scallop appetizer. She looked young and pretty with her hair tied back in a ribbon and wearing an embroidered cotton dress from the Indian market.

They were at her small villa near Chosica, in the Andean foothills. He had been spending more time with Elena recently. Good times, not just in bed. She was really a lovely woman, undemanding, intelligent, and strong. *I must be drawn to independent women!*

Elena owned a chain of specialty shops in the arcades of the fashionable hotels of Lima and Miraflores. She had started the first of them before Héctor had killed himself flying his Piper Cub into the side of a mountain. Crazy, reckless Héctor, who had been his roommate at the "B School." He and Elena had been married for four years when he flew into the cliff while buzzing the villa of an attractive divorcée.

It was just as well they hadn't had children. This way, she was free to do as she pleased. What would please her most was to marry Manuel. But what she had done was to become a successful businesswoman—no mean feat in Peru.

"Chilcano?" She handed him a glass and served the scallops in a peppery creole sauce. "I like it here without the maid," she said with a smile, as she sat on a rush chair.

"It *is* peaceful. I feel relaxed." He touched her hand briefly, and she looked fondly at him in response.

Earlier that morning, after they had made love, she

raised her head from his chest and said, "You're different lately."

"How am I different?" he asked.

Her smile was shy. "Tender . . . more gentle, I suppose."

He nodded. "So are you. You used to be a hellcat!"

She blushed. "I do whatever you require, Manuel. You should know that. If I showed you my true feelings, you might never come back. You don't like to be burdened with a woman's emotions."

Only one woman's. But how clever of her to have guessed that. "Elena . . . I do care for you. Very much. I don't know what it is about me . . . what prevents me . . . I . . ."

"Sssh . . ." she silenced him with a kiss. "I know what it is. I'll be here if you get her out of your system. But don't wait too long, Manuel. I won't be here forever."

Chapter 10

On the tip of the peninsula that juts into Lake Como at its confluence with Lake Lecco, nestled at the foot of the Alps that divide Italy from Switzerland, lies a little jewel of a village called Bellagio.

The blue of sky and water accents the jumble of yellow houses with pink-tiled roofs that climb the dense forest-green slope above the lake. Steep stone stairways, crammed with shops and *trattorias*, scale the hillside in place of streets. There is a profusion of flowers, hanging vines, and striped awnings everywhere in Bellagio, lending the little hamlet a jaunty Italian brio.

Lake Como sparkled in a blaze of afternoon sunshine as Henry Campion seated himself at one of the terrace cafés that dot the colorful lakefront. He waved as he spotted his wife, Beth, and their two sons among the passengers on board the excursion ferry. With a toot of its horn, the boat departed, flags and streamers whipping in the breeze. He would like to have joined them on this perfect summer day, but he had work to do. Henry was waiting—waiting to be summoned.

High on the promontory that divides the two lakes, Como and Lecco, set in lush formal gardens crowned by a conifer forest, the Villa Montebello provides a serene habitat for scholars and statesmen to meet in privacy, without the distractions of public fora. If the villagers who passed the imposing wrought iron gates of the villa were curious about the black diplomatic limousines that had driven through its guarded entrance at regular intervals the previous day, they gave no sign. The citizens of Bellagio had become accustomed to the arrival of luminaries at the villa—the *"villa cittadina inglese,"* as it was sometimes called, in reference to the English widow of the last prince of the house of Montebello, who had given it to the American foundation. Only a foreign wife would part with a palazzo that had been in her husband's family for over two hundred and fifty years!

Henry found the luxury of the villa tedious. The eighteenth-century splendor of its huge parlors was somewhat intimidating. Dining with a footman standing at attention behind his chair was unnerving. He was a simple man with rather spartan tastes, and the opulence of his surroundings seemed wasteful.

Beth and the boys were not permitted to stay there, so he returned to their modest lakeside hotel every evening after dinner. The villa's manager had invited Beth to bring the boys for tea the previous afternoon. To while away the time with two active children, Beth had walked up the mountain with them to see the spectacular view of the lakes. The boys had gathered some huge evergreen cones they found lying on the ground, intending to take them home. Beth was horrified—they had resin all over their hands and clean shirts. She had wiped them off with one of those disposable towelettes she had saved from the airplane and managed to make them presentable. They left the pine cones carefully stacked under a hedge when they went in for tea. When they had returned half an hour later, the cones had disappeared—whisked away by the groundskeepers.

Henry had a young wife. His earlier marriage, to a woman who had decided she could not live on the salary of a doctor who worked for the CDC, had ended in divorce. He had left Atlanta for Philadelphia, and met Beth during his first week at Penn. They were married six months later and had been sublimely happy for seven years.

Last night in bed, they had laughed together over the incident with the pine cones. "The old place will never be the same, darling! I think they must be the first kids who've ever been invited to the villa for tea," Henry said.

"And I bet they'll be the *last!* I hope they didn't disgrace you, Henry."

"No chance of that. The manager takes herself much too seriously. You'd never know she grew up in Youngstown, Ohio. Living here has made her feel she's to the villa born!"

"Are you sure you don't mind sleeping down here with us? You could be enjoying all that luxury, too."

"Yes, but just think what I'd be *missing* if I had chosen the luxury." He reached for her and drew her body close to his. "I really ought to take you on more of my trips," he murmured.

The meeting taking place in the ornate rooms of the villa during the third week of June 1973 would have significant long-term effects on health programs around the world.

It was a high-powered group that had assembled here. Present were the chief executive officers of the large American foundations, the United States Agency for International Development (USAID), the international assistance agencies of Canada and the European countries, the World Health Organizatin (WHO), the World Bank, and the UNDP—the United Nations Development Programme.

Henry Campion had spent three days in Bellagio before the meeting began, conferring with the study and feasibility teams assigned to his proposal, and now he was on hand to give the formal presentation. He was nervous.

The group of agency heads who met at Lake Como had known before traveling to Italy what the outcome would be, but Henry did not realize that. These busy men would not have come together to debate or disagree. Their role was to give the nod of approval, to send a clear signal of support down through the ranks of their organizations, and to pledge the financial backing needed for the task that brought them together. Or, in Henry's words, "come up with the dough."

This meeting was long overdue. Its purpose was to further cooperation and coordination of activities among disease control programs in the poor nations of the Third World—Africa, Asia, and Latin America.

It was time for the health agencies to work together, to stop their internal bickering and external competition, and join hands in a combined effort to halt the spread of disease and alleviate the sufferings of people in the developing world.

Too much valuable time had been lost and too many

opportunities missed for cooperation in malaria control, in cholera treatment, even in the smallpox eradication program launched by the WHO seven years before—so far, the best example of a cooperative international health effort the world had seen.

After a day of background papers and discussions, the elite group unanimously adopted Henry Campion's innovative proposal. A new organization was born—the International Health Task Force. In the diplomatic world of acronyms it would be known as the IHTF.

Henry was satisfied. "A good day's work," he summed it up over drinks that night. This was his baby and he couldn't *wait* to get going!

It was a whole new approach, really, as he had explained to Lloyd Rankin, the deputy director of the World Health Organization, who was the meeting's chairman. They had been on an airplane together, returning from a meeting in Nairobi, when Henry first sounded him out on the concept. That had been over a year ago. These things took time.

Henry's idea had been to create a resource group, a brain trust, whose members would do research in specialties like virology and immunology, field test vaccines, consult with and provide technical assistance to existing programs in the developing world.

"A unit like the one I have in mind would be able to cut through all the red tape and get to the nitty-gritty, Lloyd. It's *got* to be *free of politics*. The sole criterion for selecting members would be their proven ability and their interest in medical problems of the developing world."

"They can't all be Americans, though, Henry," Lloyd had cautioned. "That just won't wash."

"Who said anything about Americans? I'm reserving a spot for *one* American—not including myself. But I would just be directing the show."

"If it were within the UN framework, you might not get away with an American heading it up."

"That's why it *has* to be independent of the WHO in organization, Lloyd. I don't want to have to worry about who's from the eastern bloc, or whether we've got geographical representation from your regional offices, and all that crap! I intend to get things *done*."

Dr. Rankin had been sold on the idea. He knew better

than anyone all the problems involved in working within the UN framework. His hands were tied in many program areas.

Henry thought about his appointees. This bunch of kids he had collected from around the world were tops. No question, they were the best young people in their fields. Mostly, he had found them in the departments and labs of his old friends and colleagues at universities in places like Lagos, Taipei, Belgrade, the Karolinska . . .

There was Prem Mehta, the microbiologist from the All-India Institute in New Delhi—smart as they come, he might win a Nobel one day. And Luís Ribera at the National Institute of Nutrition in Mexico, sharp-witted, a leader, who was doing important research in nutrition and child development.

Of course, as far as Henry was concerned, the star of the group was his own fellow, Andrew Tower, but maybe he was prejudiced. Drew was the only American besides himself, but it had been agreed ahead of time that it was all right. He needed Drew. Best damn virologist he'd ever had as a student, he was going to come up with a monoclonal antibody one of these days.

A couple of the selectees had been in the epidemiology course at the CDC. The best of that lot was the young pediatrician from Peru, Nicole Légende. She had really taken to the idea of the IHTF. What a cumbersome name! Henry had gotten into the habit of calling it the Task Force. He had a devil of a time keeping all those acronyms sorted. You had to talk a sort of double-speak to get along in this UN crowd.

Henry looked around the elaborate grand salon where they were gathered for cocktails. The villa wasn't half bad, once you got used to it. In fact, he wouldn't mind coming back sometime and staying here, when Beth wasn't along. It sure was a helluva place for a boy from Dubuque to end up. Life was funny. Nice of them to have included Beth tonight for cocktails and dinner. Look at her over there, talking to the heads of SIDA and the World Bank. They seemed to be hanging on her every word.

This was sort of a celebration tonight. It is not every day a new international group like this is created. Tomorrow it would be official.

Hot damn, it had worked! They were going to do it. Ten Young Turks, all under thirty-five, from ten different nations and, except for those from Paris and Stockholm and his own student Drew Tower, they were all from developing countries. But not a compromise among them, Henry, he congratulated himself. They're all first-rate.

On their last morning at the Villa Montebello, the agency heads approved the appointment of the ten individuals hand-picked by Dr. Campion from a list of over fifty suggested candidates.

The ten million dollars Henry had requested was pledged, an amount sufficient to assure ample funding for the first five years. The World Bank would collect and manage the funds, and the WHO would provide administrative back-up in Geneva for its new independent affiliate.

In the first week of July, a cablegram arrived at the office of the Department of Maternal and Child Health, San Martín University Hospital. It was addressed to Dr. Nicole Légende and it was marked "Priority."

Nicole opened the cable while she went over the afternoon schedule on her desk. As she glanced at its contents, she reached behind her for a chair and sat down. Once again, she read the message:

YOU ARE INVITED TO BECOME MEMBER INTERNATIONAL HEALTH TASK FORCE (IHTF). FIRST MEETING SCHEDULED 10–14 SEPTEMBER 1973, UNITED NATIONS HEADQUARTERS, NEW YORK. PLEASE CABLE ACCEPTANCE HENRY CAMPION, CHAIRMAN, IHTF-CAMP, NEW YORK, SOONEST POSSIBLE. TRAVEL DOCUMENTS AND INFORMATION WILL FOLLOW.

It was difficult to fall asleep that night. She had a sense of both anticipation and apprehension. Change always does this to me, she thought. For she had no doubt that this was the beginning of a new chapter in her life.

BOOK II

East Wind

Chapter 11

On St. Valentine's Day in 1972, a week before her twenty-third birthday, Julie Benjamin Tower died of cancer in the arms of her husband, Drew.

Drew continued to hold her after she stopped breathing, stroking the soft new growth of wavy copper-colored hair, rocking her emaciated body, while he placed gentle kisses on her face and whispered over and over, "I love you, I love you, I love you. . . ."

The hospital odor of disinfectant, boiled linens, and adhesive was overpowered by the sweet floral scent of roses. Drew raised his head and saw the vase of a dozen American Beauty roses he had brought for Valentine's Day. Forever after, he would hate the smell of roses.

Julie died of a fulminating carcinoma of the reproductive tract. Her first symptoms appeared in March 1971, but the disease had its beginning twenty-three years before that date, when she was a fetus in her mother's uterus. Julie's cancer was caused by overzealous medical care.

Less than a year before Julie's death, Drew was working in the University of Pennsylvania's virology lab one afternoon when his beeper sounded.

"Dr. Tower," said the operator, "Dr. Branch would like you to call him. He said it's important." Philip Branch was Professor of Obstetrics and Gynecology at Penn. His department was on the other side of the medical complex from Drew's lab, in the Dulles building of the university hospital.

I wonder what Phil wants, Drew thought as he dialed. Dr. Branch, ordinarily a gracious man, did not bother with pleasantries. "Drew, I'd like to see you in my office as soon as possible. Can you come right over?"

He had been in the middle of a tissue culture. "Can it wait for about an hour, Phil?"

There was a pause. "I think you'd better come now."

As he walked down Spruce Street, Drew asked himself what it could be. He was not aware of a case he was on that Phil Branch would be involved in. They occasionally consulted each other about a patient. Drew's residency was in medicine and his Ph.D. in virology made him a good resource person for other members of the staff.

Branch was a top-notch gynecologist. Julie used him as her GYN man for annual check-ups.

Julie? She mentioned recently that she was going to make an appointment with Phil. It was just for a routine check-up, though, and she hadn't said anything about seeing him today.

Drew had slept at the hospital for the past three nights because he was on call, and there were a couple of difficult cases. He had phoned Julie last night. She always waited for his call before she went to bed.

"It's my fix," she told him. "I can't fall asleep unless I hear your voice."

"If I were there, I'd give you another kind of fix!"

"Ummm, I wish you *were* here. I miss you, Drew. Tomorrow night—I can't wait!"

"That's a date, ma'am." He hung up feeling deprived. Medicine, he thought. You've got to be crazy to choose this life.

Julie would have mentioned to him if she were going to see Phil Branch today, probably suggesting they meet for a quick lunch. No, it couldn't have anything to do with Julie.

But it did. It had everything to do with Julie. Half an hour later, when he left Dr. Branch's office, his life was turned upside down.

He didn't tell her right away. He just couldn't bring himself to spoil their first time together in three nights. They made love as soon as he reached home, and Julie wanted him again after dinner, but he wasn't able to have another erection. By then, it had begun to sink in.

It was the weekend, and Dr. Branch had said she would not have to check into the hospital until Monday.

"We'll repeat all the tests and do open biopsies. But I

think there's no doubt about the outcome." He had been full of compassion. "God, Drew, I wish I didn't have to tell you this! Of course, I've called for a consultation. You don't go into something like this without getting several opinions."

"She never told me there was a problem. I didn't even know she'd already seen you. I thought she was coming in for a routine check-up sometime next week."

"Her only symptom was a tenderness on palpation. She asked me not to say anything until I got the results. I guess she didn't want to worry you. All I've told her was that I wanted to do some tests because her Pap smear wasn't a hundred percent. I haven't spoken to her yet . . . I thought you might prefer to do that."

As Drew was leaving, Dr. Branch said, "I asked her whether her mother had taken any medication during pregnancy. She didn't know. She said her mother isn't alive."

"Yes, both her parents died in an automobile accident in 1966, when she was sixteen. My folks were her guardians, so she came to live with them. My stepfather was her family doctor for years. Perhaps he would know the answer to your question. Why are you asking? What sort of medication did you have in mind . . . ?" He stopped, remembering something he had read in the *New England Journal of Medicine.* "It's DES, isn't it?" He felt ill.

"Yes. We're beginning to see a significant number of clear cell adenomas in young women whose mothers took diethylstilbestrol during their pregnancies."

Drew called his stepfather, Arthur Hillman, in Wilkes-Barre. Arthur was still practicing medicine there at the age of seventy. Drew did not want to alarm his mother, Molly, so he asked Arthur to keep the call confidential.

"Of course, Drew. What is it, son?" Drew liked the way Arthur treated him like he was his own child. He felt extremely close to his mother's husband.

"Would you have any of the medical records of Julie's parents in your old files, Dad?"

"I doubt it, Drew. Ruth and David have been gone for five years now. There might be some boxes of old files in the basement. I can ask my secretary. Mind telling me why you want them?"

Drew swallowed. He tried to keep his voice steady. "I
. . . uh . . . I need to know whether Julie's mother took
any hormones when she was pregnant with Julie."

At the other end of the wire, Arthur Hillman felt a
chill on the back of his neck, and he was overcome with a
sense of dread.

A scene flashed through his mind, a memory from long
ago, back in the '40s, a few years after the war. Ruth
Benjamin was four months pregnant, and he had referred
her to the bright young obstetrician who had opened a
practice in town after his marriage to a local girl. A nice
young doctor, Harvard-trained, who kept up with the
Boston group where he did his residency.

Julie's father, David Benjamin, was one of Arthur's
closest friends, a distinguished member of the Pennsylvania bar. The Benjamins had been childless throughout
their twenty-three year marriage when Ruth discovered
that she was pregnant. The two of them took a lot of
razzing about that.

That was before Arthur's first wife, Emily, had died.
They met the Benjamins for dinner at Wolf's Head Country Club on a Saturday night. . . . Arthur remembered
asking Ruth how the pregnancy was going and she told
him it was fine. "I take three kinds of pills a day, so this
baby ought to be pretty healthy!"

"What pills?" Arthur inquired, not liking the sound of
that. Vitamins, calcium, and something with a name she
couldn't pronounce that was supposed to keep her from
miscarrying, she answered.

Surprised, he said, "I didn't know you were threatening to miscarry, Ruth."

"Oh, I'm not, Arthur. But I had a little spotting one
day, so the doctor thought it would be a good idea, just
in case."

Then she lowered her voice so David would not hear.
"My doctor knows I absolutely *cannot lose this child!*"

Arthur called the obstetrician to ask him about the
medication. "She's my patient, doctor," he told the younger man. "I referred her to you, so I feel a responsibility."

The young man had sounded so confident, a little
patronizing of smalltown docs, if the truth could be told.

"We found up in Boston, Dr. Hillman, that five milli-
grams of diethylstilbestrol, given prophylactically to preg-

nant women, increases the baby's birth weight and adds
to a general sense of well-being. You might say it makes
a normal pregnancy more normal."

Arthur had not minced words. "That is the biggest
bunch of bullshit I ever heard, doctor. There is no such
thing as 'more normal!' I want her taken off that drug
immediately."

You don't often interfere in a case. But Arthur had no
hesitation on that occasion. He was relieved as hell when
Ruth was safely delivered and the baby was fine.

And now, Drew . . . ! Drew and Julie were married,
and Drew was asking this question. *God. Please don't let
that be the reason.*

He cleared his throat. "Ruth *did* take hormones for a
part of her early pregnancy, Drew. I remember, because . . ." and he told Drew the story. When Drew did
not respond, Arthur said, "I hope nothing's wrong."

"Well, we're not quite sure about the extent of it,
Dad, but we'll know in a few days." In a subdued voice,
he told Arthur what Dr. Branch had found.

When Drew hung up, Dr. Hillman sat staring out the
window. He thought about Julie, that lovely, blithe, vibrant young woman. . . . His heart ached for them. How
he wished he could take on the burden, spare them this
awful ordeal.

Tears came to his eyes, and that is how Molly found
him when she came into the study.

*How do you tell your twenty-two-year-old wife that she
must lose her uterus, ovaries, and vagina?*

The results of the biopsies could not have been worse.
They removed the primary tumor, but the cancer had
already spread. More surgery was necessary—the most
aggressive kind. Julie was given a course of radiation and
chemotherapy. More would be given after the radical
surgery, in an all-out attempt to arrest the metastasis.

Why put her through all this, he asked himself, when
she would most likely die of cancer in any case? But he
knew the answer. If there was the *slightest* chance to save
her, they had to take it.

She was so brave. She cried when he said her hair
would fall out. "I know it sounds terribly vain," she told
him between sobs, "but my hair has always been the one

thing that was right about me. When I was skinny and
flatchested and wore braces, at least I could always count
on my hair being okay."

"Everything about you is okay. You're the most okay
thing I've ever seen!" He grabbed her and kissed her
until she couldn't catch her breath.

But *this* was different, this radical operation. Hair grew
back. . . .

She was in bed in their apartment, finishing some
sketches for her sculpture studio. This was her senior
year of college, and she was desperately trying to finish
her course work in order to graduate with her class. He
had spoken to her advisors himself and they promised to
do everything possible to see that she received her degree. Her professors had waived the final exams, but
Julie was determined to hand in every assignment.

He sat talking while she worked. She was so talented.
It put him in awe of her to see what she could do with
charcoal or pastels. Surely someone who could create
such beauty, who brought so much goodness to life and
suffered the loss she had when her parents were killed
. . . surely Julie should not be made to endure more. He
didn't believe in God, but whatever system of order ruled
the universe, this defied all logic, all justice.

Julie put down her sketch pad. She gave him a tremulous smile. "Are you going to tell me?"

"Tell you . . .?"

"I know you've heard something. What is it?"

And so he told her. In the most gentle way he could.
He tried to describe the radical procedure to make it
sound less frightening, but Julie was too smart for that.
Besides, it was her body and she had a right to know . . .
and the right to choose.

She looked grave. "So that means, essentially, that I
will be a castrate female."

He closed his eyes. "Julie, that's a harsh way to describe it. You'll be as feminine as you ever were."

"I'll never be able to have children now."

"We can adopt, darling. We would love any baby we
took care of. It doesn't have to be our biological child.
Look at my father—I mean Arthur. He didn't even know
me as a baby, yet I believe he really loves me. And I love
him."

She moistened her lips. "When you say . . . when you describe it as a 'resection' of the vagina . . . exactly what does that mean?"

He sucked in his lips to keep his mouth steady. Reaching out for her, his expression told her the answer even before he found the words.

She wrenched away from him. *"No!* No, I won't *let* them do that to me!"

He had to fight to keep from crying. "You'll still have sensation, Julie. They might even be able to leave . . . to create an opening."

"Oh, swell! They might even be able to *create an opening!* I'm certain your male doctor friends will try everything in their power to be damn sure you can still screw your wife, Drew!"

She began to cry in that same awful tearing way she had cried when her parents died. He had never heard anyone but Julie cry like that. It sounded like someone who has already seen beyond the grave.

"Julie . . . darling . . . please, darling, I love you so much . . ." But she would not let him touch her.

"Get out! Leave me alone!" she screamed. "I have a right to be alone with this."

He went into the living room and poured himself a stiff Scotch. He almost never drank hard liquor. After Dartmouth, he figured he'd done enough damage to his liver for a lifetime. He sat on the sofa, his head back, wondering whether this could really be happening to them, this awful thing.

He also felt guilty. Julie wasn't wrong. Wasn't he feeling sorry for himself? When a guy is twenty-five, it's not exactly heaven to know his wife is going to be rendered incapable of having normal sex.

God. What a bastard I am!

Once, he tried to go back into the bedroom, but Julie had locked the door and she was either asleep or would not answer when he called her name. Finally, he turned out the lights and fell asleep on the couch, pulling an afghan over himself.

In the middle of the night, he felt her put her arms around him, saying his name and touching him all over. Half asleep, he made love to her and then followed her back to their bed.

*   *   *

Julie finished the last of her art workshop assignments at the end of March. The next day she was scheduled for a radical hysterectomy with vaginectomy. "April Fool's Day," she said. "Maybe they'll tell me it's a joke."

There were some good times left. Julie graduated with her class in June. She wore a wig to commencement because her hair had not grown back yet.

They were supposed to have spent a month in Atlanta that summer of 1971, while he did some work at the Center for Disease Control. Henry Campion had asked him to give a talk on viruses to the epidemiology course, and at the same time Drew wanted to learn a new immuno-assay technique in the live virus lab at the CDC. Julie was in the hospital for more chemotherapy then. He went down for only two days, gave the lecture, spent some time in the lab, and flew back to Philadelphia. Julie encouraged him to stay longer, but he could not stand to be away from her.

She had this drive to bare herself to him.

"What did you think of me the first time you met me?" she asked. They had met in 1962 at his mother's wedding to Arthur Hillman. Julie's father, Justice Benjamin, had performed the ceremony because Arthur was Jewish and Molly was Catholic, albeit a lapsed Catholic.

"I thought you were a cute little girl," he answered.

"Little girl! I would have *died* if I'd known that. I had the hots for you even then."

"C'mon, Julie," he laughed. "You were only thirteen years old."

"I was precocious." He kissed her and fondled her. He did that often. It was important for her to feel desirable.

"Everyone always thought I was so good, but I was a terrible kid," she continued. "They never knew what I was like underneath."

"Yeah, I'll bet."

"Really! Want me to tell you some things about myself that will surprise you?"

"Tell me."

"I seduced you."

"What do you mean, *you* seduced *me? I* seduced *you!*"

"No, Drew. I planned the whole thing. I dropped the books on the stairs and I was going to pretend to fall and hurt myself."

"You *did* hurt yourself. Your ankle was all swollen and bruised."

"I know. But that was an accident. I stepped on a book that slid out from under me."

"Why, you little scheming seductress! . . . taking advantage of me." He grabbed for her and began to feel her breasts. She lay back, encouraging him to continue.

"I did some other bad things. . . ."

"What things?" he asked absentmindedly, as he stroked her thighs.

"I went through your room, read your love letters."

He lifted his head. "Julie! Did you really?"

Pleased that she got a rise out of him, she said, "Yep. I went on a panty raid. Took clothes from your drawers to keep . . . sort of like a fetish. I used to go into your closet, too, and hug your sports coats on the hangers, pretending it was you. It smelled like you . . . you know how a closet smells like the person." He wrinkled his nose. "I used to go there to cry."

"You cried?"

"Yes. I cried a lot. My parents were dead, and even though Molly and Arthur were great, I was miserable. The only thing I liked was that I was living in *your* house. But you were away at college most of the time. What I really hated was when you brought your girl friends home. I *despised* them. I was mad with jealousy. I used to plan mean things to do to them, but I was afraid you'd find out." She looked down at her hands. "I was always in love with you."

"Why are you telling me all this?"

"I want you to know everything about me."

Some of what she said surprised him. That time he had gone home to Wilkes-Barre just to get a few days rest, for instance. . . . He'd been working like hell. The combined M.D./Ph.D. program at Penn was a killer. Molly and Arthur were in Europe, and the house was closed up because the housekeeper had gone away for a month. When he drove back to the garage, he was surprised to see Julie's car parked in the driveway. She was a freshman at Mt. Holyoke and he hadn't expected her to be home.

Julie was in the kitchen eating cookies and going through a pile of mail. "You scared me," she said when he walked in.

"I didn't know you would be here, Julie. I came home for a few days to get some sleep. I just about made it through mid-terms."

"Yeah," she said, giving him an appraising look. "You look like maybe you *didn't* make it." The remark irritated him. Later, he looked in his bathroom mirror to see what she meant.

Julie had a date that night with a boy from Kingston who went to Lehigh. She came home at two o'clock. *What the hell is there to do in Wilkes-Barre until 2 A.M. on a Thursday night?* he thought angrily. He could hear them laughing outside his open window. Then there was the murmur of low voices followed by a long silence. Julie laughed again, and Drew punched his pillow and turned over. He could not fall asleep until he heard her close the door and saw the lights go out.

He slept late the next morning. He was in the kitchen drinking coffee when Julie came down wearing shorts and an Amherst T-shirt. *Boy, the kid really gets around.*

"Are you going out again tonight?" he asked. His voice had an edge of sarcasm.

"I don't know. I might." She poured herself some orange juice. "Why do you ask?"

"Well . . . I thought we might . . . I don't know . . . go to a movie or something?" He couldn't believe what he had just said.

She regarded him thoughtfully and put the bottle of juice in the refrigerator. Bending over, she rummaged in the vegetable drawer. He tried to keep his attention off the sight of Julie's bottom in short shorts.

"Well?" he asked, feeling like a fool.

She straightened up and closed the refrigerator door. "Why don't I make some dinner here, and then we'll see?"

"Fine." He felt terrific, full of energy. Nothing like a good night's sleep, he told himself. "Feel like some tennis?"

They played tennis at the neighbors' courts next door.

They hung around the house all afternoon, reading in the sun parlor. Julie made spaghetti and meatballs for dinner. Then they watched TV.

At eleven o'clock, he yawned. "I guess I'll hit the sack." She sure was a cute kid, he thought. Interesting, too. The evening hadn't been half bad.

They said good night.

He had almost fallen asleep when he heard a loud tumbling noise and a muffled scream. Startled, he jumped out of bed. He slept skinny, so he grabbed his jeans and put them on, then ran out in the hall.

"Julie?" he called. "What happened?" The door to her room was open and the light was on, but she was not in there. "Where are you, Julie?"

"Here. . . ." It came from somewhere out in the hall.

She was wearing skimpy blue shorty pajamas, sitting at the bottom of the attic stairs, holding her foot and grimacing. A carton of books had spilled down the stairway.

"What in the world are you doing? Are you hurt?"

She nodded, biting her lower lip.

"Here . . . let me see."

Her ankle was swelling down into the instep. She had given it a nasty twist, maybe torn a ligament.

He carried her into her room and put her on the double canopy bed, then went down to get ice. He spent half an hour holding ice on the wrenched ankle and rubbing the leg above it.

He had never seen skin like hers on anyone else. Satiny soft, it was pale and smooth, with pink blushes, like a Renoir painting. This must be what's meant by peaches and cream, he thought.

Julie looked like a confection, her wide, turquoise eyes matching the robin's-egg blue pajamas. He could see the outline of her breasts through the fabric. Her hair lay over her shoulders, long and straight, shining in the dim lamplight. Drew had thought of it as red, but it was really an extraordinary color, like old gold with rosy glints.

He never was sure how it happened, but he was kissing her. She opened her mouth and he was drowning in her kisses. His hands were moving over her body beneath the ridiculous little pajamas, and it was right somehow. She responded with wondrous abandon and Drew knew this was the woman he would love for the rest of his life.

When he entered her, it was the answer to all the questions he had ever asked about himself. What was the meaning of this transcendent feeling? It was Julie . . . Julie who was the missing segment in the puzzle of his life.

"Did you know this?" he whispered afterward when they were lying quietly, at rest.

Her laugh was low and wise. "Yes," she answered him. "Always!"

Did he have a premonition that she might not live long? They were married the following June. Julie was only twenty, and she transferred to Penn for her final two years of college. Drew had another year of medical school to complete after finishing his Ph.D. dissertation.

Molly thought Julie was too young for marriage.

"We know it's right, Mother," he insisted. "Please don't try to talk us into waiting."

"You know we love Julie, Drew. I feel a responsibility to her parents. I have to be sure it's the right thing for *her*, as well as you."

"Are you trying to tell me I'm not good enough for her?" he teased.

Arthur was the one who convinced Molly. Drew did not know what he told her, but she came around full circle. She helped Julie plan the wedding. It was a beautiful, happy wedding, in the garden of the Hillman house on Grandview Terrace—where Molly and Arthur had been married.

Arthur gave them a two-week trip to Europe for a wedding gift. "You've worked hard, Drew. And you'll work even harder these next years during your residency. You deserve a romantic honeymoon."

They went to Paris, Rome, Venice, and Florence. It was Julie's dreams come true, reveling in all the works of art she had studied and was seeing for the first time.

They settled into their apartment on Walnut Street, and for two years they knew what it was to be completely happy. *Complete happiness.* Well, maybe people aren't supposed to be that happy. One thing he knew for sure, he would never find it again. He didn't even want to try.

Julie came home one last time for almost a month after

her third hospitalization. By that time, she was too sick for pretense. She was content to be there. She did not want a nurse, so he took care of her himself, working half-days and no nights. The other residents in the department were great, covering for him. Drew took daily bloods to measure her levels, and she was seen by the oncologist once a week.

The day came when Phil Branch said, "We have to bring her back in, Drew."

"She wants to die at home," he answered in a monotone.

"That's a romantic notion. But you and I know what it would be like. We can make her more comfortable in the hospital, Drew. It can't be done at home. You're going to kill yourself, the way you look."

Julie moved around the apartment, touching things . . . her piano, her easel, the end tables and club chairs that had belonged to her parents. Comfortable old friends she had known all her life.

When she realized he knew what she was doing, she gave a little self-conscious laugh that ended in a hiccup. "I love this place so much, Drew! It's been a happy home."

He put his arms around her, rubbing his cheek against her hair. It had grown in again in curling tendrils, giving her a child-like appeal.

"Promise me something?" Her voice was muffled against him.

"Anything . . . *anything!*" he answered fiercely, the tears running down his cheeks and into her hair.

"Promise me you'll be there when I die. Be sure to hold me in your arms until you know I'm dead. I once read that you can hear everything and understand what's happening for a few minutes after you stop breathing. I won't be so afraid if you're holding me."

And so he held her, and kept telling her he loved her . . . until there was no doubt in his mind that she was really dead.

Chapter 12

Henry Campion gathered the scattered pages of Drew's report and stacked them into a neat pile, fastening it with a clamp. "Terrific job, Drew! It's just what I needed. I'll get Beth to polish it up a little. She's my editor—used to teach English before we were married."

He had asked Drew to draft the section on viral diseases for the proposal he was sending to the World Health Organization. He could have done it himself, but he thought it would be a good idea to involve Drew in the early stages of the proposed Task Force. Besides, he needed something to take his mind off things.

Henry regarded the young man for a moment. Drew looked better. Still pale and drawn, but his eyes were alive again. What a tragedy Julie's death had been. They were such a nice young couple. Drew needed to lose himself in his work for a time, Henry thought. A scientific collaboration in the lab would be good for him.

"There's an Indian microbiologist who's been out at Michigan on a fellowship, working on vaccines. He's coming to Penn for a few months before returning to India. I'd like to get the two of you together. Interested?"

"Sure. I'm about ready for something new."

An enormous depression had settled on Drew in the past six months. When Julie was still alive, her need had kept him going, kept his energy level high. Now, making it through each day was an effort. Just getting up in the morning took every ounce of strength he could muster. He would welcome anything that could take his mind off himself.

Prem Mehta was just the sort of person he liked. Smart, friendly, confident. At Dartmouth, Drew had known several Indians and Pakistanis, none of them well.

They were all the sons of wealthy expatriates and had an elitist attitude.

Prem was different. He had been educated in India before he came to the University of Michigan for his graduate work. Offered a teaching position there, he had turned it down in order to go home to India.

"I imagine I shall be sorry a year from now," he told Drew one day when they were in the lab. "But if everyone who studied abroad didn't go back, there would be little hope for Indian science." He grinned. "Besides, I'm getting married soon."

"Married? Congratulations! Someone you knew before?"

"No. Actually, we met here. She was at Michigan, too. But we had a devil of a time with the families. We're Punjabis and they're Sindhis. Her family had someone else picked out for her—and my family wanted me to marry a girl from the same community."

"That sounds pretty complicated to me. So you still have arranged marriages in India?"

Prem nodded. "Yes, but many of us *arrange* to have ours arranged! I convinced my father to approach her family, so now it's all set. We'll have the betrothal when I reach home and be married a few months after that."

"It sounds sensible—unromantic, but well-ordered," Drew laughed.

"Not as unromantic as you may suppose!" Prem smiled widely. He was quiet for a moment. "You ought to remarry soon, Drew. It would help you."

Drew shook his head. "I don't think so, Prem. Things don't work that way here. We marry for love—at least, most of us do."

"And when that love doesn't last? I've met many divorced people in the States."

"I know. That's why I don't want to marry again."

Drew had long been intrigued with India. His stepbrother, Robert Hillman, one of Arthur's twin sons, lived in New Delhi and worked for the Ford Foundation. Robert had urged Drew to come visit him and his wife Jane after Julie's death. Someday he might do that, especially now that he knew Prem.

There was a farewell party given for Prem in March, on the Saturday night before he left for home. It was held at the house of a technician from the lab, one of those tiny row houses that abound in Philadelphia, with a front stoop and a back porch, each identical to the others.

Drew arrived late. He had been working out in the gym, trying to get himself back in shape. Before her illness, he and Julie used to run together, and they always played tennis on the weekends.

The place was jammed. He pushed his way through to the kitchen to get a beer. A woman was bending down, trying to prime the keg.

"May I help?" he asked.

"It was going fine 'til *I* got here! My usual effect on machinery. My car's always in the shop." She straightened up. "Oh, hi! I remember you."

She looked vaguely familiar. Freckled face, snub nose, and a nice smile. He couldn't place her. "I'm Drew Tower," he said.

"Of course you are! I'm Gail McPherson." And when he didn't react, she added, "I used to be Ben's wife."

He finished pumping the coils, siphoned off some foam, and handed her a beer. "Used to be?" he repeated.

"Yes." She took a long swallow of beer. "We split." She licked the foam off her upper lip.

"Oh. Too bad."

"No, not really. But it got a bit uncomfortable with the two of us out at Northwestern, so I came back to Penn." She gave a little shrug and grinned. "Well, what the hell, I always did like Philly more than Chicago."

Drew smiled. "I would say Penn came out ahead on that one." She was cute, and Ben McPherson had been decidedly uncute, a real crud.

They moved together into the dining room, where the table was laden with dips, potato chips, and chunks of Swiss cheese on toothpicks stuck into a grapefruit. Prem waved from the other side of the room.

"Have you met the guest of honor?" he asked Gail. She shook her head. "Come on, I'll introduce you." He took her arm and led the way.

"I was wondering whether you would come," Prem told him.

"I wouldn't have missed it. I was lifting weights, and then I swam a few laps." He slapped his midriff. "Gotta get rid of this flab."

Gail eyed him up and down, then made a fist and pretended to punch him in the gut. "Oww! the iron man," she cried. Prem laughed and gave Drew a questioning glance.

He ignored the look. "How do you feel about leaving?" he asked Prem.

"Oddly enough, I feel sad. After four years at Michigan, it was understandable that I should regret leaving there, but I've been at Penn for only six months."

Gail had turned to speak to some other people. "I'll miss you, Prem," Drew said, looking into his glass, "I haven't exactly been the most cheerful soul in the lab, but I've enjoyed working with you."

"So have I, Drew. I hope you'll come to Delhi one day. You'd always be welcome at my parents' house. And you should visit your step-brother."

"Be sure to call Robert and Jane when you reach home," Drew reminded him.

Gail took his arm. "Want some pizza? They have some out in the kitchen."

Drew rested his hand on Prem's shoulder. "I'll see you later."

They replenished their beers and, taking slices of pizza on paper plates, sat on the narrow stairs.

"You worked with Prem Mehta in the lab?" she asked. He nodded, his mouth full. "Doing what?"

"Trying to make an antibody for hepatitis. He's a microbiologist, one of the best. And that's not just *my* opinion."

"What will he do back in India? Other than go crazy."

"Not this guy!" Drew said firmly. "He's the kind who will make it work, if anyone can."

He changed the subject. "Tell me about you," he said. He listened while she told him she had taken the course at the CDC, followed by an assignment in infectious diseases out in Colorado, and then the return to Northwestern to a bad marriage.

He was curious about her. She had something—an elusive quality that reminded him a little of Julie. There was a sauciness about her, a dedicated irreverence. Her hazel eyes turned up at the corners, and the short auburn curls framed her face in much the same way that Julie's hair had after the chemotherapy. It made him feel good to think about Julie tonight, to compare this spirited woman to Julie.

"You aren't listening." He had wandered off, and she was looking at him seriously now, a little anxiously. "Am I boring you?"

"Not at all," he replied. "I heard everything you said." He sighed. "You just made me think of . . . other things."

"I heard about your wife," she said quietly. "I'm really very sorry."

He smiled softly. "Thank you."

"Would you take me home?" she asked impulsively.

"I . . ." he drew in his breath and stared at her long enough for her to blush and say, "Forget it. That was one of my poorer ideas."

"No!" He put his hand on top of hers. "No, Gail. It was a fine idea. I'm just not sure what will happen."

She smiled at him, her eyes crinkling at the corners. "Nothing has to happen, Drew. Let's go!"

It was snowing. He scraped the windows of his car, then let the motor idle to warm up. Gail's apartment was on the second floor of a brick house near the veterinary school. He found a parking space on the same block. They stamped the snow off their feet in the small entry before climbing the stairs.

"It's a mess. I wasn't planning on having company," she apologized, as she picked up newspapers and slippers from the floor of the living room.

"That's okay. You should see *my* place."

"All right!" she said, then laughed nervously. "That was dumb."

She took his coat and hung it on a brass coat rack with hers. "Drink?" she asked. "Scotch, beer—coke?" He shook his head, looking around with curiosity. "Shall I make some coffee?"

"Yes. That sounds nice." He sat on the rust tweed convertible sofa and wondered why he was there.

The room was small. One wall held do-it-yourself book-shelves filled with medical books, some left over college texts, and a stereo. A coffee table was made from cinder blocks painted white and a slab of black ersatz marble. There were black canvas directors chairs, some flimsy end tables, and a pair of matching white pottery lamps. It was fairiy typical of student apartments, but Gail was five years out of medical school. Presumably she and Ben had owned some decent furniture when they were married. This did not look like it had been used very long.

"Here we are." Gail returned with an electric percolator and a plate of brownies. "It's the best I could do. I baked them yesterday."

"That's great," he said. "I love brownies."

She put on some Johnny Mathis records, then came to sit on the couch. "It's a lousy apartment, isn't it?"

"It's not so bad."

"Oh, come on, Drew. It stinks. You can say it. I can't afford to fix it up yet. I had to buy the cheapest stuff I could find. Sears special!"

"What happened to the furniture you had when you were married?"

She was looking down at her coffee mug. "Ben kept it."

"Everything?"

She nodded. "Every last thing. China, linens, the eight place settings of sterling that were gifts from his relatives. The French Provincial living room set his mother insisted on choosing for us."

"Yeah, but, Gail . . . how long were you married?"

"Almost six years. Except we haven't been together for the last three."

She put her mug on the coffee table and sat with her hands folded in her lap like a well-bred school girl.

"Ben never wanted me to take the fellowship at the CDC. I almost turned it down, but then he was offered a chance to go out to California to work with the heart transplant team at Stanford for a year. So, I didn't see why I should have to stay in Chicago.

"I was in Atlanta for two years—in fact, I was there when you came down to give that talk—and then, when I went back to Northwestern, Ben informed me he had met another woman out in Palo Alto. The daughter of one of the surgeons he was training with. Very social, very rich, very beautiful. Exactly what his mother always wanted for him." She laughed. "And she is *crazy* about French Provincial!"

"Well, that still doesn't explain why you're in such straits, Gail. How did Ben end up with everything?"

"I went out to Colorado for three months after Ben

told me he wanted a divorce. That, plus my two years in Atlanta, meant *I* had left *him*." She let out a long shaky breath. "I can't afford expensive lawyers, Drew. I'm still paying off a $25,000 loan for med school. My mother's a widow. She lives in Maine, and I have three younger brothers who have to be educated."

"Ben's a bastard! The whole thing sucks."

Gail did not reply. Her head was bent, her hands still folded in her lap. A tremor went through her body.

"Gail?" Drew touched her shoulder tentatively. She turned her head and he saw that she was crying. "Ah, Gail, don't cry."

He put his arms around her and she buried her face against his chest. *How did this happen?* he wondered as he tightened his embrace. It seemed both strange and natural for him to be comforting a weeping woman.

They lay on the couch, her clothes in disarray, his tie and jacket discarded. Her tears had long dried and her lips were ripe with kissing. "Shall we go to bed?" she asked huskily, when his hand found her breasts.

"I'd like to," he answered.

In the bedroom, she kissed him and unbuttoned his shirt. "I don't have anything . . . a condom," he said, as unaccustomed to this as if he had never been with a woman.

"That's all right. I have a diaphragm. That's one thing Ben let me keep!" She laughed. He wished she had not mentioned Ben at that moment.

For several minutes he savored the luxury of lying in bed with a woman, feeling her naked flesh against his. Gail had a lovely body, firm and smooth, with small round breasts and slim hips. She was eager for him, wanting him to take the lead, ready to respond. But he could tell it wasn't going to work.

He rolled onto his back. "I'm sorry, Gail. It's not . . . I'm not. . . ."

"That's all right, Drew. I told you nothing had to happen, remember?"

She was hiding her disappointment.

"Gail . . . I don't want you to think it's you. It's my fault."

"It's not your *fault*. It's something you can't help. I

never thought of a man's problems before. I always thought
about how hard it was for a woman—to have satisfying
sex, I mean."

"I've never thought about either one, to tell you the
truth!"

"Is this the first time . . . since your wife?" she asked
hesitantly.

"Yes. I just haven't had any interest in sex. It's kind of
complicated, but I hope it's not a permanent condition."
He smiled at her in the semidarkness. "Well, I guess I
better go. It's really late, and it's snowing hard."

"Why don't you stay over?"

"No, I don't think so."

He dressed and she said goodbye to him at the door,
wearing a blue chenille bathrobe and fluffy slippers.

"The snow looks deep," she called down the stairs
when he opened the front door.

A few minutes later he rang the doorbell. "Hey, lady,
do you have a shovel?" he asked, grinning when she
answered the door. "I'm snowed in."

"No. Maybe one of my neighbors does, but it's
two-thirty."

He spread his hands in a helpless gesture. "Is it still
okay if I stay?"

It was the first morning in eighteen months that he had
awakened in the same bed with a woman.

"Hi!" She was leaning on one elbow looking at him.
"You're beautiful when you sleep."

He smiled groggily. "I'm supposed to be saying that to
you."

"I said it first."

He stretched, then winced at the pain in his muscles.

"What's wrong?"

"My whole body aches—from working out." She rubbed
his shoulder. "Mmm, that feels good."

"Turn over. I'll give you a massage."

She knelt beside him and began to knead his neck and
shoulders, then his back. He felt himself stirring.

After a while he murmured, "You know what?"

"What?" she asked, guessing the answer.

"You're not so bad with machinery."

They came together and they made love, and it was good.

"You see," she said. "There's nothing wrong with you. Nothing at all."

They had a late breakfast and sat around reading the Sunday papers. "I'll call you soon," he told her when he left in the early afternoon. They both wondered whether he meant it.

The apartment improved. Gail made new curtains. Drew gave her a small chest of drawers and an easy chair from the attic in his parents' house, and when they visited the Museum of Fine Arts one Sunday afternoon, he bought two prints she admired, which she framed and hung on the living room wall.

He didn't want to get involved and she understood. When he couldn't stand to be by himself, and when the lab didn't offer consolation, he would call her and go over there, and she would make dinner for him and take him to her bed.

Sometimes she called him. And sometimes two or three weeks would pass without their seeing each other.

In the last week of June, he asked her to go to a concert at Robin Hood Dell. She invited him to come home with her at the end of the evening. After they had made love, she sent him away.

"I'm beginning to care too much, Drew. Please don't call me again."

"But, Gail—" he protested mildly.

"Drew, I'm not that dumb. You'll never fall for me, and I'm afraid I might be in love with you. Good night!" She pushed him out the door.

He was both saddened and relieved when it was over. Gail had helped to heal him, and he would always think of her with gratitude and affection.

The following week, Drew received his official appointment to the International Health Task Force.

Chapter 13

She walked from the Avenue Foch to l'Etoile, stepping briskly along the Champs Élysées with its rush of morning traffic, turning left on Rue de Berri to the Faubourg-Saint-Honoré, pausing at Le Bristol, then impulsively entering the hotel through the revolving doors.

It was the same lobby with its crystal chandeliers and little groups of velvet upholstered Louis XV chairs, the same bar to the left on the raised platform, the same gilded lift in its tube of glass. This had been her first home in Paris when she was still young enough to expect happy endings.

She continued on her way. There was not even the burn of unshed tears when she confronted the splendor of Place Vendôme. She could not permit herself to respond to her memories or she would be overwhelmed.

Through the ormolu gates she passed, up the Persian-carpeted staircase with the statue of Tupaq Amaru Inca on the landing beneath the domed skylight. Hesitating only for a moment, she entered the distinctive doors of hammered bronze, the world headquarters of Légende et Cie.

The concierge was a stranger. So was the receptionist. When she gave her name in a soft voice, there was a stir, a stiffening of spines, a rising to feet, a murmur of apologies.

"We didn't expect you until tomorrow, Mademoiselle Légende."

"I wanted to see . . . to spend some time in my father's office," she explained. "Do you have the key?"

"Of course!"

She followed the secretary past the rows of glass cabinets in which were displayed the Légende product lines: Inca pour les Hommes, Flor del Viento pour les Femmes;

the fragrances Tina and Nicole, in their prize-winning crystal phials; Légende Baume de Beauté, Légende Tonique . . . the dozens of extravagant health and beauty items that had their origins in the valley of the flamesword and in the creative genius of Daniel Légende.

Down the hallway she walked, her footsteps falling silent on lush silvery carpeting. At the paneled door of the executive suite she held out her hand, taking the key ring.

"I'd like to be alone for a while." The woman nodded understandingly.

The door closed silently behind her and she surveyed the shadowed room. The draperies were drawn and there were dust covers on the couches and chairs. Throwing off the shrouds, she dropped them on the floor, then moved to the windows and pulled the cords, letting in bright daylight.

There was a table made of cherry wood on which stood framed photographs of her mother and herself. And two little boys. Several faded old snapshots taken at Huaranca showed her father and grandfather with a group of *campesinos*. The pictures with heads of state and university presidents, showing Daniel receiving medals and honorary degrees, were not on display.

She moved to the massive desk, running her hand over its tooled leather surface, touching the monogrammed silver letter opener, the embossed cover of the appointments diary. She sat in the burgundy leather chair molded by years of his occupancy as the head of this great enterprise.

At last, she put her face in her hands and wept.

An hour passed. There was a discreet knock at the door. *"Entrez,"* she called. Manuel entered the room.

"They said you've been here for a long time." He scrutinized her face. "Am I disturbing you?"

She sighed, pushing herself away from the desk and rising. "No, Manuel. I just had to come here alone first. Before the meeting."

"I understand. Shall I leave you?"

"No, I'm all right now. I'll just wash my face." She went through her father's private dressing room to the bath. His toiletries were there and it smelled of his per-

sonal custom-made soap and shaving cologne. It was a
new onslaught of nostalgia, but now she was prepared for
it.

She splashed her face with cold water. Looking in the
mirror, she thought, I will not go to the Left Bank. I
have had enough of memories. But she knew she had to
go, because she must visit her former professor at the
Hôpital Necker. And she must see Isabelle Somme. She
has promised Daniel.

She smoothed her hair with both hands. Pulling herself
to her full height, she returned to Manuel.

"Why don't we have lunch at the Ritz?" Manuel held
her hand as they crossed the Place Vendôme.

"Do you remember the first time I brought you here
for tea?" he asked when they were seated behind a
screen of palms at a table spread with pink linen.

Nicole smiled. "I was so young!"

"And so beautiful . . . almost as beautiful as you are
now." He took her hand and kissed it. Then he reached
into his pocket and removed a small gift-wrapped box,
placing it in front of her. "Here's a birthday gift."

"But . . . it isn't my birthday."

He laughed indulgently. "Open it."

It was from Cartier. A marvelous bracelet of large oval
turquoises set in braided gold links.

"Manuel. . . ." She shook her head. "I can't accept
this from you."

"You don't like it?" He was amused.

"*Like* it? Who wouldn't like it? It's exquisite! But . . .
but, I can't let you give it to me."

Lowering his head, he looked at her from the top of
his eyes. "Nicole. If it gives me pleasure to present you
with a pretty bracelet, and still more pleasure to see you
wear it, why can't you accept it graciously and say 'Thank
you, Manuel,' and let it go at that? There are no strings
attached to my gift."

She ran her fingers up and down the stem of her wine
glass, as she regarded him steadily. *I must be crazy,* she
thought. *He's everything any woman would want, and I
can't love him.*

Manuel cocked one eyebrow quizzically, and she could
not help smiling. "Thank you, Manuel," she said de-

murely. He reached over and fastened the bracelet on her wrist.

"Splendid!" he pronounced. "It belongs on you." He raised his glass in salute.

This was the first full board meeting of Légende et Cie since the death of Daniel Légende. All of the members wore little black ribbons in their lapels. Nicole was touched by that, but at the same time she wondered whether it was not a diplomatic ploy. Except for Manuel and Claude Montagne, Daniel's partner in the original company, none of the directors was an intimate family friend.

I'm becoming cynical, she thought. One reason Manuel had insisted she should attend this meeting, even though she had argued that she was not ready, was to help ensure that Claude would take over as Chief Executive Officer.

The executive committee had met earlier to discuss the succession. The Swiss had a candidate and so did the Americans.

"That would be like the tail wagging the dog, Nicole," Manuel had said, in reference to the subsidiaries. "Claude is the only one who understands the company perfectly. He'll guide it with leadership similar to your father's. But we need your presence, not just your proxy. It will help to prevent an open revolt."

She had been nervous about attending. She was the only woman, and ironically enough, the only one besides Manuel not wearing a symbol of mourning. *Thank heaven I came here yesterday and got my emotions under control!*

Claude Montagne, as Vice President and Chief Counsel, presided. Manuel sat next to Nicole, explaining everything as they went along. Surprisingly, she found the meeting fascinating. She said little until after the luncheon, prepared by a chef from Fouquet's and served in the directors' dining room.

In the afternoon, as planned, she nominated Claude Montagne to replace her father as the head of Légende et Cie, giving a graceful speech, prepared weeks ago with Manuel's help. She ended by saying, "Gentlemen, I am really acting as the voice of Daniel Légende. This was my father's wish, to be succeeded by the man who was instrumental in the founding of this company."

Claude, Uncle Claude! He had always been one of her favorite people. She remembered when he used to take her to the Bois de Boulogne for Sunday afternoon concerts and *glace.* Now he gave her a subdued smile from the head of the table. Manuel seconded the nomination and the board unanimously agreed.

"They couldn't have done anything else," Manuel said at dinner with Claude that evening. "Not with Nicole there."

"We haven't heard the last of it," Claude told them. "They're already plotting how they'll force me out. I'll give them a good fight!"

Manuel joined Nicole for dinner at the little house in Neuilly where Françoise Bercy lived with her new husband.

"Alain has two children by his first marriage," Françoise explained when she and Nicole were alone in the kitchen, "so it was better to have a country place, for when they visit."

"You look happy, Françoise. I'm so pleased for you."

Impulsively, Françoise hugged her. *"You* look beautiful! My elegant friend . . . no one would *believe* you were that awkward schoolgirl with pigtails who began with me at the Faculté de Médecine!"

"Really, chérie!"

Françoise stirred red wine into a saucepan. "Tell me about Manuel," she said quietly, with a glance over her shoulder, to be certain they were not overheard. "Is he the only man in your life?"

Nicole smiled ruefully. "It would seem so. The fact is, Françoise, there *is* no man—not in the way you mean."

"But that's terrible!"

"Ah, how French you are!" she laughed. "In some ways, perhaps you're right. But it's safe."

Françoise studied her. "Nicole. You're not still thinking about Erik? That was a war. It will never happen again. And it was a long time ago."

The next morning, she went to visit Isabelle Somme in her apartment overlooking the Jardin du Luxembourg. Lovely Isabelle, she thought, as they embraced.

With tears in her eyes, the woman who had been Daniel's frequent companion for more than ten years asked, "Did he suffer?"

Nicole shook her head. "Not so much, Isabelle. He wasn't conscious at the end."

"He never told me, the last time we were together." She wept, then apologized for her tears. "I'm sorry, Nicole. But I did love him very much."

"I know. He loved you, too," she said softly.

"He was so generous! Did you know?"

"Yes, he told me. No more than he should have been."

She said goodbye to Isabelle, then walked the streets of student Paris, her Paris, for the first time since she had left here five years before. Boulevard Saint Germain, Rue des Écoles, Rue des Saints Pères, and finally the Rue du Bac, where she stood in the street looking up at a window in a room on the third floor where she had fallen in love with Erik Sonnenborg . . . a hundred years ago.

I've had enough of tears, she thought. *I will put this behind me now.*

By the time she was back in the apartment, Nicole's mind had turned to her visit the next day at the Hôpital Necker. And to the meeting in New York the following week—the initial meeting of the new International Health Task Force.

New York rang strident and pulsating with energy, a brash upstart after Paris. A marvel of excess compared to Lima. Only at night, when the city lights glittered like a million candles, did Nicole find it beautiful.

"Taxi, miss?" asked the doorman as she left her hotel.

"No, thank you. I'm going to walk."

He tipped his hat. "Have a nice day."

She preferred the sonorous speech of London or the soft, drawn out politesse of Atlanta to the nasal flatness of New York. When she had not been thinking in English for so long, the language settled on her gradually, a stringing together of sibilants.

She felt free and unfettered in this city. Walking across United Nations Plaza toward UN Headquarters, she was stirred by the curving line of flags of the member nations fluttering in the breeze off the East River. At the gate, she showed her identity pass to the uniformed security guard. Past the squat structure of the General Assembly, she headed for the tall glass tower of the Secretariat Building.

While waiting for the elevator, Nicole studied a photographic display of UNICEF powdered milk distribution centers in Asia. As she read the captions under the pictures, she realized that, despite all the capitals and embassies she had visited in her life, she was awed at being connected, if only in a peripheral way, with this effort in world government, the United Nations.

"Impressive, isn't it?"

Nicole started at the unexpected voice. She looked around to see a tall, striking, dark-haired man with deep blue eyes. He smiled, and she realized that this was Andrew Tower, the man who had lectured at the Center for Disease Control when she was a trainee in the epidemiology course. She wanted to tell him she recognized him, but she felt unaccountably shy.

"Yes, very impressive," she answered. The elevator arrived and he stepped aside to let her enter first. Nicole pushed the button for the twenty-fourth floor.

"It looks like we're headed for the same meeting. The Task Force?"

When she nodded, he put out his hand. "I'm Andrew Tower."

"My name is Nicole Légende."

"From Peru! Henry Campion has told me about your work in the slums—the *barriadas*. Is that the right word?"

He had an easy warmth that she found appealing. Nodding, she returned his smile. "Not bad! That's the right word." He seemed to expect something more of her. "You're at the University of Pennsylvania with Dr. Campion?"

How stupid of me to act as if I hadn't remembered, she thought. He must realize I know where all the members of the IHTF come from. "I heard you speak at the CDC when I was there. I think it was in 1970." That was better.

He raised his head, as if listening for a sound. "It was 1971," he said. "In June."

There was strength in his square jaw and sureness in the firm, sculpted mouth. When his face was in repose, his eyes harbored an unhappy secret.

The elevator doors opened. Nicole pretended to be absorbed in her notes as they walked separately down the corridor to the conference room.

Henry Campion called the first meeting of the Interna-

tional Health Task Force to order. Not an overly demon-
strative man, he was inspired to orate as he looked around
the long oval conference table at the youthful faces of the
seven men and three women representing ten different
nations.

"This is the beginning of a great experiment," he told
them. "We're not here to impress each other or anyone
else with how smart we are—although I will say that
you're here because you *are* smart." Everyone laughed.

"We're going to be an informal group. You'll be encouraged to express yourselves freely at every meeting
. . . in fact, you'll be expected to contribute with opinions and objections, if you have them. Argue with one
another—disagree!

"What will set us apart is that we won't need to take
credit for our successes . . . although I imagine we'll
receive plenty of blame for our failures. We'll study,
collect data, do research, aid field programs—whatever
and whenever the need is there.

"I don't have to introduce myself to any of you, because each one of you is someone I've met and talked
with at some length. But you don't know one another, so
we'll go around the table and you can introduce yourself
and briefly tell the others what you've done and what
your major interest is. Prem, why don't we start with
you?"

The group shifted position to direct their attention to
an attractive, light-skinned Indian. "I'm Prem Mehta, from
New Delhi. I'm a microbiologist at the All-India Institute
of Medical Sciences—better known as the AIIMS—"

Nicole listened carefully as her new colleagues told the
group about themselves. When her turn came, she mentioned having been at the CDC and told about her work
at San Martín and in the mobile clinics.

After the last of the ten had spoken, Henry Campion
said, "Now I'm going to pass around a list of requests for
our assistance. I think you'll be pleasantly surprised when
you see how many people want our help."

He gave them time to read the document. "Okay, let's
talk about priorities. Just to get us going, I suggest we
define five areas on which to concentrate for this meeting
. . . any suggestions?"

There were a number of suggestions, and the group

finally agreed to discuss malnutrition, water-born bacterial diseases, smallpox eradication, malaria, and parasitic infections.

They began slowly, hesitantly, but by the end of the morning, the discussion had become lively. Nicole had a sense of excitement. Not since her days at the CDC had she known this kind of intellectual stimulation. Henry Campion had been right when he told her she would enjoy the IHTF.

The telephone was ringing when Nicole entered her room at the UN Plaza Hotel at six-thirty on Wednesday evening. With only one more day of meetings, the Task Force had just ended the afternoon session.

"Nicole! I've been trying to reach you." Manuel's familiar voice was alien here. Her heart sank. She had forgotten about him. Forgotten he was arriving in New York today. She closed her eyes, willing herself not to sound impatient.

"Hello, Manuel. We just finished. When did you get in?"

"This morning, on the Concorde. Can you be ready by seven-thirty? I accepted dinner at the Hammonds'. They dress."

"I didn't bring a long gown, Manuel." Damn! She did not feel like one of his stuffy business dinners tonight.

"It doesn't matter. New York women wear anything. I'll pick you up in an hour."

When she hung up, she reflected that Manuel was becoming a constant presence in her life. In Lima, in Paris, and now in New York. There was little she could do about it without a rupture in their friendship. Or was she perhaps allowing it to continue at this level for another reason? She did not like to think she was the kind of woman who would keep a man dangling because it was convenient.

As she dressed, she thought with regret that she would be unable to join any of the IHTF people for dinner tonight. Some of them were going to a Broadway show, but she knew there would be a few downstairs in the restaurant.

They had all dined together for the past two evenings. Henry had reserved the wine cellar at Pierre's last night. It had been a wonderful evening.

He insisted that they all call him Henry. "Enough of this Professor bit," he exclaimed the first afternoon. "You make me feel like I'm ready to cash it in!" Nicole had to explain his slang to Anija, the Yugoslavian woman, whose English was not colloquial.

Only those of the group who had spent an extended period in the States were prepared for the informality. Nicole remembered what a short time it had taken her to feel comfortable with her instructors at the CDC. After a few of these meetings, all of them would relax.

The Mexican was certainly at ease! He had sat at her left at dinner and had been openly admiring. Luís Ribera was what the English would call a blade. Nicole could recognize machismo a mile away, even when it was disguised as gallantry, which he practiced with the three women in the group. Beneath his cordiality, though, it was obvious that he did not regard them as equal members. On two separate occasions Andrew Tower had chided him for dismissing one of the women's contributions to the discussions.

Last night Luís had said to her at dinner, "Have you been enjoying the shops? When my wife comes to New York, she spends all her time on Fifth Avenue."

"Alas! I've just come from Paris and have no patience for Fifth Avenue," she had replied. Let him think whatever he wished.

Drew was having a drink in the lounge with Prem Mehta and Luís Ribera when Nicole glided past, stylishly dressed in a black silk sheath, a double rope of lustrous pearls clasped with rubies at the corner of her neckline. There was a pause in the conversation as the three of them watched her leave the hotel with a distinguished-looking man.

"Ho, ho-o-o!" remarked Luís. "Our lovely lady from Peru is out on the town."

"Well, why not?" replied Drew irritably.

Luís raised his eyebrows at Prem.

On the last morning, they received their assignments. Nicole's research project in her home university was a comprehensive maternal and child health care program for the poor. Its objective was to collect data and provide health care, immunizations, and family planning services.

Each of the members of the Task Force was given a field assignment for a three-month period, in addition to their regular on-going project. From February through April 1974, Nicole would be going to India as a medical officer in the Smallpox Eradication Program. Her team partner was Andrew Tower.

The group had decided that smallpox eradication should be a number one priority in field work. There was much to be learned from working in the WHO's global program to eradicate smallpox, the first of its kind. Before the IHTF meeting adjourned, Henry Campion, pursuing his favorite subject, gave them a pep talk about the progress in eliminating variola, the medical term for the disease.

"This is an important time to become involved in smallpox eradication. We're very near the goal. At this moment, the western hemisphere is free of smallpox. Except for the Horn of Africa, all the endemic smallpox in the world is in four Asian countries—India, Bangladesh, Pakistan, and Nepal. The greatest number of cases by far is in India, with its enormous population. Therefore, India will be the focus of our attention.

"The strategy has changed from mass vaccination to one of surveillance and containment—hunting down cases, isolating them, and vaccinating all contacts. It worked in Nigeria when Bill Foege did it, and it will work on the subcontinent. . . .

"Good luck to all of you. We'll next meet in Geneva in January. Keep in touch. If you have any problems, let me know."

As the group began to leave the conference room, Andrew Tower walked over to Nicole. "If we're going to be working together, Nicole, we should have some preliminary meetings and coordinate our calendars."

"I'll be in New York for the rest of this week," she answered. "I have appointments in the mornings, but the afternoons are free."

"And what about the evenings?" he smiled.

Nicole stiffened. "I like to keep my professional and private lives separated, Dr. Tower."

"My friends call me Drew," he answered pleasantly.

Her look said she was judging him and found him wanting. "I shall call you Andrew."

Surprisingly, he laughed. "When my mother called me Andrew, I knew I was in trouble."

He was a confident male. So confident and so good looking that he undermined her own confidence. She realized she was behaving in an insufferably priggish manner, but she did not know how to handle this man.

"Tomorrow or Friday would be convenient," she said, trying to regain her equilibrium.

"Shall we say tomorrow at twelve-thirty? I would suggest lunch, unless that's too frivolous an idea." She realized he was teasing her.

"Lunch would be fine."

His mood altered abruptly, as if he was bored with their banter. "Good. Meet me in the Ambassador Grill." Calling to Prem Mehta to wait for him, he gathered his papers and left the conference room.

Nicole opened her attaché case and slowly arranged the stack of memos and reports in folders. She had an uncomfortable feeling about working with Andrew Tower. She did not understand her reaction to him. It was not dislike, because he was likeable—although there *had* been times during the discussions when he seemed a bit impatient and overbearing. Smart, well-informed, articulate, he was the one of this group who impressed her most of all. But for some reason he had an unsettling effect on her, and she preferred to be in complete control of herself at all times.

The lunch next day was not a success. After agreeing that they would see each other at the January meeting in Geneva and then proceed to India together, they had nothing more to say to each other.

How strange, she thought, as she studied the menu. We should have a great deal in common. The meetings, our joint assignment, an admiration for Henry Campion. It's going to be a grim three months trudging around Indian villages if this is an example of how we'll get along.

Chapter 14

There was ground fog and snow in Frankfurt, delaying the takeoff of Pan American's Round-the-World Flight 2. Having left Geneva before dawn, they waited in the Clipper Club at Frankfurt am Main Airport for almost three hours until the flight was finally called.

When the plane reached its cruising altitude, Drew reclined his seat and wondered what lay ahead. Merely leaving home was not going to lift his depression, but he hoped the change of scene and the new work would help him pull himself out of his lingering malaise.

In Geneva at the IHTF meeting, they had all greeted one another like long lost friends. Henry Campion had been pleased. "I'm tickled with the way the Task Force is shaping up, Drew," he said when they met privately before departure.

Drew agreed. "It's great when all the members of a group can interact like this."

Henry had looked at Drew quizzically. "What do you think of Nicole Légende? Strictly off the record." He could ask Drew a question like that. Theirs was a close friendship of five years.

"She's okay. Kind of cold, but we'll be all right." He shrugged. "It doesn't really matter, does it?"

"It would be better if you liked each other. She's very able, Drew. I'm sure you'll grow to respect her." He sat back and put his hands behind his head. "The young woman I knew in Atlanta was softer. There was a . . . tenderness about her then. Brilliant, of course. I wonder whether she would have been tough enough to carry out this assignment, though. She's developed a strength, a resilience that I didn't notice back then."

Drew and Nicole were not sitting together on the plane because it was a long way to New Delhi. Since the first class section of the 747 was practically empty, they would be able to stretch out to sleep during the eighteen-hour flight.

The stewards were preparing cocktails and canapés to precede the elaborate meal that was served to first class passengers on this flight. He should go sit with Nicole for a while. She had been friendlier these past few days in Geneva, within the conviviality of the Task Force.

Henry was right. It would help if they liked each other. The fact was, he *did* like her—or found her attractive, which was not the same thing. What they needed to have was a good working relationship. Period.

Nicole removed the arm dividing the two seats in order to make up a bed with blankets and pillows, but she was too excited to fall asleep. After dozing briefly, she sat up and opened a French novel she had picked up in the airport in Geneva. It was an unaccustomed luxury for her to have absolutely nothing to do for all these hours. Nothing to do except think, or indulge herself in frivolous reading.

Not for years had she experienced this sense of carefree independence. Wearing slacks and a comfortable turtleneck sweater, she had changed her boots for low-heeled walking shoes, and her hair was pulled back in a single braid, the way she wore it in Huaranca. Andrew had looked surprised that early morning when she appeared in the lobby of their Geneva hotel dressed casually for the trip. Surprised and approving.

"You look comfortable. That was smart of you."

She had taken it as a compliment, but her reaction bothered her. Why should she care what he thought about her or her appearance?

She stretched. What a marvelous feeling! At twenty-seven years of age, she was about to have the most freedom she had ever enjoyed in her entire life. Was that not bizarre? But the truth was, there had been someone there watching over her, someone to account to, for as long as she could remember. Her governess in Lima, Mademoiselle in Paris, and always, her father. Even now there was Manuel.

She had put off telling him about this trip for the

longest time. But as the departure date approached she finally had to say something.

"I'll be going to India after Geneva," she mentioned casually one evening when they were having dinner together.

"For how long?"

"Three months."

"*Three months in India?* Nicole . . . you must be joking!"

"No, Manuel, I'm perfectly serious. We all have a three-month field assignment."

"Where will you go? Who will be with you?"

She tried not to show her irritation, speaking in a reasonable tone. "I shall *go* wherever they send me. I shall *be* with my fellow workers."

"And who might they be, if I may ask?"

For some reason, she had not wanted to mention Andrew Tower.

"How can I possibly know people I have not yet met? They'll be WHO doctors and Indian government workers." She was angry. "What's gotten into you? You're acting like an over-protective father."

He was silent, staring moodily into space. Finally he said, "You no longer have a father, Nicole. You need a man to protect you. Sometimes you make foolish decisions—like going alone into the *barriadas,* or . . ." He stopped.

"*Or?*" Nicole's jaw hardened. "You were saying?"

"Or going outside of Lima to the pueblos!"

How would Manuel know about that? she wondered. She had met some Peace Corps volunteers through Pepe and Carlos. They were running a health and sanitation education program for peasants in the countryside, and she had visited three of the pueblos to advise them on how to improve the project.

She wanted to ask Manuel how he had heard about it, but she hesitated. It was not exactly that she was *afraid* to ask. There was nothing to fear. Yet, she had stopped herself.

"Oh, Manuel," she answered airily, "you worry too much."

But now, peering down at the cottony cloud cover that obscured the land mass of Europe, Nicole wondered once again, who could have told Manuel about her visits to the pueblos?

Her thoughts were interrupted by a deep male voice. "May I join you for lunch?" Andrew had come forward from his seat two rows behind.

"Of course." She removed the blankets and pillows from the seat next to hers. Without the arm in between it was like the small couch Americans called a love seat.

The steward served pâté de foie gras and smoked salmon with capers. "Champagne?" he asked.

Before she could reply, Andrew said, "I think this is an occasion that calls for champagne, don't you?" He had a wonderful smile, she noted, a little crooked, with creases on either side of his mouth. In a sweater, without a tie and jacket, he looked younger and less intimidating.

"*Definitely* champagne," she answered.

He raised his glass. "Here's to three months of good teamwork!" She felt her face grow warm as they touched glasses and sipped.

The next two hours passed quickly. They had more champagne, then red wine with the chateaubriand, and cognac after dessert.

"I think I should not have so much to drink," she said, feeling giddy.

His eyes regarded her. "You need to relax, Nicole. You seem to take life very seriously."

"I've had a serious life, for the most part."

His smile faded. "I hope I didn't offend you."

She shook her head. "No. But do you always speak your mind? You seem to be such a definite person, someone who doesn't worry about what others think. I envy you that."

He laughed ruefully. "That's always been my problem! The Brothers at St. Ben's used to tell me I was arrogant."

"St. Ben's . . .?"

"St. Benedict's, the boarding school I attended in Ireland one year when I was young."

"Ireland? That's an unusual place to send a boy to school."

"Not if he's Irish it isn't," he laughed.

"You're Irish? I thought you were born in the States," she said in surprise.

"No. I was born in Dublin. My mother's an American, though, and I chose to be one."

"And your father?"

Drew leaned his head back against the seat. "Oh, *he* was Irish, all right. . . . Was he ever Irish!" He shook his head, giving a silent laugh. "It landed him in prison. The Brits thought he might cause trouble during the Second World War, so they locked him up. He had symptoms of MS then, but they didn't start treating him early enough, or maybe they just didn't diagnose it. My mother returned from the war—she was a Red Cross nurse—to find him in a wheelchair." He sipped his brandy.

"How terrible! How old were you then?" She was puzzled. Why would his mother have left her son at such an early age?

"I wasn't born yet. I came along nine months later." He grinned. "Got in just under the gun, you might say! After I was born, they moved to Geneva—for the medical care. My father lived for another eight years, in and out of hospitals." Drew paused. "I can't remember him too well. I mean, as a person. I remember how helpless he was, and the pain. . . ."

Nicole watched him as he spoke. She realized there was a surprising sensitivity under his handsome, masculine appearance.

"That's a sad story, Andrew."

He smiled at her. "It was so long ago. I don't want you to think I had an unhappy childhood, Nicole. It was great, except for the time my mother decided I should go to school in Ireland so I would feel more Irish. That was a mistake. It was so awful I only lasted for one term. I was twelve years old. Can you imagine sending a kid away from home at twelve?"

"No, I can't." Nicole was horrified. "When *I* went to school, my father came along."

"You're kidding!"

"Really. He just moved us to Paris. I think he wanted to get away from Lima, truthfully. He wasn't happy there in those years. My mother had died, and he never really forgot her. . . ." She stopped suddenly, remembering what she had heard about Drew losing his wife.

He turned his head. "No," he said, "you never do

forget." There was a look of such pain in his eyes that
she wanted to take him in her arms to comfort him.

"I'm so sorry. I spoke without thinking." She touched
his hand, then quickly withdrew hers.

"It's all right," he murmured. He stood up. "Well, I
think I'll try to get some sleep. See you in a while."

That's too bad, she thought. I was enjoying our conversation. But, I don't *want* to enjoy you, Andrew Tower!
Take care, Nicole. The last thing you need is to become
too fond of him.

Long plane trips always made him introspective. When
he was busy in the hospital or the lab, he did not have to
think about himself.

It was strange that he had talked about Sean with
Nicole. He almost never spoke about his real father, at
least not in that way. And St. Ben's! When was the last
time he had even *thought* about it? The anticipation of
beginning this new assignment together, the proximity of
the long plane trip, the relaxation of wine and food, had
caused him to let down his guard.

Drew closed his eyes and tried to sleep, but his mind
kept drifting to the imponderable that used to trouble
him when he was a boy. He had always sensed there was
a mystery about himself. During that terribly lonely year
when he had been at school in Ireland, he would often
dwell on it before falling asleep at night. It had to do
with Ireland and the Catholic Church, with his mother
and his dead father . . . and secret matters which he was
never meant to know.

There was a dreamlike memory, but he knew it had
not been a dream. He would try to recapture the dim
vision, but it always eluded him. The house in Geneva
. . . his father lying in a hospital bed in an alcove off the
parlor, paralyzed with multiple sclerosis . . . seven-year-
old Drew dozing on a couch, inadvertently overhearing a
conversation between his parents. . . .

"Does he look like his father?" Sean asked.

And Molly answered, "No, not really. Sometimes he
smiles in a certain way, or gestures . . . and I get a
feeling, like *déjà vu,* when I think there's a resemblance."

How had Drew known they were talking about him?

Sean said, "You've never told me much about him, Molly? What sort of man is he?"

"It's hard for me to speak of him, Sean. He's a good man . . . kind, idealistic. . . ."

"Handsome?" he teased.

She laughed then. "Yes, of course! Very handsome."

"He *would* be, to have a boy like that." She reached for Sean's hand and he said sadly, "You know, I've always loved you, Molly. Loved you so much."

"I know you have, dear. I *know* it. I'm sorry . . . the way it's all been."

"It's been *fine*. Molly. More than I ever hoped for. And we've had Drew. I love him, too. You know that, don't you?"

"Yes," she had whispered, laying her cheek along his.

What were they talking about? Was he adopted? Of course not! Everyone said he was the spitting image of his mother. He could look in a mirror and see it was true.

His father had died not long after that, and Drew had never asked his mother about the strange conversation to which he had been an unsuspected witness.

The first thing that happened when they landed at New Delhi's Palam Airport was the appearance of a barefoot, undernourished man clothed in a tattered khaki *dhoti*, who sprayed the interior of the plane's cabin with insecticide. Then an Indian health inspector walked the aisle, peering at the passengers. After that, they were allowed to disembark.

It was 2 A.M. As they walked across the tarmac from the 747, Drew noticed the terminal building was surrounded by figures lying asleep on the ground. The night was chilly, and he felt a pang of compassion at his first encounter with Third World poverty.

Robert Hillman was waiting for them in the customs area. He had shaved off the beard he had worn last time Drew had seen him. Blonde and tanned, with the same sea-blue eyes as Arthur, he was delighted to see Drew.

The two men embraced. "You're looking terrific, Rob! I think I like you better without the whiskers. Makes you look younger."

Robert grinned. "That was Jane's intention. I'm going to have my fortieth birthday in two months."

Drew introduced Nicole. "I've reserved a room for you at the foundation guest house, Nicole. I thought you would find that comfortable. Jane and I are expecting you at our house for dinner tonight, and any other time you care to join us."

Nicole thanked him. Although they were stepbrothers, she thought Robert had the same spontaneous warmth and self-confidence as Drew.

"Jane is waiting for us at home," he told Drew. "We don't have an *ayah*, so she didn't want to leave the kids alone."

"We have some cartons of supplies in unaccompanied baggage," said Drew. "Can we pick it up tonight?"

"Not a chance," Robert laughed. "Your first encounter with Indian red tape. You'll have to come back at least twice before you get it. If there're any problems, we have a trouble-shooter at the foundation just for that sort of thing."

Robert drove a white Ford Falcon along the dark airport road. Again, they noticed sleeping bodies on the ground, the more fortunate of them rolled in blankets.

"Are those the homeless?" Drew asked.

"No. Most of them are construction workers who come from the villages. They stay as long as they can find employment, then they return to their families for a time. The homeless you've read about—the ones who live on the pavements—are mainly in Calcutta. The government worries about appearances in the capital. Not that Delhi doesn't have its share of beggars."

"Yes, but . . . to sleep like that, on the ground, with no shelter!"

Robert nodded and turned to look at Drew. "That's just the beginning. You have a lot to learn."

They circled around Chanakyapuri, the Diplomatic Enclave, where the embassies of most of the affluent western nations were located in garden compounds, behind high walls and locked gates. The U.S. Embassy was prominent, a tall, white marble structure that Robert told them had been designed by Edward Stone, the noted American architect. The circle of illumination bathing its facade, with the Great Seal of the United States suspended above the portals at the top of the stairs, gave the building a spectral magnificence in the darkness.

Robert pointed to an enormous pink sandstone structure with many wings. "That's the Ashoka, the government hotel. You have to go inside, just to see it. When you realize all the construction work was done by manual labor, you'll understand why everything takes so long in India."

They left Nicole in the comfort of the guest house, set in a landscaped compound with the foundation's offices. As tired as they were, they could appreciate its beauty. "Some people think it's a little elaborate for a developing country," said Robert self-consciously.

Turning into a road that ran along the fringe of a golf course, Robert stopped in front of a walled garden. "Here we are."

From the shadows, a blanket-wrapped *chowkidar* appeared. Raising his hand to his forehead in greeting, he pulled open the gates and Robert drove along a tree-lined driveway to the side entrance of a bougainvillea-covered, Anglo-Indian bungalow. A spreading white stucco house with a tile roof, it was surrounded by verandahs.

Jane Hillman greeted them at the door, wearing a bathrobe. She was a statuesque, dark-haired woman with ample breasts and hips. When she smiled, her wide mouth softened and the strong bone structure of her face relaxed.

"How are you, Drew?" she asked, a note of concern in her voice.

"Better, thanks." He kissed her cheek.

"You must be exhausted after that trip. Come have something to eat, and then you can sleep off the jet lag."

Over a breakfast of blood oranges, bitter black tea laced with buffalo milk, and vegetable *samosas*, Drew told Robert and Jane all the family news.

They had not been in the States on home leave since the summer of '72, after the disastrous flood in Wilkes-Barre, when the Susquehanna River had overflowed. The Hillman house had been badly damaged when the flood waters had risen to a level just below its second story.

"The house is as good as new," Drew told them. "Which is more than I can say for the city. It will take a long time for that area to get over the flood."

"I can't understand why Molly and Dad are still living in that big house," said Robert.

"They want to stay. I guess it's hard to change when you get older."

Drew had a great affection for Robert. Rob's twin brother Jeff, who lacked a certain generosity of nature, had not especially welcomed Drew into the family when their father married Molly Tower—but Robert had made him feel like he was one of them from the first time they'd met.

Drew pushed his chair away from the table. He was feeling the effects of his long trip, for he had not completely adjusted to Geneva time in the past few days. There was a ten and a half hour time difference between Philadelphia and New Delhi.

Jane showed him to his room, where the bed had been turned down. After showering in the gray marble bathroom, he slid beneath the sheets, stretching his long body.

He felt tired, but happy to be here—happier than he had been at any time since he had lost Julie. As his eyes closed, the first light of the rising sun streaked the sky over the Indian capital.

Chapter 15

Nicole awakened at five o'clock on Monday morning, her third day in India. A pale pink dawn filtered through the sheer curtains. She had forgotten to draw the draperies last night after returning from dinner at Robert and Jane Hillman's house.

It had been a pleasant evening. They were a warmly affectionate family with three children. It struck a poignant chord within her to see Robert's blonde head bent close to that of his older daughter as they examined a map together. It reminded her of Daniel and their closeness, and she realized how much she still missed him.

She liked the way the younger two clung to Andrew, sitting on his lap while he read to them, hanging onto his neck for a piggy-back ride. He had a gentle, sweet way with them that was touching. You could see that he would make a wonderful father.

This was silly, to lie here musing about the paternal qualities of Andrew Tower and his brother! She got out of bed and went to the window.

From her room she had a view of Lodi Gardens, with the domed tombs of the pre-Moghul kings rising among the treetops. She was surprised to see a number of people walking at this early hour. Well-dressed couples with children strolled into the park, laborers with baskets on their heads hurried along the roadway. Nicole opened the window. In the distance she could hear the sounds of morning traffic. India's day had already begun. Hurriedly, she showered and dressed in a tan poplin skirt and short-sleeved white shirt.

Downstairs in the parlor, a boy was sweeping the carpet with a short-handled broom, squatting on his haunches as he moved across the floor. He touched his hand to his forehead, rising to greet her. Immediately, another servant dressed in white appeared, one of the bearers from the dining room.

"Good morning, madam. Breakfast?"

"Good morning. I'm going to take a walk first. In the garden."

"Very well, madam. Take care that you do not wander too far from the entrance. It is better to stay near other people."

Yes, thought Nicole. I well know what a temptation it is to poor people when a prosperous-looking foreigner walks alone.

Forever after she would be able to close her eyes and conjure up the heady perfume of early morning India. Dew on sweet jasmine and crushed grasses, pungent marigold and bougainvillea, sandalwood, cardamon, and coriander, dust and dung and *chik* fires.

In the garden she found two little Sikh boys squatting near the steps of a tomb, one with his hair gathered in a topknot covered by a white cloth, the other with braids tied up in red ribbons. They smiled when they saw her, displaying tiny, even teeth of blinding whiteness. Taking some sticks from a bundle, they performed sleight-of-hand tricks of such dexterity that, try as she might, she was unable to detect the secret.

She sat on the grass-covered steps of the ancient tomb, enjoying them. A few curious spectators gathered, more interested in Nicole than in the small magicians. She smiled at them, and they nodded in shy friendliness.

Slowly, from different directions, others appeared, but these were children—tattered and dirty and unsmiling. Like shadows, they sidled up behind trees and bushes to peer at her. A young girl of six or seven, wrapped in a length of filthy cloth, balancing a rheumy-eyed infant on her hip, drew close, bolder than the rest. Nicole became aware of a low, whining murmur, pleading eyes, an outstretched palm.

The ring of children was closing in, while the few men and women who were taking an early morning stroll had begun to move off. Nicole rose, and the little Sikh boys increased the tempo of their act.

"Just see! Just see!" cried one.

"More tricks, memsahib," called the other.

They were adorable entrepreneurs and they had put on a good show. They deserved something for their pains. But, despite their bare feet, they were neatly dressed in clean clothing. Their teeth were strong and healthy. And someone had attended to their hair.

The circle of beggar children watched, their eyes wide and sickly. She read hunger and fear in their faces, but no hostility. A resigned submission to their fate, with little hope that the coming day would bring anything to alter it.

She knew that the moment she reached into her bag there would be a scramble. This was not the *barriada* of Lima, where in spite of dire poverty there was hope and spirit. This was an extreme of poverty she had never before encountered, not in Peru, nor even on trips to Mexico.

She began to walk toward the entrance. With a motion of her head, she indicated that the two performers of magic should follow. As she had expected, the entire troop of children moved along with them. Like a pied piper, Nicole made her way, a procession of children in her wake.

"Memsahib, memsahib. . . . *Baksheesh*. . . ." they pleaded, pointing to sores on their arms and legs, to sightless eyes, the stump of a lost arm. The volume and intensity of their pleas increased as they neared the park's gateway, as the chance of reward faded. Confident in having been chosen, the two Sikh children skipped along beside Nicole, trying to make conversation with the few English words at their command.

At the entrance she turned, taking stock of the children. There were thirteen of them, including two infants. The Government of India asked foreigners not to give *baksheesh* . . . it encouraged beggars and their exploiters.

Pointing her finger, she directed the smallest to stand in front of her. The others rushed forward. She shook her head. First the smallest, then the next smallest . . . they immediately grasped the idea and began to sort themselves out by size. Soon there was a line of little beggars. Some of them had lost their woebegone looks and were smiling, their eyes sparkling in their dirty faces under the filthy matted hair.

One by one, she gave them each a rupee note. They

leapt for joy, gleefully dancing away, showing the rupees to the others, then secreting them somewhere within their rags. The magicians were looking mystified and dubious.

When all the beggars had left, she gave each of the Sikh boys two rupees, smiled, and walked quickly away in the direction of the guest house.

Seventeen rupees was a little more than two American dollars.

In the dining room, with its immaculate white-linened tables, the bearer served breakfast. A large glass of fresh orange juice, a wedge of papaya with lemon, scrambled eggs and two slices of crisp bacon, freshly brewed coffee, and a basket of toast and rolls with three kinds of jam and imported Danish butter.

As Robert had predicted, they had some trouble at customs getting them to release the lab supplies Drew had brought along. Finally, in desperation after a wasted morning, they asked the man in charge of shipments for the Ford Foundation office to go out to the airport with them.

"What are these?" asked a turbaned Sikh customs officer, fingering some glass tubules.

Exasperated, Drew said, "Those are Christmas tree ornaments!"

To their amazement, the man stamped all of the packages and waved them on with a haughty stare.

When they had finished laughing, Nicole asked, "Shouldn't we check in with the WHO Regional Office today?"

"That's not a bad idea. Just to let them know we've arrived."

They were scheduled to go on project site visits for the first week—Nicole to tour primary health centers in rural districts and Drew to virology labs, where he would observe the work and give lectures. After that, they would proceed to whichever state smallpox eradication program they were assigned.

No one at the regional office of the WHO had heard of them.

"I'm sorry, sir, I am not finding IHTF on the list of approved WHO programs," said an officious clerk at the third desk.

"Of course not," answered Drew. "It isn't a WHO program. It's an independent."

"We are not handling NGOs here. Very sorry, sir." Nicole knew that NGO stood for non-governmental organization.

"Look," said Drew, opening his attaché case. "I have a letter here stating that we are expected to join the Smallpox Eradication Program."

The man scanned the letter. "Then you must be going to the NSEP."

Drew rolled his eyes at Nicole. She was afraid he was losing his cool.

"What is the NSEP and *where* is it and *whom* should we see there?" she asked rapidly.

This clerk reminded her of the government employees in Peru. The only way to get around them was to intimidate them.

He stared at her with some hostility for a moment, then wrote something on a slip of paper and handed it to Drew.

"National Smallpox Eradication Program," he read. There was an address and a woman's name.

At the NSEP office, they were told the woman they wanted to see was out of station.

"When will she return?" they asked.

"Next month."

"Well, is there someone else who can help us?"

The secretary shook his head. "It would be best for you to go to the WHO," he said.

Drew slapped the desk in frustration. "We've just come from there! They sent us here."

"I'm sorry, sir. There is nothing I am doing."

"That's for sure!" He turned to Nicole. "What the hell? How are we going to find out where we should go?"

Drew would have to learn to curb his impatience if he was going to make it in India. "Maybe Robert can help," she suggested. "He knows how to get things done here."

On the way over to the Ford Foundation, Nicole patted Drew's arm sympathetically. "I think perhaps you need a glass of champagne. Relax, Andrew. This is not the efficient United States."

In the comfort of Robert's carpeted, attractively furnished office, they drank tea while his secretary applied herself to the task of finding a contact for them.

"That's the problem of coming here without a backup organization," Robert told them.

"The WHO is supposed to be our backup." said Drew. "Something funny's going on. We were all squared away in Geneva."

They had spent an entire day at the Geneva headquarters of WHO, getting briefed on the smallpox campaign, making sure they had all the proper papers and visas and knew how to proceed once they reached India.

Robert's secretary stuck her head in the door. "Excuse me, Dr. Tower. They want to know whether you worked through Dr. Schmidt's office in Geneva."

Nicole and Drew looked at each other in astonishment. When they had been in Geneva, each member of the Task Force had received a memo from a Dr. Alton Schmidt, director of something called the Special Unit for Communicable Diseases.

"Hmm . . . it orders any personnel assigned to field programs in communicable diseases to be processed through their office," Drew had said to Nicole after reading the memo. "I never even heard of them."

Henry Campion had taken a copy of the memo to the office of the deputy director, Lloyd Rankin.

"Ignore it," Rankin told him, and Henry had repeated that to the Task Force later, adding, "This is just the kind of red tape we're meant to avoid."

They explained what happened to Robert.

"Tell them that it was cleared through the office of the Director General," Robert instructed his secretary.

A minute later, she returned. "It will have to wait for the Deputy Regional Director's approval. He's away and will return next week."

"Next week!" Drew was outraged.

"Calm down, Drew." said Robert. "Look, you have work to do. And I would really recommend that you take the orientation course set up for foreigners coming to work in India. It will give you a good overview of Indian culture and customs." He winked at Nicole. "Too many people come out here without understanding enough about the country and its people. By the end of that, you'll be all set." As an afterthought, he added, "It's a good thing you didn't wait until next week to go over to the regional office!"

Drew looked at Robert, the scowl on his face slowly becoming a sheepish grin. "That was Nicole's idea."

Robert stood up. "Come on, let's go home for lunch. Please join us, Nicole. You've both had a bad morning. I'd like to be able to say this isn't typical, but I wouldn't be telling you the truth."

Prem Mehta returned to Delhi the following day. He had visited some labs in Europe on his way home from Geneva. Prem was going to Dacca to the Cholera Lab, where he would assist the Oral Rehydration Program for Diarrheal Diseases as part of his IHTF work, but fortunately he was spending a few days at home in Delhi before leaving again.

He took Nicole and Drew on a tour of the All-India Institute of Medical Sciences, ending in his own department. They were impressed with the way Prem had set up his lab, not letting the unavailability of modern technology deter him. He had ordered equipment made to his own specifications from local craftsmen. There was a glassblower to make flasks and pipettes, a tinsmith to construct cages for laboratory animals, and a carpenter to build lab benches.

Both Nicole and Drew agreed to give lectures to the medical students. They were so eager to learn, these bright-faced, friendly young men and women, and almost too respectful of the visitors.

Prem's bride had gone to the south to visit her family, since Prem would be away for a month. On Sunday morning, he invited Nicole and Drew to go riding with him at the Delhi Polo Club. Afterward, he took them home to his family's big, high-ceilinged bungalow in what used to be the Civil Lines of Old Delhi in the days of the British Raj.

Prem's mother plied Nicole and Drew with food, standing behind them while they ate the delicious vegetarian meal. The Mehtas did not eat meat, although Drew knew that Prem relished roast beef and steaks and missed them since he had returned from the States.

On Monday, Nicole left for the villages in the company of a woman from the Central Health Ministry, an arrangement Robert had made before his departure on one of his frequent tours of foundation programs. The next few days passed quickly.

After dinner on Wednesday evening, Drew sat with
Jane on brightly upholstered willow lounge furniture in
the screened patio. The turbaned bearer brought a brass
tray with coffee service and demitasse. Drew admired the
graciousness of the Hillmans' lifestyle as foreign service
people. The house was inviting, with large, airy, high-
ceilinged rooms. Jane had furnished it comfortably with
locally made teak furniture, copies of Scandinavian de-
sign. She and Rob had collected a number of hand-made
carpets from Kashmir, and ornamental copper and brass
lamps and bowls that lent a distinctive Indian flavor to
the rooms. Wood carvings and framed batiks lined the
walls of the many rooms and hallways.

Jane laughed it off when Drew complimented her on
her taste. "You won't think it very original after you've
been to a few more foreign houses," she told him. "We
all do the same thing. Our Indian friends are always
amused to see a water jug holding flowers. But everything is hand made and the artisans take such pride in
decorating even the most ordinary object."

"I can see why you enjoy living here, Jane. It's a
wonderful country. I really like the people."

"Yes, Drew. So do I. Rob adores his work . . . in fact,
he's in love with India. I sometimes think we shall never
leave."

Drew studied Jane's face. It was a plain face in repose,
but when she smiled, she was almost beautiful. She had
deepset brown eyes above a high arched nose, and that
generous, friendly mouth. Despite her self-possession,
Drew had noticed how Jane's glance kept returning to
her husband when they were with other people, as if
seeking reassurance there. They complemented each other
well. Drew thought it was sensible of Robert, who was
certainly attractive to women, to have chosen a wife like
Jane.

"Arthur has a friend here in Delhi whom he wanted
me to see—an Indian Army doctor he knew during the
war when he was stationed in Assam," Drew said. "You
and Rob must know him. Colonel Ranjit Kar?"

Jane seemed to shrink. She reached for her coffee cup.
"Yes, we know Colonel Kar. He has retired from the
Health Ministry. We don't see much of him these days
. . . he's aging."

"I'd like to call him if you can tell me where to reach him. I couldn't find him listed in the telephone directory."

"Yes, of course. I have it in my book."

Jane was tense now. She had lost her easy, relaxed manner. "What do you do with your time when Robert travels?" Drew asked, wondering what had disturbed her tranquility.

"Go crazy, sometimes! I'm thinking of teaching again. You know, I was a teacher at the International School in Kathmandu when Rob and I became engaged. Now that the baby's in kindergarten, I would like a job." She looked out at the fading light. "It does get lonely when he's away."

They finished their coffee and Jane excused herself to put the children to bed. Drew went to his room to work on his lecture for the following day. At nine o'clock there was a knock on his door. It was Jane.

"Here's Colonel Kar's address and telephone number," she said. "He lives in a colony for retired army officers. You know," she added, "he was a prince before India was independent. His father was a rajah, but the government took away most of their wealth following Independence."

After she left, Drew could not get back to work. Something definitely was troubling Jane, something to do with Colonel Kar.

Jane lay in the double bed trying to fall asleep. The atonal melody of wedding music came through the darkness. This was an auspicious season for Indian marriages, and a few of the large bungalows nearby were rented out for weddings.

She missed Robert. Accustomed to reaching out for him at night, she hated the emptiness in the bed beside her when he was gone. Having Drew here was nice, but it depressed her to think how lonely his life must be without Julie.

Was that why she was melancholy? *No, you know it isn't.* It was Drew's mentioning Colonel Kar that had altered her mood. It had taken her back to that evening, how many years ago? She had been pregnant with their second child and she thought she was the happiest woman alive, married to Robert, whom she had wanted from the

day she met him—twelve years ago at that teachers'
conference in Connecticut.

When he called her in New York and asked her to
have dinner with him, she was delirious with joy. But he
seemed more interested in her father's connections with
the Peace Corps than he was in making out with her. She
would have gone to bed with him the first night in her
apartment if he had asked, but after talking until two in
the morning, he kissed her cheek and said goodbye.

Not long after that, she had left for her new teaching
job in Kathmandu, thinking she would never see him
again. He wrote once, telling her he was going to India
with the Peace Corps. A year later he appeared in Nepal
to do some trekking and climbing with Peace Corps friends.
When she saw him, after all that time, she knew she was
in love with him.

Another six months passed. Soon her contract would
be up for renewal, but Jane had decided to return to the
States. She had given up any hope of hearing from Rob-
ert Hillman again. Then suddenly he called her from
Delhi and asked whether he could come to Kathmandu.
She made a reservation for him at the Palace Hotel.

Robert spent only one night in that hotel room. She
smiled to herself when she remembered how it had happened, the way he looked at her when he took her back
to her apartment the second evening after dinner . . .
how they had reached for each other at the same moment.

When they kissed, it was a soft, tentative kiss, Robert
putting his arms around her awkwardly, like a gangly
school boy on his first date. His lips adjusted themselves
to hers and their centers found each other. Jane had been
engulfed with him, her limbs turning warm and mallea-
ble. She became totally lost in the wonder of being loved
by Robert.

"What are you thinking?" he had asked.

"That it was exactly the way I knew it would be . . .
slow and tender, then great and powerful."

"I wasn't very thoughtful, Jane. I'm sorry. It happened
so unexpectedly . . . I mean, suddenly here we were, and
I didn't even think about it being your first time."

She laughed. "Maybe that's why it was so good!"

"Do I have to go back to my hotel, or may I stay
here?"

"Stay. I want you to." They made love late into the night, then slept. The next morning he had asked her to marry him.

Had she known about Leila Kar then? She couldn't remember, but if so, she probably hadn't attached any significance to their friendship. Not that Robert had purposely kept it from her. It was one of those personal things that he never discussed. Robert was a private man.

It was during the fourth year of their marriage, and they had just returned from the States to take up residence in India, when they had attended a party. . . .

In the garden of the Canadian High Commission, twinkling Diwali lights created a fairy world in the darkness of night. The strong-colored patchwork *shamianah*, muted in the candleglow, enclosed them under a canopy of embroidered mirrorwork. As they moved through the crowded tent, Jane was conscious of Robert's prideful look. He had told her she was becoming a poised and elegant woman. She had tried hard to do so. He was such a personable man, and she'd always felt a little awkward with attractive men.

The guests were a mixture of diplomats, people from the international development community, and high-placed Indians from government and industry.

Jane became separated from Robert. She was concentrating on the rapid delivery of a gentleman from Bombay when she noticed an exquisite Indian woman standing a few feet away, alone, her attention riveted on someone and an expression of adulation on her face. Jane followed the woman's gaze . . . and the shock of it was stunning!

As she watched, Robert turned and became aware of the woman staring at him. Jane saw her husband move toward this exotic beauty, his hands reach out to take hers, his eyes and the line of his jaw softening in a tenderness that, until that moment, she thought reserved for her.

He's in love with her, thought Jane. *And she loves him.* The impact of it made her feel faint. In a daze, she saw him bend to kiss the petal-fresh cheek, saw the kohl-outlined eyes briefly close, then widen with emotion as they sparkled at him. He smiled down at her, that joyful, shimmering smile that made Jane's heart turn over each time she saw it. And Jane thought she would die of her heartbroken knowledge.

The chattering Bombay official decided he was wasting the opportunity to make important contacts and broke away from this tall, inattentive American wife.

Holding onto one small delicate hand, Robert drew the graceful, silk-draped woman toward Jane. "You must meet my wife, Leila. Jane, this is Leila Roy—Colonel Kar's daughter. Leila was my guide when I first came to India. Thanks to her, it was love at first sight."

Yes, I can see that!

"I'm overjoyed to meet you, Jane! How wonderful to find you and Robert here. We've only just returned from London, and I had no *idea* we would see you. Come, you must meet Rahman, my husband. He'll be delighted. . . ."

The lilting music of Leila's voice, the magnetism of her beauty and her warmth had reached the frozen place within Jane's chest. It was impossible to resist this shining woman, who linked arms with her and brought her through the maze of conversational groups that parted before her as if she were of royal blood—which, in fact, she was.

"Rahman, look who I've found!" Leila addressed a tall, distinguished Indian man.

Jane cast a glance of confusion at Robert, who stood slack-armed and discomfited. He saw the understanding in her eyes and realized she knew, and that it was something that would always be there between them.

When they were at home later that night, Robert had made love with a desperation that could have meant he was mad with desire for her. But by then Jane knew better. She wondered whether in the darkness he pretended that she was an Indian princess with long satiny hair and luminous eyes, and centuries of pleasuring a man bred into her blood.

Chapter 16

The Ford Eagle sped eastward across the Indian subcontinent. So low were they flying that Nicole could distinctly see details of villages and fields and the figures of women walking along roads with bundles on their heads.

They were on their way to report to the Smallpox Eradication Program, Division of Communicable Diseases, Health Ministry of the State of Bihar, where they would receive further orders. Fortunately for them, the foundation's plane had to go to Calcutta to pick up some program officers, and they had hitched a ride to Patna, the state capital of Bihar.

"The plane is a great convenience," Robert had mentioned, always a little defensive about the foundation being accused of throwing money around. "Our people can go all over the country on the Eagle, even places where there isn't regular air service."

"Like Patna?" joked Drew.

"No. You can fly to Patna on the commercial airline . . . twice a week."

"The Ford Foundation seems to be a little island of super efficiency here in Delhi."

Robert nodded. "Yeah. That was especially true back in the sixties, when I first came to India. They had an amazing representative then who had an interesting philosophy. He thought it was a waste of time and money to get a bunch of consultants out here and expect them to worry about things like housing or transportation. Of course, some people called it neo-colonialism, and it bred a certain elitism, the usual thing when foreigners come to India and play at being sahibs and memsahibs. But, the foundation really got things done in those days. And for a long time, it had the same status as many governments,

171

with import privileges and such. All that's changed, of
course, since Vietnam—and Nixon, whom Mrs. Gandhi
dislikes. American experts are not as, uh, welcome, I
guess you'd say, as they used to be."

Deposited at the Patna airport with their gear, Nicole
and Drew said goodbye to the Ford Eagle and her pilot,
then went to the terminal building to find transportation
to town. There was no bus at this hour, they were told,
but they were in luck. A car with a driver had just
delivered some passengers to a private plane, and they
could hire him.

At the Health Ministry, they found the WHO regional
coordinator, who told them they were to proceed to
Darbhanga, which lay to the north, toward Nepal. He
examined their passports. "I see you have visas for Bangladesh. I would strongly advise you to also get them for
Nepal. You never know if you're going to have to cross
the border. Once you leave Patna, it would be impossible
to obtain visas."

A secretary told them they could get a ride to Darbhanga
that afternoon on a truck leaving at four o'clock with
supplies for the field teams. Nicole glanced at her wrist-
watch. "If we hurry, Andrew, we can be back in time.
It's not yet 2:30."

"Let's go."

Nepal House proved to be on the outskirts of Patna,
on the other side of the old walled city, a good half
hour's drive. When they neared their destination, the
driver had to stop for directions.

"Can this possibly be correct?" asked Nicole. "It seems
a strange area for a consulate."

They had crossed a muddy stream, smelling of sewage,
and were bumping along a narrow dirt road with hovels on
either side. A sharp turn left took them into an even narrower lane, a neighborhood bazaar. The shops were open-
fronted raised platforms, crammed together, the merchan-
dise piled in haphazard fashion or hanging from hooks
on posts.

Men chewed red beetel and spat on the ground where
naked children played in the roadway, splashing in the
shallow drainage ditch and picking up refuse to eat. Sari-
wrapped housewives haggled with merchants over a hand-

ful of dried-out vegetables or chunks of fly-covered meat whose nature was hard to determine.

Nicole and Drew grew silent. Even Old Delhi was not as dirty and congested as this. They could have been in a space capsule, transported back in time to the fourteenth century. Except, they were in an automobile of Indian manufacture, with antimacassars on the upholstery and Madras cotton curtains on the windows, and it was 1974.

The car was hurtling through the narrow streets at an alarming rate. Suddenly it came to a strident halt, blocked by an abandoned bullock cart. Their driver sounded the horn repeatedly, shouting out the window. Some laborers who had been lounging on the side of the road got up and moved toward the cart at their own pace, while others ran off in the direction of a large and neglected building of ancient yellow sandstone, discolored by centuries of monsoons. It stood alone in a walled garden, with boarded windows and crumbling columns.

Nicole turned to Drew. He had slid down in the seat with his head back and a look of despair on his face. She began to laugh.

"We'd best start thinking of this as an interesting experience, Andrew. I have a feeling it's not going to improve."

The cart was finally pulled out of the way—a purposeful barricade, they later decided—to give the sleepy-eyed individual who emerged from the dilapidated house a chance to prepare himself for visitors. The gate was dragged open on its rusty hinges, and the car crawled into an overgrown courtyard.

Cracked inlaid marble formed the porticoed verandah, where the barefoot man awaited them in his undershirt and loose trousers, the Indian pajama. A number of bright, curious eyes belonging to women and children peeked from behind the partially opened doors and shutters of the house, which must once have been the palace of a minor local prince.

"We have come to see the Consul of Nepal," announced Drew, rather grandly.

"Yes," the man answered in English.

"Is he here?"

The man tilted his head sideways in the affirmative. "Yes, you are standing before him."

Mon dieu! No one would believe this. Nicole could not look at Drew and keep a straight face.

"We would like visas, sir, if you please. Immediately, if possible."

The man seated himself at a wooden table while two peons came running with chairs for Nicole and Drew. Folding his hands on the table, the consul sat back and smiled at them, prepared for a long interview. "What is the purpose of your visit?" he asked.

"We are medical doctors assigned to the Smallpox Eradication Program by the World Health Organization." Drew handed him their official assignment papers.

Oh no, thought Nicole. *That was a mistake.* He should have said we were tourists. This will make it more complicated.

The consul studied the documents, reading every word, examining the letterheads and signatures. The letters were identical, except for the names of the appointees, yet he gave them equal attention.

"Which is Nicolee Légendee, M.D.?" he asked.

"I am," Nicole answered.

"May I see your passport?"

While she opened her shoulder bag to find her passport, Drew took his from his case and handed it to the man, who ignored it.

The passport received even more thorough attention than the letters. He read every page, examining each entry stamp, turning it this way and that to read those that were upside down or sideways, squinting, holding it up to the light.

"France!" he said, pointing to her French visa.

Nicole smiled. "Yes, I went to France."

"And here again!" he exclaimed, a few pages later.

"That's right. I went *twice*—to France," she encouraged him. She was beginning to enjoy this.

Drew, on the other hand, was not enjoying it. She could see how impatient he was becoming. *Americans!* They could never learn to slow down.

"We're going to miss the truck," he told her in an agitated whisper.

She shrugged. "Well, we shall just have to go on the next one."

By the time the visa forms had been filled in, signed

and countersigned, they had lost any hope of catching the transport. At last, the official took out an ink pad and two rubber stamps and carefully, painstakingly affixed them to the documents and the passports. It was four-fifteen.

Back in the automobile, they examined their passports. They found they were in possession of visas number 1 and 2 issued at Patna.

"Well," said Nicole. "We've made his career."

"Not an auspicious beginning," commented Drew.

It was six o'clock by the time they reached the Health Ministry. Rush hour in Patna made Lima seem orderly by comparison. Of course, the truck had departed without them. When was the next one going? Drew inquired.

"Perhaps in one week or two."

Nicole steadied Drew with one hand while she asked, "Is there another way to get there?"

"Yes, madam, tomorrow morning, by train. It will save time, though, to go part way by car."

At the Shalimar Hotel they were shown the only vacancy available, a suite of two cramped rooms—a sitting room and a bedroom, both painted a bright orangey pink. The bedroom had two single cots placed side by side. There was a private bathroom, the manager pointed out. It had a sink, a spigot with a drain for bathing, and an Indian style toilet, consisting of a hole in the floor with indentations on either side for the feet. A cup and hand towel hung on a hook next to a large jug of water.

"You don't have two separate rooms?" asked Drew.

The manager spread his hands. "Alas! No, sir."

He sighed, "All right, we'll take it."

"And we're not even in the villages yet," he remarked when the manager left.

Nicole was looking around curiously, seemingly unperturbed by their accommodations.

"I'll sleep in the parlor," said Drew. "I can move one of the beds in here."

She regarded him steadily. "I think, Andrew, if we are going to work together for the next three months as colleagues and as equals, we must begin to put aside such formalities. Otherwise, it will become impossibly complicated." She looked him up and down, then said lightly, "I believe I can control myself, if you can."

He stared at her for a long moment, expressionless. Then he slowly smiled. "You're all right, Légende," he said, slapping her on the back. He threw down his duffle bag. "Do you suppose we can find some decent food in this town?"

"Remember—only cooked vegetables, check the bottled water before drinking, and no ice," Drew reminded her.

They had lamb kabob, a delicious vegetable curry, and *pilau* rice. The *chapatis* were piping hot. They washed it all down with Golden Eagle beer, served in liter bottles.

"When Henry promised us a great adventure," Nicole remarked, "I didn't realize what he had in mind."

"No," Drew shook his head emphatically, "even Henry's imagination couldn't have come up with today."

Nicole lay in the dark on the hard narrow bed, listening to the grind of the air conditioner. For all the good it did, they might have turned it off and opened a window. At least it blocked out the noises below. Although Patna did not have large numbers of motor vehicles, the Indian habit of constantly sounding the horn while driving created a nerve-racking din.

She was becoming accustomed to the street melodies of India—the cries of merchants and hawkers in the crooked alleys of the bazaars, the cacophony of main thoroughfares, where hurtling lorries driven by daredevil turbaned Sikhs passed slower-moving bullock carts and tongas with complete disregard for life.

The teeming humanity of an old Indian city like Patna had more of an impact on Drew than it did on her. After all, she was acquainted with poverty in Peru, which was also a developing nation. For Drew, an American who had never before visited a Third World country, this must be an assault on his senses. She would have to keep reminding herself of that if he continued to behave with superior impatience. His intolerance for the inefficiencies and delays they'd encountered thus far were not his most endearing quality.

She turned to look at him in the bluish neon light cast by the hotel sign outside the window. He was lying on his side, turned away from her, close enough for her to reach out and touch his bare back.

She had a sudden thought. *If Manuel Caldeiro-León*

could see me now! She had to press the pillow against her mouth to keep from laughing aloud.

This was the most uncomfortable bed she had ever slept in. The hotel was simply dreadful—she had never seen such dirty, insect-infested rooms. Yet, she felt euphoric, with a sense of anticipation such as she hadn't known for years. *Why am I so happy?* She turned over, closed her eyes, and immediately fell fast asleep.

When the car began to overheat an hour out of Patna, Drew suggested they stop at a roadside bazaar where they noticed a shop displaying automotive parts, but their driver said it was not necessary. After the fan belt broke on an uninhabited stretch of country road, they hailed a passing bullock cart loaded with grain.

Leaving the angry driver to deal with his disabled automobile, they piled their bedrolls and duffle bags on top of the two-wheeled wagon, then climbed up to sit beside the farmer, a leathery-faced, turbaned man who smiled at them through rotting teeth. Nicole tried the few words of Hindi she had learned and discovered he was forty years old and had eight living children, but unfortunately only three were sons.

At the railroad crossing, they waited for two hours for the train to Darbhanga. They were the objects of curiosity for the itinerant families who sat patiently, enjoying the sociability of the platform, in no hurry to board the third class boxcars where no one would bother to collect tickets. They offered to share food with Nicole and Drew, plying them with the sort of questions asked only by the most tactless relatives in more modern societies: How old were they? What was Drew's work? How much money did he make? How many children did they have?

They naturally assumed that Nicole was Drew's wife, for no self-respecting woman would be traveling with a man in this fashion unless they were married. Glee was their response when they understood that both were doctors and would travel to villages with Indian health officers working on the smallpox campaign. In that case, why did they not get married to each other?

At last a steam engine pulling a dozen cars halted at the siding. There was a chorus of shouts from food vendors, a scramble of passengers and coolies. Drew grabbed

Nicole's hand, helping her up and directing a coolie to stow the luggage in their second class carriage. They sat on hard benches in the slow-moving train, eating oranges and drinking hot tea poured into their enamel cups by the tea wallah. Three hours later, after a long, inexplicable standstill between stops, they pulled into Darbhanga station.

For the last five miles, they boarded a listing bus that spewed dark, evil-smelling fumes and was loaded with chickens, goats, and fat Muslim women wearing black *bourkhas* that covered them from head to toe.

Three Indian public health officers from the State Health Ministry shook hands with them when they arrived at the Darbhanga District Headquarters. A woman health worker made a *namaste*, the graceful Hindu sign of greeting and was introduced as Parvati Narain. There were two WHO medical officers. One was a Russian and the other a wiry, energetic American with rusty brown hair named Dick Gentry.

"We'd about given you up," said Dr. Gentry.

"We would have been here a week ago if your office in Delhi had cooperated!" Drew was in no mood to humor anyone after their trip.

"Cooperated? What happened?"

"It seems that a certain Dr. Schmidt in Geneva hadn't cleared us."

Gentry shook his head angrily. "Goddammit! Schmidt again. Why the hell did anyone ever agree to let his office process assignments?"

"We could easily have gone there when we were in Geneva, but we were told it wasn't necessary," said Nicole. "If only we'd known."

"I think he prefers it this way. Last time it was field kits that were rushed over because we were running short. They got sidetracked to a godown in Delhi. I don't believe these things are accidental."

"But why?" asked Nicole.

"UN politics, and I don't mean among nations. You wouldn't believe the pettiness and power struggles that go on. Schmidt is director of a special program that has something to do with communicable diseases. I'm not sure anyone remembers why it was created in the first place. It just perpetuates year after year."

"Why doesn't someone bring it to an end?" asked Drew.

"That's not easy in the UN system. It's almost impossible to fire someone without bringing charges of incompetence or misconduct. There has to be a hearing—it gets to be a real hassle. Sometimes it's just easier to work around him or to give him a job where he can't do much harm."

"That's disgraceful!" said Nicole.

"Yes, it is. Well, Schmidt hasn't heard the last of this."

He started for the door, then paused. "When did you have your last vaccinations?"

"Last week in Geneva, at the WHO," they both said.

"Let's have a look."

Nicole raised her sleeve to show him the scab that had formed on her upper arm. "A take. When was the previous one?"

"Four years ago, but no take," she replied.

"That may have meant the vaccine was no good. We're getting virtually a hundred percent results now with the freeze-dried vaccine and the bifurcated needles. Let's get going. Has either of you ever seen a case of smallpox?"

"Only in the training film in Geneva," replied Drew.

"Then we'll visit an isolation hospital and let you get acquainted with the enemy."

"This is the severe Asian form of the disease, *variola major*. The African variety isn't nearly as ugly," Dick Gentry commented when they were walking through the crowded isolation ward. "It's been called the most hideous disease on earth—with good reason."

Lines of patients were lying on the floor on pallets. "It's preferable to isolate patients in their own homes, but these cases were brought to the health center from outlying areas. Hospitalization is always risky—it puts workers and other patients in jeopardy."

The children were the worst. Confused, frightened, in pain, most cried pathetically, while others were too ill to do more than silently endure in the arms of their mothers. Covered from head to foot with large pustules, many had lesions in their eyes that would leave them blind, or complications that would kill them. And those who survived would be badly scarred for life. The parents of the girls were especially horrified because the disease would make their daughters less marriageable, a matter of consideration from the moment a child was born in India.

Nicole's attention was caught by one mother who sat staring into space, despair written on her features, as she cradled a two-year-old child with a case so severe that its eyes were swollen shut. The pustules crowded one another, leaving no unmarked skin on the face. Dr. Gentry imperceptibly shook his head when Nicole raised her eyes in question. The child would die, and there was nothing they could do other than try to make it more comfortable.

Emerging from the barracks-like building badly shaken, Nicole did not trust herself to speak. She walked off alone to the side of the hospital, where some workers were laying the foundation for a new structure. Pretending to be absorbed in watching them, she fought back tears. She heard footsteps behind her and hurriedly wiped her eyes.

"That's got to be the worst thing I have ever seen." It was Drew. He placed an arm around her shoulders. "Don't be embarrassed, Nicole. It got to me, too."

She gave him a grateful look. "It's the others, Andrew. They've just met me, and I don't want them to think I can't take it. I'll be all right."

He smiled understandingly. "I know you will. You've done a lot better than I have so far on this trip."

His words cheered her. She was beginning to feel close to him, as if the two of them had already become a team.

"We are in desperate need of trained epidemiologists," Dr. Gentry told them that evening as they ate dinner in the circuit house.

"Now that we've organized our surveillance strategy and are conducting thorough searches, were finding ten, maybe twenty times the number of active cases of smallpox than were formerly reported, and many different lines of infection. The disease spreads slowly, but it moves with travelers. And this is a country with a constantly migrating population. We are in the midst of an epidemic in Bihar State, and this is just the beginning of the worst season for the disease."

At first, Nicole had been put off by Dick Gentry's

abrupt manner, but as they sat around the table listening to him talk about some of the problems they could expect to encounter in their field work, she found him more likeable. It was obvious that he was a dedicated professional, and she suspected his blunt approach was meant to hide a deeper vulnerability. His round, earnest expression softened when she asked him where his home was. After a brief hesitation, he said, "That's a good question. I brought my family out to India last year, but it didn't work. My wife has just taken the children back to the States."

As if regretting the momentary lapse into personal areas, Gentry turned the conversation back to their work. He explained to Nicole and Drew that they would each spend the next few days working in the field with an experienced epidemiologist in order to become familiar with the methods of ferreting out hidden cases of smallpox, isolating the focus of infection, and vaccinating all unprotected individuals.

"After that, the two of you, with Parvati as your assistant and interpreter, will be assigned a jeep and driver."

Their posting was Jaynagar district, close to the Indian border with Nepal. Because of its numerous isolated villages, it was well suited to Nicole's epidemiology study and Drew's project of testing a new immunological method of diagnosis using the smallpox virus.

That night they slept on rope *charpoys*. Nicole and Parvati were given a small room together, since it had a curtain over the door and afforded some privacy. Nicole was so tired that she did not bother to inflate the air mattress she had been issued but followed Parvati's method of laying one of her two blankets over the *charpoy* as padding, with a sheet on top of that. It was too warm for covers, but they did use their mosquito nets.

These were the most comfortable lodgings they would find for the next two and a half months.

Chapter 17

The jeep bumped over the rutted road, keeping a distance between them and the cloud of dust raised by the surveillance team's vehicle. Nicole and Parvati sat in the rear seat, fanning themselves. In the front seat, Drew spoke to the driver, pointing to a cluster of mud huts in the distance.

It was too hot for conversation. The air danced with heat waves as the temperature hovered at 104 degrees, with not a breath of wind stirring. On either side of the road, as far as they could see, the flat Northern Plains stretched, plot after plot of farmland—wheat and rice and pulses, the staple crops of the north Indian diet. Even in the hottest hours of the day, men and women toiled in the fields, employing the same farming methods that had been used for centuries.

For weeks, they had been crisscrossing east and west, back and forth across northern Bihar, an area of twenty-five hundred square miles. They had visited countless villages, ranging in size from a few huts and fifty people to a *pukka* village of a thousand with a proper bazaar and *panchayat,* the council of elders who governed a community.

In the market towns, smallpox surveillance workers learned about suspicious cases of fever with rash when people came to trade from remote areas that had no bazaar. At temples or religious festivals, when worshipers arrived from outlying districts, health workers and vaccinators mingled with the crowds, asking questions about illness, showing the smallpox identification cards with photographs of children and adults stricken with the disfiguring disease. They checked for vaccination scars, especially among young children under school age, vaccinating on the spot those without visible proof of immunization.

Following up every rumor of illness accompanied by rash, no matter how far they had to travel, the health workers would call for a WHO medical team if there was a doubt about the diagnosis—as they had in this instance.

Nicole and Drew had received a radio message from Darbhanga alerting them to the death of a child who had been examined by a rural health officer and diagnosed as having chickenpox. It was essential to rule out smallpox as the cause of the child's death, especially because this area had formerly been smallpox-free.

The village headman and the entire *panchayat* were there to greet them. Standing behind were all the men of the village, gathered to see the foreigners. Grinning children stared at them wide-eyed, elbowing each other and tittering at the strange spectacle of the big, red-faced, pale-eyed man and a woman in trousers, with her bared head and immodest manner.

Nicole and Parvati walked behind the men—the village elders, Drew, and the members of the smallpox surveillance team. Although Nicole found this subservience of women irritating, it was necessary to follow the customs.

Those of the village women who were not sequestered in their homes had come to see the excitement. They carried their babies on their hips, drawing up the ends of their saris to cover their faces as the visitors passed. Nicole smiled at them, pressing her palms together in greeting. They returned her smile, their eyes dancing and friendly.

It was obligatory to sit on the floor in the meeting room of the *panchayat,* drinking tea, while the public health workers discussed their reasons for being there with the elders and gained their cooperation. After a lengthy discussion, it was agreed that every person in the village could be examined, including the women in purdah, who would be seen by Nicole and Parvati.

The body of the child who had died had been cremated, in accordance with Hindu custom, so it was not possible to determine the cause of death. Several other people in the village had fever, they learned. Smallpox victims develop a rash two or three days after the onset of illness, thus it was possible these people could already be victims of the disease.

The search began with the fever patients. All the people in the family of the deceased child had been vaccinated at some time, with the exception of a one-year-old
boy. He had a fever with a rash-like eruption on his
body, but only a few red patches on his face—not a
typical smallpox rash.

Nicole examined the baby. Sometimes a flat atypical
rash like this one indicated an especially virulent form of
smallpox, ending in internal hemorrhage and death. It
was difficult to make a diagnosis from the little boy's
appearance. They would have to rely on Drew's new
experimental technique.

Drew took blood from a vein in the child's leg. He
would know in two hours whether there was a positive
reaction with the antibodies developed at the Center for
Disease Control's virus lab. He also collected fluid from
a blister-like eruption on the child's trunk to be sent with
blood samples to the Institute of Communicable Diseases
in Delhi, where they would identify the virus with proven
laboratory tests and an electron microscope.

"I need a control, Nicole. How about drawing blood
from me?"

She wrapped the tourniquet around his arm, patting
the inside of his elbow to raise the vein. He made a fist
and she swabbed with alcohol, before sliding the needle
in and releasing the rubber tubing. As he bent his head
near hers to watch, she suddenly became aware of the
intimacy of their contact.

"You have a nice technique, doctor," he said, his voice
light. "I hardly felt that."

She smiled spontaneously. "That's because I usually do
children. They require a delicate touch." There was a
fluttering near her heart as his eyes seemed to caress her
face.

Nicole watched Drew separate out the red cells by
spinning down the blood in a small hand centrifuge,
which he cranked like mad. Clamped to a table, it held
four tapered glass tubes, two vials of the young patient's
blood and two of his own. Into the clear blood serum he
mixed a small amount of the freeze-dried antiserum prepared at the CDC.

"That should stand for an hour and a half, Nicole.
Then, we'll see." He carefully cleaned the used tubes and

syringes before putting them into a portable sterilizer for boiling at the end of the day, then scrubbed his hands.

"Do you always use such a careful technique when handling blood?" she asked.

"When you work with Hepatitis B as much as I have, you gain a very healthy respect for viruses," he replied.

After examining the residents of the next five houses, Nicole looked for Drew, wanting to know the results of his immuno-assay. She found him in the village meeting house, where they had established a temporary headquarters.

He looked at his watch. "I guess it's time. Keep your fingers crossed. It's so bloody hot, it might not work."

He cranked the centrifuge vigorously for three minutes, and when it stopped spinning, lifted the first of the sick child's blood serum samples, holding it up to the window. Nicole looked over his shoulder. She knew it took a practiced eye to determine the result. The elongated tip of the glass tube looked cloudy, but there was no definite precipitate. Drew frowned, but made no comment.

Peering at the second tube, he grunted, a satisfied sound. "You see here," he pointed out to her. "There's a small amount of white powder that's formed in the bottom. That's a positive, for sure. The virus has combined with the antiserum and precipitated out." He turned to the other samples. "Now let's see the controls."

The centrifuge tubes containing his own blood serum remained perfectly clear. Although the test was experimental, Drew was convinced that the disease they had encountered was *variola major,* the virulent Asian form of smallpox!

The surveillance team went into action. Now that a diagnosis had been made, it was imperative to contain this new outbreak in a previously smallpox-free area.

Two other members of the child's large extended family had fever, although they had not yet developed other symptoms. However, they bore the scars of old vaccinations.

"We have to assume that they had only partial protection and have developed a mild case," Nicole told the head of the surveillance team.

A twenty-four-hour guard was posted at the affected house. No one with fever or rash could leave the house. Every person in the village and within a five-mile radius

had to be vaccinated. A house-to-house search began,
and as the men came in from the fields and the women
returned from the village well, each person was questioned, examined, and vaccinated until the entire village
had been covered.

The villagers told them that a man and wife and their
unvaccinated infant had left early that morning, heading
for Muzaffarpur, where they planned to take a train to
Patna and then to Rajasthan, a state that had been free
of smallpox for several years.

The alarm went out. A messenger was sent to the
district police who would alert the authorities at all points
along the way. Using their radio, Drew contacted the
health office in Darbhanga and told them to inform Patna
and Delhi. The couple and their baby would have to be
apprehended and isolated, for if one of them should
develop smallpox, it would be enough to start a whole
new line of transmission wherever they traveled.

Nicole and Parvati finished visiting the last of the village's purdah houses, where the women lived in seclu-
sion, emerging only occasionally and then veiled from
head to foot. Nicole was appalled at the physical condition of these women, especially the older ones, who were
obese because of inactivity and the starchy diet of the
plains. It was hard to say who was less fortunate, the
women who labored ceaselessly in the fields or those who
were confined to the walls of their huts.

"It's discouraging to see how the village women live,
isn't it, Nicole?" Parvati remarked when they had dropped
exhausted on the floor of the headman's house, where
they would spend the night.

"Those women seem to be no better off than their
animals, Parvati. The water buffaloes also get to live in
the houses, and at least *they* can go out!" Gratefully, she
accepted a cup of hot tea and, after a moment's hesitation, slices of melon offered by the headman's wife.

"You're right," agreed Parvati. "It seems as strange to
me as it does to you. This is one of the most backward
areas we've visited."

Living was always difficult for them in a village like
this, with no running water or latrines. They did not wish
to offend their hosts by refusing food, but the risk of

picking up an intestinal infection was great. Virtually no one in this village was free of some parasite, Nicole knew.

She ate with her fingers, like the others, scooping up rice and *dal* with a *chapati,* and then she took a bowl of cool curds because they looked refreshing and Parvati was eating them. The men were in another part of the house, segregated from the women, so Drew was not there to chide her for eating uncooked fruit or unpasteurized dairy products.

Soon it was dark. By the light of a lantern, they visited the field where the women went to relieve themselves. They washed from an earthen jug of water, using the carbolic soap they always carried with them, and worked the foot pump to inflate their air mattresses, which they made into beds on the dirt floor of the mud-walled house.

Nicole and Parvati lay side by side talking, as they often did before falling asleep. Nicole had become fond of the young woman who was their co-worker. She was intelligent, sweet-tempered, and untiring in her sharing of the long arduous hours. Parvati had told her she attended a woman's college in Lucknow, where her family had fled from their native Lahore at the time of Partition. Once successful merchants, they had left everything behind in Pakistan and had to begin again.

Parvati spoke to Nicole in a low voice so they would not disturb the women of the house. "My father has arranged for my marriage."

Nicole was surprised. She had never heard Parvati mention an engagement. "Who is your fiancé?" she asked.

"I have not yet met him. He is the son of an acquaintance of my father's . . . from a good family."

Nicole was shocked. Of course, she knew that marriages were arranged in India—Drew had told her about Prem Mehta and his wife, how they had planned to have their parents arrange their marriage—but she couldn't believe that Parvati, a college graduate who traveled independently for her work, would actually marry someone she had never met.

"How do you feel about it . . . getting married?" Nicole asked.

"A little nervous," Parvati confessed. "But also, excited."

"Do you . . . *mind* marrying someone you don't know? Someone you aren't in love with?"

"Mind? Of course not, at least I don't think so. I suppose I won't know until I meet him. You see, Nicole, we are taught from the earliest years that we will grow to care for our husbands, particularly when we have children together."

"But . . . marriage is such a personal relationship. What if afterward you find you don't like each other . . . aren't attracted to each other?"

Parvati nodded in the darkness, her voice serious. "Of course, that does happen. I hope it won't be so in my case." She seemed to be considering this possibility for the first time, and Nicole was almost sorry she had spoken so frankly.

Parvati's voice was philosophical, if not cheerful, when she said, "I have a dear father, Nicole. He is quite considerate. He made sure that the groom's family is not only wealthy, but congenial. That's very important, you see. We shall have to live with his parents and brothers. A mother-in-law can make things most unpleasant for her son's wife if she doesn't like her."

Nicole lay awake after their conversation ended, considering what it meant to be born female in this part of the world. Which was preferable? To be an educated woman like Parvati, whose father nevertheless had found her a husband, or a woman of rural India, who expected nothing more than the limitations of village life?

The women of the headman's family were asleep, some of them lying in raised niches that were formed in the mud walls of the house, while others had climbed to the flat roof, where it was cooler. They were, in every sense, chattels of their husbands—possessions, like the family cow. Of course, there was no question in her mind about which women were more fortunate. But was it not ironic that in one of the few nations of the world where a woman was head of state, females were considered of such little consequence?

Nicole could hear the drone of male voices and see the reflection of firelight outside the house, but in this village the evening conversation did not include her. She may have been a respected visitor and a doctor, but she was not welcome to join Drew and the men.

They had been bouncing around the Northern Plains in the four-wheel drive jeep for the past month, hiking for long stretches when the road stopped ten kilometers from their destination, sleeping wherever they found themselves at the end of the day. The temperature was often unbearable; this was the hot season and there would be no relief until the monsoons came in July. They all worked twelve and fourteen hours a day, seven days a week, going wherever the rumor of smallpox took them, acting in whatever capacity was called for on the occasion.

Nicole recalled Henry Campion's words in Geneva. "You must learn to be flexible, to improvise, to constantly reevaluate, and be willing to change. Apply the knowledge you gain to other problems, other situations."

They had followed his advice. Nicole had even delivered two babies when complications set in, performed an appendectomy assisted by Drew and Parvati, and treated children for everything from trachoma to scabies. The saddest part for her was that there was no treatment for the disease they were stalking—smallpox.

Living together as they did, the team had grown close. Parvati was almost like a sister. And Drew? She still called him Andrew, but she had begun to think of him as Drew. Well, he certainly wasn't like a brother, at least not in her most private thoughts. On a night like this, when she couldn't fall asleep, when she was conscious of him nearby, talking and laughing with the other men, she could imagine how it would be to love a man like him . . . and to be loved by him.

They had developed an attachment in the time they had spent working together. Since they had been in the villages, she had not seen a display of the old impatience. He seemed to have left his stubbornness and arrogance behind.

She admired him in many ways. He was a skilled, compassionate doctor and a brilliant virologist. He was a leader, strong and decisive. She did not hesitate to follow his judgment—in fact, she accepted him as the senior member of the team, she realized, although she would never have admitted it to anyone.

But most of all, he was her friend. Her humorous, good-natured, irreverent, handsome . . . lovable friend. And there was no one, not even Parvati, with whom she could share her feelings.

*   *   *

Dick Gentry caught up with them in a place called
Dapali, toward the Bangladesh border. He was contacting the epidemiologists already in the field to direct them
toward new outbreaks of smallpox in isolated villages
until reinforcements arrived. The Russian epidemiologist
had left for Bangladesh, he told them. There were now a
Swiss, an Indonesian, and two Indians traveling with
him.

Nicole, Drew, and Parvati had not properly bathed for
two weeks when they pulled into the depot. They were
dirty and sweaty, and Drew was unshaven. Nicole and
Parvati excused themselves to find a shower. When they
returned to the one-room building, the men were in
heated debate.

"It's no place for women, I tell you," one of the Indian
doctors was saying. "You don't understand what it's like
there! They've never seen Westerners."

"I don't think Dr. Légende should go," said the second Indian, who was a public health official.

"Why don't we ask Nicole how she feels about it?"
said Drew, seeing her appear in the doorway.

"How I feel about what?"

Dick Gentry held up his hands as everyone began to
speak at once. "Wait. Let me explain it to her. Nicole,
we have to send a team to a tribal area northeast of here.
We've had reports of smallpox there, and the people are
resistant to vaccination. I'm going, and Drew's going
with me, but we don't think you and Parvati should
come. I want to reassign you to another group."

"*Why?* Why can't we go?" she exclaimed, unable to
hide her dismay.

"It's rough country, and the people there could be
hostile. Of course, we'll be with an Indian public health
group—I don't want to make it sound worse than it is.
But it might be wiser if you were sent somewhere else."

Drew interrupted. "Nicole, do you want to go? Or will
you be content to stay behind?"

"I *want* to go!" she said vehemently. "You don't have
to worry about me. I've been in rugged terrain all my
life."

Drew turned to the others. "Dr. Légende is part of the
team. Where we go, she goes." And it was settled.

Parvati insisted on coming, too. "I've always wanted to visit a tribal area," she confided to Nicole later that night. "I'm sure there's no real danger."

The next morning they said goodbye to the others, who were heading back to Darbhanga. The driver was servicing a larger staff car while they replenished the field kits from the supplies Dick had brought with him. As they drove away from Dapali, Gentry mentioned that they were meeting the team of public health workers in another sector to the northeast, at a shrine dedicated to Shitala Mata, the Smallpox Goddess.

"They've been searching this district for three weeks," said Dick when they were approaching the hill country. "There are over two hundred villages, most of them with fewer than fifty inhabitants. The settlements are scattered in the hills, the people don't speak Hindi, and they live at a subsistence level, with almost no cultivated crops."

They passed a group of tents guarded by an Indian Army sentry, one of several base camps established by the smallpox teams. "The searchers go by foot from there," Gentry explained. "The villages are inaccessible by jeep. Once the rains begin, forget it."

"I've never seen a smallpox temple before," said Parvati, as they neared their destination. "This should be interesting."

Wherever there was religion, there was exploitation, Nicole observed as they walked up a long flight of terraced steps to the shrine dedicated to the goddess of smallpox. At the foot of the steps and at regular intervals along the way were stalls offering religious paraphernalia for sale—picture cards of Shitala Mata, garlands of limp, dead marigolds, and incense for offerings.

They saw lepers and swollen-limbed victims of filariasis begging for *baksheesh*. *Sadhus,* the wandering holy men of India, sat cross-legged in prayer, bowls at their feet to receive the ill-afforded *paise* given by superstitious pilgrims.

Those who came to the shrine to appease the deity believed that Shitala Mata caused smallpox by a tipping of the basket of grain balanced on her head. If she washed the scattered grains with water, the patient would survive, but with a sweep of her dry broom a victim was condemned to death. Because people with active cases were sometimes brought here, or those who thought they might have been infected, the surveillance teams visited the temple on a regular basis.

They rendezvoused with the supervisor of the searchers who, after registering surprise when he saw the women, guided them to the base camp that would be their headquarters for the next two weeks. Over tea, he brought them up to date on the special surveillance activities his teams had been conducting and advised them on the nature of the people in the tribal area.

The leaders of the third village strongly objected to the presence of Nicole and Parvati. Several men confronted the team, fierce and wiry men with knotted legs, dressed in loincloths, turbans, and nothing else. They stood there arguing with the interpreter, holding long staffs, machete-like blades hanging at their waists.

The worried health workers turned to Dr. Gentry. "They refuse to allow the women to come into the village."

Parvati spoke to the Indian team members in Hindi. They had a long conversation, and then the interpreter turned to the tribesmen and held a dialogue in their language. After a ten-minute exchange, the hillmen laughed together and nodded, not looking at the women, but coming to an agreement.

"All right," said the surveillance leader. "They may come, but they should stay close to us and not go off alone."

"What did you say to them?" Dick asked Parvati in amazement.

She smiled delightedly, her eyes sparkling, as she answered in her musical voice, "I merely told them that it would take the strength of *two women* to combat the power of the goddess Shitala Mata. Evidently, they agreed!"

The child should not be so debilitated, thought Nicole. This isn't smallpox, just a simple skin rash. Yet he lay there with a glazed look in his eyes, exhausted from crying, his voice a croak. The mother squatted at his side, looking sadly at her prostrate son, who was on a mat, swaddled in a filthy strip of cloth.

"May I examine the baby?" Nicole asked, pointing to the child. Drew had come into the hut with her, taking seriously the instructions of the health worker not to leave either of the women alone.

The mother nodded, moving aside as Nicole knelt next to the baby. She unwound the rag, turning him to remove it . . . and came close to dropping the child, so shocked was she by what she saw.

"Drew!" she gasped, her voice registering horror.

Low on the abdomen, in the tender flesh just above the tiny penis, was a deep festering, crescent-shaped wound that had been deliberately inflicted by a red-hot branding iron.

"Please get one of the interpreters," she said, struggling to keep her tone level.

She could not bring herself to look at the mother. Gently, she put the child down and began to search in her kit for an anesthetic topical ointment for burns.

The interpreter, accompanied by an English speaking health worker, entered the hut.

"Ask her who did this to her son," Nicole instructed in a firm voice.

The health worker looked troubled, but translated.

"She says the healer branded him to drive away his sickness," he told them.

"What sickness? This rash? It's just a skin rash from heat and filth!"

The interpreter spoke to the woman for several minutes, while Nicole cleaned the infected wound and applied an antiseptic. The child whimpered, but lay still. Drew was preparing a dressing.

"The baby was unable to pass water without pain and there was 'bad matter,' she says—probably pus from an infection," the health worker told her.

"Well, they damn well didn't have to torture the child in order to cure a urinary infection! *He could die from this.* I've never heard of anything so hideous, have you?"

"Yes, Dr. Légende. Branding is illegal, but it's still practiced in the back country. The branders are like witch doctors. They're powerful and they prey on superstition. Unfortunately, the people believe in them."

She injected the child with antibiotics and fed him Furadantin, a drug for urinary tract infections, spooning it into his mouth. He drooled and swallowed the fruit-flavored liquid.

"Tell her we're leaving this medicine here with her. She must give it to him—one teaspoonful four times a day at regular intervals until the bottle is gone. It will cure his infection."

When the interpreter had finished speaking, Nicole noted the dumb look in the woman's eyes. "Do you think she understands?" Nicole asked.

The health worker shook his head. "I'm not sure, Dr. Légende. These people . . . they are so backward. I don't think she trusts us."

"Tell her it's the *brander* she shouldn't trust! *He almost killed her son.* Doesn't that mean anything to her? He didn't cure the baby's sickness, but he gave him a third degree burn, and he'll be scarred for the rest of his life."

She was shouting, incensed at the heartlessness of the evil person who practiced this form of cruelty and exploitation. "Tell her my power is greater than the brander's. If it's magic she believes in, tell her *my magic will work!*"

With an admiring glance, the young man spoke to the interpreter. The woman nodded and picked up her infant, who had fallen asleep.

Subdued, Nicole marched through the thick growth of tangled forest with Drew and the others, back to the base camp. She liked walking beside him. They had grown closer since coming here to the hills. They were friends now in a way they had not been before. Everything was different here—faster, more intense, more personal. There was something special about being together like this, in this wild and remote country, with the threat of danger around them.

At night, outside the main tent, they would sit talking near the fires that kept wild animals away. Two army *chowkidars,* weapons at hand, were always on guard.

"Why the guns?" Drew had asked Dick on the first evening.

"They're not taking any chances," Gentry had replied. "The tribesmen have been known to cause trouble."

In other villages, they saw more children who had been branded. One of the public health officers brought back reports of a child who had died of shock and infection from branding. Dick protested to the village headman, telling him that he would lodge a formal complaint with the authorities when he returned to Darbhanga.

"Have you noticed that we haven't seen any adults with fresh brands—or even old scars, Andrew?" Nicole said when the two of them were sitting alone one night.

"Yes, I've been aware of that. I bet many of the children who are branded don't survive. I doubt that someone old enough to know what it means would subject himself to such treatment."

"It's one of the most inhumane customs I've ever come across. The Quechuas in Peru use hallucinogens and believe in shamans, but they would never harm a defenseless infant!" She stared at the fire before she spoke again. "Thanks for supporting me, Andrew. I mean, about coming along with you."

He squeezed her shoulder. "It wouldn't have been the same without you."

They sat companionably, not speaking. She was unaware of Drew's eyes on her, of how beautiful she looked in the firelight.

"Where did the name Légende come from?" he asked. "It's French for legend, isn't it?"

She nodded. "I'm not sure how the family took that name. My father was a French Jew." She told him how Daniel had sailed to Peru when the Nazis invaded France and how he came to marry Maria Christina.

"Do you look like your mother?" Drew asked.

"No. I wish I did! She was so beautiful—petite and soft, with perfectly formed features. Even though she was half Indian, she was the classic Spanish beauty."

He was silent for a moment. "I would have thought that described you," he said quietly.

Nicole turned to look at him, an uncertain smile lighting her face. She had a sudden desire to put out her hand to touch him. Her fingers seemed to feel the texture of his skin, the outline of his mouth.

"Tell me about yourself . . . about your wife," she said impetuously.

It was all right in this setting to ask questions she would never have asked under different circumstances, to reach out in ways she otherwise would not have dared. She wanted to know about him, was curious about this sad, appealing, defensive man with secrets he did not want to share.

He paused for only a minute and then began talking

about Julie and his family. She watched his face as he spoke, thinking how warmhearted and gentle he was beneath his strong exterior.

Drew stopped talking and was looking at her. "You've never been married?" he asked.

"No." Her eyes moved away from his.

"I find that hard to understand. You must have had many suitors."

"Not so many." She was acutely uncomfortable.

"Then that can only mean that you discourage them."

"I suppose you could say that," she replied. She stood up and tossed a stick into the fire. "Well . . ." she smiled awkwardly at him and shrugged her shoulders. "It's getting late."

Drew sat on alone by the fire. He rubbed his hand over the *morah*, the low stool woven of rushes, vacated by Nicole. It still held the warmth of her body. He felt a flicker of excitement as he imagined how she would feel in his arms. He had been thinking of that a good deal in the past weeks. Perhaps it was natural. After all, he was a normal man and she was an unusually attractive woman.

He had a great curiosity about her. She was the most exotically remote woman he had ever known—and yet, the longer they were together, the more she relaxed in his company, the more he realized how tender and vulnerable she was. She was not at all like Julie. But, given another time and place, he might have . . . what? Fallen in love with her? That was something he did not want to consider.

He was indulging too much in self-contemplation lately. He had always appeared to others to be a happy, uncomplicated person, but there was a dark side to him. Julie had kept him from brooding. Since her death, he had once again become introspective.

He would have to be more careful with Nicole. She had not liked it when he asked her that about marriage. She was sensitive, and he didn't want to disrupt the harmony of their working together.

His thoughts were interrupted by the sound of the guards speaking to each other. One of them shouldered a gun and walked around the tents. The surrounding forest was dark and forbidding in the reflection of the fire. He rose and stretched. It was time for sleep.

In the tent he shared with Dick, Drew lay on his cot wondering what it was like to be one of those men who lived all their lives in the hills, scarcely touched by civilization. Clearly, they resented the intrusion of the smallpox teams. They grudgingly accepted the authority of the Government of India, but they felt no gratitude for its efforts to improve their health. Although they permitted the epidemiologists to enter their villages, there was never a moment when he was not aware of their barely contained hostility.

Nicole and Parvati had stayed at the base camp. The teams were nearing the end of their work in this district, fanning out to villages far from the cluster of tents. Although the two women had not wanted to stay behind, they realized how taxing the long foot journey would be, and they did not want to slow the men down.

They spent the day doing laundry and washing their hair. Nicole sat at a table bringing her diary notes up to date for the report she would write at the end of the tour. Just before noon, some villagers appeared and shyly indicated that they would like medicines and dressings for various minor ailments. Soon they were running a dispensary for more than two dozen patients, mostly women and children.

"If we could stay here for a year, Parvati, wouldn't that be wonderful? Think of what we could accomplish!"

Parvati smiled. "I would like to work with you always, Nicole. I wish you lived in India."

I could take a job with the WHO, thought Nicole. *I'd like that. There's so much to be done all over the world. If I didn't have my patients in Lima, if there weren't as much need in Peru, I would come here.* At least being a member of the IHTF would give her an opportunity to serve beyond her own country. *I hope I can spend the rest of my life doing work like this.*

As the sun slanted low, casting long shadows, the hill people returned to their villages, slipping away into the forest. Nicole and Parvati closed up their impromptu clinic, packing the supplies and disposing of the refuse. Parvati was sterilizing the syringes and instruments in boiling water when Dick Gentry returned with one of the vaccinators and an interpreter.

"Boy, you two ought to be glad you didn't come with us today," he said, dropping onto a *morah* and unlacing his boots.

"Hard going?" asked Nicole, handing him a cup of tea.

"The worst yet. Terrible terrain—and *impossible* people. We're going to have to get the army in there to force them to accept vaccination." He drank the tea. "I could use a real drink."

"I'm afraid we haven't got anything, unless you want rubbing alcohol," Nicole laughed. "Where's Andrew?" she asked, realizing that he had not followed Dick into the camp.

"Oh, we separated. Thought we could cover more territory that way. He and two of the health workers were going to four villages. They'll be along soon."

"No interpreter?" She felt a nagging worry.

"They had a native guide who understands Hindi. Prakash and Francis, the two health workers, have a lot of experience around these parts. There won't be any problems," he assured her. "Well, I guess I'll wash up. They'll be back by the time I'm finished."

But they had not arrived half an hour later when Dick had washed and changed his clothes. Nor were they there by the time the sun was a red glow on the horizon. The coolies brought wood and lit a fire, and the cooks had begun preparations for dinner when Gentry and the vaccinator spoke to the sentries about the three men who had not returned. By this time, Nicole and Parvati did not bother to conceal their alarm.

"We have to send a search party for them, Dick."

"It would be impossible at night, Nicole. It will be dark soon. I'm sure they decided they were too far from camp and are staying in a village overnight."

"But the people are so unfriendly! They would never invite them into their homes."

"Maybe they'll be more hospitable to the men when we're not there, Nicole," Parvati tried to reassure her.

Night fell, and still there was no sign of them. Nicole could not eat any dinner. She sat up half the night, hoping she would see Drew and the two health officers come walking out of the forest.

At first light the next day, they sent two search parties, each with an army sentry, to look for the men. Dick and

Nicole went to the other base camps to alert the teams that part of their crew had not returned. Everyone agreed they would try to locate them wherever they went that day. Dr. Gentry also sent a radio message to the WHO coordinator in Patna, informing him of the situation but explaining that the men would probably show up that day.

By late afternoon, the two search parties returned. They had gone to all four of the villages. Drew and his co-workers had visited one of them yesterday morning with a guide, but no one in the other three villages admitted to having seen them. Dick radioed again, for police or army scouts to come to their aid. The reply came that a unit would set out immediately, but would not reach them until sometime in the middle of the next day.

Nicole was overwhelmed with a sense of dread. *What if he's been killed?* she thought. There could have been wild animals—these hills were full of tigers, wild boars, and bears. *What if they fell into a trap set for game and can't get out?* All during that second night, she dozed fitfully, awakening frequently to imagine the horrible things that could have happened to Drew.

Why had they not stuck together? Why had Drew gone off without Dick? They *knew* they were headed for the most remote and difficult terrain. Of all times to leave each other!

She found herself wishing it had been Dick Gentry who was missing instead of Drew. There was a heaviness in her chest. She couldn't be bothered analyzing its cause or her feelings for him. All she knew was that she was in the grip of a dire fear that she would never see him again. All through the night she pictured him, wanting him there with her, praying for his safe return. She found herself reciting the long-forgotten charms learned from Rosa in her childhood, making promises to the mountain gods of Huascarán, the *apus*, if they would only bring Drew back safely . . . back safely to her.

On the third morning, all work was abandoned in the camps. An army unit arrived in a military truck by mid-morning. Seeing the soldiers, a squad of military police, caused Nicole even further alarm rather than raising her hopes because now it was acknowledged that something dire had happened to the three men. Either they were lost in the dense forest, had met with an accident, or had been attacked by beasts of prey.

"Or they could have been captured by *dacoits*," suggested the commander of the unit.

"What are *dacoits?*" asked Nicole.

"Bandits," replied Parvati. "They are active in the hills."

"But why would they capture a medical team? They don't have any valuables."

"Possibly for ransom," said Dick.

"Then they would have sent a *demand* for ransom!" Nicole was on the verge of tears. She went into the tent to get hold of herself. She knew Dick must think she was a hysterical woman or in love with Drew, but she didn't care what he thought if only Drew was found alive.

By late afternoon they had heard nothing. The soldiers had not returned to camp yet, but they would soon begin coming in. Parvati, who sensed that Nicole did not want company, was talking with the other health workers.

Alone in the tent, Nicole experienced the too-familiar feeling of loss. Once again someone who had become special to her was gone. She remembered little things about Drew, the smile that shone like the sun coming out, how he looked with his brow wrinkled in concentration, the habit he had of pushing back his hair when it fell forward, the way he brushed her arm with his fingers when they had a moment of special accord. . . . Would she ever see him again? In panic, she realized she was losing hope. The more time passed, the less chance there was the men would be found.

Out in the camp, she heard the sound of men's voices. She rushed out, but it was only some soldiers returning.

"You look all in, Nicole," said Dick. "Why don't you try to get some sleep?"

"I think we're all nervous," she answered. "Maybe I will go take a nap. Be sure to call me if there's any news." Dick watched her go, a look of concern crossing his face.

Nicole pulled off her hiking boots and lay on the cot. In the oppressive heat of the tent, her eyelids soon grew heavy.

*   *   *

They had been tied up and gagged for over twelve hours—since their captors had left, barring the door behind them. Drew's arms and legs were numb, and he was finding it difficult to breathe in the close air of the godown.

Francis, the younger health worker, a medical student, had been badly beaten the first day. Drew was afraid he might have some broken bones. In the dim light that filtered down through the ventilation slots at ceiling height, he could see that the boy's face was bruised and swollen. His breathing was harsh and ragged in the silence, but that might have been because he had fallen asleep.

How long had they been here? He had lost track of time because he had been blindfolded for long intervals. So far, he could only be sure that two nights and two days had passed since they were taken by surprise in the forest.

They had left the first village and were heading east along a clearly marked trail when the underbrush parted and four men armed with automatic rifles stepped out to surround them. Francis panicked and tried to run, and they beat him senseless with the butt of a gun. The other health worker, Prakash, older and more experienced with these tribesmen, had prevailed upon them to stop when the boy lost consciousness and most probably had saved his life. Prakash knew enough words in common with their kidnappers to be able to communicate with them, luckily, since the guide—probably in league with them—had been taken away almost immediately.

The thugs emptied their captives' pockets, taking their watches and Drew's Dartmouth ring. How odd that he had worn it. It had lain in a drawer for years . . . he had come across it when he was packing for the trip and, on a whim, put it on.

He did not fear death. After watching Julie die, after seeing so many patients go, it was not death he feared. It was the process of dying. Somehow he knew that these captors would not put a clean, quick end to lives. Not from what he had seen of them.

There was one slim hope. Before the three of them had been gagged, Drew told Prakash to offer the *dacoits,* as he called them, twice as much money to let them go as the branders were willing to pay for their capture. He counted on the bandits' greed to overcome their loyalty to the people who hired them. On the other hand, they would have to continue to live in the hills with those people, and they may have decided the risk was too great.

Drew closed his eyes and turned his thoughts to the one subject that had helped him keep his sanity since he had been thrown into this dark hole . . . Nicole.

In another hour darkness would fall. This would be the third night. Everyone in the camp acknowledged that the three men were probably dead by now. The military police would continue to search the forest and every village for their remains, but whatever had happened to them, it was unlikely they would ever be seen alive again.

Between the smoke of the cooking fires and the milling around of the army men, no one spied the two men who appeared on a ridge above the clearing. One of them sank back into the woods, while the other stumbled down an embankment and fell, sliding halfway, until he regained his footing. He had reached the edge of the emcampment before he was noticed.

Parvati was the first to see him. "Drew!" she cried and ran to him.

Dick Gentry threw down his pipe and leapt to his feet. "Thank the Lord!" he exclaimed. "Where the hell have you been, Tower? Where are the others?" He threw his arms around Drew's shoulders, then caught him as he staggered. "Hey, he's not in such good shape," he said with concern.

Drew let them lead him to the main tent, where he sat down. "Water, please," he said hoarsely.

When he had drunk, Dick said. "Let me take a look at you."

Drew shook his head. "I'm all right. Now please, you've got to listen to me . . . ."

He told them of their capture and how the *dacoits* had finally agreed to free them for a ransom. Prakash had convinced them that the only way the foreigners would believe their good intentions was if they let Drew be the one to carry their demands.

"They want three thousand rupees for the release of the other two. I promised they would have it, with no recriminations."

Everyone was silent. Three thousand rupees, less than five hundred American dollars, was more than a year's salary for a public health worker in India.

"Who's going to pay it?" asked one of the health team.

"I am," said Drew. "We have until noon, day after tomorrow, to give them the money." He looked at Gentry. "They mean business, Dick. I don't want to argue with anyone. Just get me the money, and I'll pay it back when I reach Delhi."

Gentry nodded. "All right. We'll talk about who pays it some other time. I'll speak to the police commander." The police would have to get hold of the cash for them. They might not agree to do it, probably preferring to storm the kidnappers' hideout.

"They'll never find it. And if by some chance they did, they would have two dead health workers on their hands," Drew protested.

"What makes you think they won't kill them anyway?"

"I don't think they would have let me go if they intended to do that."

"Now will you tell us what happened?" said Gentry.

Drew explained that the branders, hearing they were going to be reported, paid the bandits to kidnap one of the smallpox teams. As a warning, they had intended to kill the prisoners and dump their bodies somewhere where they would be found.

"We bargained with them and settled on three thousand rupees." Drew drank some hot tea. "Three thousand rupees . . . and vaccinations for all of them!" He looked around. "Where's Nicole?" he asked.

"In our tent," said Parvati. "I think she may have fallen asleep. She hasn't slept at all since you were gone—" she stopped suddenly, as if she had uttered an indiscretion, looking at Dr. Gentry.

"She's been pretty broken up about this, Drew," said Dick.

Without saying another word, Drew went to find Nicole. She was asleep, lying on her side facing him. Even in sleep, she looked exhausted. By the light of a lantern, he could see dark circles under her eyes. He knelt at the side of the cot, thinking he should let her sleep, but he touched her cheek gently and stroked her arm.

She opened her eyes slowly, looking confused, and when she focused, she stared at him in disbelief.

"Hi," he said softly.

She tried to sit up, but he caught her in his arms and buried his face in her hair, holding her, not speaking.

Her arms went around his neck and he heard her gasp, *"Oh, Drew!"* He realized she was crying, tears running down her cheeks.

"Don't cry, Nicole. I'm back. Everything's going to be all right."

"What happened to you? I was so worried," she asked, her voice catching.

He drew back to look at her and then he brought his mouth down on hers, kissing her long and deeply, the way he had a hundred times in his imagination. When at last he let her go, he said, "I've been promising myself for the past three days I would do that if I lived through this thing."

Later that night, after he had been bathed, shaven and deloused by the army barber and fed hot soup and roasted lamb by the mess cook, he felt reasonable, though exhausted.

"I'm glad you made it, Drew," Gentry said sincerely when they were alone in their tent. Then he grinned. "I don't know what I would have done with Nicole if you hadn't!"

Drew did not smile. His voice was serious when he said, "I can assure you there has been nothing unprofessional in my relationship with Nicole, Dick."

"Hey, Drew . . . I wasn't suggesting there was. I have the highest regard for your professionalism—for both of you. Boy, I really put my foot in it, didn't I? It's just that I've been here, I can see that she . . ."

"That she what?"

"Hell, it's obvious she cares about you. Cares a lot."

He was silent. "I care for her, too. She's an amazing person. But I can't let myself get involved with a woman now, especially when it's an impossible situation."

"You said you lost your wife . . . is that why?"

"I guess so. The thing is, I've finally got my bearings again. Falling in love could really screw up my life."

"Tell me about it!"

"I know you're married, Dick. . . ."

"Yeah. I can't remember the last time I spent twenty-four hours with my wife. I guess my marriage is a casualty of the smallpox campaign. My wife couldn't take it in Patna—not that I blame her. Even the best house I could find was impossible, and I was gone for days at a time. You saw Patna."

"Where is she now?"

"She was in Delhi for a while, but she went home before the start of the hot weather. By home, I mean back to Maryland. That's where her folks live."

"What are you going to do? Just let her go?"

"It's a choice of that, or give up here."

"Do you want my advice?" Gentry nodded. "Take a leave of absence and patch up your marriage. Unless you don't care."

"I care. But I'm not sure there's anything left to patch up."

Two days later, at noon, Drew went alone to an agreed upon rendezvous, where he was met by a scout sent by the *dacoits*. After an elaborate, circuitous foot journey through uncharted jungle, the money was handed over, and a short time later Prakash appeared, leading Francis, who was bruised but not seriously injured. The scout led the three of them by another route to a point above the base camp, then melted away into the forest from which he had come.

The following day, after the WHO medical team had left the area, a detachment of military police marched through the woods in search of the *dacoits*, but they were never able to locate the godown where Drew and the others had been held captive.

Chapter 18

They were pushing on toward Jaynagar, hoping to reach the district headquarters before dark.

The ordeal in the hills was almost forgotten. The State Health Ministry had provided the ransom and intended to continue trying to apprehend the kidnappers, although Drew told them he thought they would never succeed. He was certain the *dacoits* had quit the district immediately after they received the money.

They had said goodbye to Dick Gentry at Dapali two weeks ago. Ever since then, they had been driving west, covering the regions around Jogbani and Nirmali, sleeping in villages under some of the most trying conditions they had encountered. Every one of the crew was overtaxed, and now they were eager to return to the Jaynagar health station, as primitive as it was. At least there would be water for a bath, a decent latrine, and a *charpoy* to lie on instead of a hard-packed dirt floor.

Nicole had been suffering from dysentery for several days. She thought it was nothing serious, the usual problem the epidemiologists encountered when working in the field. She gritted her teeth as the jeep rattled over the pitted road. Every bone in her body ached, and her head felt like it would fall forward if she did not make a conscious effort to hold it up. She had also been feeling nauseated all afternoon, and her stomach was beginning to cramp. It's a question of mind over matter, she told herself. I won't give in. Soon, in a few hours, I'll be able to take a bath and go to sleep. I won't even have dinner.

The thought of food made her feel even worse. She was suddenly overcome with a dreadful nausea. Turning to Drew, she said, "Would you please ask the driver to stop? I don't feel so well. . . ." She gagged, holding her hand to her mouth.

Drew leaned forward. "Pull over," he said. "Doctor is sick."

She made it to a ditch just in time, leaned over and retched convulsively, while Drew held her shoulders. When she stopped vomiting, drained of all strength, she leaned against him, shivering and tinged with green.

"Oh, Drew," was all she could say.

"Feeling better?" he asked, wiping her face with his handkerchief, which he had wet from a thermos of water Parvati had brought from the jeep.

"A little," she lied. The fact was, she was feeling horrible. The landscape seemed to be moving in on her. She was seized with intestinal cramps and another wave of nausea. "I wish there were a latrine."

They were not near a village. The road ran along a stretch of dry wasteland dotted with clusters of trees and scrub.

"You can go behind some bushes," Drew said.

"No . . ." she groaned.

"It's all right, honey. Parvati will go with you."

"Yes, Nicole," said Parvati, in a cheerful tone. "Don't worry about it. Come!"

When they returned to the jeep, Drew placed his arm around her, drawing her head against his chest as if she were a child. "You'll be okay soon," he whispered, as they drove off.

They had to stop four more times before they reached Jaynagar. By then, mortification at her condition had been replaced by sheer physical misery. There was no bearable position. She was too weak to sit up, but became dizzy lying flat. Drew put her across his lap in the back of the jeep, holding her in a reclining position with her head supported on his arm. Gently he stroked her face, brushing the hair back from her brow while telling her they would soon reach their destination. What kept her from being completely demoralized was his voice and the strength of his arms around her.

Arriving at Jaynagar at last, Drew carried Nicole into the darkened dispensary, ordering the *chowkidar* to bring two *charpoys*. Laying her on one of the cots, they made the other into a bed, using an air mattress and padding it with blankets and a sheet, folding another blanket to pillow her head.

"Parvati, will you bathe her and get her into something more comfortable?"

While Parvati went to get a basin of water, he took Nicole's temperature and was alarmed to see it was above 105. She lay with her eyes closed, her hands crossed over her chest, breathing rapidly. It frightened him to see her in that position. In the dim light of the kerosene lamp she looked like a cadaver.

"God, I hope she doesn't have ameba! It seems too short a time—"

Parvati shook her head. "I don't think it's amebiasis," she whispered. "I just hope it isn't—"

He looked up. "Isn't what?"

"I was thinking of typhoid . . . or cholera."

He shook his head, "It couldn't be! She had shots for both of those before coming to India."

They knew there were no guarantees with inoculations, especially for those diseases. It could be any one of a number of serious possibilities. In the villages there was no such thing as sanitation. The water and the soil were polluted. Vegetables were fertilized with human feces, and every inhabitant harbored some active disease organisms.

There was one thing for sure. This was no simple case of traveler's diarrhea. Her symptoms were too severe. What would he do?

The first thing was to get some fluids into her, for she would soon become dehydrated. Drew remembered Prem's report about oral rehydration at the cholera lab in Dacca, the simple sugar and salt solution that could save lives. It was easy to make, using boiled water. If Nicole could keep enough of the mixture down to obtain initial rehydration, he knew the vomiting would abate. He supported her, coaxing her to sip and swallow, but she was unable to tolerate anything by mouth, becoming violently ill.

Drew considered their predicament. They were 300 miles from the nearest hospital. The roads were so poor it would take hours to reach even the rural health center at Darbhanga. That was not much better equipped than this place, and as ill as she was, it would be cruel to subject her to the trip. To make matters worse, their radio had given out yesterday, and he had been unable to repair it.

He *had* to get to a telephone or telegraph! Maybe they could send an ambulance for her. Or a plane. But the closest airfield was in Patna.

Nicole was seized with another fit of vomiting. By now, there was nothing to bring up. She was limp as he sponged her off and gently laid her back on the cot. If this continued, she would go into shock from fluid loss. She was shivering and appeared almost comatose to him, her eyes unfocused, seeming not to realize he was there. He had never seen anyone deteriorate so rapidly. For a moment, he couldn't decide what to do. Overcome with panic, he thought, *My God, she could die. No! I won't let her die! I won't.*

He had to get fluids into her parenterally. There were no intravenous supplies in this bare infirmary, which was used only sporadically when the State Health Ministry sent a doctor to the district. He began going through their own supplies to see what medications he had for dysentery. Not much. Some broad spectrum antibiotics and sulfadiazine, both in capsule form. It would help to know the cause of her disease, but there was no time to identify the organism. He would have to use both drugs, and hope one of them would attack whatever it was. If he mixed the powdered contents of the antibiotic and sulfa capsules with the rehydration solution, he hoped she would stabilize enough to be moved to a hospital. If only he could devise a way to get it into her.

In the disorganized shelves of the dispensary's *almirahs,* he found what he wanted. Three large bottles with screw tops and some rubber tubing. He had hollow needles in his own field kit, and sterile filter paper. . . .

"Parvati," he called, "boil up a *dekshi* of water!"

Parvati came in, bringing food for him. "Not in here, Parvati. We're going to treat this as if it's highly infectious, just in case. Everything gets boiled—dishes, glasses, utensils, clothing. Disinfect everything—especially body wastes. We can't afford to have either one of us or the driver get sick. If Nicole doesn't improve in another twenty-four hours, we'll *have* to move her."

"I think she'll improve by tomorrow," Parvati said to comfort him.

Drew stayed with Nicole until dawn. He sat next to the cot, holding her hands, chafing them, bathing her face and body with tepid water to bring down the fever. Now and then he dozed off, and in the twilight between sleeping and waking, he dreamed of Julie and she became one with Nicole, lying near death with tubes coming out of her. He wakened with a start, his heart hammering, leaning forward to make certain she was still breathing.

Nicole slept fitfully, muttering incoherent phrases in a language he did not recognize. She kept repeating the same words in Spanish, something about flowers . . . and the wind.

"Poor darling, you're delirious," he whispered.

If only the homemade drip would control the infection and keep her fluids in balance until she was stabilized enough to move. He checked her arm, making certain the solution was not infiltrating the tissue where the needle went into the vein. Bringing the limp hand to his lips, he closed his eyes, realizing how much she had come to mean to him.

Don't die, Nicole. Please, darling, don't die.

It was their driver who told them about the mission hospital. They had sent him to the district police station with a message to be telephoned to the WHO coordinator in Patna, informing them of Nicole's illness and requesting an ambulance. He returned in the middle of the afternoon to report that the telephone lines were down.

If only their radio would work. "I never realized how isolated we are," Drew said to Parvati, his apprehension increasing.

She was having an animated conversation with the driver. "Drew, he says they told him there are some American missionary doctors who run a surgery three hours' drive from here!"

"Three hours! How come we haven't heard of it before this?"

She looked crestfallen as the driver continued speaking. "It's at Malangwa, over the border, in Nepal. They'll never let us in without visas."

*   *   *

"I am now an international criminal," exclaimed Drew, when they had left the border station behind.

"I don't know how you managed that," Parvati told him with an admiring glance.

"I guess they don't have many visitors entering Nepal this way. At least Nicole and I have valid visas, so only the two of you will go to jail! I could kiss that man in Patna, with all his stamps."

Aided by the two hundred-rupee notes he produced, Drew had convinced the border guards to accept the WHO letters bearing the stamp of the Nepalese Consul in Patna as entry permits for Parvati and the driver. When they questioned the nature of Nicole's illness, Drew instructed Parvati to tell them she was going to the mission hospital to have her appendix removed. Nicole was asleep at the time, Drew having given her a sedative for the trip. The guards had accepted the story.

They had made a bed for Nicole in the jeep by removing the front passenger seat and installing two air mattresses, one on top of the other. Parvati and Drew were squeezed together in the rear seat.

Driving across the swampy plain of southern Nepal at the base of the Himalayan foothills, they could see the hazy silhouette of the world's highest mountain range in the distance. Drew kept an anxious eye on Nicole. Although there had been some improvement in her condition that morning, her temperature still intermittently rose above 102 and she was extremely weak. She was lucid and had agreed when he told her what they were planning to do. Fortunately, the improvised intravenous drip was working, keeping her electrolytes in balance. Drew was a little nervous about the sterility of the IV, even though he had taken extreme care in its preparation. He would be relieved when they reached the mission. A surgical hospital, even one on this remote frontier, should have intravenous equipment and medications.

That is, if it truly is a hospital, he thought. He had learned not to take anything for granted in this far corner of the earth. He hoped they would have communications to the outside world, for he intended to call Robert and ask him to send a plane for Nicole.

They reached Malangwa in mid-afternoon, five hours after they set out. The road ended abruptly twenty miles short of their destination, and the driver had to cut across the rising terrain, driving the jeep along footpaths and stream beds, which were low in this pre-monsoon season.

The Malangwa Mission Hospital stood on a hill in a picturesque grove of oak and chestnut trees, its architecture steep-roofed and curiously Elizabethan. A line of poles with telephone and electric wires was the first distinguishing feature Drew noticed.

Alma and Spurgeon Russell were husband and wife, both of them Baptist missionary doctors. In this remote outpost, they provided the only medical care in Nepal south of Kathmandu for a distance of two hundred miles, east to west.

Within half an hour, Nicole was lying on clean, sun-dried hospital sheets in a comfortable bed with intravenous solutions going. "We won't remove your needle, Dr. Tower. It's just fine and no need to stick her twice," said Dr. Alma Russell.

"We'll take blood and stool samples, but because of the antibiotics, we may not get a good culture going," her husband told Drew. "Doesn't matter. As long as the medication works."

They ruled out typhoid, cholera, and other infectious diseases. "My guess is Flexner's *Shigella*, and we have a specific medication for that. She should respond in very short order," said Dr. Alma.

The Russells were happy to have visitors. They seldom saw foreigners, especially Americans. Spurgeon told Drew his father had run a mission hospital in Burma before the Second World War. "So, I was accustomed to the life, you see. The Russells are a medical family. And some of us are doing the Lord's work as well."

The Lord's work, thought Drew. He had never been so appreciative of the missionary spirit.

The next day, in the Russells' bungalow, Drew was able to get a call through to Robert Hillman in Delhi. "Nepal! What are you doing there?" asked Rob.

Drew explained what had happened. It was a poor connection, full of static, and they were disconnected at one point, but he managed to tell Robert where they were and how he could be reached.

"I'll have to see whether the plane can fly into Nepal," he told Drew. "Is there an air field nearby?"

Spurgeon told him there was an old Gurkha encampment with an airstrip, somewhat rundown, but usable for light aircraft. Robert said he would call Drew the following day after checking with the pilot and the Nepalese embassy.

When he had finished shouting into the phone at Rob, he tried, without success, to call the WHO team in Darbhanga and the Health Ministry in Patna.

"We don't always have the best telephone service down here," said Spurgeon with a chuckle.

Down? thought Drew. I suppose it's all in your perspective. To him, this was the top of the world.

"Your patient is asking for you," Alma told him when he walked across the compound to the hospital building.

Nicole was lying with her head raised against the pillows, looking wan but smiling.

He touched her hand, his fingers lingering there. "How are you?" he asked softly.

"I think I feel human," she answered in a weak voice. "Thank you, Drew. For everything." Her eyes were large with emotion. He felt a tightness in his chest.

"You gave me a scare," he said, his hand still covering hers.

"I'm sorry. It's my own fault. I wasn't very careful about food in the last couple of villages."

He shook his head. "We all took chances. You just had some bad luck. I'm glad you're feeling better." He squeezed her hand, then let it go. "I think they'll send the Ford Eagle up here to take you back to Delhi as soon as you can leave."

"Oh, no!" she cried in dismay. "What about our work?"

Drew laughed. "Do you really think you're in any condition to work?" When he saw that she was truly distressed, he said, "There's only one more week before we were due back in Delhi, Nicole. You have all the data you need. I'll keep diary notes for you."

"You're not going back with me?" she asked in a small voice.

He felt that constricted sensation in his chest again. She seemed so vulnerable, lying there, looking young and pale. He wanted to go with her . . . he didn't want to be separated from her.

"I'll be there soon. By next week you'll be all recovered, and we can spend a few days enjoying India," he ran a finger down her arm, ". . . now that we're friends."

"Friends?" She did not understand.

He grinned. "I once told you that my friends call me Drew." He suddenly looked shy. "You'd better get some rest now. I'll see you later." He left the room quickly.

The Ford Eagle landed at the old Gurkha station, guided to the airstrip by the flashing headlights of the jeep and the Russells' ambulance, a converted weapons carrier. The plane's door opened, and out sprang a tall, smiling nun, her dark brown habit flapping around her ankles.

"Hello there! I'm Dr. George," she told the astonished group. "From Holy Family Hospital in Delhi. Where's the patient?"

Drew was the first to recover. "She's back at the hospital. We can get her ready to leave in a few minutes, Dr. George." He introduced himself and Spurgeon Russell.

They shook hands with the pilot, who casually said, "I need to charge my battery. It seems to be low, and the spare is missing."

Drew had a sinking feeling. "This isn't exactly an international airport! How can you charge an airplane battery here?"

"Oh, the jeep will do," he answered cavalierly.

An hour later, when they brought Nicole to the airstrip in the ambulance, it was an unnerving sight for Drew to see the Cessna attached by a set of cables to the jeep, whose driver was sitting behind the wheel, gunning the motor.

As he watched the little plane gather speed on the bumpy airstrip and lift off, then bank and turn west, Drew was terrified. It seemed as if everything in the world he cared about was contained within that fragile fuselage.

On board the plane, Nicole lay on a stretcher, considering the strange twists of fate. Here she was, flying back to Delhi from a mission hospital in Nepal five days after becoming ill in a remote Indian village, unchanged for the past four centuries. This was surely one of the more bizarre paths her life had taken.

But it was of Parvati Narain Nicole was thinking. Of what Parvati had said in the hospital room before they parted, when they were waiting for the others to come . . . Parvati's words that had an electrifying effect on her.

"Thank you for taking such good care of me, Parvati," she told her friend. "I'm sure I wouldn't have survived if it weren't for you."

"Oh, it wasn't *I* who nursed you, Nicole," Parvati laughed. "It was *Drew*. He sat up with you for three nights in a row—wouldn't let me do anything. He was out of his mind with worry. I think he's gone quite daft over you!"

Before Nicole could answer, or protest, Drew arrived to take her off to the airfield in the ambulance. Parvati stood on the verandah of the Malangwa Mission Hospital, her sari fluttering in the breeze, as she smiled a tearful farewell.

Chapter 19

Nandipur is in the hills, near the Vindhya mountains," Prem told them, turning from his place in the front seat. "Good game country—jungle and tiger grass."

"Sounds exciting!" said Nicole.

"Yes. We'll see wild elephant, and even a tiger if we're lucky. They had regular *shikars* there in the old days. The British were fond of the hunt, as you know."

They were driving south from Gwalior, where they had visited a comprehensive health services project. To wind up their stay in India, Prem had asked a friend to arrange a private tour for them at one of India's most famous wildlife sanctuaries, the former game preserve of a maharajah.

Nicole dozed off for an hour, and when she awakened, they had left the plains behind and were climbing through a growth of sal trees. They turned off the main road, heading west. The way became narrower and rutted, the forest thicker.

"We shall soon be in Pulbah, and that's the end of the road," said Prem. "The game warden will meet us there. From Pulbah, it's elephant back up to Nandipur." Prem pointed to the west. "It always impresses foreigners when they hear that all the land thirty miles in that direction and about another twenty to the north formerly belonged to one man."

Drew whistled. "Six hundred square miles. That would be a national park in the States."

"Well, nowadays it is in India. They *were* decadent, though, weren't they?"

"What's happened to the maharajahs since India has been independent?"

"The government gives them an annual purse. Some of

them have transformed their palaces into hotels. Others live abroad. But a few, like the Maharajah of Kashmir, have turned good citizen. He's the Indian Minister of Health and Family Planning."

The game warden was waiting with their elephant when they reached Pulbah. They climbed a ladder to a wooden platform, from which they easily stepped onto the *howdah*, sitting two on each side. The *mahout*, who spends his entire life with one elephant, which he has personally trained from the time of its capture, sat in front of them on the animal's neck. Secured by an iron bar that locked in place across their laps, they moved off up the rocky track toward Nandipur, swaying with the lumbering gait of the huge beast.

Is this really happening? thought Nicole. Two weeks ago I was so sick, I thought I was going to die. And here I am, feeling absolutely wonderful, riding on a maharajah's elephant with Drew Tower, who looks like he should be a prince!

At the game sanctuary, they found a group of three lodges with steep thatched roofs. The buildings were raised on stilts, the game warden explained, to protect them from scorpions, snakes, and prowling animals.

It was late afternoon. "Let's get settled in our rooms," suggested Prem. "You can have a rest, then wash up for tea—or something stronger, if you wish. I managed to bring a little whiskey along—strictly illegal! *Aacha?*"

Their lodge had a spacious, high-ceilinged anteroom furnished with rattan chairs and tables. The bedrooms were on the far side of the structure, each with a private bath. There was no plumbing, of course, but ingenious methods had been devised to overcome this. A great galvanized tub stood in one corner, with a drain fitted into the wooden floor next to it. When she wanted to take a bath, the *bheesti* would bring the water. Once it had been used, however, a different person was responsible for emptying the tub.

In the opposite corner of the bathroom, Nicole found a throne-like chair with a hinged seat. Lifting up the cover, she looked down through a hole under which rested a chamber pot, which could be removed through a little trap door in the wall behind—presumably by one of the untouchables who performed such functions. Not as instantaneous as flushing, but equally effective.

*   *   *

They sat in the screened loggia of the main lodge after a dinner of *pakoras,* hot curry, *pilau* made with sultanas and fried almonds, *dahi, dal,* mango chutney, and *puris.* They were forced to stop eating long before they had consumed a third of the prepared food.

"Prem, how can they expect us to eat this much?"

"They don't, Nicole," he laughed. "In fact, they would be very disappointed if we did!" He explained that those of the servants who were lower-caste got to eat what was left, or what was important, their families did. It was a more or less quiet understanding. "And why not? They have so little compared to us."

Nicole wore a sweater over her shoulders against the sudden chill of evening. One moment the sun had been a large fiery crimson ball, hanging on the rim of the near mounded hilltops. A brief purple interlude with darker plum shadows followed and, finally, inky darkness. A myriad of stars sparkled before the rising of the moon.

The bearer moved around them, barefoot and silent on the dhurrie-covered floor, serving small cups of bitter dark coffee. Prem produced his precious bottle of Scotch. After placing a brazier of charcoals in the copperhooded firepit, the bearer left them to sip their whiskey and regard the glowing coals.

"It's hard for me to believe we're in the same India, Prem," said Drew. "This is so tranquil, I have a hard time reconciling it with some of the disturbing sights. Despite all the beauty in this country, I've seen a great deal that worries me. I wonder how India can ever hope to overcome its problems."

Prem nodded in the dark. "Yes, I know how you feel. Sometimes I get so desperately discouraged, I'm ready to throw it in and go back to the States. But then, I think of all that has to be done. I ask myself what's more important—making a contribution here, where it counts, or having a fancy lab and living well in Michigan."

The sobering conversation seemed to put Prem in a melancholy frame of mind. He rambled on in a detached tone, a faraway look in his eyes, telling them bizarre tales of rural India—animistic legends that illustrated the backwardness of the people, eerie accounts of secret sects who worshiped the goddess of destruction, Kali, in clandestine rituals, sometimes taking human lives. He told of reports that circulated from time to time about the disappearance of children who were drugged, blinded or mutilated, then set to beg by their captors.

There were weirder stories, reflecting the perils of the exotic fauna of the subcontinent. One, which Nicole hoped was an apocryphal tale, was about a missionary couple serving in an outpost who left the bridge table one evening to check on their infant in the nursery. "All they found was its skeleton, bones picked clean by flesh-eating ants," said Prem. "I've seen such insects."

Nicole could not blot out the mental picture of the unwavering, pulsating black column moving across a lawn, up a bungalow wall, over the windowsill, and down toward the crib where they consumed a sleeping child with malevolent efficiency. She shivered, too upset by the stories to comment. Drew touched her arm reassuringly. His hand remained there for a moment, and she turned to look at him, wishing they were alone, the two of them.

Prem downed the last of his whiskey. "Sorry, Nicole," he apologized. "I don't know what put me on this morbid course." He stretched. "Well, friends, shall we turn in? It's up before dawn tomorrow to see the animals."

Drew climbed into the narrow bed, a thin mattress on a hard wooden plank, firm and comfortable, he discovered. He turned down the lamp and pulled the enveloping mosquito netting closed again. The bearer had sprayed the rooms with Flit, then gone around swinging a perforated brass pomander of burning sandal to mask the odor of the insecticide. The result was a mingled blend of Flit and incense, and the elusive perfume of the jungle night.

The *chowkidar* was making his rounds, knocking his stick against the corner post of the lodge to reassure them that he had not fallen asleep while on duty. As Drew drifted off to sleep, the last sound to reach his ears was the modal whimsy of a reed instrument somewhere in the night.

"Drew! Drew!" an urgent voice whispered. He felt a hand shaking his shoulder. Still half asleep, he mumbled, "What . . . who is it?"

"Drew, it's Nicole. Please wake up."

He came fully awake and sat up. "Nicole? What time is it?"

"I don't know. But Drew, I heard something outside. Something is prowling out there. Something large that breathes heavily and growls."

"You're just imagining things, Nicole," he said, not unkindly. "After those spooky stories tonight, you're hearing things that aren't there."

"No, *really*, Drew. I've been lying awake for a long time. There *is* something out there. I want to stay in here with you. I know nothing can get in, but I won't sleep a wink if I'm alone."

"That's silly, Nicole."

"Well, *I'm staying here*, whether or not you think I'm silly." She swept across the room to the other bed, pulled back the mosquito net and got under the coverlet.

Drew put his pillow up against the wall and leaned back against it, straining his ears. Nothing. He couldn't hear a thing except dogs barking and baying at the waning moon in the distant village. Now he was wide awake and probably wouldn't be able to fall back to sleep. Wasn't that like a woman to wake him for nothing! Why hadn't she just crawled into the damn bed and let him sleep?

He had a vaguely uncomfortable feeling about her being here in the same room with him. He realized how illogical that was. They had been together under the most intimate circumstances for the past twelve weeks. Why should he care if she slept in here? It was because of Prem, of course. He didn't want their friend and colleague on the Task Force to get the wrong idea about them.

"Nicole . . . ?"

"What?"

"Are you mad?"

"*Yes*, I'm mad! What do you suppose?"

Just then there was a low, reverberating, angry snarl that echoed somewhere from the west side of the encampment, through the surrounding jungle.

Drew felt the hairs rise on his neck. "What was that?"

"*That*," said Nicole, "is what I have been hearing for the past half hour." She turned on her side away from him.

Drew got out of bed and went to the window. He looked out but could see nothing unusual. He listened for the *chowkidar*. There was nothing but the peaceful sounds of the night.

It was getting cooler, his feet were cold. Sighing, he moved back to the bed, pulling the covers up around his shoulders. He lay there, terribly aware of Nicole across the room, wishing that he could reach out for her. This nearness was almost more than he could bear.

"Nicole?" he whispered.

There was no answer. Just the regular, even breathing of someone who is sound asleep.

"Chota hazri," said the bearer in his low monotone as he entered the room in the pre-dawn darkness, set down two trays with tea and fruit, and left.

Nicole came awake, realized where she was, and sat up. The tray of bed tea was on a low table next to her. She siped the hot, dark brew. I shall miss this, she thought. It's a good way to begin the day.

Drew swung his feet over the side of his bed. "Good morning, Nicole."

"Good morning." She slipped into her robe.

They were silent, Drew sitting on the edge of his bed, drinking hot tea, Nicole on the rattan chair, cradling a cup in her hands. She rose, looking down at him from the side of her eyes. In dignified silence, she walked out of the room.

In the bathroom the metal tub was filled with tepid water. Like a wraith, the *bheesti* had come and gone through a door connecting the room to the outside. The total lack of privacy still disconcerted Drew. Was there nothing sacrosanct?

After submerging, he dried himself and dressed quickly. Nicole came out of her room as he entered the anteroom. They looked at each other for a moment, uncertain how to act.

Drew grinned and went over to her. "Sorry I was such a grouch," he said, taking both of her hands in his. "Peace?"

"Peace," she echoed. He kissed the top of her head and together they walked out into the morning dew.

Their elephant was waiting, a different one this time, with colored chalk designs around her eyes, forehead, and on her flanks. She was a female, they were assured by the game warden, who spoke hardly any English.

Prem interpreted, "He says, never fear, this is a pregnant female, so the rogue bull won't come after her."

"I wasn't worried, until he said that," Nicole laughed.
"Does she have a name?"

"She is called Shanti," said the warden.

"What a beautiful name."

The *mahout,* standing at the elephant's side, smiled
broadly and saluted them. He touched Shanti on her
enormous foreleg with his *hawkus,* the wooden prod with
a hook on its point. The elephant knelt and extended her
trunk for them to mount, which Prem did to show them
how.

"You next, Drew, so Nicole can sit in front of you and
see everything."

The game warden helped Nicole up, then in one lithe
movement mounted opposite, next to Prem, followed by
the *mahout,* who settled himself on Shanti's neck. A
turbaned attendant handed the game warden a large shotgun. Drew had noticed two rifles strapped to the under-
carriage of the *howdah.*

Shanti covered the ground through the tall grass to the
jungle's edge in a surprisingly short time. The *mahout*
patted her, speaking caressingly, and she slowed her gait
to a dignified gliding motion.

"Animals smell only elephant," the game warden said
in halting English. Again he spoke to Prem in Hindi.

"He says we must be very quiet so the animals won't
know we're here. They'll see only the elephant. The
elephant odor overpowers the human scent. He says that
even the tiger, with its keen sense of smell and sight, will
not detect us."

Nicole leaned close to Drew and whispered, "How
does *he* know? Is he a tiger?"

If there was a track, it was invisible to them. Silently,
the *mahout* communicated with Shanti by touching an ear
or the side of her head. He sat with one leg folded up
under him, the other dangling down against the elephant's flank. They entered the forest and were swallowed by a dense stand of teak and sal, jacarandra and
sandal, and exotic vine-covered trees with flowers and
fruits they had never seen.

Their heads were level with the low-hanging branches.
The air about them was moist with dew and pleasantly
cool. Soon the silvery pre-dawn light turned to a pinkish
glow, and with it, the silence of the jungle was broken by

the warbles and chirps of the earliest risers—the tropical birds who flitted from the trees in bright slashes of color, searching for food and water. Within minutes the jungle had come alive—a chattering, cawing, whooping, scratching, clamorous chorus surrounding them on all sides.

In the roof of foliage overhead, silver-capped langur monkeys swung from branch to branch. Every female had a baby clinging to its body, each wizened little face almost human, staring and wide-eyed. Prem touched their forearms, pointing to the left. Through the meadow of long grasses they saw a lake. This was the destination of all the scurrying beasts and flying birds. Shanti stood still, stretching her trunk up for the tender leaves on top of a sapling, then stuffing them in her mouth. They could hear the rumbling of her stomach and grinding of her teeth as she dined on the dainty morsel. Nicole, fascinated to see that the elephant's hide was bleeding from an insect bite, wondered what could penetrate that wrinkled, leathery gray skin.

They watched, entranced, while the still pool sprang to life with monkeys, sambar, chital, wild pig, swamp deer, antelope, and swooping birds of the most brilliant hue—flaming tangerine, lemon yellow, turquoise, and sea blue. On the far side of the lake, long-legged cranes stood in the shallows, their heads turning slowly in all directions, then quickly darting into the water in quest of food. Golden arrows of light pierced the jungle, playing on the surface of the water, and as they watched, the dawn rose up over the tree tops to blaze the dew-tipped greenery in a sheen of sunlit splendor.

Onward they rambled, through tiger grass that came to Shanti's flanks and brushed their ankles. The *mahout* now patted Shanti soothingly, at the same time extending his prod to the end of her trunk. For they had reached the bathing pool of the wild elephants, and he did not want Shanti to forget that long ago she had forsaken the herd to live in the world of humans. Once that step has been taken, even though not of her own choosing, it must not be altered, for tame, domesticated Shanti could never again survive in the wild.

The watering hole was a deep, muddy pool in which elephants of all sizes, from newborn calves to immense bulls, splashed and romped, rolled and sprayed, squirting

each other and squealing with delight. It was all Nicole
and Drew could do to keep from exclaiming aloud at the
antics of the huge, ungainly beasts who, despite their
size, cavorted with amazing grace.

On through the forest they moved, the sun now fully
risen, filtering down through the leafy green overhead.
The peace of the jungle surrounded them.

Suddenly Shanti came to a halt. She took several steps
backward, shaking her head from side to side. The *mahout*
signaled her with his foot, prodding her flank with the
hooked instrument and holding on to the flap of her ear.
But she was clearly agitated over something. They heard
the game warden engage his shotgun, and sensed the
tension in the two men on the other side of the *howdah*.

There was a thrashing in the thickest part of the grove
in front of them, and a great black elephant thundered
into view. It was a rogue—the most feared male, for he
had been ousted by the herd as an anti-social member.
He was a killer.

Shanti was now flapping her ears violently, raising her
trunk in the air, and in danger of rearing up on her hind
feet. The *mahout* broke the silence and spoke to her,
leaning down to cajole her, while keeping his eyes on the
dangerous rogue. The game warden raised his shotgun
and was sighting the wild bull along the length of the
barrel. Drew hoped he was a good shot.

The rogue was uprooting small trees with his trunk,
chewing off the tender top leaves and throwing the trunks
to the ground, stamping on them in rage. He battered
down a larger tree, charging it with his head, knocking it
over with an ease that sent a thrill of terror through the
five people watching him from Shanti's heaving back.

The rogue was no more than fifty yards from them,
Drew judged. All at once, he swerved in their direction
and for the first time seemed to be aware of Shanti. He
stood there, swinging his long trunk, holding it low,
swaying from side to side. Suddenly, he reared up on his
hind legs, throwing his trunk in the air and letting out a
blood-curdling challenge that rent the still air of the
jungle.

Out of the corner of his eye, Drew saw the game
warden stiffen and correct his aim, prepared for the great
creature's imminent charge. Instinctively, Drew reached

out to hold Nicole, although she seemed unafraid, mesmerized by the fantastic spectacle. Just as they braced themselves for the inevitable attack, the rogue arrested the forward thrust of his body and turned tail, crashing off into the dark recesses of the jungle. The echo of his shrill call reached back to them, reverberating through the thicket.

They stared at the place where he had been, then at each other, open-mouthed and weak with relief. They had not noticed Prem slip the rifle he was holding out of its straps. He rolled his eyes at them and flashed a grin. "Close call!" he whispered.

They returned to the encampment without incident. The jungle was now filled with the noisy din of animals feeding and caring for their young, swinging through branches overhead and skittering along the ground underfoot.

When they reached the clearing, Prem broke the silence. "I say! I thought we were in for it. I was wondering how I was going to explain to Henry if I lost two members of the Task Force. Thought it would be just as well if I didn't survive myself." They all laughed heartily—the laugh of people who have had a brush with danger and come through unscathed.

Dismounting near the lodges, they were greeted by a contingent of villagers who had been waiting since first light to speak to the game warden.

Last night, they told him, a lame female tiger who had been plaguing the district had roamed. A member of the village *panchayat* reported that his prized water buffalo had been killed and dragged into the jungle. However, the tiger had been interrupted by the barking of dogs and fled before she had eaten her fill. In the early hours before dawn, a young bride had gone into the fields to the banks of a *nullah*, where she became the tiger's next victim.

Not to be outdone, *chowkidar* told of discovering the pug marks of the lame tigress just this morning, scarcely fifty meters from the lodge where the visitors were sleeping.

Nicole threw Drew a significant glance.

The game warden had to leave them. He was going with the villagers to organize a hunt for the Man-eater. It must be done without delay, that night, for none of the villagers was safe in the fields as long as the lame tigress remained at large. Having tasted human flesh, she would become bolder and bolder.

A work force was delegated to build a *machan*, the high platform in the branches of a strong tree from which the *shikari*, a professional hunter, would await the tigress. They would bring the bait, a tender young goat, to be tied to a stake on the ground. Beaters would be deployed in outlying parts to drive the tiger inward toward the spot where the armed men would lie in wait.

Prem decided to depart with the game warden, for he had an appointment that afternoon at the University of Jaipur. "Do you two mind staying here until tomorrow morning? I'll send the jeep back for you. You'll be perfectly safe. They'll post guards around the lodges."

They assured him they would enjoy remaining. After breakfast, they waved goodbye as Prem and the game warden rode off on elephant back.

Nicole watched Drew making notes by the light of a kerosene lamp. She noticed how his lashes cast long shadows on his cheeks. The firm, sculpted lips drew in as he wrote. He leaned one arm on the table, his hand occasionally brushing back a lock of hair, his forehead wrinkled in concentration. He was a strong and virile man, yet in the soft glow of the lamp, his face had a romantic quality. His physical presence pulled at her. In these last few weeks, she had become increasingly aware of him.

He raised his head, rubbing his neck.

"You look tired," she said.

He smiled wearily. "I am, a little."

Their eyes met and they gazed at each other.

A feeling of tenderness and longing swept through Nicole. Her hand instinctively raised, as if it would reach out to touch him of its own volition. Closing it, she made a fist and brought it against her chest. She knew she should leave before he was able to read her thoughts.

"I think I'll go to bed now," she said, rising. "Good night, Drew."

He wanted to tell her to stay, but instead he said, "Good night, Nicole. See you in the morning."

He sat staring after her, at the place where she had

stood. All evening he had been conscious of her beauty and his desire for her. It had been an effort, just then, not to rise and take her in his arms. What would have happened if he had? Would she have welcomed him?

She intruded on all of his thoughts now. They had been together for three months, and he constantly had to fight his wish to be close to her.

He turned the lamp down to a dull glow.

Moonlight shone through the screens into the lodge, beckoning him. Opening the door, he walked onto the verandah, looking out over the moondrenched clearing. The bush sang to him . . . crickets in the tall grasses, the hoot of an owl, the howling of jackals in the distance. Heat lightning forked across the sky, high above the surrounding mountains.

Drew raised his head to scan the far horizon. The moon was a golden globe in the endless night sky. He could see scattered brush fires in the hills. Soon the monsoons would come, but now the drought drove predators like the lame tigress down to the lowlands.

How strange that he should be here in this beautiful, troubled land with a lovely woman. She had come into his life when he wanted nothing of women. And yet, he was undeniably drawn to her.

Soon they would part. Back to their own countries, to their dissimilar, separate lives. He would miss her. She had filled an emptiness in him, a need he had not realized was there . . . the need to still his restless heart.

A sharp wind blew across the campground, catching the edge of a wooden shutter, slamming it shut and breaking his reverie.

Leaning against the banister post, he closed his eyes, trying to recall his vision of Julie. Always, he had been able to picture her, to hear her voice, to imagine her standing beside him. Tears welled as he realized he was losing her . . . her image was fading.

What he saw was Nicole. Nicole, holding a dying child in her arms . . . the tenderness of her mouth, the light in her emerald eyes, the soothing melody of her voice.

From a distance now, barely heard, came a thrumming, low and constant, fading in and out on the wind. It was the sound of the beaters stalking the tigress, driving her through the jungle to the center of a circle where the *shikari* awaited his prey.

* * *

Nicole washed in the primitive bathroom. She would not bother to call the *bheesti* to refill the tub with hot water. She had become expert at dousing herself with a bucket, then soaping all over and rinsing afterward. It was simple and effective, as were all customs formed out of necessity.

Soon enough she would be living with the hundreds of unnecessary luxuries she had taken for granted all of her life. It seemed impossible that next week she would be at Casa Loma again, working each day in the department at San Martín Hospital, giving lectures to the students, going on rounds, attending staff meetings, discussing cases with Jorge Alvares, placating Nurse Ramos. Lima, Huaranca, Paris . . . her entire other world seemed an illusion. This was the reality.

Four days. Only four more days until they would leave India. She realized she was not looking forward to returning home. In fact, she wished this trip were just beginning. She would be happy to relive every hour of it, even the time of her illness, for through the haze of weakness and misery she had been aware of Drew's face above her, the anxiety in his eyes, the gentle touch of his hands.

What had happened to her? Every time she looked at him now, she wanted to be held in those arms, wanted to be kissed by those lips. It no longer angered her to know she felt this way. But, except for that one kiss after he had been freed by the kidnappers, he had given not the slightest sign of being attracted to her, despite what Parvati had said.

I'm setting quite a record, she thought wryly. In less than a year, I have practically *offered* myself to two handsome men—and they've both tucked me up and said goodnight!

She put on pajamas and pulled the pins from her hair, unraveling the braid. As she stood vigorously brushing, she heard a loud noise from the front of the lodge. Putting on her robe, she padded barefoot out to the sitting area.

The room was almost dark, the lamp turned low on the table where Drew had been working. He must have gone to bed. Whatever the noise had been, it was quiet now.

A brisk wind stirred the papers on the table and a shutter banged. That must have been what she had heard.

There was a spicy, fresh fragrance on the breeze. She saw the flicker of lightning. Maybe it would rain. Did it ever rain before the monsoons, she wondered. Opening the door, she stepped onto the verandah. The moon had risen, washing the game park with a soft luminescence.

At first, she did not notice Drew standing there, leaning his head against a pillar. He turned at the sound of the door closing, and she could see the gleam of unshed tears in his eyes.

He stood for a moment, his chest rising and falling, the sound of his breathing audible. Then, taking a step toward her, he pulled her into his arms, his mouth coming down to cover hers. Her lips opened to his kiss, releasing all of her pent up passion.

"*Nicole* . . ." his voice was a searing whisper, "I've wanted you so much."

"*Yes . . . oh, yes!*" Her senses were reeling.

Inside the lodge, he kissed her again, crushing her against him. She could feel the beating of his heart against hers. "Your place or mine," he murmured, smiling down at her.

She laughed softly. "Mine has a double bed."

Closing the door to her room, he slid the bolt in place.

She lay in his arms, touching his eyes, his cheek, his lips, the way she had dreamed of doing so many times.

"What is it?" he asked, sensing what was in her mind as she gazed at him. "Are you afraid?"

She nodded, mute.

"So am I, darling. I think I'm in love with you—and that scares the hell out of me." He held her closer.

"Oh, Drew!" She pressed her face against his chest. His arms felt strong around her, his body was warm and perfect, entwined with hers. She wanted to love him, but she couldn't bring herself to form the words. It was as if it was a betrayal of her creed to say *I love you*.

She had never before experienced the lust of a man in his full maturity. The girl who had loved a boy in Paris had been naive and unskilled, and so had the boy, despite his sweet pretensions. This . . . this *oneness* was beyond anything she had ever imagined. When Drew touched her, she could not have stopped herself from responding. Her mouth was as hungry as his, her hands as eager to explore him in all the beauty of his manhood. She felt she could never have enough of him.

"I hurt you, didn't I?" he asked.

"A little, just for a moment, but it wasn't really pain."

"I didn't realize . . . think you would be a virgin."

"I wasn't! It's just been a long time . . . seven years." She sighed, wanting to tell him. "I was twenty and he was twenty-four, and we were in love. I was a medical student in Paris then. . . . Do you know what it's like to be young and in love in Paris?"

Gently, "They write songs about that."

"Well, that's the way it was—like a love song."

"What happened?"

"He was killed. In Israel, in the Six Day War. Only, he died on the sixteenth day, after it was all over. It left me with a terrifying bitterness—and a fear of ever falling in love again."

Softly he caressed her face, smoothed the length of her hair. His lips touched her eyelids and throat, and then he kissed her deeply as his hands moved over her body.

"Don't be afraid, Nicole," he whispered. "Let's help each other not to fear love." Drew began to love her again, touching and kissing her body with a slow tenderness. He was seized with a passion that was far beyond mere physical attraction. He had a compulsion to know her soul, to immerse himself in her heart and thoughts, her entire being.

When at last they slept in the hour before dawn, they did not hear the distant shots ring out, the brief space of silence that followed, and then the echo of shouts sounding through the jungle, from the center of the circle.

Chapter 20

Drew sat with Nicole in her room at the guest house while she used a borrowed typewriter to draft her report for the Task Force.

"If I don't get this done now, it won't be fresh in my mind," she told him. "Besides, I'll be swamped when I return to Lima."

He smiled. "I like it when you use American slang. It always comes as a surprise."

"You forget, I spent two years in the States!" She pulled the final page from the typewriter, stacking the papers with an air of satisfaction. "I'll proof it later. Right now, I could use a bath and a nap."

He looked at her longingly. "I wish I could join you. How strict are they here?" He took her in his arms.

"It's probably not such a good idea," she said regretfully.

"I'm accustomed to you now, seeing you every day. How will I stand being away from you?"

She looked into the warm, ocean blue of his eyes, loving the happiness there. His habitual scowl, that troubled expression she'd seen when she first met him, had vanished, leaving him younger looking, handsomer.

"I'll miss you, too, chéri. But, we'll see each other at least three times a year, at the IHTF meetings."

"That's not enough. I want to be with you *always*."

He was serious! She touched his lips with her fingers. "Shhh. . . . Don't spoil the little time we have left. Let's pretend the distance and the time in between aren't as great. That will make it easier."

But Drew knew nothing would make it easy for him. He was in love with Nicole. Completely and impossibly in love.

Last night, lying alone in his bed at Robert and Jane's house in Lodi Estates, his arms had felt empty. *One night.* One night with her had done this to him! Made him acknowledge something he had been fighting for the past three months, fighting daily, because as he reviewed their time working together, he realized how often he had hungered for her, pretending to himself that he was simply sexually deprived and would find any woman attractive.

It was ironic. Here was the one woman he wanted, the only woman in the world, and he was not at all certain she would ever be his. They lived a hemisphere apart. If it were not for the extraordinary circumstances that had brought them together, they would never even have met.

Robert was waiting for him in his automobile when he said goodbye to Nicole in the entryway of the guest house. Watching them together, Rob evidently detected the intense emotion between them.

"You two aren't fooling anyone!" he said when Drew got into the car. "Even I—dense as Jane says I am about such matters—can see what's going on with you and Nicole!"

Drew laughed, flushing. "She's just about the most wonderful thing that's ever happened to me, Rob."

Robert grinned. "Fantastic! She's a great woman, Drew. Are you going to get married?"

"I don't know. It's not that easy. Her work is in Peru, and mine's in Philadelphia. One of us would have to make a change."

Robert nodded. "Or both of you."

"What do you mean?"

"I mean, if you both left your present jobs and went to work for the WHO or one of the other international agencies—or even a foundation—that would be a compromise."

Drew regarded Robert thoughtfully. "That's a very interesting idea. How come I didn't think of it?"

Robert laughed. "Simple. I'm a lot smarter than you are!"

It *was* a good idea, but he knew he didn't want to leave Penn. His work there, combining research and clinical medicine, was perfect and he wasn't about to give it up. *Someone's* work had to have priority, and he thought it should be his. Nicole would have to be the one to make a move. He was sure she would, once she agreed to marry him. . . .

That night sitting in the screened patio after Robert and Jane had retired, they realized they could not say goodbye, not yet. There would have to be a few more days together, stolen days, somewhere enroute.

"We could go to Bombay," Drew suggested.

"Too hot."

"How about spring skiing in Austria?"

"Too cold."

"Where then? You decide."

"I know! Come to Paris with me. We can stay at my apartment."

"Sensational!"

Their kisses aroused in him the deepest passion and need. With his heart pounding, he held her against himself, scarcely able to breathe. They belonged to each other now. If only he could convince her that it could be no other way, that their lives were destined to be lived together. Overcome with emotion, he stared at her in wonder. She was quite simply the most beautiful woman he had ever known.

Leisurely Sunday afternoons had been introduced to India by the British during the Raj, never to be taken away.

Families were picnicking in Lodi Gardens, despite the hot weather, strolling beneath the shade of banyan trees or sitting on the grass-carpeted steps of the tombs. The hot dry breath of the *loo,* the pre-monsoon wind that blows from the Great Indian Desert depositing fine particles of dust everywhere, produces a stupor in foreigners who are unused to the intense heat, but the Indians persevere.

Drew squinted in the glare. A cloud of red dust rose in front of the automobile in the wake of a motor scooter carrying husband, wife, and two children. The ideal Indian family, he thought. A son, a daughter. *Ek, do, bas.* as the family planning posters said. One, two, enough!

He was on his way to visit Colonel Ranjit Kar, Indian Army Medical Corps, Retired. Colonel Kar had been a friend of his stepfather's during World War II, when Arthur Hillman was stationed in India with the U.S.

Army Medical Corps. It had been difficult to arrange a
meeting with the colonel, but Drew had promised Arthur
he would see him.

The Kar bungalow was spacious, furnished with hints
of the luxury Ranjit Kar must have known growing up as
the son of a rajah. Upholstered couches of English manufacture and lustrous carpets from Kashmir and Afghani-
stan softened the starkness of polished marble floors.
Modern oil paintings and antique Indian wood carvings
adorned the walls. Someone with a good eye and a knowledge of Western art had designed these rooms.

A beam of light from a window fell on the colonel's
disfigured face. Drew's stepfather had told him how Ranjit
Kar had been severely burned in a gas explosion near the
end of the war. Through a fortunate coincidence, Arthur
had been able to arrange for an American eye surgeon to
operate, saving the sight in one eye. Later, Colonel Kar
had gone to the States, where additional surgery had
restored partial vision in the second eye.

"So you are the youngest son," said the colonel. His
speech was clipped British English, and in his white bush
jacket, he had an impressive bearing, despite the feeble-
ness of advancing years. Removing a pair of dark glasses,
he placed them on a rosewood table inlaid with mother-
of-pearl.

"My wife is in Bombay visiting her sister. She'll be
sorry to have missed you. How much longer will you be
in Delhi, Andrew?"

"I leave tomorrow. I'm sorry not to have seen you
earlier, sir, but I wasn't able to reach you."

"I was away. Visiting my children. My daughter's husband is a diplomat at our embassy in Stockholm."

A bearer served drinks and puffed lotus seeds. Colonel
Kar had whiskey and soda, Drew *nimbupani*.

For a while they chatted about Drew's work. Colonel
Kar was interested in the smallpox eradication campaign,
knowing a great deal about it from his days in the Indian
Health Ministry.

"Tell me," Kar inquired, "how are your parents?"

"They're fine. They both send their regards."

"Wonderful chap, Arthur! Molly, too. *Lovely* woman,
Molly. We had some fine times together during the war,
the three of us. That was quite a period in our lives."

The *three* of them? Drew hadn't realized his mother was acquainted with Colonel Kar then. He thought they had met for the first time when Molly and Arthur visited India in 1962, *after* their marriage. The colonel's memory must be getting hazy.

"During the war, sir?"

"Yes! We managed to enjoy ourselves between the duty. When Arthur was recuperating from his wounds, we got away. My wife stayed in Bombay until I had my accident, but Arthur and Molly kept me company. I remember going off to the hills together. . . ."

The most eery sensation came over Drew as he listened to the colonel's words. He had the feeling that a door was opening.

Why had he never heard that Molly and Arthur had met in India during the war? He knew they both had served here . . . but not *together*, not in the same place! He held his breath, waiting, *willing* Kar to go on.

The colonel spoke half to himself, his eyes on a distant horizon. "I was so pleased when they finally married," he said. "They should have been married back then, you know . . . it would have been the right thing. They loved each other. Any fool could have seen that. . . ."

The man seemed to be dozing, his lowered lids hooding the damaged eyes with their dilated pupils. The unscarred hemisphere of his face was turned toward Drew, the profile noble. He had been a handsome man in his youth, one could tell. Before the accident.

"Where were they?" Drew prompted gently, his voice barely above a whisper.

"In Calcutta . . . and Darjeeling. We had a tea garden there, my family's. The two of them went up alone for a spell. The war was almost over by then. . . ." He sighed, looking up. "Ah well, all's right in the end. Each thing in its appointed season, eh? *Karma . . . destiny.*" He suddenly appeared years younger, a sprightliness in the set of his shoulders, a gleam in the dim eyes.

Stunned, Drew sat there immobilized, unable to speak.

Regretfully, the colonel rose. "It's time for my rest, Andrew. I'm glad you came. I like to have young people around. Your brother used to visit . . . I always liked Robert."

My brother!

Drew left the Kar bungalow in a daze.

There had always been so many questions. *Was this the answer?*

He had *known* that Sean Tower could not have been his real father! He had seen the medical reports when he helped his mother pack up the house in Geneva. . . . Sean had been ill by the time Drew was born, too ill to father a child. His trunk and lower extremities were already paralyzed with multiple sclerosis.

Was Arthur Hillman his father?

Drew could hardly ask his mother that question. It was probably wishful thinking, anyway.

But . . . *if they had been together in India near the end of the war?*

The Second World War had ended in the summer of '45. . . . The date of his birth was December 15, 1945.

BOOK III

Tempest

Chapter 21

She was a changed person. When she left Peru in January, Nicole could not have foreseen the transformation this assignment would make in her. More purposeful, self-confident, and questioning, she knew that India and the experiences of the last three months had given her strength, knowledge, and skills she had never before possessed. She was determined to put her newly gained expertise to work in her own country, for that was the purpose of the International Health Task Force—to improve medical care throughout the underprivileged world by sharing the experiences and knowledge they gained in their research and field work, adapting and applying them to the needs of each country.

She was eager to begin.

With soaring spirit, she peered down from the 747's cruising altitude of 36,000 feet onto the splendor of the jagged white spine of the Cordillera Blanca. Filled with a profound pride, she contemplated the kingdom of her Inca heritage. Majestic and forbidding though they were, the mountains welcomed her after the endless flight over the dense green carpet of the Amazon. It was May. She had always found autumn the most beautiful time of year in the Andes, and as she gazed at the sparkling pinnacles, she hungered for Flor del Viento.

The plane's cabin was thick with the odor of cigarette smoke. Even though she was sitting in the no-smoking section, her lungs felt as if they needed airing. She had almost forgotten how constantly Europeans and South Americans smoked.

They would reach Lima in less than an hour. She had called home from Caracas, asking Vera to send Pedro with a car to fetch her. Vera said that Señor Caldeiro had already called to tell her not to have the chauffeur go, because he would drive to the airport himself to meet the señorita. That had annoyed Nicole, but she was glad it had not come as a surprise. This way, there was time to prepare herself for seeing Manuel again.

How did he always manage to know when she was arriving? Each time she returned from a trip abroad, Manuel would be waiting for her when she came through Passport Control. Last week, she had changed her original reservations when she and Drew had decided to stop in Paris.

Paris!

She let her mind dwell on the past five days, the stolen hours that had been the most blissful of her life. And this, perhaps, had wrought an even more remarkable change in her. For, emotionally, she had opened like a flower to the strength and intimacy of Drew's love. She marveled at her response to him. To his sweetness, his tenderness, the way he curbed his own desire to bring her to fulfillment.

And not just in their lovemaking was this so. Every moment together had been magical, even the simplest act having importance and meaning, as long as they were together. There had come a certain moment yesterday afternoon when her joy was almost uncontainable. It had been a sublime spring day, the kind of weather that makes Paris its most delightful. They wandered in and out of shops and art galleries on the Ile St. Louis, stopping for an aperitif at a tiny café. Arms around each other, they ambled across the footbridge to the Cité, feeding the last of their *glaces* to pigeons, and pausing to watch a street mime in the park behind Notre Dame.

Drew turned his head to look down at her and said, "Do you know, this is the first time I have ever seen you really have *fun?*"

She caught hold of his hand and kissed it, closing her eyes and wanting to hold onto that fragment of time, realizing the truth of his words. It was as if a pall had lifted, freeing the joyful spirit imprisoned within her for so long. Drew reveled in her animation and vivacity, encouraging her to tell him about the years of her girlhood in this beautiful, romantic city. He responded to her merriment with laughter, as she regaled him with stories about her father's attempts to come to terms with rearing an adolescent daughter.

"He would never allow me to cut my hair! Can you imagine what it was like to have *pigtails* in my first year of medical school?"

"If I'd been there, I would have dipped them in the inkwell," he responded teasingly, hugging her.

And later, back in the apartment, wrapped in each other's arms, he had sunk his strong hands into the shining black mass of her unraveled hair, burying his face in the silky waves. His voice was heavy with desire as he murmured, "I'm glad your hair was never cut. It's the most erotic part of the many beautiful parts of you that I love."

Saying goodbye to him this morning had been painful. They would not see each other again until the end of June, when the Task Force met in Geneva. It was going to be difficult hiding their involvement from the other members of the IHTF, but she thought it was necessary.

Drew had not agreed. "What difference does it make, darling?"

"It matters, Drew. The first time they send a man and a woman out in the field together, to have this happen—you know what they'd say."

"It didn't happen until the end, and it didn't interfere with our work—not for a minute!"

"That's true," she acknowledged.

"What about the other women in the group?"

"What about them? They're both married!"

He had promised, for her sake, to say nothing. They would not be given a field assignment again for a long time, in any case, and then probably not together.

She had a sinking feeling when she thought of the many weeks until they would see each other again. She recalled her father's words about his love affair with Isabelle: *Some relationships thrive on separations.* Somehow, she did not feel that would be true of hers and Drew's.

Nor did he. The first day in Paris, he suddenly said, "We could get married, Nicole."

And for a moment, she was so supremely happy that she wanted to hold the feeling, the inrush of surprised air, the quickening of her heartbeat. But all she had answered was, "It's too soon, chéri. Let's wait. There are so many things to work out."

Drew had not mentioned marriage again. That was just as well, she reasoned, for she would have had a difficult time resisting him. And resist she must, no matter how hard, for she had her work to do and she was committed to it. It would be a betrayal of all the faith and hope Jorge Alvares had placed in her if she deserted the program in Peru. Henry Campion, too, would be disappointed in her, for he had selected her for the Task Force as a representative from Peru, a country that was part of the developing world.

Life sometimes demanded sacrifices. She had told herself many times over the years that she would never marry, and although she questioned that decision from time to time, she had never before been seriously tempted to change her mind.

This time it was different, though. Drew had touched a place within her that no one else had been able to reach since Erik. There had been moments in Paris when she wanted nothing more than to spend the rest of her life with him. In the past week, when she awakened in the mornings to find him warm and eager beside her, when he stirred her flesh with his hands and mouth and looked at her with adoration, she was carried to such supreme heights that she wondered how she could ever bear to leave him when the time came.

Yet, despite the strength of her feelings, she had not told him she loved him. Like the tears she had been unable to weep as a child at the graves of her loved ones, the language of love remained locked inside her, as if to release it would leave her open to still more grief and sorrow. It was her last defense, to withhold those words.

Her plane was scheduled to leave Paris an hour before Drew's. When they kissed goodbye at the airport, the realization that they would not spend the next day together, or the day after that, had brought tears to her eyes.

"God, I'll miss you," Drew whispered as he put his arms around her.

She left him standing at the gate, hands in pockets, with that sweet-sad look of need that had first churned her emotions in a sweltering health station on the northern plains of India.

Now there was Lima.

With trepidation, she wondered what awaited her at San Martín Hospital. She had the feeling she was on the brink of a new phase in her professional life. . . . How had the mobile clinics progressed while she was away? How had her absence affected her relationships with her colleagues? Had this assignment in India been viewed as further proof of her elitist position? All of the challenges and problems at the hospital came back to her in a rush of familiarity, like a discarded possession discovered after months of disuse.

The pilot announced their approach to Lima. There was a flurry of activity in the cabin as passengers put aside blankets and pillows, smoothed hair, straightened ties, and gathered reading material and personal belongings from the pockets of their seats.

Nicole checked her handbag to be certain her passport and landing card were together. On an impulse, she opened her wallet to look at the snapshot of herself with Drew and Parvati in an Indian village near Darbhanga. The photograph was not very good, but it showed Drew's face clearly, his rugged good looks pronounced. He was smiling, and the characteristic way he had of holding his head a little to the side caused a sudden wave of longing to course through her.

I do love him, she thought. *I must be in love with him, the way he makes me feel!*

The seat belt sign had flashed on, followed by the no-smoking sign. Nicole looked out the window as the plane circled over the blue Pacific and came in on a straight approach for landing. It was a rare clear day above Lima.

At the instant the wheels touched Peruvian soil, Nicole was struck anew by the knowledge that, with her father gone, she was coming home to no one.

Manuel Caldeiro paced nervously back and forth in the customs office at Jorge Chavez International Airport. A look of concern darkened his gray-blue eyes, casting a saturnine shadow over his aristocratically handsome features. Stubbing out a cigarette, he lit another, the long planes of his cheeks drawing in as he inhaled.

Nicole's flight was three hours late. She did not expect

him to meet her, but his secretary had pulled strings to check the manifests of all arriving flights that week, and Nicole's name was on today's Air France flight from Paris via Caracas.

Would she be happy to see him, he wondered, or would she resent his being there? Nicole was unpredictable. On those occasions when she was receptive and affectionate, it reinforced his conviction that if he hung in, he would win her in the end. But often, particularly during the weeks just before she had left on this trip, she had been aloof. In all the time she had been gone, he had received only one short letter and some post cards from New Delhi. For over a month, he had heard nothing at all.

At times he almost hated her, when he reflected on the years of his life consumed with wanting her. There had been a certain relief in her absence from Lima. These had been tranquil months for him. Since there was no possibility of seeing her, he was not continually thinking about her. When she was here, a phone call away, a few miles distant, she was constantly on his mind, giving his life a sense of urgency and expectation. Or despair.

What would he do about Elena?

Recently they had been spending most nights together and taking many long, leisurely weekends at her villa. Their retreats had not even interfered with the secret negotiations, the plans he and his fellow conspirators were devising. They had to be careful. All political activities were forbidden by the military government. The villa, accessible but secluded, was a convenient hideaway for a private meeting with one or two of his confederates. Elena was discreet and completely loyal.

The time had been sweet, and if it were not for Nicole, he would marry Elena and be content for the rest of his life. He had tried to tell Elena how he felt, to explain what he did not understand himself. Her answer had only increased his enormous guilt.

"Once I said I wouldn't wait forever, but that's not true, Manuel. Whatever I can have of you, my darling, I'll take. Because without you, there's nothing for me." The strangest part of it was, he really could not imagine his life without Elena.

They were announcing the flight from Caracas. Nicole

was here! He was aware of that old thrill surging through his body. And dread.

How patrician she was, he thought, as she extended her cheeks in greeting. Despite the simplicity of her taupe woolen slacks and silk shirt, she was the elegant Nicole he had anticipated. Her sleek smoothness belied the fact that she had been traveling all day. Cool and imperturbable, she was the enigma that had intrigued him from the first time he had seen her.

"Lima wasn't the same without you," he told her, his long cheeks creased in a smile.

"How did you know when I was arriving?" she asked, a laugh in her voice. "Thank you for meeting me," she added. He hoped she meant it.

In the car, he raised the dividing glass, giving them privacy in the rear. "You'll find Lima changed," he said. "All everyone talks about these days is politics."

"That sounds like nothing has changed," she answered. "As I remember, that was all anyone *ever* talked about!"

"No, but it's different now. You'll see what I mean."

They drove past creeping adobe slums that mingled with the starkness of the buff-colored hills outlining the city. "It all looks the same to me," said Nicole.

At the door of Casa Loma Vera greeted them with tears, thankful for Nicole's safe return. She had worried about her mistress, so far away in that godforsaken, heathen corner of the world. Only four servants were left, she told them, in addition to Pedro and the gardener. The others had departed for the countryside to return to their families in these troubled times. It was better this way, Vera assured Nicole. Fewer people to supervise, to make certain they were not stealing.

Manuel accepted Nicole's half hearted invitation to stay for dinner. He knew she was tired and would probably prefer him to take his leave, but she could rest tomorrow. Tonight he wanted to be with her. He pushed from his mind the thought of Elena, waiting at her house for his call.

After dinner, they had coffee and cognac in the library, where a fragrant eucalyptus fire was lit against the chill of evening. The flames cast a rosy glow on the warm rubbed walnut panelling and the walls of books and pre-Columbian artifacts. They sat separately on deep, pillowed, rust velvet couches, facing each other across the fireplace.

All through dinner Nicole had fought sleep. Her eyelids felt leaden as she answered Manuel's searching questions about India and her work there. "Just today in the paper I read that India is having one of the worst smallpox epidemics in years," he said. "How can you say they're nearing the goal of eradication?"

"It's a question of where the disease is occurring, Manuel, and how effectively it is being contained," she answered wearily. "More than half of all the world's smallpox is in India. The reason we're finding so many cases is that the system of reporting has improved. They were always there—they just weren't being recorded. The disease *will* be prevented from spreading." Tolerant of his skeptical smile, she said, "It won't be long, I assure you. In a year or two, the world will have seen the last of smallpox."

"I'll believe it when it happens." Manuel put out his cigarette. "Well, little one, I should let you get to bed. You're probably exhausted."

"Yes, I am. I'm still working on Delhi time."

"You must have adjusted a little in Paris," he said casually, as they walked through the tapestry-hung gallery. "How long were you there?"

Tired as she was, her antennae bristled. She sensed he was testing her veracity.

"Just a few days," she answered. "But I was so wound up, I didn't really sleep well." Was it possible that Manuel had some way of knowing when she had arrived at her apartment in Paris? And if so, what else did he know?

They had reached the front door.

"When do you go back to work?" he asked.

"First thing Monday morning. And I can imagine what's awaiting me in the department!"

"I don't like to bring this up now, knowing how sensitive you are on the subject." He hesitated.

"Yes?"

"It's no longer safe for you to drive yourself around Lima, Nicole. While you've been gone, there have been a number of abductions . . . and murders. A young woman who is known to be from the upper class is a prime target."

"Manuel, I'm really very tired tonight. Can't we discuss this another time?" Nicole tried to contain her irritation.

"Yes, of course we can. But I can assure you I'm serious. You don't have to take my word for it—just ask anyone. Most people we know have bodyguards now, or at least their drivers are armed."

Nicole laughed. "Can you imagine poor old Pedro carrying a gun?" She patted his arm. "Good night, Manuel. I'll speak to you in a few days."

Sitting in his car, he realized he had been *dismissed!* He felt angry with her, a rage welling in his breast.

Why was she so pig-headed when he made a simple suggestion that was for her safety? She had no understanding of what had been happening in Lima, in all of Peru—even before she had gone off on her globe-trotting mission. He had been telling her the truth. All of the wealthy people he knew in Lima had hired armed guards to protect them when they rode in their limousines.

What if something were to happen to Nicole? The daughter of a well-known banker had been abducted, held for ransom, and after the ransom had been paid, they had found her body, raped and mutilated by torture, on a roadside in the sierra. A leftist guerrilla group had claimed responsibility for the atrocity. The government was, of course, unable to stop them—as it was powerless to cope with all the immense political and economic problems of the country!

He lit a cigarette, inhaling deeply to calm himself. The thought of such an outrage inflicted on Nicole had unnerved him. He could not bear the idea of another man laying a hand on her in violence . . . or in love. Seeing her again, spending these few hours with her, had rekindled his ardor, enflamed his desire to possess her, completely and unalterably.

She had been distant, but she was tired after her long flight. There was a strain between them, which was natural after their separation. He must give her time to readjust to being at home, to feeling comfortable with him again.

Perhaps he *had* been behaving in too overbearing a fashion with her before she went away. She had accused him of taking a paternal attitude, of watching over her as if he were her guardian. But why wouldn't he? Daniel had appointed him an executor and trustee of his estate. In truth, he *did* consider himself her guardian, for hadn't he given his word to her father that he would be her protector?

He had been more than surprised at the maturity and tenacity with which Nicole had performed her various duties related to Daniel's holdings. Not only in connection with the terms of the will, but on the board of Légende et Cie.

Tonight she had seemed older, more assured. Traveling alone around the world, working under the rigorous conditions she had described, had made her even more independent than she had always been. He knew with certainty that he would have a difficult time persuading her that she had to take precautions to protect herself from harm in Lima and when she traveled to the hacienda in Huaranca. And he must convince her that there was no longer any possibility of her going alone to the *barriadas* or out to villages in the countryside, as she had insisted on doing in the past.

But there was something else he had noticed about Nicole, from the moment she had stepped off the plane this afternoon. He couldn't pinpoint it, because it was an elusive quality. There was a luminescence about her, a vibrancy that was new. It was an inner excitement that emanated from her, and he had never seen it before in all the years he had known her.

Something was different about Nicole. What was it? There was no doubt in his mind that she had changed. It increased her allure for him, leaving him all the more resolved to make her his own.

Chapter 22

The *garua* clung to the city like a shroud.

Early morning traffic moved in a slow, ghostly procession. Its headlights barely penetrating the winter fog, a bus stopped in front of San Martín University Hospital to discharge a single passenger.

With shoulders hunched against the dampness, Pepe hurried past the sentries to the hospital's service entrance. Once inside, he pulled a handcart from the basement hallway and rolled it into the open elevator, closing the gates and releasing the lever. The elevator slowly rose to the second floor, where cart and passenger emerged, turning right down a corridor to the Department of Maternal and Child Health.

In the rear of the department, Pepe unlocked a storage closet. One of the overhead lights was burned out and he had trouble reading the labels on cartons stored in the recesses of the windowless room.

He consulted the list again: syringes, broad spectrum antibiotics, isoniazid, pediatric vaccines . . . antiseptics, analgesic salves, dressings and bandages. After loading the boxes on the cart, he made sure the lights were off and relocked the door.

As he backed from the elevator on the ground floor, pulling the heavily loaded cart, a woman's voice called, "Where are you going with those, young man?"

Pepe looked around to meet the cold eyes of Mona Ramos, the head nurse of the clinics, standing in her familiar attitude, arms folded, a ring of keys hanging at her waist.

"Oh! S-señorita Ramos," he stuttered. Why should he be nervous? He wasn't doing anything wrong, but Nurse Ramos had an unnerving effect on him.

She folded her arms. "I asked you a question."

"We're holding a mobile clinic in Villamaria today, but some of our vaccines and bandages haven't arrived, so I'm taking these temporarily . . ." His voice trailed off.

"On whose authority?"

"I have an order here somewhere." He fished in his trousers pocket and handed her a slip of paper.

The nurse put on spectacles and studied the wrinkled form. "Doctora Légende," she enunciated slowly. Without raising her head, her eyes moved up to regard Pepe.

He shifted uncomfortably. "May I go now, señorita? They're waiting at the clinic." He smiled weakly, hating himself for his lack of spine.

She pocketed the requisition and waved him away. "Go."

His eyes followed her uneasily as she strode down the corridor. When she had turned the corner, he pushed the laden handcart out to the receiving area. Walking across to the parking spaces, he climbed into a van and backed it up to the loading dock.

As he transferred the medical supplies to the van, Pepe did not glance up at a window overlooking the courtyard. If he had, he might have been disquieted to see the figure of Señorita Ramos, who watched with folded arms and a speculative expression on her face until he drove away.

Jorge Alvares appeared weary when he ushered Nicole into his office, but it was an improvement over the way he had looked a month ago. When she returned from India, she had been shocked at how much he had aged during her absence. Nicole heard from one of the other doctors that Alvares had been under pressure from the university's chancellor, a junta appointee, who had accused the professor of anti-government sympathies. There was an increasing sentiment against the United States in official Peru these days, and since Alvares's department had received grants from North American foundations to support its research and clinical programs, that was enough to cast suspicion on him.

Nicole knew there was another reason why Jorge Alvares had cause to resent and fear the junta. Alvares was the youngest son of one of Peru's great, traditional landholding families, the Forty-five Families of the oligarchy, who had long controlled all of Peru's land, resources, and major industries.

When he was a young man, instead of joining one of his family's business enterprises, Jorge had decided to study medicine. The family arranged for him to attend medical school in the United States, expecting their son to return to Lima to open a prestigious medical practice catering to the elite of the capital. They were scandalized when he announced his intention of teaching at San Martín University Medical School and attaching himself to the Maternal and Child Health Clinic for the poor. Jorge further alienated himself from them when he adopted the use of one of his mother's family names, so that he would not be identified with the oligarchy.

With the advent of the junta, Alvares's family had been broken in wealth and landholdings. Despite their estrangement, Nicole thought he must still have a filial affection for them and feel grieved at their misfortunes.

"I don't know how much longer we can support the mobile clinics, Nicole," Alvares now told her with regret. "It wouldn't be wise to renew our grant from the Cartwright Foundation at this time, and the government won't give us more money. They can't, truthfully. They're on the verge of bankruptcy." He shook his head. "How has this happened to a country with the great natural resources we have? But, I mustn't talk about this here—" he let his eyes wander around the room and laughed, "the walls have ears!"

Nicole was startled. Surely he didn't mean that his office was bugged?

"I'll be going to Geneva in a few weeks for a Task Force meeting, Dr. Alvares. Shall I inquire about applying for WHO support for the clinics?"

"That would be perfect! Non-aligned, and above reproach."

"Meanwhile, may we continue to borrow supplies from the department? We're always a week or two behind in receiving our shipments."

Concern furrowed his brow. "How many times have you done that?"

She thought for a minute. "Only twice, in addition to the day you first suggested it. We always return everything as soon as the orders arrive. The department isn't at all short of inventory."

He gave her a significant look. "You know how bureaucratic the administration can be. Don't take anything unless it's absolutely necessary."

He must be referring to Mona Ramos, she thought. No one else in the administration would know or care.

Professor Alvares handed her a folder. "Here are your articles, my dear. There are a few notes in the margins. I've made no important changes, except to remove my name as a co-author from the report on the Lima project." He cocked his head and said, with a sparkle of humor in his eye, "You know I had nothing to do with the study, Nicole."

"It's customary . . ." she began.

He waved it aside. "Yes, I know. It's customary for a chief to be given co-authorship when one of his staff writes a paper, whether or not he makes a contribution. I have never approved of that practice. I have a rule that I don't allow my name to be listed unless I've actually done part of the work."

Nicole smiled in admiration. "Thanks. That's generous of you."

She scanned the title page of the first paper: "The Smallpox Eradication Program in Bihar State, India, as a Model for Comprehensive Rural Health Care in Developing Countries." Drew and Parvati were listed as coauthors. This was an expanded report of their work in India, to be published as an article in the *WHO Chronicle.* She was submitting a second paper, focusing on the epidemiological aspects of smallpox eradication, to the *International Journal of Epidemiology.*

"I'm delighted that you're publishing, Nicole. It's very important, both for you and for the department."

Nicole thanked him again as she took her leave. She felt a true affection for Alvares. He was brilliant, selflessly dedicated, and one of the most modest men she had encountered in medicine. As she walked through the lab to her office, she thought how good it was to see him looking happier than he had four weeks before.

Back at her desk, she was going over Professor Alvares's marginal notes on the papers when her telephone rang. The secretary had left for the day, so she picked up the receiver.

"Back from the mysterious East, I see." Nicole recognized Lucy Monaco's low voice.

"Lucy! I've tried to reach you a couple of times. I returned weeks ago."

"Let's have lunch. I want to hear about India."

"Lunch is difficult. I can never get away from the hospital. Would you like to come here?"

A few days later, Lucy arrived at Nicole's office in time for the midday meal. Nicole was glad to see her. She enjoyed Lucy's droll humor and lively conversation.

In the dining room, Lucy listened with interest while Nicole talked about her three months in India. Over coffee, she said, "Someday I'd like to see one of your mobile clinics—remember, you promised me?"

"You've come at a good time. I'm going out to check on a clinic this afternoon. Want to come along?"

Lucy looked at her watch. "Splendid! I have until 4:30, when I pick up Francisco, my little boy, at his school."

They drove to the *barriada* in Nicole's car. Along the way, Nicole told Lucy about the problems they were having with the clinic program, explaining how short of money they were because their government funds had dried up.

"We only need a few thousand *soles* a week for maintenance and medical supplies," she said. "There aren't any salaries to pay—we depend on medical students and house staff to volunteer their time. And the vans were donated by a private foundation. It's such a short-sighted policy!"

"Sometimes the policy has nothing to do with the real reasons," said Lucy.

"What do you mean?"

"I've heard rumors that the clinics are considered . . . subversive."

Nicole could not contain her surprise and anger. "*Subversive!* What can be subversive about bringing health care into the slums, where it's most needed?"

"I agree with you, but there are some people who think their *real* purpose is to provide health care for dissidents."

"Lucy!" Nicole did not try to disguise her shock and unease. "That just isn't true! Why would anyone think that?"

Lucy shrugged her shoulders. "Nicole, you've been very visible about going out into the countryside . . ."

"I've been visible about it because I have nothing to hide! I've gone with our students and some Peace Corps volunteers."

"The military sees either the CIA or a Maoist plot behind everything these days, especially where students are involved. And that includes the Peace Corps."

"Well, they're wrong about the mobile clinics. *I'm* the one who planned them, and I can assure you I'm neither an agent for the CIA nor a Maoist!"

Lucy was deadly serious. "Just be careful, Nicole. You're known by the company you keep."

"Everyone has become so cautious in Lima. That's all I've heard since I came home—be careful."

"With good reason," said Lucy. She told Nicole that she had more than thirty clients from all walks of life who had been arrested, some of them still being held without specific charges. "I'm feeling most pessimistic about legal rights in Peru, Nicole. This country has a history of military regimes, but it's been a long time since there have been the kinds of abuses I find these days."

"Why now?" asked Nicole. "The government seems firmly in power."

"That's an illusion. The economy is on the brink of disaster. The junta doesn't have popular support from any faction. They say theirs is a leftist revolution, but they're scared to death of the communists. In fact, they're afraid of everyone. Ever since Allende was overthrown in Chile last year they expect the Americans will try to stage a countercoup here."

"I've never been interested in politics, Lucy. I never thought I had to be. As a doctor, I don't get involved with political factions. I'm just concerned with *people.*"

Lucy shook her head. "That sounds easy, but it's not that simple. Sooner or later, everyone gets involved in politics."

As they entered the clinic, held in a storefront, with the van used as a dispensary, Nicole pointed out Pepe and Carlos, who were examining babies. "Those are the medical students I mentioned to you. Pepe, the shorter boy, is the one who was beaten up." Nicole had told her friend about that day and her visit to Pepe's apartment.

Lucy now looked at Pepe with interest. "Introduce me when we go over there," she said. "He'll probably be in trouble again, and he may want a lawyer."

That's just what Lucy needs, thought Nicole, another impoverished student for a client.

By the time they were ready to leave the clinic, it was later than they had expected. Nicole offered to call for Lucy's son on their way back to the hospital, where Lucy had parked her car.

"I'm surprised you're going around without a driver, Nicole," Lucy said when they were in the automobile. "Very few women do these days."

"So Manuel Caldeiro informed me," she said, before she could prevent herself. "He almost insisted I hire a bodyguard, as well as use a driver."

Lucy regarded her thoughtfully. "That's not such a bad idea. I think you might consider it."

"You're kidding!" Nicole was amazed.

"No, I'm quite serious. I know . . . I don't follow my own advice, but it's different for me. I doubt that anyone is going to kidnap me and hold me for ransom. I'm known as the lawyer lady who defends those guys!"

Nicole did not reply. She was more than surprised that Lucy would tell her she should follow Manuel's suggestion to hire a bodyguard. Coming from Lucy, perhaps it *should* be given serious consideration.

Nicole recalled how threatened she had felt upon finding her car smeared with excrement on the afternoon she had visited Pepe after he was attacked. Afterward, when she discussed it with Lucy, she had come to believe that it was a sinister act by someone who had been watching and observed her going into the building. The sense of violation and vulnerability it had caused was similar to her feelings of helplessness during the days of Drew's abduction on the Indian frontier. Violence had never been a part of her life. It took getting used to.

Changing the subject, she asked, "How old is Francisco?"

Lucy brightened perceptibly. "He just turned six, and what a wonderful age this is!" And then she said, "I'm sure you've heard about me and Horacio Salamanca."

"Well . . ." Nicole didn't know what to say.

"Oh, you needn't feel uncomfortable about it, Nicole. It's quite true. We were lovers. We lived together for five years, and he *is* Francisco's father." Lucy lit a cigarette.

"Horacio doesn't believe in marriage, at least not for himself, but he's a good father and Francisco loves him."

"I read that he's in trouble with the government," said Nicole.

"Always! But I think he may have gone too far this time. He's been outrageous lately, and he just had another article published in *The New York Times* criticizing the junta." Lucy lit a second cigarette. "We're no longer together . . . now we're just good friends. But I'll always love him."

"I'm sorry, Lucy. This must be so difficult for you, and Francisco."

Parked in front of the school, Nicole waited in the car while Lucy went to find her son. She felt a twinge of envy when a thin, anxious-looking boy with huge dark eyes and tousled hair broke from the crowd of children and threw himself against Lucy, hugging her. His somber face came alive with an infectious grin as his mother laughed down at him and said something, pointing to Nicole in the Renault. It was a revelation to see the sophisticated, acerb Lucy, her sharp features tender with love for her child, as they walked hand in hand toward the automobile.

A week later, Nicole was disturbed and felt a personal involvement when she saw the headlines in one of the few remaining independent newspapers. Horacio Sala-manca Rosenn, Peru's most respected journalist, had been sent into political exile by the military government.

She called Lucy and invited her to bring Francisco to spend Sunday with her at Casa Loma. "Francisco will enjoy it. We can play tennis, and the pool is heated."

"Never mind Francisco—*I'll* love it!" Lucy replied.

The two women relaxed on chaises at the side of the pool while Francisco and the gardener's son splashed each other and dived into the water over and over again. Nicole had thought of including the other child that morning, when she realized Francisco might want a playmate.

"This was so good of you, Nicole," said Lucy. "Horacio always spent Sundays with Francisco. It promised to be a gloomy day."

Nicole noticed that Lucy was smoking more than usual. She appeared calm on the surface, but occasionally a distraught expression crept into her eyes.

"It makes me furious to think they would deport such

an eminent writer, Lucy. Peru must be the laughingstock of the world.''

Lucy agreed. "There have been editorials in most of the major newspapers around the world. It doesn't seem to affect the junta, though.''

"Well, at least it's better than prison.''

"From our viewpoint it is, Nicole. But Horacio wouldn't agree with you. When a writer is in jail he becomes a symbol, and he can usually smuggle out articles. Exile for a patriot like Horacio is a terrible punishment.''

Nicole began seeing Lucy more frequently. She was extremely fond of her. Lucy was smart, well-informed, an amusing, irreverent conversationalist, and although it was apparent she was deeply in love with Horacio Salamanca, she did not indulge in self-pity. Nicole admired the strength and gallantry of the woman who had become her best friend.

Manuel Caldeiro-León was growing to be a major nuisance! What right did he have to hire a guard for her?

Nicole was seething with anger when the bulky, muscular *cholo* presented himself at the service entrance to the mansion. Vera sent one of the servants to fetch Nicole, and the two women stood with her in the back entry while she questioned the man and read the chit Manuel had sent.

"Querida Nicole," he had written. "This is Fabricio, whom I have taken the liberty of engaging as your security escort. His salary is paid for the next two months. Please don't be angry with me. I will have peace of mind if he accompanies you when you go out." He had signed it "Devotedly, Manuel.''

She would have turned the man away, two months salary notwithstanding, if Lucy Monaco's words had not echoed in her mind. Lucy certainly was not a hysterical woman, and she had indicated she thought Nicole should have a guard. There had been a number of robberies at gunpoint lately, usually when affluent women or couples were driving alone in their automobiles and stopped at traffic signals. Well, maybe she would try the guard for one month, just to humor Manuel.

"See that Fabricio is given coffee and rolls," she told the maids. "I shall be leaving for the hospital in half an hour.''

During the afternoon Manuel called her at work. She was not in a good mood. One of the nurses had come to her in tears, threatening to quit her job because Mona Ramos had given her a dressing down in front of everyone in the Maternal and Child clinic. Manuel's call came through just as Nicole was soothing the nurse's feelings, and knowing that she would have to have it out with Señorita Ramos, dreading the encounter.

"You sound snappish," he said. "Are you angry about Fabricio?"

"I'm angry, but not about that," she answered. "It's something here at the hospital."

"How would you like to invite me to dinner this evening?" he asked. "I would suggest going out, but this is a meatless day." No beef could be sold for the first two weeks of each month. The government had imposed food rationing in an attempt to curb the runaway inflation.

"All right, Manuel," she said, anxious to bring the phone call to an end. "Come at eight-thirty."

Nicole hung up and went in search of the head nurse. She had no choice but to ask her not to meddle in the affairs of the department.

Drew called that evening, as he usually did on Friday. Nicole was preparing to dress for dinner. She wrapped a midnight-blue terry velour robe around her still-damp body and padded barefoot across the room to the telephone.

"Can you hear me, darling? This isn't the best connection," Drew's deep voice came over the wire.

She was, as always, thrilled to speak to him. "You sound like you're next door! How are you, chéri?"

"Wonderful, except that I miss you terribly. Did you get my letters?"

"Yes, I received two letters this week."

"*Two?* I've written about five! What's happened to them?"

"Sometimes the mails get held up. They'll get here eventually—probably all at once. What about my letters to you—have they come?"

"Not lately. There's been nothing from you for two weeks."

Why had he not received her letters? She had mailed

them from the hospital. The mails were often delayed in Peru, and frequently packages were lost or stolen, but letters usually got through, especially to and from the hospital. Was her mail being taken by someone? *No!* That was idiotic. How foolish of her to jump to such conclusions. It was all part of the ridiculous political climate of fear that had developed in the capital.

"We'll see each other in two weeks," she told Drew joyfully. "I can hardly wait, chéri."

"When can you get away? I'd like to spend the week-end with you before the meeting."

She consulted her calendar. "I can leave on Thursday . . . that's June 20th."

"Terrific! Then it will be *less* than two weeks." His voice was warm and low. "Tell me where you are, so I can picture you."

She laughed indulgently. "Well, I just took a bath, and I put on my robe without drying myself so that I could talk to you."

She could hear his mock groan. "That's not fair . . . I should be there with you. What are you doing tonight?"

Hesitantly, she said, "Having dinner at home." And then, because she could not lie to him, "With my friend Manuel. I've told you about him, haven't I?"

"You mean the lawyer, the one who was your father's favorite?" She could hear a tightness in his voice. What had she told him about Manuel? She couldn't remember. It amused her to think that Drew might be jealous of Manuel Caldeiro.

She had to hurry once they said goodbye, since Manuel was always prompt. One of the maids knocked on her bedroom door to announce his arrival as Nicole sat at the dressing table peering into a hand mirror to secure two jade hairpins in her chignon. She wore a heavy silk mandarin hostess pajama in celadon green with green brocade slippers. Jade earrings and a long necklace of carved jade medallions interspersed with antique cloisonné beads completed the elegant costume, which accented the green of her eyes. The elated mood caused by Drew's call lingered as she hastened down the stairway.

"You're looking marvelous, as always, *querida*" Manuel greeted her, kissing her on both cheeks. "Shall I fix us a drink?"

Vera had placed a serving cart for cocktails in the corner of the small sitting room. Since her father's death, Nicole almost never used the more formal drawing room. Manuel poured a glass of white wine for Nicole and mixed himself a martini. Vera came in bearing a silver platter of hot *empanadas*. She had asked the cook to make them especially for Manuel, who was fond of the crisp, cheese-filled pastries. Nicole was aware that her housekeeper pampered Manuel, particularly now that Daniel was gone. It would certainly make Vera happy if her mistress married Señor Caldeiro-León.

Nicole half-listened to Manuel as she thought about her conversation with Drew. The excitement she felt at the sound of his voice was still with her. In two weeks, they would be together in Geneva!

Manuel had asked her a question. "I'm sorry, Manuel. My mind was wandering. What did you say?"

"You haven't chewed me out about Fabricio. I wonder whether you're mellowing, Nicole."

She laughed. "All right, you win! I'll try him. But I reserve my final decision about a bodyguard until the end of the two months."

In view of the meatless days, the cook had made a seafood dinner. The appetizer of ceviche was followed by a light lobster bisque, and then *huachinango asado*—red snapper baked with onions, peppers, and olives.

"Your father imported some magnificent wines," Manuel said appreciatively, twirling the Baccarat crystal goblet of montrachet.

Nicole lifted her head and spread her hands in an encompassing gesture. "Everywhere I turn in this house, I see his touch. He always selected the best, in everything."

Manuel's expression softened. "You still miss him, don't you?"

"Dreadfully."

His eyes devoured her. He lowered them to prevent her from reading the longing in his soul.

Chapter 23

Salle C, Fifth Floor, June 24—27, International Health Task Force; Private."

It was the second listing on the directory in the new building of the Organisation Mondiale de la Santé (OMS), the Headquarters of the World Health Organization in Geneva.

Outside, across from the building, the O bus came to a stop at the turnaround of Avenue Appia, the end of the line. Luís Ribera stepped off, extending his hand to Nicole. In the company of Prem Mehta and other colleagues from the IHTF whom they had met in the lobby of their hotel, they crossed the driveway and entered through the huge glass doors that are engraved with the organization's name in all the world's major languages.

Drew was not among them. He was staying in an apartment owned by his mother in the Vieille Ville, on the left bank of Lake Geneva.

Inside the WHO, the long marble lobby, leafy with potted trees and interior plantings, was crowded with diplomats clustered in conversational groups. An occasional woman in a sari or an African in national dress provided colorful focal points amongst the uniform dark gray of the mostly male delegates.

The Task Force group stopped at the newsstand to buy the *Herald Tribune* or *Le Monde* before proceeding into the lounge for coffee. Through the glass walls, the green of rolling lawns and beautifully attended gardens stretched invitingly on either side. Luís joined Nicole for coffee, eager to hear about her field assignment in India, while Prem sat listening as she described some of their more exciting experiences in his homeland.

Luís had been amused the night before when he observed Nicole alighting from a taxi at the rear door of the

Hotel Alba, the modest establishment near the Gare de Cornavin where rooms had been reserved for them. Simply dressed in casual slacks and raincoat, she had carried her single small suitcase, as if she weren't the heiress to the vast Légende fortune. She probably enjoyed playing the role of just another working member of the Task Force . . . the same as she pretended to have come directly from the airport to the hotel!

Luís had seen her the *previous* evening walking arm in arm with Drew Tower on the Grande Rue, the two of them oblivious to him as he left a restaurant and got into a taxi. He was glad now that he had not hailed them, spoiling their weekend tryst.

Luís loved romance, and a more handsome pair than Nicole and Drew he could not imagine. This just confirmed his opinion, though, that you can't send a man off on a mission with a beautiful woman without a sexual attraction developing!

Some of the men—and all of the women—in the group kidded him about his macho philosophy. Once, in the middle of a bull session, he said, "The male sexual response cannot be repressed. Men are not biologically programmed to be monogamous. The need to pass on his chromosomes is part of the genetic makeup of the male. The species would never have survived without it."

It was Drew who had responded, "Some people will use any excuse for their own behavior!"

Henry Campion was standing at the door of the meeting room when they left the elevator at the fifth floor. "It's wonderful to see you, Nicole," he exclaimed, kissing her. "Your diary notes were fantastic! I'm tickled pink about your tour in India."

Henry often sounded to Luís like a refugee from a fifties film. "Henry, you *do* use the quaintest expressions," he said. "Does that mean you've become a fellow traveler?"

Henry laughed good naturedly. "We all travel in the same ship here at the UN." Luís rolled his eyes.

Drew was already in the room, engaged in conversation, trying to act as if he were not aware of Nicole. Luís further entertained himself by observing the way they greeted each other casually, with the appropriate degree of restraint, and yet with the enthusiasm one shows for a colleague. He thought that, of the two, it was Drew who had a more difficult time preventing his feelings from showing. The way his eyes melted when she spoke to him. Dios, *I believe he's really gone on her!*

As soon as the others had taken their seats at the U-shaped conference tables, Henry called the meeting to order. Luís pushed aside the earphones for simultaneous translations, usually provided by linguists who sat in the glassed-in booths above. In this group, everyone spoke English, and since there were no Russians to insist on them, translators were unnecessary.

He noticed that Drew and Nicole sat at opposite ends of the room. It's going to be fun to watch those two, he thought. But shortly he forgot about them, for he was completely absorbed in the discussion of the impact of Oral Rehydration Therapy (ORT) on debilitating diarrheal diseases in children of the Third World.

As usual, the meeting had an informal quality, full of banter, fast moving, and productive. Even Anija, the Yugoslavian woman, had reached her stride with the group, Luís realized, as she disagreed with Prem's conclusions.

"Why are you calling ORT a bandaid operation?" she argued. "The Rockefeller Foundation study in Indonesia shows that in eighty percent of the acute episodes oral rehydration controlled diarrhea. A simple thing like a little package of salts and a measuring spoon can bring down infant mortality all over the world!"

The mild-mannered Prem was becoming exercised. "Look, no one has ever proven that ORT will reduce infant mortality! For sure, it stops diarrhea. But if you send the baby home, where the same conditions exist, it gets another infection, and it's just a matter of time before it succumbs!"

"So you don't believe ORT is useful?" she asked stubbornly.

"Of course it's useful! I'm not *against* oral rehydration. It's a remarkable therapy. But in Bangladesh, the Matlab study showed that it has no effect whatsoever on the infant death rate. If we want to make an impact on infant mortality, ORT must be incorporated into broader health education and primary health care."

"That's the concept in Nicole's program in Peru," Luís interjected.

"Exactly!" Prem continued. "You've got to get the people to stop using open wells so their water supply isn't polluted with human and animal wastes. Mothers have to learn to boil water before giving it to infants. They have to breast feed longer and not use supplemental feedings that can be contaminated easily."

"We try to get our mothers to weigh the babies," said Nicole. "Every village has scales, or it's easy enough to rig a simple balance for making sure a baby isn't losing weight."

"We try that, too. You may be dealing with a more receptive population, Nicole. Education in health and sanitation sometimes goes against customs. Well, you know—you've spent enough time in Indian villages." Prem grinned. "Teaching mothers to recognize symptoms early and to get their children to a health center—these are the methods that must be used along with oral rehydration if we want to bring down infant mortality. And that's what we're really after. Isn't it?"

The secretary had turned on her tape recorder because it was impossible to keep up with the sharp minds—and tongues—of the IHTF.

They were reluctant to break at one o'clock. "Quick lunch, everyone, so we can get right back to this," announced Henry. "Let's wrap it up and begin on Nicole's and Drew's smallpox report this afternoon."

Luís could tell from Campion's tone of satisfaction that the Task Force was fulfilling his expectations.

On Thursday afternoon the meetings came to an end. They all stopped at La Perle du Lac for a final drink together before going their separate ways. On the flower-decked terrace of the Orangerie under blue umbrellas, they had a ringside view of the Ski Nautique Club, where water-skiers in wet suits practiced jumps and spectacular turns, sending up fans of rainbow-tinged water from the glacier-fed lake.

Until the next time, they toasted. They were becoming fond of one another, regarding these meetings, held three times a year, as a reunion of friends and not just another professional obligation. It was a bittersweet moment an hour later when they said goodbye in the hotel lobby. Drew had taken his leave at the café, choosing to walk across the Pont du Mont-Blanc to the other side of the lake, where he was staying.

In her monastic room containing a narrow single bed, Nicole showered and dressed for the evening, choosing a lightweight gray cashmere knit dress with a tee neckline. It was cool in Geneva for this time of year, particularly at night. Sitting at the desk, she read through the documents from the meeting, planning to wait a while before joining Drew, to be certain all of their colleagues had left the hotel. She felt a little guilty about deceiving them. After all, they were friends and would probably be delighted that she and Drew were in love.

In love? Was she in love?

Drew had asked once, "Do you love me?" and she had replied, "I care deeply about you, more than I care for anyone, but whether or not it's love, I don't know. I'm afraid of love, Drew."

He had covered her hand with his. "It's enough for now." He never asked again.

Drew seemed to have no doubts about love, but she still did not trust her feelings—or her luck. That was what it was, really. Superstition. If she pretended not to be in love, not to count on that love for happiness, maybe—just *maybe*—the gods would overlook it and let her keep him.

Drew was waiting for her at the apartment. The private courtyard to 5 Place de Ville, at the end of a cul-de-sac, was entered through a door in a large wooden gate. Inside were half a dozen cooperative apartments within an ancient stone building that was actually built on the bastion wall of the Old City of Geneva. To own one of these was a rare bit of luck. His mother had lived there until her marriage to Arthur Hillman, and every time she thought of selling it, Drew persuaded her not to. For a number of years it had been rented to a couple from the Red Cross, but recently the tenants had left and he now used it whenever he came to Geneva.

The moment Nicole stepped through the door, Drew's arms were around her, crushing her against him, his lips hungry on hers. "I didn't think I could stand it until you got here," he said, his voice muffled in her hair. "Do you know what agony it is for me to sleep in the same city with you and to be apart?"

"Mmm, for me, too," she answered, soft and pliant in his arms. "I've missed you all week."

"We have an hour and a half until dinner," he murmured. They clung to each other, walking up the narrow stairway, feeling the heat of arousal.

When he looked down at her, he said, "Have I ever told you that you have the most ravishing smile in all the world?"

They were late arriving for their dinner reservation, but a corner table was waiting. The waiter immediately brought flutes of Champagne Framboise.

Le Chandelier is Geneva's most romantic restaurant. Dark and intimate, its beams are hung with copper pots reflecting the soft glow of candlelight. Contributing to the ambience are labels from memorable vintages, displayed on a board next to the wine cellar. The food and wines are superb and the waiters attentive but not intrusive.

Drew touched his glass to Nicole's, his eyes never leaving hers as he sipped. How exotically beautiful she looked tonight, he thought, studying her expressive face. The silky black mass of hair was caught back in a loose, careless arrangement, allowing waving tendrils to escape at the brow and in front of her ears. In the candle glow, her ivory skin was polished to satiny perfection. She had changed to a jade silk shirt dress that accentuated the gold-shot emerald of her unbelievable eyes. When she looked down, the long fringe of curling lashes cast romantic shadows on the high, rounded apples of her cheeks. In the aftermath of their lovemaking, she had the passionate, seductive glow of a Manet painting.

A surge of feeling went through him and he realized he desired her again. He wanted to spend forever making love to her! Two lifetimes would not be sufficient.

If only they were already married, assured of being together for the rest of their lives. Sometimes he had this ominous feeling that he wasn't meant for happiness. He didn't usually indulge himself in melancholy, but the more he loved Nicole, the more he feared that love would slip away from him.

"At this moment I am the happiest I have ever been,"

he said. Nicole's eyes moistened with emotion at his words. She put her fingers to her lips and touched them to his.

The waiter approached. They had not yet read tne menu, so Drew consulted with the man and ordered his suggestions.

"It always surprises me to hear your fluent French," said Nicole. "Even though it's Swiss French! You're so American, it's as if it were someone else speaking."

"So American, the lady says! I used to be given a hard time at Andover about my so-called British accent."

Except for his brief misadventure at St. Ben's, Drew had lived in Geneva for most of his youth, attending an English school, until he had gone to the States for his last two years of prep school. He liked coming back to this city, although he had few contacts remaining here. The Swiss kept to themselves, as a rule, so most of his boyhood friends had been from the foreign community.

Their meal was served, a delectable smoked trout with *sauce raifort,* followed by rack of lamb *à la fleur de thym.* The *sommelier* filled their goblets with Dôle de Chandelier, the private house reserve. Drew ate with relish, but Nicole paid little attention to her food.

"Don't you like it?"

"Yes, it's delicious," she replied. "I just can't seem to eat much tonight, chéri."

They sipped cognac and sat close on the banquette, hands joined, gazing at each other.

"Do you know what I want?" His eyes caressed her. She nodded.

"Do you want the same thing?"

"Desperately," she answered, her voice breathy.

He motioned for the check.

Out on the Grande Rue, they walked hand in hand down the incline, pretending not to hurry. They paused to look into the window of an antique shop and then into another, containing nursery furniture—ruffled bassinets, cradles, tiny tables and chairs.

Drew's hand moved up to the nape of her neck. "I hope someday we'll have a child together, you and I."

Her eyes closed briefly, almost in ecstasy. "Please, let's go home," she whispered.

His lips lightly brushed hers and they continued on

their way, turning right, to the end of the short narrow
street, where they stepped through the wall.

Once inside the little hallway, they fell into each other's arms, hands and lips searching. When they broke
apart, Nicole backed away, extending her arms to him.
Their eyes locked as she led him to the bedroom and
began to unbutton his shirt.

All too soon it was over.

"Why can't it last for hours and hours?" she asked.

"I'd probably die if it did! No one could sustain that
intense excitement for so long." He held her and stroked
her back. "I love it when you speak in tongues, Nicole . . . when we make love." She did not answer. "I
recognize the French and Spanish, but there's something
else. What is it?"

"Quechua. Sometimes it seems more natural. I don't
know why." Her voice was low and hesitant. "I wasn't
really aware that I did that."

"I hope you won't stop. I didn't mean to make you
self-conscious, darling."

"I'm never self-conscious with you, Drew."

He threw back the covers to look at her in the dim
light. The shining length of her blue-black hair rippled
across the pillow like a silken shawl. Heavily lashed and
almond-shaped, the exotic emerald eyes, their pupils huge
in the darkness, glowed at him. His gaze swept the length
of her. Slowly, with the utmost tenderness, his hands
molded her body. Gentle and certain, his fingers traced
the slim smoothness of her shoulders, the ovoid perfection of her breasts, the god's eye of her navel . . . and
moved on. Through partially closed, quivering lids her
eyes gleamed as she made undulating motions with her
hips in response to his touch.

The curve of her throat, long and sweet, was stretched
by her uptilted chin. The delicate nostrils distended, her
breath came in short gasps from between parted lips. She
moaned his name.

"Put your hands on me, darling," he whispered.

Half comprehending, she followed him, knowing only
this pulsating, cresting need to reach a goal long abandoned. At last he joined his body to hers, and as the
tremendous force seized her, she began to weep. Wracked

with sobs, her voice rose, crying, "I love you, I love you! Oh, Drew, I love you so much. . . ."

For a long while, he held her, letting her cry. He understood what was happening to her, to both of them. Like wanderers in a desert, they had craved the slaking of their thirst for love. When love had revealed itself, it was like an oasis, beckoning to them, promising salvation. He had put his trust in that vision, but Nicole had been afraid, fearing it was a mirage that would vanish and leave her more deprived than ever.

Soon her breathing slowed and became even.

He moved away, looking down at her. The exquisite planes of her face were in repose. With the back of his hand, he gently caressed her cheek. Her eyes slowly opened and regarded him with awe.

"Is it so painful for you, to say you love me?" he asked softly.

She shook her head in denial, her brows drawing together with emotion. "Oh, no, my darling . . . if only you knew how I feel. If you could understand how *free* . . . how *wonderful* it is to be able to love you!"

Once again they were saying goodbye, this time for three months. Drew watched as the jumbo jet was hauled back from the ramp and turned. As Nicole's plane taxied away, a mood of depression settled on him.

He knew that as soon as he returned to Philadelphia and the virology lab, it would not be as bad. He was usually able to lose himself in his work. However, when he had come back from India, work had not been sufficient to erase the ache of loneliness he felt for Nicole. After this beautiful time together, he would miss her even more.

They planned to meet next in Paris in early October. She had to go there for the board meeting of Légende et Cie a week before the next IHTF meeting in Geneva.

Until they were married, this was what they could expect—stolen moments in various places around the world, brief interludes of ecstasy in a basically lonely existence. What a profound effect love had. His life now seemed incomplete without Nicole. He was convinced that she loved him, but he also realized she was not ready

to commit herself to that love. She still did not believe it
was real.

"It's too soon," she said when he had again broached
the subject of marriage last night. "We've been together
under the most extraordinary circumstances. We've had a
fantastic adventure together . . . it's like a dream, for
both of us."

"It's real enough for me, darling. I have no problem
separating reality from dreams."

All the way across the Atlantic he savored the remembered warmth of that reality.

Chapter 24

It had been a "minor cerebral accident," Molly told Drew when she called from Wilkes-Barre.

His immediate reaction was to try to convince his mother to bring Arthur to the University of Pennsylvania Hospital by ambulance, if he was able to be moved. Arthur would not want to leave St. Anne's Hospital, where he had been on the staff for all of his professional life, she said. Perhaps when he was feeling stronger he would agree to go down for a consultation, but right now she did not wish to upset him by discussing anything controversial.

Drew left immediately for Wyoming Valley, driving over the northeast extension of the Pennsylvania Turnpike and going directly to the hospital, in south Wilkes-Barre. St. Anne's was a Catholic institution and considered the best hospital in this part of Pennsylvania. When he was younger, Arthur Hillman had been chief of staff here. It was also in this hospital that he had first met a beautiful young nurse named Molly Shea, forty-six years ago.

Drew entered the private room with apprehension. It was a shock for him to see the silver haired patient lying in a hospital bed, an oxygen tube in his nose. Smiling faintly and holding out his right arm to Drew, Arthur made a futile little gesture with the left.

"How are you, Drew?" His speech was slightly slurred. Minor or not, the stroke had left him debilitated. For as long as Drew had known him, Arthur had been in good health. He had aged well, appearing much younger than his seventy-three years—until now.

"Dad!" Drew had a difficult time holding back tears as he bent to hug him. He loved this man, and after what he

had been told by Ranjit Kar in India, he was almost
certain this was his real father.

Drew had not been able to discuss that conversation
yet with either of his parents. It was such a difficult
subject to raise. He had not wanted to hit them with
what was bound to be a startling and sensitive matter the
first time he saw them after his return from India. Since
then, he had been waiting for the right opportunity. But
seeing Arthur in this weakened condition, with his left
side partially paralyzed, he was afraid it was too late. It
might be too traumatic for him to discuss such an emotional subject. Now Drew would never be able to tell him
he knew the truth, a truth he believed Arthur would
welcome his knowing.

"Drew! How wonderful to see you, darling!" Molly,
looking fresh and summery in a blue linen dress, hurried
into the room. Dropping purse and white gloves on a
chair, she embraced her tall, broad-shouldered son and
then turned to Arthur. "Hello, my love." She kissed him
and leaned closer as his good arm tightened around her.

Molly perched on the edge of the bed. She beckoned
to Drew, who pulled a chair over next to them and sat
down. The resemblance between mother and son was
striking. Molly's dark hair was streaked with gray now,
but the straight, expressive brows above violet blue eyes
were the original of Drew's. The resolute, sculpted lips,
the firm and determined chins, were identical. And both
had the Riordan smile—that flashing, heart-catching Irish
magnetism of Molly's maternal family—with sparkling,
perfect teeth.

"What do you think of our patient?" she asked brightly,
smiling at Drew and reaching out to touch Arthur's hand.
She was trying hard to be brave and she played the part
well, given her years of nursing, but Drew saw the fear
behind her eyes and the almost imperceptible quiver of
her mouth.

"I think he looks pretty good," he said lightly. Then,
realizing how ridiculous it was to act as if Arthur were
not a physician and part of this, he addressed himself to
him. "When will your doctor be coming in? I'd like to
talk to him, if that's all right with you."

Arthur nodded, looking pleased. "The internist should
be here sometime later this morning. I have a cardiolo-

gist and a neurologist, too. Whole bunch of people looking after me." His speech was slower. Drew could see
that he was tiring.

"Dad, why don't you rest for a while? Mum and I will
keep each other company. We'll be here whenever you
feel like talking."

As soon as Arthur closed his eyes, Drew noticed the
sorrowful expression that came over his mother's face.

Drew remained in Wilkes-Barre for the rest of the
week, until it was obvious that his father was stabilized.
All of Arthur's children came—Ellen, Jeffrey, and Robert, who flew in from Delhi—prompting Arthur to say,
"I'm delighted to see everyone, but I wish you wouldn't
all go around with such long faces. I'm not planning to
kick off yet!"

"I'm glad to see you've got your sense of humor intact,
Dad," said Robert. Arthur held on to Rob's hand, profoundly moved to have him at his bedside. "That's the
main problem with working overseas," Robert said to
Drew later when they were alone. "When something like
this happens, you're so damn far away."

"You shouldn't feel guilty about that, Rob. Arthur's
terribly proud of you and what you're doing," Drew
replied. "How are Jane and the kids?"

"Everyone in the family is fine—they send their love."
He hesitated for a moment. "Colonel Kar died of a heart
attack the other day. I decided not to mention it to Dad.
It would upset him."

"*Kar!*" Drew pretended to be searching for something
in his pocket to hide his startled reaction. Robert would
wonder why he should be more than mildly sympathetic
about a man he had met once for half an hour. What *did*
it mean to him? That the one person beside his parents
who seemed to know he was Arthur's son was no longer
alive. He wasn't even sure that Ranjit had realized it,
had understood what he was revealing—he was practically in his dotage when he had spoken of his memories
of Molly and Arthur.

"Why are you so surprised? You knew he had been ill,
didn't you?" Robert had the most peculiar expression on
his face—a combination of affection and, *yes*, embarrass-
ment! Had the colonel revealed something to him, too?
Had Rob guessed? Drew's heart skipped irregularly.

"I suppose I shouldn't be surprised," he answered. "Well, I hardly knew him, but he was awfully nice to me."

Robert gazed at him, then heaved a deep breath. *Here it comes,* thought Drew. "Did you know I once wanted to marry his daughter?" asked Robert.

Drew was so relieved that he sounded almost too enthusiastic. "Kar's daughter? No, I didn't know that!"

"Yes. Back in '62 when I was in the Peace Corps. I fell in love with her. It took me a long time to get over it."

"Was she in love with you?"

Robert nodded. "Yes, but she was already engaged to her husband. In India, once they have the betrothal ceremony, it's almost as binding as a wedding."

"Jane . . . does she know?"

"Unfortunately, yes." He smiled with regret. "I was still in love with Leila when I married Jane, Drew. I'm not any longer, but I think Jane will never believe it."

Rob reminded him so much of Arthur, with the same gentleness and warmth to his personality. "Jane is terrific, Rob. You're lucky to have a wife like her."

"I know I am, and I tell her that all the time!" Robert smiled, then cocked his head. "What about Nicole? Are you two still. . . ."

Drew laughed. "Yes, we are. But it doesn't look like marriage for a while."

"For Christ's sake why not? You don't find someone you want to marry every day."

"It's like I said in Delhi, she lives in Lima and I'm in Philadelphia."

"Drew—I told you what to do about that. There's the WHO, USAID, the Ford Foundation. . . . There are *lots* of solutions."

Drew sighed. "I guess if the truth is known, I don't want to leave Penn. Hell, Rob, I've carved out a great spot for myself there. I love the lab, I have a terrific boss, and I'll be in line for tenure in a few more years."

"Jobs come and go, Drew. Good marriages aren't that easy to find."

One day soon he would remember Robert's words.

Drew spent hours at a time with Arthur, who especially liked to discuss medicine and his career with him.

The second morning, Drew had entered the room without his father noticing him. Dr. Hillman was lying in bed staring out the window, his face sagging with dejection.

"Good morning, Dad. Here's a present for you!" He withdrew a soft rubber ball from his pocket. Placing it in the palm of Arthur's left hand, Drew said, "I want you to hold that all day and squeeze it over and over, as often as you can. It'll help reeducate those muscles. I'm going to talk to your doctors about getting started with physical therapy."

Later that day, with Drew supporting his left side, Arthur stood and took a few steps across the room, dragging the left leg, in which he had sensation and some movement.

"You're doing fine," exclaimed Drew. "I bet you'll be walking alone in no time." With Drew and Molly's encouragement, Arthur's spirits lifted immeasurably.

Drew consulted with the doctors and they agreed to begin physical therapy immediately. At some future date, he was determined to take Arthur down to Penn for a cardio-vascular work-up and an arteriogram. They had one of the country's best cardiology departments, using the most advanced developments in diagnosis, treatment, and surgery.

Drew went back to work in Philadelphia, but returned the following weekend to find Arthur much improved. Sitting alone together in the hospital room, Arthur studied Drew, then asked, "Is there another woman, Drew?"

Drew hesitated for only a minute, then nodded. "Yes. How did you know?"

"You no longer have that haunted look. I recognized what it was, or at least I hoped that was it," said Arthur. "Love is important, Drew. I'm just as much in love with your mother now as I was the day I married her. The old can love, too, you know. In fact, I believe we value love more, having discovered how ephemeral it is." Then he smiled apologetically, realizing that Drew had made that sad discovery in his youth.

Drew had not been planning to discuss Nicole with his parents. Not until she had agreed to marry him. But suddenly he wanted to talk about her. "You'll love her, Dad! We're on the Task Force together. . . ." He told Arthur all about Nicole and their three months in India

together, his face alive with excitement as he described
the woman he loved.

At the rate he was recovering, Arthur would soon be
discharged from the hospital. Reassured at his father's
condition, Robert said goodbye and prepared to embark
for India. Drew took him to the airport, seeing him off
on the first leg of the long trip back to Delhi.

Both Ellen and Jeff had left after their second visits.
Drew did not plan to drive to Philadelphia until the next
morning because he knew his mother would feel lonely
that night if everyone departed at once. Returning from
the airport, he let himself in the side door of his parents'
home. Molly was sitting in the library working on needle-
point. Kissing her, he noticed how drawn she appeared in
the lamplight.

"You look tired," he said, his hand resting affection-
ately on her shoulder.

She smiled up at him. "I'm fine, dear. If only Arthur
will be all right." Her eyes sought reassurance in his face.
"Do you think he'll recover the full use of his arm and
leg?"

Drew nodded. "I think so. His speech has come back
perfectly and he's doing extremely well with the physical
therapy. That side will always be weaker, so it's important
to keep up the exercises." He grinned. "He's lucky. He
has his own live-in nurse!"

She laughed and put aside her needlework. "Can I get
you something to eat, dear?"

"No thanks, but maybe a brandy?" He started toward
the bar, but Molly was there ahead of him.

"I'll fix it," she said. "That sounds like a good idea. I
think I'll join you." Opening a cabinet, she selected two
glasses and bent to take out a bottle of Courvoisier from
a shelf below.

"Mother, did Robert mention that Colonel Kar had
died?" Drew kept his eyes on her back. Was it his imagination, or had her shoulders become rigid for an instant?

"Yes, he told me. I was so terribly sad to hear that.
Ranjit was a wonderful man, and a dear friend of—of
Arthur's." She handed him a brandy snifter and returned
to the bar.

He ran his finger over the rim of the glass as he

carefully considered his words. "I didn't realize you knew Colonel Kar during World War II. I thought you met him after you married Arthur."

Molly's hands fluttered at the bottles of liqueurs, resting first on one, then another, as if she could not make up her mind what to have. "Oh, did I not tell you that, dear?" Her voice sounded high and unnatural. She kept her back turned to him. "Well, I suppose it never seemed important. I met him when I was nursing in Calcutta with the Red Cross. He was a medical officer . . . he . . ."

"The colonel told me he was the one who brought Arthur to the hospital in Calcutta when he was wounded."

Molly faced him, her eyes meeting his steadily. "Yes," she said in a firm voice. "He was a devoted friend. Arthur wouldn't be alive if it weren't for Ranjit."

"Ranjit said he wouldn't have lived if it weren't for *you.*"

She folded her hands and brought them up to her face, pressing them against her mouth, but continuing to regard him.

He could not ask the question! He opened his mouth several times to speak, but the words would not form on his lips.

"What is it you want to say, Drew?" Molly asked quietly.

"Mum . . . is Arthur my father?"

She closed her eyes, looking stricken, and Drew feared he had committed an unpardonable sin. In an instant he was at her side.

"I'm sorry, Mother! Don't . . . please." She leaned against him, laying her head on his shoulder. He put his arms around her, hating himself for what he was doing, *but he had to know!*

After a few minutes, Molly breathed deeply and stood back, facing him squarely. "Yes," she said, "he is." Drew saw that there were tears in her eyes. "But he never knew about you, Drew! *I kept it from him.*"

Molly moved to a chair and motioned for him to be seated. She had regained her composure. She told him how she had first met Arthur Hillman and fallen in love with him when she was a young nurse and he had just started to practice medicine in Wyoming Valley. Despite the religious difference, they had planned to be married, but her father's uncle, a bishop, had intervened.

"The Church was absolutely rigid in those days, Drew. If I had married Arthur, I would have been excommunicated unless he converted to Catholicism." She sighed. "So, I went to Ireland and married Sean."

"How awful!"

"Sean was a wonderful man, dear. It wouldn't have been awful if. . . . Well, you might as well know it all. Sean was unable to father children. He . . . he was impotent. It was probably an early symptom of the multiple sclerosis. In any case, we never lived together normally, as man and wife."

"Mother . . . I feel as if I've intruded. I should never have asked you about this."

Molly sighed. "No, darling. You have a right to know. I probably should have told you long ago, but—" She looked down at her hands. "By the time Arthur and I met again, in India, he had a wife and three children." She gave a little laugh. "Not that it prevented us from falling in love all over again! Arthur wanted to divorce Emily and marry me—and I could have obtained an annulment. But when I discovered I was pregnant, I realized it would be too late by the time you were born.

"There were other reasons. His family, and mine too. It would have been impossible for us to come back to Wilkes-Barre. Things were different then, Drew. Not only my reputation would have been ruined, but Arthur's as well—and our child, *you*, would have suffered. So I went home to Sean without telling Arthur I was expecting a baby. And you know the rest."

"Did Ranjit Kar know?"

"He probably guessed. I asked him to do a pregnancy test—for a friend. We never discussed it, though." Molly shook her head. "Well, you can imagine that I never expected either of us would see Ranjit ever again!"

Drew leaned his head against the back of the wing chair. So, this was the story of his birth. Strangely enough, knowing the truth was almost anticlimactic.

"What will you do, now that you know?" Molly asked.

He looked at her in surprise. "Why, nothing. What would you expect me to do?"

"I don't know. Tell everyone, I suppose."

Molly was actually willing to let him make that decision! What would be gained, he wondered, by telling anyone? Drew did not want his mother made vulnerable to the scorn of other people. Things had not changed that much. The woman was always the one to pay the penalty. How would Arthur's family react to this startling revelation? Of the three Hillman children, Drew thought only Robert would be understanding—and even he might resent Arthur's infidelity to his first wife, who had, after all, been Rob's mother.

"No, Mother. It's enough that I know."

There was a look of relief on Molly's face, lovely even at this age. "What about Arthur? Aren't you going to tell him?"

What difference would it make? He had regarded Arthur Hillman as his father ever since his mother had married him, and Arthur treated him like a son. And yet, he *wanted* to tell him.

"Someday, when he has fully recovered. I don't think this is the time."

And then Drew remembered. "There *is* one person who should know, if you don't mind."

"Who?"

"The woman I hope to marry. I've been meaning to tell you about her. . . ."

Chapter 25

In the last week of July 1974, the President of Peru, General Juan Velasco Alvarado, announced the takeover of Lima's major independent newspapers, shocking all of the Americas with this flagrant denial of freedom of expression.

Castigated in editorials by *The New York Times* and other leading American newspapers for its censorship of the press, the Peruvian government answered that its seizure of the publications was part of an over-all plan to remove power from the old establishment and put it in the hands of the people. This excuse for censorship was greeted with protests by the students of Lima's universities.

Nicole had already retired on Saturday night and was reading in bed, when Vera appeared at her bedroom door, frightened. "There are some boys at the door who insist they must talk to you, Señorita Nicole. I tried to send them away, but they refuse to leave. One said to tell you it's Carlos."

Nicole slipped a woolen robe over her nightgown. Carlos? Whatever could he want at this hour of the night? She followed Vera down the back stairs to the pantry and out to the rear entry.

There was a courtyard outside the service entrance where deliveries were made. Nicole seldom ventured there. As a young girl, she used to play ball and jump rope in the enclosure because it had large squares of stone that made a perfect surface for games. From the yard, a back driveway opened onto a seldom-used alley connected to the winding road that led down to Costa Verde, the coastal highway.

Peering through the glass of the door, Nicole could make out a huddle of figures in the darkness. Carlos stepped forward into a beam of light shining from a window.

"It's all right, Vera. You can open the door," Nicole assured the nervous housekeeper.

Carlos was accompanied by another youth whom Nicole didn't recognize. Between them they supported Pepe.

"Bring him in," she said quickly. "What happened to him?"

"He's been shot! We were at a rally and the police came with high pressure hoses to break it up. Then they began making arrests, so we ran. We managed to get away before the trucks came to take everyone to prison. But they shot at us, and Pepe was hit."

"You should have taken him to the hospital!" she told him in dismay.

"They would report him to the police and he'd end up in jail! Please, Nicole, can't you help him?"

She sighed. "Bring him upstairs, Carlos. Vera, we'll have to use one of the maids' rooms."

"*No*, Señorita Nicole! You *must not!* This will mean trouble."

"Vera, I can't refuse to help them. They've done nothing wrong." She attempted to soothe the agitated woman, but she was feeling far from calm herself. It was a crime for a doctor not to report a gunshot wound.

They carried him up to a spare servant's room, with a disapproving Vera leading the way.

She hoped no one had seen them. The night watchman was probably sound asleep at his post at the front gate. Pedro and the gardener had cottages on the property, but they were on the other side of the garages, so it had been easy for the three students to slip in the back way unnoticed. Nicole was relieved that the other maids went home at night. Following the departure of most of the household staff, Vera was the only one of the servants to sleep in the main house with her.

A single bullet had caught Pepe in the fleshy part of the left shoulder, lodging near a bone, but fortunately not shattering it. He was grimacing from pain and fright, but not seriously injured.

"I keep a sterile pack at home for emergencies," she told them. "Luckily, he hasn't lost much blood. Carlos, get him undressed. Your friend can help Vera. Will you please boil two pots of water?" she asked the house-keeper. "I'll go get my bag."

Pepe screamed with pain when she probed the wound. "There's some chloroform in the bag, Carlos. We'll have to give him a whiff." Carlos saturated a gauze and held it to Pepe's nose, while the other boy threw open a window to dissipate the fumes.

In a matter of minutes Nicole loosened the projectile. With pincers, she drew out the bullet of an automatic rifle. "A few inches lower and he might have been killed," she remarked, holding it up for them to see.

"It was a peaceful demonstration, Nicole. We were carrying signs and chanting about freedom of the press—but it was orderly. The police turned on their hoses and started beating us on the heads with clubs. That was when some *chicos* began throwing stones, and then all hell broke loose."

Shooting unarmed students in the back! Her hands shook as she cleaned the wound. While she applied a dressing, she said, "You could have done this yourself, Carlos. Why did you bring him here?"

"I don't have any instruments, Nicole." Carlos muttered an apology but would not look at her. He had an annoying habit of cracking his knuckles.

"Why, Carlos?"

"I didn't know where else to go," he said lamely. "We couldn't go to the apartment. They're watching us, and all our friends." She heard Vera gasp in the corner of the room. They all knew what that meant, who "they" were: the PIP.

PIP stood for Policias Investigaciónes del Peru, disparagingly and appropriately pronounced "peep." They were feared with good reason. Like all secret police organizations, they considered themselves above the law and often overstepped their authority.

"Are you certain you weren't followed?"

"Positive! We drove around for a long time."

"Drove? Do you have a car?"

He looked down. "I used one of the vans."

She was aghast. "From *the clinics?"*

Shamefaced, he nodded, pulling at his fingers. "I didn't know what else to do, and Pepe had the keys in his pocket. We were right there, in the plaza near the hospital."

"You're lucky you weren't stopped."

"I shouldn't have used the van. I'm sorry, Nicole."

She shrugged. "You took a chance."

Their friend left, telling them he would return the van to the hospital parking lot before it was missed. As soon as she was alone with Carlos she said, "You know that I'm required by law to report this, don't you?"

He paled. *"Nicole!* You won't, will you? I swear, no one else will ever know. They'd lock Pepe up for years—and he's done nothing wrong. *Please*, Nicole!"

She sighed with resignation. "I won't report him, Carlos."

He smiled with relief.

Pepe stirred and opened his eyes. He was in pain and felt ill from the chloroform. Nicole gave him some medication. "That will make him sleep. He should be all right in the morning."

Carlos said he would look after Pepe so Nicole could get some rest.

"You can stay here tomorrow," Nicole told him. "The servants don't come in on Sunday. But you're going to have to leave before Monday morning—someone might talk." Carlos looked pointedly at Vera's retreating back as she left the room. "You don't have to worry about Vera. She's completely loyal and trustworthy. Although she doesn't approve."

He grasped her arm as she reached the door. "You're a real friend, Nicole."

She thought for a moment. "Carlos . . . that time Pepe was beaten up. Was it the police?"

He nodded. "It was goons from the PIP. They've been watching our house, and sometimes they harass visitors."

That's who smeared my windshield, Nicole thought. They must have made a note of her license plate number!

She was exhausted. It was past three o'clock. Telling Carlos he could sleep on the other twin bed in the room, she said good night. She would have to drive them somewhere tomorrow. But where? If their apartment was being watched, they couldn't go there until Pepe had recovered.

In the morning, Pepe was feeling stonger. His shoulder

throbbed, but he was not running a fever. Nicole insisted he take some antibiotic capsules to prevent an infection. Then in the early afternoon, after sending Pedro on an errand to get him out of the way, she took another car from the garage and drove the two young men to a bus stop on the other side of Lima. They said they were going to stay with friends.

"Thank you, Nicole," Pepe told her. "I won't ever forget this."

I hope I can forget it, she thought. *I wish it had never happened.*

All through the month of August and into September there were demonstrations against the government's suppression of the press. Middle class people who had never before campaigned for any cause or taken much interest in political affairs marched in the streets of Lima.

The police were called out to control violence, and instead they created it. Over five hundred demonstrators were detained and held in jail. Lashing out in a desperate measure to put down unrest, the government accused opposition leaders of planning organized violence in order to produce chaos in the capital city.

Nicole was packing to leave for Paris, where she would be attending the board meeting of Légende et Cie before going on to Geneva, when Lima was rocked with a scandal over police torture. The leading newspapers, although now under the direction of the government, called for a thorough investigation of the brutality and an end to the practice of torture.

Nicole called Lucy Monaco. "What's happening, Lucy? It sounds alarming."

"On the contrary," answered her friend. "It's out in the open now. Torture has been going on for years without anyone's being able to stop it. We're hoping this will be the beginning of a return to legal rights."

Lucy went on to tell her excitedly about the document she was helping to prepare, with other members of the Lima Bar Association, petitioning the Ministry of Justice to uphold guarantees that had been lost when the junta set aside the Constitution.

As Peruvians gathered to commemorate the first anniversary of the overthrow of Chile's President Allende,

Peru's junta seemed stronger than ever. President Velasco issued a statement extolling the accomplishments of his administration and predicting it would take at least another six years to achieve the goals of the revolution. In the resulting reordered society, he told them, there would be a return to elective government and constitutional law.

Many citizens did not believe him. Those who did thought six more years was too long to wait.

Chapter 26

It was a celebration of culture, fashion, and *le Grand monde* unique even for Paris. Balmain, Schiaparelli, Chanel, Christian Dior—all the great couturiers—had joined with Cartier and Hermès in a Salut à Légende, a festival of fashion and fragrance in honor of the thirtieth year of France's most illustrious house of beauty.

The gathering of five hundred included various assorted princesses, countesses, and a baroness or two. The officers and board of Légende et Cie were guests of honor at a gala dinner and *fête des beaux arts* held in Le Grand Palais. The hall was transformed into an Inca temple with plaster reproductions of the famous statue of the Inca that was Daniel's trademark. Privately, Nicole thought the lavish decorations rather garish, but it was typical of French exuberance to create this extravaganza. After dinner, she accepted the special plaque in memory of her father presented by the Minister of Culture and another from the Minister of Trade. How proud Daniel would have been if he were alive for this event. There had been many honors in the past, of course, but this was special.

Nicole was sorry she hadn't invited Drew to be here tonight, sharing this with her. Instead, he was flying from New York to Paris and would arrive early tomorrow morning. To be in Paris without him increased her longing. All week long, missing him, wanting him, her body had been aching for his. If he were present, it would have created an awkward situation, though.

Her eyes swept the length of the banquet table, and she smiled as she caught Manuel watching her. He was hurt and a little angry, she knew, that they had not been spending the evenings together. As far as she was concerned, it was enough that she had flown from Lima to

Paris with Manuel and had been in his company for the past two days of board meetings! And of course she was not responsible for the seating arrangements tonight. The Minister of Culture was at her left and Baron de Reginaude, a Légende Director and Patron of the Paris Festival Commission, on her right.

Tomorrow morning was their last business conference, a short session of the executive committee to review the preliminary packaging designs for the prospective youth line. Claude Montagne had hired new blood. An innovative staff had introduced the marvelous idea for a new product division that would tap the market of affluent young people on their way up. It was to be called Légende d'Or. Nicole thought the plans exciting.

Claude was proving to be a dynamic CEO. Since he had taken over the leadership of Légende et Cie, he seemed years younger. Last night at dinner he and Isabelle Somme had dropped a bombshell. They were getting married!

"I have long loved Isabelle," he confessed to Nicole. "But, when your father was alive, I could never reveal my feelings. I hope, Nicole, you don't misunderstand."

She hugged him and said, "Uncle Claude! I'm so happy for both of you. And Papá would be happy too."

Even at their age, she noticed how love cast its glow on them. Surely, if Claude and Isabelle could commit themselves to each other for the rest of their lives, I shouldn't hesitate. . . . Her thoughts had stopped there.

At the end of the long evening, when the speeches were over and the brilliant parade of costumes had ceased, there was dancing to the accompaniment of a string orchestra. She had finished talking with the functionaries and the other board members when Manuel finally came over to her.

"You've been avoiding me, *querida*," he said, arching an eyebrow.

"Now, Manuel, why do you say that? You know I have no control over these affairs."

"I meant all this week. Every night you have another engagement."

"But I must accept dinner invitations when I come to Paris."

He had too much pride to remind her that on other

occasions she had included him when her Paris friends
invited her. The first night, she had dined with Françoise
and Alain, without him. And even last night, with Claude
and Isabelle, she had not invited Manuel along.

"May I take you home?" he asked, when people began
to leave.

She hesitated. "My car is waiting."

"Then I'll send my driver away and come with yours,"
he answered smoothly.

As they drove along the Seine in silence, the lights of
the Pont Alexandre III were reflected in the river. It
made her happy tonight to see the Arc de Triomphe
bathed in floodlight. Paris was a city that held so many
associations for her. Only lately had it become her place
with Drew.

Manuel interrupted her thoughts. "It was a splendid
evening. You must have been thinking a great deal about
your father. I know I was."

She looked at him, her expression soft. "Yes. This
would have meant so much to him."

In front of her building on the Avenue Foch, she
turned to him in the car. "Would you mind, Manuel, if I
don't invite you to come up? I'm dreadfully tired, and we
do have that early meeting tomorrow morning."

Surprised and caught off guard, he began to protest,
but she was ahead of him. "Don't bother getting out,"
she said, quickly leaving when the chauffeur opened the
door. "Good night, Manuel." She was through the gate
and up the stairs to the entrance before he could follow.

The following morning, when Drew arrived at the Avenue Foch by taxi, a Peugeot limousine stood waiting for
Nicole. The liveried chauffeur touched the brim of his
hat as Drew shouldered his garment bag and opened the
iron gate to Number 17.

Nicole was there in the foyer when the lift reached the
sixth floor. Drew enveloped her in his embrace, kissing
her hard on the mouth. "I rushed like mad to get here
before you left," he told her.

"And I waited until the last minute! I'm afraid I'm
going to be late for my meeting." She held him at arm's
length. "Let me look at you." She noticed the lines of

fatigue. "You need sleep. I've left breakfast for you. I told the maid not to come in today."

She led the way to the master bedroom, opening one of the closets. "This is yours."

"And yours?" he asked.

She laughed. "I still keep my things in my old room, but I'll stay in here with you, chéri."

He was charmed by the blush of color in her cheeks. "Good. None of this separate bedrooms nonsense for us."

They kissed again, and his hands moved down her back and over her hips. Nicole broke away. "I really do have to go now, chéri. I'll be back right after lunch. Try to get some sleep."

Without her, it was an apartment of beautiful empty rooms. Drew went into the small breakfast room where Nicole had set a place for him. After eating melon, croissant, and coffee, he washed the dishes and set them to drain. He liked French kitchens. They reminded him of his childhood in Geneva.

Upstairs, he was tempted by the immense sunken tub with its whirlpool but showered instead, turning on the steam head. The black marble bathroom had a mirrored wall, ornate silver faucets, and glass shelves holding an array of Légende toiletries for men and plush terry bath sheets with the Légende monogram. A teak-lined excercise room with sauna and massage table connected to the bath. The opulence of this suite went beyond anything Drew had ever seen. The bedroom itself was furnished in exquisite understatement in a hand-blocked fabric in shades of gray with burgundy. All of the furniture was Directoire. The walls, upholstered in a muted coordinating fabric, were hung with a series of rare Delacroix drawings. An adjoining sitting room had functioned as a home office when Daniel had lived here with Nicole. Now it was an orderly, unused, silent room.

Naked, Drew slid beneath the covers of the large double bed that Nicole had turned down for him. He stretched to his full length and still his toes did not touch the footboard. Nicole had told him her father had this bed custom designed for himself, and he had been a big man. With a sigh of contentment, Drew closed his eyes and slept.

*   *   *

Three hours later, Nicole quietly let herself into the apartment. She had stayed for part of the luncheon but slipped out early. Fortunately, Manuel had an appointment in the afternoon at Lazard Frères. She had managed to elude him for the rest of the week, telling him she had to prepare for the Geneva meeting and would see him back in Lima the week after next. It was becoming more and more difficult for her to handle Manuel's persistence.

Stepping softly, she entered the bedroom. Covers thrown back, Drew was sprawled asleep on the big bed, resembling a fallen Greek statue. She enjoyed looking at him, loving the way he was made. Quickly she shed her clothing, flinging it on a chaise, and removed the pins from her hair. He was not fully awake when he began to respond to her caresses.

They dined late that evening, at Taillevent, where Daniel had always had his special table. The staff made a quiet fuss over Nicole. With the appetizer of *langoustines aux pâtes fraiches,* Drew ordered a 1970 Meursault. In a magnanimous gesture of sentimentality, the owner sent a bottle of 1966 Romanée-Conti for them to have with their *caneton au cassis.* Bending to discreetly murmur the vintage, the waiter poured a small amount into Drew's glass for him to taste. Gravely he nodded his approval.

"I'm impressed," he whispered when the waiter had left.

Nicole reached for his hand and squeezed it. *"I'm* impressed, too!" She gave him a long look, drawing in her cheeks.

He grinned. They had made love over and over again all afternoon and into the evening. "I think we may have set a new world record," he told her.

They lingered at the restaurant over coffee and cognac, as content and at peace as either of them had ever been.

Later, lost in each other, they did not notice the black Mercedes parked beneath the trees on the divided slope of the Avenue Foch three blocks north of the Etoile. In the darkness, it blended with the night.

Manuel sat behind the wheel, looking up at the windows of the two-story penthouse of Number 17. There was soft light in the front rooms. Was she there?

Again she had begged off his invitation to join him tonight for dinner with friends in St.-Cloud. Not one evening since they had arrived together in Paris had she consented to go out with him!

How vibrant she had looked this morning, that same luminosity shining from her that he had noticed when she returned from India. She seemed to be in the grip of an inner force these days. She had a *sensual* quality. It was a sexual energy that emanated from her. He recognized it and responded to it. All day he had thought of her, dreamed of her, wanted her.

Should he go up? *Yes.* He could not sit back any longer. He must act. *Dios* . . . they had been more intimate two years ago than they were now!

For too long he had been patient, waiting for her to realize that her destiny lay with him—as his wife. He would make love to her! What a fool he had been to play the honorable gentleman that night at the hacienda. She had wanted him, and if he had taken her then, they would have been married by now.

Manuel could almost sense her presence nearby. He ground out his cigarette in the ashtray, determined to go up to the apartment and confront her.

A taxi stopped at the end of the block to discharge its passengers, then drove away into the Rue de Traktir. Manuel saw two people, a man and a woman, walking up the hill with their arms around each other. They paused and their profiles merged in the darkness under the trees. There was that aura of love in their stance, in their leaning into each other, as if ready for coupling. They continued up the hill, closer, and as they broke from the shadows, Manuel slowly removed his hand from the handle of the automobile door.

He recognized Nicole in the wash of the street light but not the tall man with his head bent toward her in an attitude of devotion. They reached the gate of Number 17 and the man removed a key from his pocket, inserting it in the lock with a familiar air, as if he had fitted that key into that particular lock before and knew the consequences of his act.

Feeling the constriction of rage in his chest, Manuel's

eyes burned with tears of frustration. Sick with the bile of jealousy, he saw them walk through the garden, mount the steps, and enter the building. His hand shaking violently, he lit another cigarette and sat with narrowed eyes peering up through the threads of smoke.

He watched as the penthouse windows brightened. He continued to stare when the lights winked off on the lower level, and only the front bedroom windows on the top floor remained lit.

"No!" he cried aloud, as the light dimmed and the windows became a dull glow. And still he waited, keeping watch, long after the last of the lights had gone out.

Chapter 27

Nicole had led a solitary life during the past month. She took pleasure from the time alone to reflect on herself and her growing love for Drew.

Much to her relief, Manuel had kept his distance since Paris. When they spoke, there was a coolness in his manner that she attributed to hurt pride. He was feeling rebuffed for now, but she hoped they would eventually resume their friendship.

Thus, she was pleased on a warm Sunday afternoon in November when Manuel called, asking if he could come by to see her. They spent the afternoon pleasantly enough, playing two sets of tennis on the grass court—still perfectly maintained by the gardener, although seldom used—and cooling off with a swim in the pool afterward.

Manuel stayed on for an early Sunday night supper. After he left, Nicole sat alone in the study.

Tonight they had quarreled.

Fabricio was the ostensible cause of their disagreement, but it had gone far beyond that. It began when Nicole told Manuel she no longer needed the bodyguard, that she felt self-conscious driving around in her automobile with someone riding shotgun.

Manuel replied that she was acting like a frivolous woman and did not understand the seriousness of the situation in Lima these days. So insistent was he that, just to keep peace, she agreed to retain Fabricio.

Taut with having given in, she bristled when he asked, "Have you continued to visit the Peace Corps projects in the pueblos?"

"No, I haven't," she answered, barely hiding her annoyance. "I've been too busy." She would never admit that she had avoided going because Lucy warned her not to.

"Good."

His obvious relief was irritating to her. She chose another subject, one that would put him on the defensive.

"Will you join the protest in support of your colleagues at the bar?" she asked.

Five leading attorneys, all active in Lima's Bar Association, had been arrested for openly debating the legality of the government's foreign trade agreements. Many lawyers had rallied to their cause. Nicole was fairly certain that Manuel was not one of them. She thought he was far too cautious and self-protective to allow himself to be involved in the defense efforts on their behalf.

Looking down, he rubbed his cigarette back and forth in an ashtray. "You know I'm not a political man, Nicole," he said lightly. "It's just not my style."

She had overestimated her ability to throw him off balance. He was well trained in conducting an argument. When challenged, the best defense is an offense.

"The International Health Task Force—how long will you continue your association with this organization?" he inquired.

Surprised, she answered, "As long as they want me. My contract was just renewed. They'll probably keep me on for five years."

"I think you would be wise to drop out at the end of the current period."

Her voice was icy. "Oh? Is that so, Manuel? I hardly think it's any concern of yours."

They argued for several minutes, with Nicole telling him he had no business meddling in her professional affairs and Manuel saying it was risky for her to travel alone so often.

Realizing they were at a stalemate, he said, "I hadn't planned to tell you this, Nicole, but . . ." he took a deep breath, "our government suspects the IHTF of being a front for the Central Intelligence Agency."

Incredulous, she stared at him. "That's the most outrageous accusation I have ever heard! Manuel, you can't possibly believe that!"

"I'm not saying I believe it, Nicole. But then, what *I* believe isn't important. The fact is there are other people who do believe it—and what they think does matter."

At first, she thought his words absurd, but immediately

that was replaced by apprehension. *Is this the beginning of something terrible?* she wondered. She looked at Manuel's face. He was unsmiling, even stern. The hollows in his cheeks and the cool gray of his eyes could have belonged to a cruel man.

Quietly she said, "I know you're just trying to protect me, Manuel, but I can assure you the idea that anyone in that group is . . . is a *spy!* Well, it's highly unlikely."

His eyes narrowed as he regarded her with a lift of his head. "Are you certain, Nicole? Think about it for a minute. Didn't you tell me that many of them have had fellowships in the States? Isn't it possible that at least some of them may have been asked to cooperate with the CIA? For example, if a young scientist from another country went to the National Institutes of Health . . ."

"Or the Center for Disease Control," she interrupted. "Is that what you're trying to say, Manuel? *A young woman doctor from Peru, for instance?*" She glared at him.

Manuel studied the ash of his cigarette. "I didn't say that, but I wouldn't be at all surprised if others have so concluded."

She shook her head in disbelief. "By that reasoning, anyone who studied in the States could be accused—including you! What would make them come to such a conclusion?"

"The junta is suspicious of any group that is dominated by Americans."

"You see how foolish that is? Their suspicions are groundless. Except for Dr. Campion, there's only *one* American on the IHTF—Andrew Tower, a virologist. And in fact, he was born in Ireland."

His face had closed and his tone chilled her when he said, "I am well informed about Dr. Tower, Nicole. People are not always what they seem to be."

Manuel tried to end the evening on a more conciliatory note. "Nicole, I have no wish to argue with you. You're in jeopardy, my dear. You don't seem to realize what's going on in Peru. If you persist in acting foolishly, I may not always be in a position to protect you."

When he finally left, her anger would not dissipate. She refused to call it fear. Stifled, she felt like everything was closing in on her. Especially with Manuel did she sense it. It seemed she couldn't make a move without his finding out about it and questioning her.

How did he know the IHTF was suspected by the government? Could the charges possibly be true? But that was crazy! She would be aware of anything suspicious, wouldn't she? What kind of information could a bunch of doctors and scientists collect that would be of interest to an intelligence service? The whole idea was simply preposterous.

There had been something threatening about Manuel tonight. Why was he privy to inside information? For some time she had wondered how he was aware of her movements. Where did he pick up his knowledge? Could he be spying on her? she wondered. Was Fabricio's real function to collect information and report her whereabouts to Manuel? But if so, why?

Something was happening.

She had sensed it tonight. There had been an ominousness about Manuel. What was it he had said about Drew? "I am well informed about Dr. Tower. . . . People are not always what they seem." The sinister quality of the words overwhelmed her. What had he meant? What exactly did he know about Drew?

I must watch myself, she thought uneasily. From now on she would be doubly vigilant, guarding her conversation.

Especially with Manuel Caldeiro-León.

The following day, it became clear to Nicole that Manuel had known in advance of a move by the government that had grave international implications.

The Peace Corps, all 137 members, had been thrown out of Peru! The military government, in requesting their recall, stated that the American volunteers were no longer needed because their functions could be performed by Peruvians. But the Lima newspapers told a different story, charging the Peace Corps with intelligence and propaganda activities in poor and rural communities, and calling for an investigation of individuals and other organizations who attempted to undermine the revolution and advance American imperialism. Cited in an unofficial list of groups whose work was "highly suspect" was the Cartwright Foundation.

When Drew called on Friday evening, he asked about

the alarming articles he had been reading in *The New York Times* on the expulsion of the Peace Corps from Peru.

"I don't know very much about it, chéri. Just what I read in the papers. I think the disclosures about the activities of your intelligence service in Chile have created a—a lack of confidence in the United States throughout Latin America." She pointedly changed the subject. "Is it definite that the Task Force will meet in New York in February?"

"Yes, you'll be receiving a letter," he answered. "There's a conference of parliamentarians from developing countries at the UN, and we'll be involved in some of the programs. Henry and I have to be at an immunology meeting in San Francisco the following day, so I won't be able to stay in New York afterward." His voice became hesitant. "How about coming to Philadelphia first?"

Her heart missed a beat. "I . . . I'll have to let you know, chéri."

"I love you, darling," he said as he rang off.

Nicole sat staring at the telephone, trying to picture Drew at the other end. If she went to Philadelphia, it would be a commitment—in a way that staying with him in Geneva and Paris were not. He knew it, and that was why he had asked her.

Part of her wanted to make that commitment. Wanted to fly to him in Philadelphia. It would be so safe and easy to leave and never come back to Lima, where honest citizens guarded themselves with guns and fear, not knowing who was the real enemy.

It was the first time a member of the government had been attacked since the junta had taken over.

The Premier, who was also Commander in Chief of the Army and Minister of War, was not injured. Nor was the driver of his car. But the two generals riding with them, both high in the military regime, were hit when unknown gunmen fired on their vehicle and raced away.

Nicole first heard the news on Monday morning on her way to work. With Fabricio at her side, she was stopped at three roadblocks. The military police asked for identification papers and made them get out of the car to be frisked when they discovered Fabricio carried a gun.

Unnerved by this experience, Nicole arrived at the hospital to find doctors and nurses gathered in small groups, drinking coffee and discussing the attempted assassination of the head of the armed services. The motive was not clear, everyone said, since the Premier was planning to retire within a few months.

"It is the beginning," intoned Jorge Alvares. "Now you will see more violence, more restrictions, and more arrests. It is the same old story with these military men." He looked old and sounded tired, and his words echoed her father's, although Alvares lacked Daniel's fire.

Later that morning, at the weekly departmental meeting, Nicole noticed that Dr. Alvares rubbed his forehead frequently as he spoke. Afterward, they went on rounds. She kept an eye on the professor and saw him blink several times, as if his vision was blurred.

"Are you feeling all right?" she asked him, as soon as they had seen the last patient.

"I'm fine," he replied tersely. He turned away from her and walked down the hall with two of his male colleagues. Hurt by his uncharacteristically abrupt manner, Nicole reminded herself that a professor does not expect his younger associates to act familiar with him on the wards.

This time he came in uniform. There was respect and fear on the face of the receptionist when she saw him, he was pleased to note.

"*Buenas tardes,* lieutenant," Nurse Ramos greeted him. "Come in." Her eyes smiled behind the steel-rimmed glasses.

They had reached the end of their routine discussion when he turned his notebook to a fresh page and said, "The Department of Maternal and Child Health. . . ."

He saw a wary expression come over Nurse Ramos's face.

"That department, Señorita Ramos, is a special problem for my superior officer. I am hoping you can give me some facts—in addition to the helpful information you have already provided."

In another twenty minutes, the lieutenant had filled several pages of his notebook. He closed it with a satisfied air and placed notebook and pen in his pocket.

Mona Ramos rose and accompanied him to the door. He turned and shook hands. "I won't be coming to see you again, señorita. I have been promoted to the interrogation unit of the Peruvian Investigative Police."

Nurse Ramos's eyes dropped for a moment. Taking a deep breath, she looked at him directly. "Congratulations, lieutenant. I wish you success in your work."

When the lieutenant had left, the head nurse locked her office door. Closing her eyes, she brought her clenched fist against her mouth. "Dear Lord, what have I done? Blessed Mother, forgive me!"

Groping for her rosary, she dropped to her knees and bowed her head.

On the Thursday before the New Year, Jorge Alvares was found by the night custodian, slumped over his desk. Beathing unevenly, his face unnaturally florid, he regained consciousness on the gurney as they rushed him to cardiology. His condition was diagnosed as apoplexy caused by emotional strain and high blood pressure.

By the next morning, when Nicole went to see him, the professor's condition was stable. "They say it wasn't a stroke, Dr. Alvares. Just a warning. You must take it easy. I think you've been under too much strain lately."

Jorge smiled weakly. "I shall be fine, my dear. I can't imagine what happened. I was sitting at my desk and everything went blank."

"Did you have a headache?"

"Yes. But I've had headaches all my life. I get them from tension."

Many things could have caused the collapse, Nicole thought. He might even have a brain tumor. San Martín did not possess a CAT scanner, but there was one over at the Military Hospital. They needed to do a battery of modern tests on him—many of which were not available anywhere in Peru.

"Nicole, I'm counting on you to see that everything goes on as usual in the department. Make sure everyone cooperates with my next in command. I don't want to appoint an acting head because then it becomes official. I expect to be back at work within a few days—" and when she looked doubtful, he amended it, "or weeks."

And he was. Two weeks later, Jorge Alvares returned

to work, saying he had had a spell of overtiredness. He insisted he was completely fit, but Nicole continued to worry about him. She thought it had been a ministroke, and she urged him to have a CAT scan at the Military Hospital.

"In time, Nicole. I'm feeling perfect now. Really!"

"Why don't you go to the States and have a complete work-up, Dr. Alvares?"

He considered it. "That's probably the best idea. I promise to do it, but I want to wait for a few months, until we get our budget allocation and I can relax about the department's programs."

By the end of January, Professor Alvares did seem to have regained his vigor, and because he preferred not to dwell on it, Nicole seldom discussed his health with him.

"What is this I hear about your canceling your trip to New York for the Task Force meeting?" he asked when she entered his office one morning.

"I have so much work here . . ." she began.

"Nonsense! The work will be waiting."

"I don't think this will be a crucial meeting for me to attend, Dr. Alvares. I gave my project report at the last meeting, and this time we'll be involved with a Third World development conference at the UN, so I can probably get by just reading the minutes."

He gave her a level glance. "You have an obligation to the Task Force, Nicole. When you accepted that appointment, I agreed that one-third of your time would be devoted to its work. The IHTF reimburses a third of your salary to the department, as you know—and I've made that clear to anyone who has questioned the allocation of your time."

"Have many people inquired about it?" She had wanted to ask him that for a long time. She was concerned that her three-month absence last year, and the meetings she had attended since, were viewed as a special privilege.

"No, not many. One or two of our more curious colleagues, understandably. And then, the hospital administration, of course. But I believe I've satisfied everyone on that question."

He made light of it, but Nicole thought he must have had to account for his associate's travels on more than one occasion. When it was so difficult for a faculty member to get financial support to travel abroad for conferences, it was not surprising that her role in the IHTF had caused some envy.

For the past two years, ever since her father's death, Nicole had not used the vacation time to which she was entitled. That was one reason why she had no qualms about spending a few extra days with Drew before and after their meetings. Evidently her absences did not meet with the approval of someone at San Martín, though. Professor Alvares had not said it, but reading between the lines, she guessed there had been complaints.

Altogether, she thought, there were any number of reasons why she should not take the extra time to visit Drew in Philadelphia.

Chapter 28

New York was all wrong for them. To begin with, Nicole's flight was delayed and she did not arrive until Monday morning, just as the first day's session was getting underway.

Drew had borrowed a friend's apartment in the Beekman area, expecting her for the weekend. Dreadfully disappointed when she phoned him with the bad news that she could not get away early because Jorge Alvares had not fully recovered from his illness, his manner was reserved when they first greeted each other during a coffee break. But despite his suspicions that she was using Professor Alvares's health as an excuse, he joined her for cocktails at the UN Plaza Hotel at the end of the day.

"Come stay with me tonight," he urged, when they were seated for dinner in the Ambassador Restaurant.

"I've just checked in, Drew. I'm awfully tired. Maybe tomorrow." His earlier coolness had not escaped her.

The line of his jaw hardened as he stirred his drink. Looking away from her, he called Prem to join them and spent most of the dinner hour talking to him and Luís, who had also taken a seat at their table.

Nicole was quiet, contributing little to the conversation. Irrationally, she felt wounded when Drew did not try to draw her out. Pleading fatigue, she excused herself before dessert and went up to her room.

"What's wrong with the beautiful Nicole?" asked Luís archly.

"You heard her—she's tired," Drew snapped. He rose abruptly. "I'm going. I'll see you tomorrow."

Luís reached out to touch his arm, but Drew shrugged him off and left quickly.

"I think they've had a lovers' quarrel."

"You shouldn't josh him, Luís," Prem replied in quiet

reproof. "He's in love with her. And he has suffered enough, losing a wife."

Luís's eyes widened. "You don't think it's just an infatuation with him and Nicole?"

"No. He's kept his secret well, but I'm sure it's a real love affair."

"You may be right," mused Luís. "What about her? Do you think she's in love with him?"

Prem leaned forward, resting his chin against his folded hands. "That's a difficult question. She's a complicated woman, Nicole."

Striding through the lobby, Drew left the hotel. He came out on Forty-fourth Street, and turned north on First Avenue. The buildings of the United Nations were fully illuminated against the night sky. Diplomatic limousines drove in through the guarded gates, delivering guests to an official function. Tomorrow evening, the members of the Task Force were invited to a reception given by the Director of the United Nations Development Programme, in honor of the UNDP's governing board.

Packed snow and fragments of ice crunched under Drew's feet as he crossed over the avenue. He turned up his coat collar against the frigid wind that whipped along the pavement. The biting cold reminded him of Hanover. At Dartmouth, on a clear, stinging winter night like this, he would have gone skating on Occum Pond. Although he had never much cared for the old-boy, wah-hoo-wah types at Dartmouth, he had thrived in that pristine rural New England setting. That was what he liked most about the college. Ten years ago, he could not have envisioned the paths his life would follow. His ambition had been to practice medicine in a small town much like Hanover. Craving a peaceful, uncomplicated existence, he had wanted to live in proximity with nature and develop a practice where he would have close contact with his patients. It had been an honest desire, growing out of his need to belong somewhere.

For most of his life he had felt rootless. Born in Ireland, he was not truly Irish. Living in Geneva, he had always been part of the transient foreign community. Even as a student in the States, he often felt the odd man out. And as the son of two lapsed Catholics, his only real link to the Roman Catholic Church had been his mother's uncle, Father John Riordan, an open-minded priest who, before his death five years ago, had been the Dean of Students at St. Mary's University in Washington, D.C.

With Ranjit Kar's unwitting divulgence that Arthur Hillman was his father had come Drew's comprehension of *why* Sean Tower had not wanted him baptized. Drew knew Sean had conducted his own mysterious and continuing conflict with the Church. It was clear now that because Drew was half Jewish, Sean had been determined to deny Catholicism the child he accepted as his son.

At first, in the wake of his mother's confirmation of the startling revelation, Drew had lived with the expectation of a metamorphosis in himself. Such a seminal disclosure *must* have broad consequences. Surely an archangel would descend from the vaulted firmament to beknight him with an ineluctable Judaic shield! Then one day, he had studied the veins in his arms, wondering why it would matter whose genes he carried. Intellectually, he reasoned, it should have no impact on him, but from that essential core of self a caul had been removed.

Nicole would understand. He had not confided in her about his parentage, not yet. But once she agreed to marry him, she would have to know.

The longing for a solid foundation had marked the passage of his years. He thought he had found it for all time with Julie, only to have it swept away, leaving him once again bereft, like sands washed by the receding tide. Nicole was his anchor now. With her, he knew he would never again feel adrift. They were alike, the two of them, seeking where they belonged. Chance had played a remarkable role in both their lives, and fate had brought them together.

He couldn't remain angry at her. In his heart, he had already forgiven her for not coming to Philadelphia, for he perceived what had happened and why she was afraid. Professor Alvares's illness was a handy alibi to obfuscate the underlying reason for her refusal. By falling in love with Drew, her defenses had been broken down, and she was becoming as dependent on his love as he was on hers. But Nicole still feared a commitment to love, and it would be up to him to prove that giving in to it was not going to destroy her.

At Fifty-second Street he walked east to the end of the cul-de-sac high above the East River Drive. The apartment, on the tenth floor of the old Tudor building opposite the River Club, belonged to one of his classmates from Andover, who had gone overseas on an assignment for *The New York Times*. It was obviously a bachelor's apartment, possessing a spartan lack of domestic warmth, with an odd assortment of modern furniture and substantial hand-me-downs. A massive pedestal desk, cluttered with the trappings of a journalist—papers and newsclippings—stood in one corner of the living room. Stacks of back issues of *Foreign Affairs*, *The Nation*, and *The Economist* littered every surface. The bedroom had the bare essentials—a river view and a king-size bed.

After he had showered, Drew sat on the edge of the bed staring at the telephone. Finally, he picked it up and dialed the hotel.

"Were you sleeping?" he asked when he heard Nicole's voice.

"No. I couldn't fall asleep," she said softly. She sounded as if she might have been crying.

His throat tightened. "Do you still love me?"

Her voice trembled. "Of course! I'll never stop loving you . . ."

"But?"

". . . but there are so many problems."

"Only if we make them problems." He had not meant to get into this discussion now. His mother had always told him never to go to bed angry, and that was why he had called. "I wanted to tell you I love you, and to ask you again to stay with me tomorrow."

There was a pause. "I *will*, chéri! I'll stay with you."

"Good night, darling. I'll see you in the morning." As he pulled the covers over himself, the bed seemed vast and empty.

The eyes of every man—and woman—were on Nicole the following evening, as she crossed the hotel lobby to join the three attractive men in formal attire who stood waiting for her. Wearing a long slim skirt of wine velvet with a close-fitting, puff-shouldered tunic in wine lamé

shot with gold, she carried a matching velvet cape over
her arm. Coiled high on her head, the crown of glossy
black hair was twisted with thin ropes of gold. Her pa-
rures, large pendant earrings of faceted garnet set in old
gold and heavy antique bracelets to match, had belonged
to her mother.

Luís made a show of being overcome by her magnificence, holding onto Drew and Prem for support.

Nicole laughed delightedly. "What's happened to that
suave man of the world?"

He took her cloak and placed it around her, allowing
his hands to rest on her shoulders. "I'm not the *only* one
who finds you irresistible," he answered in Spanish.

He knows about us, she thought instantly. She glanced
up at Drew, who winked at her. Linking arms with Luís,
she led the way to the entrance where he signaled for a
cab.

"A taxi?" she asked, surprised. "But it's so close."

"You're far too beautiful to be blown about in this
wind. Besides, I'm freezing."

They walked through the marble lobby of the delegates' entrance to the Assembly building, riding the esca-
lator past two enormous tapestries to the upper level. At
the door of the delegates' lounge they joined the well-
known names and foreign dignitaries who moved through
the receiving line, to be greeted by a beaming director of
the UNDP and his wife.

There was a euphoric mood of triumph rippling through
the assemblage tonight, a confidence that the UNDP
would receive the financial backing for its programs during the next year. Although the governing council's deliberations would continue for the remainder of the week, and
the actual budget vote would not be taken until the final
day, it had already been determined through corridor
negotiations that the director's request for a substantial
increase would be approved. The countries counted on
for the additional funds—namely the United States and
Sweden—had indicated their willingness to make the required pledges.

Brandishing microphones, newscasters clambered over
trailing wires, and one another, to cover the event. The
guests were blinded by the lights of television crews who
lined the sides of the room to catch luminaries on cam-

era. Nicole stopped to speak with the Peruvian ambassador to the UN, Javier Pérez de Cuéllar, and his wife, introducing Luís, Prem, and Drew. She greeted others who had known her father—among them Lord Carrington and John D. Rockefeller 3rd, whose great interest was problems of the developing world.

Weaving a labyrinthine path around the islands of conversation, their senses were positively assaulted by a plethora of visual and olfactory stimuli. Saudis in flowing robes sipped fruit juice and spoke with turbaned Ibos from Nigeria. The perfumes of Araby and France mingled with spicy culinary essences from the buffet. "Cardoman and Cardin," remarked Luís.

But the headiest of all was the aroma of power. One sensed that over a Kir a deal might be made that could bring relief aid to ten thousand famine-stricken tribesmen in the Sudan—or funds for a new dam in Paraguay. Within the confines of these walls circulated the delegates of allies and enemies. The representatives of warring nations gave a wide berth to each other, but were seen speaking at different moments to the same intermediaries.

The crowded party spilled over into adjoining chambers. Except for a few celebrities, the Western women appeared strangely dowdy. One splendid blonde of statuesque proportions dripped with diamonds and was surrounded by a circle of short, dark Lotharios. Luís whispered to Nicole that she was the pilot for the private jet of a sheik. ". . . among her other qualifications, she can fly!"

They looked for the other members of the Task Force but could not spot them. Luís brought champagne and guided them toward one of the buffet tables, where cold shrimp and crab legs, smoked salmon, caviar, and pâté canapés were banked in lavish and tempting array, flanked by immense chafing dishes of dim sum and kufta kabobs.

"A United Nations of hors d'oeuvres," remarked Prem. He looked at the table thoughtfully, but Nicole noticed he ate very little. She could imagine his thoughts. Fresh from the Oral Rehydration Center in Calcutta, where patients were dying of malnutrition, the extravagant display of food in this setting must seem particularly anomalous, even obscene.

Nicole scanned the noisy throng, hearing snatches of conversations in dozens of languages. Every nation, every race, was represented here. Men and women in the national dress of Botswana, Burundi, Sierra Leone, and Zambia chatted with one another and gorged on the delicacies. They were the unlikely spokesmen for their needy peoples. Almost without exception, these diplomats had been educated in the elite institutions of the West, Moscow, or Peking. Worldly, articulate, and privileged, what did they have in common with their countrymen, most of whom could not read or write, had never traveled five miles beyond their dusty villages, and walked barefoot in the bush to hunt or root for their daily meal?

Her eyes met Prem's. He reached for her hand and gave it a reassuring squeeze. "As I once told you," he said. "It does no good to go around wringing one's hands. Despair never solved anything."

These are my family, Nicole thought suddenly, tears starting in her eyes. This group, the Task Force, especially these three men, are the people I care most about in all the world. As long as I have them, I'll never be alone.

Drew had disappeared. He returned with Henry and his wife, Beth, whom Nicole had met only once before. "My, but you're looking *swell* tonight, Nicole," Henry exclaimed in his inimitable way.

"Thank you, Henry. I think we're *all* quite marvelous. It's lovely to see you again, Beth."

"I'm going to have to convince Henry to have an IHTF meeting in Philadelphia so you can come to visit us," Beth said shyly.

"What a terrific idea," Drew interjected, giving Nicole a pointed glance.

Beth regarded the two of them for a moment. Nicole instinctively liked her. She was a reflective woman of quiet intelligence who stayed in the shadow of her husband. Tonight she was wearing a long dress of black crepe with a strand of pearls. Around her shoulders she carried a stole woven of black silk and gold thread, which Henry had brought from one of his trips to the East.

Drew hovered at Nicole's side, exerting a gentle pressure on her arm. It was easy after a time to separate from the others and lose themselves in the jostling crowd. He steered her across the room until they were no longer in view of their friends.

"Shall we skip out?" he asked. She nodded her agreement. "Pity we couldn't find them in this crush," he joked lightly. "I guess we'll just have to make our way alone."

A blustery wind caught Nicole's cape, ballooning it around her, as they left the Assembly Building. Snow flurries swirled in the crisp air of the winter night.

"I can't go dressed like this, chéri," said Nicole. "I must change."

They stopped at the hotel, where she quickly put on gray tweed pants, a gray sweater of brushed Lapland wool, and warm shearling boots. After tossing a change of clothing and her toiletries into a large Louis Vuitton handbag, she donned a hooded Norwegian lynx trench coat and hurried to the elevator.

As she rode down, she hoped they would not meet any of the IHTF people as they left the hotel, although that no longer seemed important. Somehow she felt anonymous and unfettered in New York. That was one of the things she liked most about this city.

On their way uptown, Drew asked the cabbie to wait while he ran in for the Chinese food he had ordered when she was dressing. Under the marquee of the apartment building, they stamped their feet free of snow.

"Brad keeps a well-equipped bar, but the cupboard is bare," Drew called from the kitchen, as Nicole kicked off her boots and explored the apartment in stocking feet.

He put on jeans and a sweatshirt, then lit a fire, and they sat on the living room floor eating spare ribs and Szechuan chicken, and listening to tapes from Brad's excellent collection of jazz.

He put the half-empty cartons of food in the frig and poured two brandies. Sitting close together on the soft leather sofa, they looked into the glowing coals. Drew rose to throw another log on the fire, and as Nicole watched him, Lima and all its problems seemed far away.

"Do you have any *idea* how much I love you?" he murmured as he took her in his arms, kissing her hair, her eyelids, her neck, then drawing back to look at her face.

"As much as I love you," she whispered, tracing the outline of his lips with her fingers.

"Then, why . . . ?" he began. But she silenced him with a kiss and slipped her hands beneath his clothing, erasing all thoughts of conversation from his mind.

They fell back against the pillows in each other's arms, his mouth moving on hers, his lips becoming more demanding as his passion increased. Swiftly he shed his clothing, then helped her, pausing to kiss each part of her body as it was uncovered. He stroked her breasts slowly in the way he knew she preferred, his lips following his hands as they moved over her with tantalizing delicacy. Wave after wave of ecstasy flowed through her as they moved in unison. For this moment at least, he was the center of her being, the meaning of life. She cried out for him as their love reached its culmination.

In bed, they could look south on the East River to the lights of the UN Secretariat Building. Nicole laid her cheek on Drew's chest, his arm encircling her.

"It looks like they're still at work. That place never closes down, does it?" she murmured.

"I'm not sure, darling . . . sometimes I think the UN's been politicized into uselessness. But then I remember the work of the WHO and UNICEF, which more than makes up for the rest of it."

She was so quiet that he thought she might have fallen asleep. Suddenly she said, "Drew? What would be your reaction if I told you the Task Force may be on a list of suspect organizations in Peru?"

She felt him stiffen. "Suspect organizations? Suspected of what?"

"Of being a front for US intelligence—the CIA."

He whistled. "Is that hearsay, or do you have something specific to go on?"

"Knowledgeable hearsay, I suppose. Manuel Caldeiro warned me about my association with it. I don't know how, but he does seem to know a lot about what's going on within the government. I didn't pay much attention to what he said until the news that the Peace Corps was thrown out of Peru was made public. And then I saw a column in *Correo*, the official newspaper. They published a list of other foreign organizations—mostly American—to be investigated for their suspicious activities."

"Was the IHTF on the list?" he asked in surprise.

"No. But the article made what Manuel said sound more plausible. The Cartwright Foundation was on the list. Our department has received grants from them. I prepared the last grant application."

Drew propped himself up on one elbow and looked down at her. His brow wrinkled in concern. "Nicole . . . darling, that sounds ominous. What does it mean for you?"

"Nothing, I'm sure. But I wondered what you thought . . . about the IHTF."

"I'm not one of those Americans who won't admit the CIA operates in foreign countries, Nicole. But in this case—the Task Force! You know it's absolutely clean! There is *no possibility* anyone in that group is CIA. Hell . . . who would they suspect? Either me or Henry. Who else is American?"

"I know. That's what I told Manuel."

"Well, my love, their suspicions are groundless. And I would say the same for the Cartwright Foundation. It's an old organization, respected throughout the world. There's not a chance they could be a front for anything subversive."

"I didn't think so, but I'm relieved to hear you say it."

"Maybe Manuel's jealous. What does he know about you and me?"

"Nothing! He'd be the last person I would tell." Nicole yawned and Drew could see she was having difficulty staying awake.

"We ought to go to sleep now, honey. We do have a meeting tomorrow morning." He kissed her lovingly.

This was a new worry. What if she was in danger? Military governments did not have to wait for confirmation of wrongdoing to punish someone. Chile, Argentina, and Brazil were proof of that. He had a premonition that she should leave Peru.

It was a long time until Drew slept.

"Guess what?" he said, when he awakened her with a cup of coffee early the next morning. "I'm not going to leave this afternoon. We can spend the evening together."

She sat up excitedly, "Do you mean it? I thought you had to give a paper tomorrow."

"I do. But I'll take the red-eye at midnight. I can sleep on the plane and I'll get there by morning."

"Oh, chéri! You would do that for me?"

"I would do much more than that, my love." He kissed her lingeringly. "Much, much more. . . ."

The meeting ended at noon. They had lunch at the Stanhope, then wandered through the Impressionist exhibit at the Metropolitan Museum of Art. There was great interest in the Monet painting, *Le Déjeuner sur l'Herbe,* which had been lent by the Pushkin Museum in Moscow, displayed for the first time with its twin fragments from the Louvre.

"I've seen the companion pieces in Paris many times," Nicole remarked. "Even art can't remain free of politics, it seems."

Drew studied her face, trying to read her thoughts. Was she more apprehensive about events in Peru than she had let on, he wondered. Was there any real threat to her in Lima? Probably not. In the light of day, he felt a little foolish about his concern last night. Nicole would laugh at him if she knew his thoughts. It was such a cliché. Americans always tended to think Latin American governments were unreliable. He didn't need any pretexts for taking her away from Peru. He was in love with her! That was reason enough.

They returned to the apartment. Nicole made mushroom omelettes and salad for dinner, but conscious of the passing hours, neither of them had much appetite. Soon Drew would have to leave for the airport.

He had to talk to her.

Taking her hands in his, he said, "Darling, when are we going to get married?"

Her reaction was strange, not at all what he had expected. She looked distressed. "Not yet, chéri. It . . . it isn't the right time. Maybe someday . . . but right now I have my work to do. Please don't pressure me." He could see a pulse beating in her neck.

"I'm not pressuring you. But I haven't changed my mind about marriage. Darling, I want to be with you. I want to have children with you. We haven't got forever."

No one had forever. "Marry me, Nicole! Please . . . I don't want to live without you."

She closed her eyes. "Once I said that. Those are dangerous words, Drew."

"That was *years* ago, another lifetime. You forget, I've lost someone, too. You just don't want to make a commitment to me. Is that it?"

"No, that's not what I mean. But I have *other* commitments. I've worked hard and people believe in me! I just don't see how marriage would fit into my life."

Over her shoulder he saw the hands of a clock on the mantel. Time was against them; he would have to leave soon.

"Look, don't go home tomorrow, Nicole. I'll fly back from California as soon as I give my paper. Come to Philadelphia for a few days. Stay with me there and you'll see how good we are together, by ourselves. No Paris, no India—just us."

For a moment he thought she would agree, but then she shook her head. "I can't stay, even for a few days. The department—they expect me day after tomorrow."

Despite his decision not to, he articulated the fears that had kept him awake in the night. "Darling, I'm worried about you in Peru. The whole thing could blow up overnight, like Chile. Don't stay there, Nicole! Come live with me and let me keep you safe."

"Drew! Don't be so melodramatic. You're beginning to sound like a Latin man. Peru is not on the verge of collapse and nothing is going to happen to me."

"Nicole, please be reasonable. This is crazy, being apart for months on end. I need you *here,* not thousands of miles away!"

She removed her hands from his and held herself erect. "I haven't heard you say one word about *you* making a change. Naturally you *assume* I will come to the States, don't you?"

"Well . . . you can hardly expect that I'll move to Lima!"

"Expect? No, I don't *expect* you to do that, Drew—but you *do* expect that I will move to Philadelphia without hesitation. You just take it for granted!"

"It's possible for you to work just as well out of Philadelphia. You can continue on the Task Force, be a con-

sultant to foundations or UN agencies. Lima isn't the
only place where there's a need."

"But Lima is where I *live*, where I happen to do my
work, and that's why I was chosen for the IHTF.
How can I leave Professor Alvares when I owe him
everything? If it hadn't been for him giving me the
opportunity . . ."

He seized her shoulders. *"You* are the only person
responsible for your achievements. The only thing you
owe anyone is to continue working, and that could be
almost anywhere."

"You know what a bad time we've been through at
San Martín! Why are you doing this now?" she cried.

"Because I love you. And if you really loved me, you
would want to live with me—even in Philadelphia."

"Spoken like a typical male! It always comes down to
that with a man and a woman, doesn't it? If *I* loved *you*,
then of course I should give up everything and follow you
wherever you are." She pulled away and walked across
the room to stare out a window.

His bruised pride made him angry. Dammit, he was
right . . . *she* ought to be the one to come to him! Did
she actually think he should begin again in Lima, where
he had no professional ties, under a repressive government? They would probably have him pegged as an un-
desirable alien the minute he entered the country, if they
thought the Task Force had a CIA link. His temper was
mounting, a slow, steady resentment.

"What if I told you it was over unless we get married?"
he asked stonily.

Her back was to him, so he could not see her bite her
lower lip and shut her eyes tightly. "That's your privilege. It's probably just as well, anyway. It was getting to
be a nuisance, all these stupid little weekends snatched
here and there." She started for the bedroom to pack her
bags.

This isn't happening, Drew thought. *We're fighting over
getting married!* Her words were as painful as a body
blow. Is that what she thought of their beautiful times
together, "stupid little weekends?"

He followed her to the bedroom, where their disagreement mounted. It went far beyond the main issue, as
arguments do, with words being exchanged that neither

of them meant, nor would soon forget. The result was predictable, each regarding the other hostilely, rigid and stony-eyed, too proud to give in.

Drew finished throwing his clothes into his carry-on bag in silence. In the living room, he put on his overcoat and dropped some bills on the desk, scribbling a note for the cleaning woman.

They stood looking at each other.

"I don't like parting this way, in anger." She sucked in her cheeks to keep her mouth from trembling. "Please try to understand."

He shook his head wearily. "I *am* trying, but it's not working. I think you really are afraid of love, Nicole."

Without looking at her, he picked up his bag and left. Still standing next to the desk, she heard the opening and closing of the elevator gates in the silence of the empty apartment.

Oh God, she thought, *What have I done?*

But what else could she do?

Chapter 29

Manuel was not waiting at the airport. *This is one time I wish he* were *here*, thought Nicole, as she followed the officer to a door marked "Immigration—Private—No admittance except authorized personnel."

"Just be seated, señorita, if you would be so kind," he said. "It won't take long. A formality." He was exceedingly polite, but she heard the lock turn as he left.

She had not been particularly worried at passport control when an official referred to a list of names on a clipboard and asked her to step out of line. *This is annoying*, she thought, but it would not delay her, because she would have to wait for her baggage to be unloaded in any case.

Two people standing near her were discussing some sort of civil unrest in which many people had been killed. Had there been disturbances in Lima while she was away? At that moment she had been approached by the officer from the airport police, who requested her to come with him.

She sat on a hard wooden chair, looking around at the untidy work space crammed with stacks of immigration forms and procedure manuals. What reason could they have for detaining her? Perhaps a name or a passport number similar to hers had been marked for attention. Whatever it was, if Manuel were here, he would have it straightened out immediately.

Why *now*, the one time Manuel had not come to meet her? This could have happened any time, but Manuel had always been there in the past. She had never properly appreciated how much red tape he had saved her.

Where *was* that officer? She would like to vent her anger on him, let him know that he had chosen the wrong person to interfere with! But of course, she would not do that. Still, how ironic, almost amusing, that he had selected a woman who had influential friends. He was lucky. Many people in her position would raise a fuss, costing him his job.

She drummed her fingers, tapped her feet, stood up, and walked back and forth in the close room. There were no windows. A small pane of frosted glass filled an opening in the common wall with the next office, but she could see it had been covered with paper on the other side.

The airport was crawling with military. She had heard on the plane that the Guardia Civil, the civilian police, were striking for a wage increase. There was always some strike going on in Lima nowadays.

Her weariness was oppressive.

All day long, throughout the tedious flight, she had tried to ignore the pain. She had not been able to sleep the previous night, after the angry parting with Drew. Back in her room at the hotel, she had told herself that they were not good for each other and that she was relieved it was over. Like Lucy and her lover, Horacio Salamanca, they would be better friends apart. But, finally, she acknowledged that friendship was not what she wanted from Drew. She had dissolved in tears and lay curled in bed weeping into the pillow and wondering what it was within her that made her choose the course she feared most—to be alone.

The door opened, startling Nicole, and the officer returned, accompanied by two military police guards.

"I must request, Señorita Légende, that you accompany these guards to the police headquarters in Lima."

"But why? Am I under arrest?"

"Not arrest, señorita. They merely wish to ask you a few questions," he said soothingly.

"That sounds like an arrest to me." She was frightened, but she would not allow him to see it.

The officer shrugged. "If you were arrested, señorita, you would be handcuffed. Are we not treating you with courtesy?"

"Do I have a choice about whether I may go with the police?"

"No, señorita."

"Then, señor, I say that I am under arrest!" she tried

to keep her voice light and untrembling. "May I have my passport, please?"

"Not just yet, señorita. It will be returned at the police headquarters. Your luggage will be sent to your house."

"After it has been thoroughly ransacked, I'm sure," she said, her voice heavy with sarcasm.

The man gestured indifferently.

As soon as she saw the captain, Nicole detested him. He was a squat *cholo* with a deceptively lofty manner that did not disguise his peasant background. There was none of the warmth and humor she had come to associate with the people of the pueblos, or the *campesinos* at Huaranca, however. His eyes were without emotion, unblinking. He did not appear cruel so much as uncaring.

"Am I permitted to call my lawyer?" she asked.

Feigning surprise, the captain said, "You won't need a lawyer, señorita."

"I refuse to say anything further—anything at all—until I make a call. I know that the law says I may do that."

"That is true, señorita, but—"

"I insist on using your telephone, captain."

"One call only, señorita," he was more than reluctant.

Which one should she call, Manuel or Lucy? She had only her instincts to go on. She did not entirely trust Manuel. It seemed too coincidental that he had not been at the airport on this occasion. In the police car, she had looked through her address book and, by a miracle, there were Lucy's telephone numbers, at home and at her office. Where would Lucy be now? It was too late for the office. She usually went to the school for her son at 4:30; they would be home by 5:30, surely.

With trembling fingers she dialed. There was a ring, five rings, six, . . . nine, . . .

"That is long enough, señorita," said the captain.

. . . Eleven. "Hello!" It was Lucy's voice, breathless.

Nicole's legs felt weak. "Señora Monaco?"

"Yes, yes—who is speaking, please?"

"This is, uh, Dr. Nicole Légende calling, señora."

"Nicole! I just this minute came in the door. What is this? A joke?"

"I am calling, Señora Monaco, from police headquarters. I was detained at the airport in passport control and am now being held for questioning."

The captain made an impatient sound and tried to wrest the receiver from Nicole's hand. She hung on and wrenched it away from him.

"Is this serious, Nicole?" Lucy was saying.

"Yes!"

"I'll be right there. Who is with you? Let me speak to him."

Nicole handed the receiver to the captain. He took it, giving her a look of disgust.

"Yes?"

Nicole could hear the sound of Lucy's sharp voice crackling on the line. The captain tried to interrupt several times. Finally he said, "Yes, counselor. Yes, I understand. Be assured."

Seething, he handed the receiver back to Nicole. "Lucy?"

"Listen, Nicole, I'll be there as soon as I can—thirty minutes, no more. *Do not move from that room.* Insist on staying there. You are within your rights to wait there for me. And say *nothing.* Remember that!"

"Don't worry. Thank you."

"Wouldn't you like to go somewhere more comfortable, and have some refreshments, señorita?" asked the captain when she hung up.

"No, captain. I am staying right here in this office until Señora Monaco arrives."

"That could take hours."

"So be it,"

He pushed a button. A uniformed matron appeared. "The señorita would like to use the sanitary facilities," said the captain.

"No!" shouted Nicole. "The señorita would *not* like to use any facilities. My attorney will be here within ten minutes and I insist on waiting here for her."

The matron took hold of her arm, but the captain motioned her away. "Very well," he said. "Let us begin the interrogation, then."

Nicole's heart sank. "Not until my attorney is present."

He slammed his fist on the desk, causing a water glass to bounce. "You are too proud and stubborn, Señorita Légende."

"I know my rights as a citizen."

"Constitutional rights have been rescinded."

"Not entirely, captain. There is still due process in Peru."

"I beg to differ with you, *doctora,*" he hissed. "As of yesterday, after the military was forced to crush the rebellion of the Civil Guard, all guarantees have been suspended!"

Nicole stared at him. He reminded Nicole of a jackal, lurking and devious. "Are you telling me the truth?" she whispered.

In answer, he reached behind him for a newspaper that was lying on a table and held it up. In bold banner headlines, were the words, "State of Emergency Follows Police Revolt."

Nicole reached for the paper he handed her. Swiftly she scanned the long article. It was true! The army had surrounded Lima's main police garrison with tanks to put down a rebellion. Civilian riots and looting had followed this action, with some loss of life, causing the government to declare a national emergency, a strict curfew, and a *thirty day suspension of legal rights.*

That was what the conversation in the airport had been all about. If she had not been so wrapped up in her own misery, she would have read *The New York Times* that morning and known what was happening in Peru.

Would she have stayed in the States if she had known?

"What was the nature of your trip to the United States, Señorita Légende?" the captain interrupted her thoughts.

"I told you, I won't answer any questions until my lawyer is here. After that, if she so advises me, I shall be happy to tell you anything you want to know."

He made a note on a sheet of paper and placed it in a manila file folder. Nicole craned her neck to see if the folder had her name on it. It was impossible to tell, but it looked like a substantial file.

"You travel often, señorita." He opened an envelope and withdrew some documents. Among them was her passport. Opening it, he riffled through the pages. "Very often . . . for one who is simply a doctor taking care of patients in a hospital."

Nicole ignored him. She pretended to read the paper until he stood up, came around the desk and tore it out of her hands. He loomed above her, his face menacing, with the same dead look in his eyes. "Answer me!" he growled.

The door to the outer reception hall opened and a clerk stood halfway in the room. "There is a woman lawyer here—"

He was pushed aside as Lucy flung back the door and strode into the room clutching a sheaf of papers in her hand.

"All right, captain. Here is an order for the immediate release of my client, signed by a deputy of the Public Ministry." She handed him the document. Lucy turned to face an astonished Nicole. "Are you all right, Dr. Légende? Has he threatened you?"

"No, I have not threatened her!" shouted the captain, who had turned an interesting shade of solferino.

"I'm fine, Señora Monaco. They took my passport, but they haven't told me why."

"On what grounds has my client been charged?" Lucy asked the captain.

"She has not been 'charged' with anything. We have brought her in for questioning, which is perfectly legal under the state of emergency decree. And most uncooperative she has been, too!"

"My client is not bound to cooperate with you, captain. She will cooperate fully in a court of law with counsel present, when—I repeat—*when* charges are brought. Until then, you have no right to detain her." She presented another paper. "Now, if you will sign this, please."

He looked puzzled. "What is this?"

"A writ of *habeas corpus ad subjiciendum* attesting to the fact that my client was apprehended at the airport and brought here to your office without a prior writ. For the record, captain." She smiled sweetly.

The captain studied the document, but it was apparent he could make no sense of its legal language. Not wishing to reveal his ignorance, he scribbled a signature at the bottom.

"Thank you, captain. Shall we go, Dr. Légende?"

"Not yet. Not without my passport." She turned to the captain. "May I have it?"

He looked at her with malevolent triumph. "I'm afraid

that is impossible. We have to keep your passport for now, Señorita Légende. It will be returned when it is deemed appropriate."

Nicole was dumbstruck. This was worse than she had imagined. "My passport confiscated? But I *must* have it. I can't travel without it! I go regularly to a . . . a World Health Organization meeting in Geneva. . . ." She appealed frantically to Lucy. "Tell him!"

The captain raised his hands in mock helplessness. "I know nothing of these matters, señorita. After all, I am just a simple captain." He looked directly at Lucy. "You must take it up with the political section of the Investigative Police."

"Investigative—?" Nicole began, alarm coursing through her.

"Come on, Nicole." Lucy marshaled her out of the police headquarters to her automobile, a tan two-door Chevrolet Malibu. She did not waste time on conversation until they were well along, having driven around the block, in and out of the same streets twice, to be certain they were not being followed.

"I don't trust them for a minute! I caught him off guard in there with my writ, but they're beginning to feel their power with this state of emergency."

"But, what about my passport?"

"We'll worry about the passport later. Right now, I'm more concerned about your *person.* I wanted to get you out of there before he decides he made a mistake in letting you go."

"I don't understand. What's going on?"

"He was from the Investigative Police!"

"The PIP? But he was in uniform. I thought they were plainclothes."

"Usually they are. These are not ordinary times."

"What was the writ for?"

"I wanted proof that he had detained you without a warrant. You can bet it won't be in his records."

"How did you get an order for my release so quickly?"

Lucy snorted. "I have a whole stack of them. Blanks. Perfectly legal, though. I fill in the name of the apprehended party. Believe me, with my clientele, it's necessary." Lucy turned to give her a quizzical look. "I must say, Nicole, I never figured *you* would be one of them!"

"I decided it was time you had a paying customer."

They laughed together, then Lucy sobered. "We have to talk. Where do you want to go?"

"Let's go to my house, Lucy. Vera must be going out of her mind. She was expecting me."

Indeed, Vera had passed through the first stages of alarm when Pedro called from the airport to say that all the passengers from the flight had come through customs and Nicole was not among them. On the verge of hysteria, she almost fainted from relief when Nicole and Lucy appeared.

"I didn't know what to do, Señorita Nicole!" she cried. "I tried to reach Señor Caldeiro-León. He never called this time to tell me not to send Pedro, but I thought he might have taken you before Pedro reached the airport." She looked down, a guilty expression on her face.

"Did you scold Pedro, Vera?" Nicole asked.

The woman nodded. "Yes. I'm so ashamed, but I was worried. I was afraid you had been kidnapped."

"Kidnapped?" She pondered something that had been bothering her. "Have you seen Fabricio?"

Vera shook her head. "He hasn't been here since you left."

"I see," she said thoughtfully.

Vera fluttered around them, taking Nicole's attaché case and the winter coats she carried over her arm. "Where are your suitcases?"

"They're still at the airport, in customs. Lucy, is it possible to get my luggage released? I'm afraid they'll rifle through it and steal everything."

"I'll see what I can do. May I use the phone in the study?"

Nicole told Vera to show Lucy up to her room when she had finished calling. "I'm going to take a bath. And then, maybe you would serve us something to eat up there, Vera? I don't think I'll be able to stay awake until dinner time."

Nicole felt restored after she had soaked in a soothing warm tub. Clad in slippers and robe, she joined Lucy who, cocktail in hand, was settled in the bedroom on a comfortable, overstuffed sofa next to the fireplace. Nicole poured herself a sherry from the tray Vera had placed on the Regency table, then reclined on a chaise.

Lucy leaned back, languidly sipping a *capitán* and twirling her cigarette holder, as she regarded the luxuriously appointed suite appreciatively. "Blue is such a restful color. It's especially effective with the accents of apricot. If I owned this room, I might be tempted to never leave it."

Surprised, Nicole said, "I don't spend much time here. I feel it lacks warmth."

Lucy sputtered. "It lacks a *man* . . . in that enormous bed! That's all the warmth it needs."

Nicole felt the color rise in her cheeks.

Lucy threw back her head and roared at her discomfiture. "*My God*, Nicole! You're like a shy young virgin. How old are you? Twenty eight—and a doctor, in the bargain. Don't tell me Manuel hasn't managed to seduce you. It's time you had an affair, if you haven't already."

Maybe it was because she was exhausted and wrought up over the experience at police headquarters. Or perhaps it was the strain of breaking off with Drew. Nicole dropped her face forward into her hands, overwhelmed with unhappiness.

Lucy was at her side instantly. Putting her arms around Nicole's shoulders, she said. "I think you need more than a lawyer. You need a friend you can talk to."

Flushed and wretched, Nicole found herself telling Lucy all there was to tell. About Drew and their affair, about Manuel and his relentless pursuit of her. And what he had told her of the government's suspecting the Task Force of being a CIA front. The only thing she omitted was her rising suspicion that Manuel himself might have played a role in today's episode with the police. It seemed like such an outrageous accusation that she was afraid to mention it, even to Lucy Monaco.

There was a knock at the door. Vera rolled in a tea table with sandwiches and cakes and coffee. "Pedro has arrived with the suitcases, señorita. He said the police had forced the locks and they'll have to be repaired."

"Oh, I forgot to tell you, Nicole," Lucy interrupted. "I spoke to the head of customs, who agreed to release your bags—and then, when Pedro called in, I told Vera he should collect them."

"Thank you, Lucy. And Vera, please thank Pedro. I'll

do it personally in the morning." The housekeeper was looking at her strangely. "What is it, Vera?"

"You were arrested by the police, Señorita Nicole?"

"No, no, Vera," she assured her. "They just asked me a few questions. Nothing important."

"I *warned* you, señorita. The night those boys were here! I *knew* it would cause trouble." She stared at Nicole with a doleful expression.

Nicole made a stern mouth and met Vera's eyes. "There is no connection at all between that and what happened today, Vera. Please, you must not say anything about that night or those students, *ever . . . to anyone!* Do you promise?"

She nodded, casting a frightened glance in Lucy's direction. "Don't worry about me," said Lucy. "I didn't hear a word." Vera fled from the room.

"Do you want to tell me what that was about?" asked Lucy. "Attorney-client privilege, of course. It's the same as being in the confessional."

When Nicole had completed her tale of the night the wounded Pepe had been brought to the house, Lucy said, "To think I imagined you led such a quiet, uneventful existence. And all this time you've been surrounded by handsome lovers, heartbroken suitors, and flying bullets!"

Nicole put her hands to her cheeks. "*One* bullet, Lucy! One very small bullet that should never have been shot into that young man. I could get into real trouble if anyone ever found out about it. Vera was upset tonight, or else she would never have said anything."

"Let's hope she doesn't get upset in front of the wrong people. I knew those medical students were activists the minute I met them at your clinic. They had that sweet, dumb, I've-seen-the-light look about them. They're the kind who do their cause little good but get themselves into a hell of a lot of trouble!"

"You were right about who beat up Pepe that time—remember, when my car was covered with filth?"

"I remember. I told you he would be in a jam one day, didn't I? Well, it will happen over and over again, Nicole, and as your attorney, I advise you to keep as far away from them as you can."

"They've kept *their* distance ever since the night Pepe

was shot. To protect me, I think. The only time I see them is in the clinic or on the wards."

"You can't avoid that, I suppose. But do be cautious, because you can't afford any more on your record."

In response to Nicole's questioning look, Lucy continued speaking. "As I make it out, your dossier has you. . ." she tallied on her fingers, ". . . linked with the mobile clinics, considered a likely source of aid to dissidents; present at the party for Maestro Gordo, which was undoubtedly infiltrated with police informers; appearing at Pepe's apartment after he was beaten up by police thugs; visiting Peace Corps projects in the countryside and associating with Peace Corps volunteers, who have since been expelled from Peru as pawns of the CIA; making a grant application to the highly suspect American Cartwright Foundation. To say nothing of these regular trips abroad to the notorious International Health Task Force, which is believed to be a den of espionage . . . *to which* you were appointed because of your lengthy stay in the U.S. at the Center for Disease Control, where you were undoubtedly recruited by Dr. Henry Campion, dean of the spooks!" Lucy sat back against the pillows with a cynical smile.

"Good God!" Nicole regarded Lucy with shocked wonder. "You make it sound so . . . so . . . *plausible.*"

"That's my job, love. But you can see what a case they could make, can't you? And many people would believe it. Especially after what happened in Chile." Rising, she said, "Well, I must dash. It's almost curfew."

Nicole nodded. "Haven't you forgotten someone, though?"

"Who?" asked Lucy.

"Dr. Andrew Tower. Drew."

"Oh, *him!* No, I haven't forgotten about him." Lucy picked up her briefcase, walked to the door, and turned.

"Drew is your CIA contact. He's running you."

Chapter 30

By all the rules of logic, the girl should have been dead when they brought her in.

Nicole sat in the surgery, staring at the delicate, exposed body on the table. She could have been no older than seventeen. Despite the bruised and distorted features, one could see she had been beautiful.

How had she withstood what they had done to her? What kind of person could bear to do this to another human being? In all the years of working in emergency rooms and wards, with wife beatings and child abuse, rapes and murders, Nicole had never encountered a case as horrible as this.

Someone had punched, clubbed and whipped the young woman, beating her face until it was unrecognizable. The principal bones of her hands and feet had been fractured, and both shoulders were dislocated. More than forty cigarette burns marred her body, mostly on the breasts and around the abdomen and vulva.

Her external injuries were hideous, but it had been the internal wounds that killed her. The ruptured bladder and perforated uterus.

The surgeon had hastily departed the operating room, saying little, but obviously shaken. He had done his best to make the repairs, but she had expired during the surgery. If she had been brought to the hospital earlier, instead of lying concealed in a ditch for so many hours, perhaps they could have saved her. Late in the afternoon, some workers from the *barriada* had found her and taken her to the mobile clinic, where Carlos and another intern had kept her alive and brought her to San Martín.

A nursing sister put a sheet over the mutilated body and an orderly wheeled it away to the mortuary. Nicole followed the nun to the nurses' station. Carlos was waiting there, wearing his new uniform, the white coat of an intern.

"May I speak to you, Dr. Légende?" He was always careful to observe the formalities at the hospital.

"In a moment," she told him. "Sister, did you get any identification on the woman who died?"

"No, *doctora*, there was none. It is a matter for the police." Nicole heard Carlos give a cynical snort under his breath. She flashed him a disapproving frown. "Let me know what they find out, please. She was first brought in to my service." The nun nodded.

"Come upstairs," she told Carlos. It was late and everyone had left the department. Nicole boiled some water and made two cups of tea, handing one to Carlos. "Let's go into my office."

When they were seated, she studied him over the rim of her cup. Carlos had greatly matured in the four years she had known him. With the added stature of clinical internship, he looked his age, even older, not only because he had physically broadened, but he had developed an aura of assurance and wisdom. In his calm intelligence, he reminded her of a younger Jorge Alvares. Pepe still had what Lucy had called that "sweet, dumb, I've-seen-the-light look," which made him seem young and vulnerable, hardly someone she would call a man. The Pepes would march and chant and attack the wrongs of society with shining zeal, but Nicole thought Carlos would quietly devote his life to bringing about reforms.

"That was ghastly," she said vehemently, referring to the girl who had died. "Whoever is responsible deserves to be executed!"

"I hear the police have circulated a story that she was kidnapped and tortured by Maoist terrorists."

"Who else would it be, Carlos, if not terrorists?"

"You saw her, Nicole. That was a professional job. A police job!"

"I didn't think the police dealt with prisoners that way—not after the investigations last year. Even if they did, why would they dump her on a roadside and leave her for dead? They must have other ways of disposing of a body."

"They did it for a reason, you can be sure. To place the blame on so-called urban guerrillas, or just to frighten people. They probably thought she was as good as dead, and my guess is . . . they realized who she was and were afraid of another torture scandal."

Nicole leaned forward. "Do *you* know who she was?"

He nodded. "She was a student at San Marcos University. The girlfriend of the leader of a leftist student organization. Her father is a well-to-do businessman in Arequipa."

"How do you know this, Carlos?" she asked, unable to hide the agitation she felt.

"It got around that she was arrested a few days ago. She had been shopping with a friend who went into a store, leaving her alone outside with the packages. Who knows, it may have been a set-up. Anyway, when the friend came back, the girl was gone, but the packages were still there on the pavement. A woman in the next shop said she had been forced into a car by two men. The car belonged to the PIP. The woman recognized it."

"But *why*. Carlos? Just being an activist isn't enough to get you arrested."

"They're after her boyfriend and some of his group who have left Lima. They think they're connected with the assassination attempt on the government ministers last December."

"Are they?"

"No, I'm sure they're not. Students don't go around trying to kill people, Nicole. They leave that to the police!"

"You should come forward with this information, if you really think that's who she is. Her family must be informed."

He shook his head emphatically. "The police know who she is. They'll pretend it was their excellent detective work that uncovered it. I can't go to them, Nicole, because frankly . . . I'm afraid."

I'm afraid, too, Nicole thought despairingly. She almost told Carlos about her passport being confiscated and how she had been taken to police headquarters, but she stopped herself. She realized she did not completely trust him. That is what a military dictatorship does to you. Makes you distrust even your friends. Her father had always said that and he was right. She was beginning not to trust a number of people . . . the servants, the

other doctors at the hospital, Manuel, and certainly not
Fabricio, who had resumed his duties after her return
from New York.

And now, Carlos and Pepe, too. They were Marxists,
opposed to the junta, and although they professed not to
believe in violence themselves, she retained the sharp
memory of Maestro Gordo sitting in their apartment and
preaching violent revolution.

"Whatever happened to that professor?" she asked.
"Maestro Gordo."

Carlos's eyes shifted, ever so briefly. "He was. . .
'disappeared.' "

"Disappeared? Do you think this is Argentina?"

"Sometimes, Nicole, I think it's becoming like Argentina, or Chile, or worse. People have been tortured, as
you have plainly seen. And occasionally, they simply
disappear."

Carlos cracked his knuckles. "I'm not really a communist, Nicole, but I *hate* this government. The universities
have always been centers of political activism. It's the
tradition in Peru. Where do students come from? From
the middle classes. When the government moves against
students, it's making war on the middle class!"

"That's what my father predicted would happen in
Peru. He never trusted men in uniform. My father favored socialism, although you may find that hard to
believe."

He nodded. "I remember how Gordo nailed you about
your family that night at our apartment. I was ashamed
at how he treated you, Nicole, because I knew what *you*
were, and by then I had begun to see what a fraud *he*
was."

"Maybe he has gone underground. Don't you think
that could explain his disappearance?"

"No. I think they've killed him. Like many others."

She shivered, feeling threatened by the conversation.
Against her will she was being drawn into a dark area,
terrifying in its implications.

It was late. "I should be getting home, Carlos."

She offered to drop him near his apartment on her
way, but he refused. "Thanks," he smiled sadly, "but it's
better if we're not seen together outside the hospital."

From the parking area, she watched him walk off in

the night, a dejected stoop to his shoulders. Fabricio was waiting in the Renault.

When she arrived home, she went through the mail, which contained a smaller number of invitations than usual because of the curfew. Vera told her Drew had telephoned just a few minutes before. Nicole's pulse raced at Vera's words.

"Did he leave a message? Did he say he would call again?"

"No, señorita. He just said to tell you it was Andrew Tower calling from Philadelphia." Vera, in the manner of all personal servants who have long been part of a household, had guessed that Dr. Tower was more than a professional colleague.

Nicole deliberated for almost an hour whether to call him back, and then when she tried, she could not get a line through. Her disappointment and frustration at missing his call brought tears to her eyes.

This was the second time Drew had called since they had parted in New York over a month ago. Worried about the reports of violence and martial law in Lima, he had phoned after her arrival to be sure she was safe. The conversation had been brief and cool, with both of them feeling the strain of their argument. Still wounded, she had made light of his concern, not telling him about the problems with her passport, since she had been unrealistically hopeful it would be returned to her soon. Instead, she had assured him that, except for the curfew, everything was normal in the capital.

Since then, there had scarcely been a day that passed when she had not thought of Drew longingly, hoping in vain for a letter or a telephone call. Whenever she had the impulse to write to him or call, she reasoned that the only way she could initiate contact was if she had decided she would marry him. By now, she wasn't even certain he still wanted her.

But even if she agreed to go to him now, she could not leave Peru. Until her passport was returned, she was a prisoner in her own country.

Lucy had taken her case to the Interior Ministry, which issued passports, hoping to circumvent the political division of the PIP. The situation was unbelievable! Periodically, Nicole would cease whatever activity she was engaged in, thunderstruck that she, the daughter of Peru's illustrious adoptive son, Daniel Légende, should be deprived of her travel document. There is no more precious badge of citizenship a country can bestow.

In the middle of the next week, Manuel called to ask if she could see him. In a way, she wanted not to, but their lives were intertwined to such a degree, what with Légende et Cie, her father's estate, and Lima society, that it would be awkward, if not impossible, to avoid him. "Come for dinner," she said. "We'll dine early so you can get home before curfew."

"It doesn't really matter. I have a safe conduct pass," he told her. "Still, you never know when some *sinchi* will get trigger-happy."

"No, you don't," she answered pointedly, remembering Pepe. She wondered if he might surmise her meaning, the way he seemed to divine almost everything else about her.

A year ago, Manuel Caldeiro-León had dined out five or six nights a week.

No more were the great dinner parties and receptions in palatial homes. Those who still lived in the grand manner tried to keep a low profile. At first it had been the unrest, and now the curfew, that had ruined Lima's night life. Hoteliers were complaining. Guests were virtual prisoners after dark, thus the hostelries had lost most of their tourist bookings. And since the junta had discouraged private investment in Peru, their business clientele had diminished.

That was the least of it, Manuel knew. There was a climate of fear that pervaded the capital. The country was moribund, and there was only one remedy. *The real cure for Peru's ills was a change of government*—the plan that he and his carefully chosen associates secretly supported. Meanwhile, he continued to work with the banks and the finance ministry, trying to influence the economic policies of this government. There was time enough to show his hand, and since it was his country, he would do everything in his power to keep it from going under.

Nicole was another cause of his increasing alarm. She had no idea of her vulnerability. His protection would mean nothing if she persisted in her rash actions. For example, going out to those pueblos with the young Americans from the Peace Corps last year. What a foolish and unnecessary gesture! Not for a minute did he believe they were trained agents, but they *had* been thrown out of Peru. He had seen the file and it made a good argument for irregular activities. You could twist anything around to prove a point, if you were clever and it served a purpose.

Some Americans at the embassy were CIA, of course. Everyone knew. It was even possible they had used a few of the young idealists who volunteered for the Peace Corps to gather information for them. The ridiculous part of it was that anything a Peace Corps volunteer could have furnished was readily available to anyone. It took a certain density of the mind to think like an intelligence agent.

Perhaps now that Nicole had been deprived of her passport, she would exercise better judgment. It had been for her own protection that he had not intervened. Continuing to attend the meetings of the group formed by that American professor would further implicate her in anti-government activities.

The International Health Task Force was not a United Nations agency, not really. It was an unofficial affiliate, and although its members were drawn from ten different nations, it was dominated by Americans, and American money paid for most of its work. The Peruvian government thought Nicole had been taken in by her American team members, whom they assumed to be CIA. Whether it was true or not was irrelevant. The government believed it.

Foolish girl! She would get herself in deep trouble, and one of these days she would be beyond his help. Tonight he would have it out with her, ask her to marry him for one last time. She ought to be flattered that he would still have her! How he had cursed himself for his stupidity and idealism. Standing on his honor, he had thought she would surely marry him after her father's death, and that he had owed it to Daniel, who had been a true friend, not to betray his trust by seducing his daughter.

Well, he had discovered the truth about Nicole that night in Paris six months ago! He had seen with his own eyes her shamelessness, her wanton thrusting herself against the North American. A gringo, he thought with malice, still imagining what had followed the scene he witnessed, the two mouths hungrily devouring each other, the hands seeking private places, the bodies straining like animals in heat.

Beads of perspiration formed on Manuel's forehead as he recalled the nightmare vision of himself sitting numbly in the automobile, watching them, humiliated—peering up at the penthouse, waiting for the tall American to emerge, and finally knowing that if he remained there all night, he would not see him leave.

Punishing himself still further, he had passed by 17 Avenue Foch the next day on his way to the airport. Against all probability, he had been in time to see Nicole and her lover run down the steps hand in hand, laughing together. Dressed casually in blue jeans, with a sweater tied over her shoulders, she had never appeared happier, or more desirable. In the vise of an invidious and unremitting envy, Manuel had flown home to Lima, seeking oblivion in Elena's bed.

Damn her! He had tried everything he could think of to forget Nicole, purposely avoiding her for weeks at a time, and then when they were together, provoking her to argument, when all he wanted was to take her in his arms and make her love him.

When he heard that the passport incident had gotten out of hand, ending with her being taken to police headquarters, he had been in a panic, feeling guilty that he had not taken steps to stop it. But it was to Lucy Monaco she had gone for assistance. Well, if that was where Nicole turned when she needed someone. . . . She could do worse. Lucy made a lot of noise, but she represented her clients well and he respected her.

The gates to Casa Loma were opened by the watchman. What a pathetically inadequate old man he was. He would not be worth the price of his uniform should she ever really need protection in this house! He was ushered in by a smiling Vera, transparently happy to see him. *If it were up to her, I could move in tomorrow,* he thought, as Vera showed him to the drawing room. He mixed a pitcher of martinis while he waited for Nicole.

Her voice sounded, he heard her quick, light footsteps in the gallery. And there she was, a marvel tonight in an embroidered paisley caftan of rose, lavender, and amber silk, her lustrous hair caught back with a barrett and hanging loose to the waist.

Nicole, Nicole! Love me, querida. Why won't you love me?

"Good evening, Nicole," his manner remained suave and controlled. Kissing her cheeks, he held her at arm's length. "How exotic. You must have found time for shopping in India."

Nervous, and alternately filled with resentment and desire, he drank too much. Gulping two martinis before dinner, he should have been more cautious. With the *quenelles de poisson,* they were served a 1971 Corton Charlemagne, as fine a white Burgundy as any he could have selected himself, followed by a 1949 Château Latour to accompany the grilled *filet de boeuf.* Manuel was never able to resist a truly fine wine, and Daniel's cellar was unsurpassed in all of the Americas. Nicole barely touched her glass, but Manuel consumed enough for both of them.

After dinner, they sat in his favorite room, the elegantly comfortable retreat that had been her father's study. Manuel had always thought it would be his when he married Nicole. He had planned to make only minor changes because he liked the feeling that he would occupy Daniel Légende's place.

Vera had removed the coffee tray and said good night. Manuel returned to the recessed bar, concealed behind paneled doors. Into a liqueur glass of delicate etched crystal with a sterling silver base, he poured a small amount of cointreau for Nicole. For himself, he replenished his snifter of Napoleon brandy. Wrapped in his lightheaded, falsely cheerful intoxication, he pursued a precarious subject.

"I heard you had some problems with your passport when you flew in from New York. I'm sorry I wasn't there to meet you. Perhaps I could have done something."

Her reaction surprised him. She smiled at him knowingly and said, with an edge of sarcasm, "You just happened to hear about it, is that it?"

"No, I didn't just *happen* to hear—I ran into Lucy Monaco at the ministry. It's a matter of record when a hearing is requested." She did not need to know that he had purposely asked to go into the files to see the disposition of the case. Having connections in the various ministries was one of the privileges he enjoyed.

He sat next to her on the couch. She stared at the fire, absorbed by the snap of the flames when they ignited trapped pockets of resin in the eucalyptus logs. In this room, where he had spent so many hours in the past, he was reminded of the closeness they had once known. If he approached her in just the right manner, he was certain he could recapture lost ground, reestablish their intimacy.

His eyes caressed the length of her, the tender line of throat and clavicle, the soft curve of breast and hip, the elegance of long, slim legs. *Dios!* After all these years, he wanted her with the same intensity, still captivated by her beauty, deriving sensual pleasure from examining the contours of her visage. Tonight he detected an air of melancholy about her. Could that mean she was troubled? Then might she not lean on him, be receptive to his advances?

"You seem preoccupied, Nicole."

She blinked and turned in his direction. "Oh, excuse me, Manuel. I was just . . . dreaming."

"Of what were you dreaming?" he asked softly.

She did not answer, but her eyes darkened before she looked away.

"I want to help you, Nicole. If you would marry me, my name and position would protect you."

There was repressed rage in her glance. "Are you *boasting* that your position is so secure with this government? Don't you know what they're doing to innocent people, Manuel?"

"That's what I want to prevent, my dear! I don't want them to harm you."

"Do you honestly think I would marry you for that?"

In repose, her face had been romantically tragic, reminiscent of the lovely young medical student he had discovered one chilly afternoon in Paris seven years ago. But now it was clear she was not the same woman. This Nicole challenged him with her strength and anger. She was an arrogantly beautiful goddess, a sexual creature, waiting to be tamed.

His head was buzzing from the wine and brandy he had

consumed. He moved closer, noticing how she pushed herself into a corner of the couch against the pillows. That amused him. She need not play the inexperienced maiden with him!

He took her hands in his, holding them fast when she tried to pull away, turning them over and kissing the palms.

"Please, Manuel . . ." she murmured.

Sliding the fingers of his left hand into the hair at the nape of her neck, he drew her to him.

" 'Please, Manuel' *what?*" he whispered as he bent to kiss the beating pulse in her neck.

His left hand tightened its grip on her hair as he pulled her down on the sofa and cupped her breast with his right. "Please, Manuel . . . *kiss* me? Please, Manuel . . . *touch* me? Please, Manuel, *do what I've always wanted you to do?*"

His venom became more intense as he mimicked her. He thought his head would burst with his angry frustration. Nicole's eyes widened with incomprehension and disbelief.

His voice was like a rapier: "We'll see who's better for you . . . me or your gringo!"

He heard her gasp.

She did not call for help when he released the fastenings on the shoulder of the Indian dress, pulling it down. Instead, she turned her head to the side and made denying sounds in her throat as she tried to push him away. He held her more firmly, enflamed by the allure of her unrobed skin, massaging her breast until he felt the nipple rise, covering her protesting lips with his own and thrusting his tongue deep in her mouth. These were the lips he had hungered for, this was the mouth he had wanted for his own! His hand sought her naked leg through the long slit in the gown and continued to move upward.

All sense of time and place and reason deserted him as his fingertips touched the softness between her thighs. Plummeted into carnal oblivion, the rondures of her flesh consumed him. Ravaging her with his hands and mouth, unhearing in his sybaritism, he ripped the flimsy wisp of lace from her hips. Nicole was strong, but he was too much for her, and she was encumbered by the wide sleeves and long skirt of the caftan, which were twisted around her waist and under their bodies.

Breathing hard, intent on finally possessing the body he had been denied, Manuel did not react at first when she stopped struggling. Nicole went limp in his arms. As he opened his trousers to release himself, prepared to invade her, he was halted by the steadiness of her gaze.

"Well," she said in a cold, dispassionate voice, "why don't you get on with it? Go ahead and rape me!"

He became flaccid with the horror of what he had done.

Weeks later, Nicole could still neither accept nor understand what had happened that night. She tried to blot it from her mind.

It made no sense that Manuel had behaved as he had in her house. For all the years she had known him, their acquaintance had been built on mutual respect. She had noticed how much he had to drink. But that was not an adequate explanation. Manuel held his liquor well, in true macho tradition. No. He had acted crazed, beyond all reason, and if she had not gotten through to him with her sudden switch from an attitude of defense to one of shaming him, he would have raped her. She had no doubt of it. The knowledge filled her with sadness.

Shocked out of his mindlessness, he had recoiled from her, and sat on the edge of the sofa, leaning his forehead on one hand. "Cover yourself," he had muttered.

Wordlessly she had risen from the sofa and readjusted her dress.

"Forgive me, Nicole. I have dishonored my love for you—and my friendship with your father."

He then had indulged in lugubrious self-castigations, to such extremes that she had become concerned more for him than herself. She feared he would leave the house and commit some drastic excess, such as taking his own life. It became a surreal contretemps, with Manuel decrying his evil nature and Nicole assuring him that it was the alcohol, his nerves, or something peculiar in their conversation that evening that had caused him to act in this uncharacteristic fashion. It was all perfectly ridiculous, since he had revealed to her *why* he had practically assaulted her. He somehow had found out about her love affair with Drew and was insanely jealous!

At last he had gone, permitting her to return to the study to straighten the rumpled couch and erase all signs of their struggle so the servants would not know. Retrieving the ripped panty from the floor, she used it to mop up a glass of brandy that had been overturned. In her room, removing her earrings at the dressing table, she noticed her trembling hands. Realizing how unnerved she was by the episode, she had attempted to erase the awful memory by submerging herself in a hot bath.

The next day, two dozen long-stemmed red roses had arrived, accompanied by Manuel's card with no signature. What could he have said? She did not take his call that evening, asking Vera to say that she had retired. He left a message that he was going to the United States for three weeks and could be reached through his office if she needed him.

Nicole wondered how recently he had planned the trip.

"I'm afraid the news is not good, Nicole. They won't let you have your passport. It has to come up for a special hearing and it won't be scheduled for at least three months—maybe longer."

Nicole gripped the receiver. "*Lucy!* What am I going to do? I have to go to that meeting in Geneva in June. That's in two weeks! What will I tell them?"

Lucy was silent, thinking. "I'm not sure," she finally answered. "It might not be a good idea to reveal why you can't go. The fewer people who know your passport has been revoked, the better."

Nicole caught her breath. "Is that what has happened, Lucy? *Has* my passport been revoked?"

There was a pause. "Yes, Nicole. All fancy terms aside, that's what it comes down to."

"But—but, they only do that to *criminals!*"

"Not really. I know plenty of criminals who have passports. You're not in such bad company these days. If they know a dissident wants to stay in Peru, they punish him by deportation—but in your case, they know your work requires you to travel, so they take your passport away."

"Lucy," she said firmly. "*I am not a dissident!*"

* * *

It saddened Jorge Alvares to visit the great house with
Daniel Légende gone. He had not known him well, but
he had respected Légende and admired what he had
accomplished in his life. And he adored Daniel's daughter.
If I were younger, I would be in love with her! As it
was, his shaving mirror revealed to him a short, bald,
portly man of fifty-five, possessed of a sufficient sense of
reality to stifle any such delusions.

His fantasies were harmless, hardly the conceits of a
dirty old man. Jorge's flights of fancy about Nicole re-
volved around her being his daughter. Although, when
he considered the unlikely possibility that he and his
Rubenesque wife could have given life to the divine
Nicole, he chuckled at the absurdity of the chimera.
There is that drive in all of us, he thought, to see the
realization of our dreams in the next generation. In the
absence of children of his own, Nicole's accomplishments
had come to represent that fulfillment for him.

Jorge mounted the steps of the Légende mansion, turning while he waited to look out over the well-tended
gardens, which under the mist of the winter *garua* put
him in mind of the Irish moors. It must be terribly lonely
for Nicole to live here without her father. He wondered
why she had not married. There was no question that she
was intensely feminine and extremely attractive to men.
Perhaps too attractive? A woman like Nicole would
frighten off the average man, particularly the Limeños,
who liked their women soft and submissive.

The door opened and Jorge was escorted by a maid
across the broad marble foyer, along a tapestry-hung
gallery to the library, where Nicole awaited him in front
of a leaping fire. Jorge remembered this beautiful room,
with its collection of sculptures and magnificent Persian
carpets in russets and dark blues. Against this background, Nicole made a welcoming picture, clad in a simple wool dress of harmonious burgundy.

He flushed with pleasure when she spontaneously embraced him. "How are you feeling?" she asked.

His eyes twinkled. "I always feel wonderful on weekends. It's only when you see me in the department that
you have cause for alarm!"

When they were seated on the matching velvet couches
facing each other across the fireplace, the same maid who

had answered the door served cocktails and placed a platter of assorted canapés in front of them on a low coffee table.

"Thank you, Vera. Will you see that we're not disturbed for a while?"

As soon as the servant had left the room, closing the door, Nicole began, "I hope you'll understand why I did not invite Señora Alvares to accompany you. There's a personal matter I must discuss. Something I prefer not to talk about at the hospital."

"Of course," he murmured. He sat back, sipping his whiskey and listening with mounting apprehension as Nicole related in detail what had happened almost four months ago, when she was detained by the police on her return from New York, and the events leading up to the incident.

". . . and so, my lawyer has little hope that I would be permitted to leave the country, even if I were to receive a special invitation from the United Nations. The IHTF meeting begins a week from tomorrow in Geneva." Her eyes dropped. "I won't be able to attend."

The expression of disappointment on her lovely face stabbed him. Why was it that in every generation these repressive governments had to dash the aspirations of the young? Not only in Peru. In many countries of South America, military men used strong-arm methods in doomed efforts to impose their will on the people. And all they succeeded in accomplishing was destroying the dreams and promise of the future.

Jorge wanted to say something comforting. "One meeting, Nicole. That's not a tragedy. When does your attorney expect them to return your passport?"

"I'm not sure." Her eyes met his directly. "It's possible they'll refuse to give it back, Dr. Alvares. In that case . . ."

"In that case, my dear Nicole, you would be in danger," he finished quietly. "I regret very much if your appointment to the IHTF or your work in the *barriadas* have been misconstrued by the police. As for your contact with the interns, youth has been resisting authority in Peru since the days before Pizarro. How do they expect you to teach at a medical school without associating with students? However, Carlos should never have brought

Pepe to you when he was wounded. That was a grave error. I doubt that the police know, or you would have heard about it."

"What am I going to do about the Task Force?"

"I'll be happy to explain to Henry Campion, if that's worrying you."

"Lucy Monaco, my lawyer, doesn't think I should tell him about the passport being confiscated. She said the fewer people who know, the better."

"I agree. If you embarrass the government, it will be harder for them to back down. Why don't you call Henry now and then I'll get on the line? We'll say you can't get away from the department at this time. He'll understand."

"And what if I can't go to the next meeting?"

"There's time enough to concern ourselves about that."

But Jorge had already begun to worry. He had seen this scenario before with the junta. Depriving Nicole of her passport could be the prelude to other, more serious threats. He must think of some way to protect her. Before it was too late.

Chapter 31

There was a presence about Andrew Tower. Some people call it star quality. Rangy and broad shouldered, his athlete's body, wavy dark hair, and deep blue, occasionally brooding eyes made him outrageously attractive to women. It came as no surprise to anyone that he had Irish in him.

Bound for the Swissair departure lounge, Drew hoisted his L.L. Bean garment bag over one shoulder, unaware of the interest he awakened as he strode through JFK International Airport. A dozen women followed him with their eyes, wondering who he was, certain that any man as attractive as that had to be *someone.*

The flight to Geneva had already started to board, but Henry was waiting for him. "Sorry I'm late. I was held up in traffic," Drew greeted him.

"Did you get to the Rockefeller?" Henry asked when they had moved into the cabin and stowed their carry-on luggage.

"Yes," Drew said with enthusiasm. "I'm really impressed with that beautiful campus. It's an oasis in the middle of Manhattan."

"That it is," Henry agreed. "What about the labs? You can see why it's considered a scientific mecca, can't you?"

"Yeah," Drew's tone was hesitant. "I can also see that there might be some problems for me working there."

"How so?" They settled into their seats.

"It's hard to describe—it *is* a little intimidating, with all those Nobel Prize winners and members of the National Academy floating around!"

"What's your objection to that? Are you afraid of the competition?"

"No, but I'm not sure I want to get into that sort of pressure cooker—at least, not yet."

Henry nodded knowingly. "That's the big time, Drew. Science is no different from any other field. You've got to face that if you're going to succeed in a research career."

The cornball mask had dropped from Campion. There was that keen assurance in his eyes that made you realize why he was regarded as one of the world's leading scientific movers and shakers. You could not put something over on Henry Campion. Some people might think they had, but they would be wrong.

"As I see it, the main problem for you is to make up your mind between research and clinical medicine," Henry continued. "If you want to do research, sooner or later you have to move on from Penn and start a lab of your own. An opportunity at the Rock doesn't come along often, particularly at your age and stage. You're going places, Drew! I have no doubt of that. Where you do your moving is pretty much up to you. The day will come when you'll be able to write the ticket."

Wow! That was pretty heady stuff coming from the great Campion.

"So—did they make you an offer you couldn't refuse?" Henry asked, his eyes twinkling.

Drew laughed. "There is a job for me," he admitted, "but you've got me figured out. I'm not prepared to give up clinical medicine yet."

"They have a hospital there."

"Mmmm, yeah—it's limited to research cases. I would need to have a joint appointment at New York Hospital." Drew nudged Campion with his elbow. "Looks like you're stuck with me for a while."

Henry grinned. "That's good news to me!"

He would be the last person in the world to stand in Drew's way if he wanted to work at the Rockefeller University. It never hurt to have your young people courted by other labs, and he was flattered that the RU wanted his protégé. Henry was fond of Drew and proud of him. He'd accomplished a great deal at an early age— perhaps too early, Henry reflected. Drew didn't suffer fools easily. He'd have to learn to control that arrogance of his. For a while there, he had mellowed, but lately he often seemed irritable and impatient.

They had reached cruising altitude and ordered drinks when Henry said, "Too bad Nicole can't make the meeting."

Drew took a sip of his Scotch, composing his features, before answering. "I hadn't heard about that."

Henry scrutinized him briefly. "I probably forgot to mention it. Had a call from her last week. It's a bad time to leave her department, and Jorge Alvares hasn't been feeling too well."

Jorge Alvares, my foot! I can't believe she would not come to a meeting . . . or that she didn't let me know.

All of a sudden he felt empty. The anticipation of seeing her again had elated him for weeks, *She* obviously did not want to be with *him*. Or hear from him. She had not answered any of his letters.

If Henry noticed anything, he pretended not to. All through dinner he talked about Task Force business. "There hasn't been a single case of smallpox in Pakistan this year, Drew. Hot damn! Betcher grandmother this'll be the last year for smallpox in Asia."

Pure Campion! No one could be that corny without trying. Drew often suspected that Henry affected his old-fashioned slang.

The cabin was darkened for the movie, a James Bond film, with the improbably leggy, voluptuous women and wild special effects that made them all seem alike. Henry watched the screen, completely absorbed, while Drew's mind wandered.

He reflected on Nicole's decision not to come to Geneva. It did not seem plausible that she would allow personal considerations—that is, their split—to interfere with her professional commitments. In fact, the more he thought about it, the more he was certain she would not. Yet, the excuse she had given Henry was a lame one. *All* of the members of the Task Force were always swamped with work in their departments. None of them had ever missed an IHTF meeting, though. There had to be another reason. Was she having problems? Maybe he should have called her before leaving the States.

He admitted to himself that he had been sulking. If she

wouldn't give in, he'd be damned if he would! The last
time he had spoken to her, alarmed at the news reports
of riots in Peru, she had sounded so cold, as if she was
completely indifferent to him. He had decided that two
could play that game. . . .

The movie ended with 007 wallowing in breasts and
thighs and masses of long blonde hair. Once, in Heathrow
Airport, Drew had seen Sean Connery without his tou-
pee. He remembered that whenever he saw him on screen.
Henry chuckled as he removed his earphones. "What
fantasies those crazy film people come up with! I'm glad
my boys aren't old enough to see that one. Hey, did I tell
you that Johnny's going away to summer camp?" Henry
launched into the topic of his children with enthusiasm.

Touched by Henry's pride in his young family, Drew
wondered whether he would ever have children of his
own. The thought that he might not made him painfully
sad. He'd better get himself out of this gloomy frame of
mind. They had a busy week ahead of them.

"Am I all set for Ethiopia?" he asked.

"Yes indeed. You leave July 15 for Addis. Anija will
go along. If Nicole could get away, she would be the one.
You two are really our smallpox team, you know."

That hurt.

"This Rockefeller University thing got me thinking,
Henry . . . if I *were* to change jobs, what would happen
with my appointment to the IHTF?"

"No problem," Henry replied. "The grant follows you
to whatever institution you're connected with, for the
remainder of your five years. After that, you might be
rotated off." He gave Drew a worried glance. "You're
not wanting out, I hope."

"Hell, no! It's the most exciting thing I've ever done. I
wish the appointment were for life. I can't imagine not
being part of the Task Force."

"It's hard to believe two years have gone by since we
began," Henry answered. "I'm really satisfied with some
of the things we've accomplished. Three of our demonstration projects have been taken over for general use in
developing countries—your diagnostic kit for virus identification in the field, Prem's concept of community-based
distribution of ORT packets, and Nicole's mobile clinics.

I've got high hopes for the hepatitis antibody and the distribution of the high protein wafers. And let's not overlook the dozens of ideas we've field tested and discarded as unworkable. That really clears the decks and prevents a lot of wasted time and money. People tend to forget that."

"How do you think we're rated by the WHO?"

"High marks! With everyone except Alton Schmidt's unit, that is. I hear he calls us 'Campion's Cronies.' That's a sure sign that we're doing a good job. When they can't attack you on substance, they resort to backbiting."

"He sure did give the program a hard time in India last year. Is he still making trouble?"

Henry shook his head. "I think he may finally have gotten his comeuppance. Your friend Dick Gentry really laid it on the line, complaining about Schmidt's interference to Lloyd Rankin when he was in Delhi for the smallpox evaluation meeting. It almost cost Schmidt his job."

"I thought he couldn't be fired."

"It's not easy the way things work in the UN agencies, but his position is pretty shaky. Schmidt's been hacking away at us because he's been out of a project ever since the mosquitoes in Kerala developed a resistance to DDT! It's a crime when one incompetent like that can sabotage important work."

The plane was dark and quiet as the passengers tried to sleep. They would reach Geneva at eight-thirty on Sunday morning, giving Drew and Henry a day to adjust to the time change before beginning their meeting on Monday morning.

Drew realized how much he had been counting on seeing Nicole, believing that if he could spend some time with her alone at the end of the meeting, they would make up. His thoughts full of her, he succeeded in sleeping for only part of the remaining three hours of the flight. Once dozing, he dreamed that she was nearby and in danger, that someone whose face he could not see was holding him down while she kept calling to him.

It was the first time that Drew had gone along to one of the private parties in Geneva to which the Task Force people were often invited. But then, he'd had better ways to spend the evenings in the past.

Prem and Luís insisted that he join them at the gathering in Versoix. He had planned to go back to the apartment, for there were some things he had to pack and store. A rental agent was coming to look at the place tomorrow. There was no sense in keeping it vacant any longer, now that he and Nicole . . .

Drew remembered when he was a teenager that his mother had known and socialized with all the international agencies crowd. In those days, he imagined, they were a lot more decorous!

The old chalet on the outskirts of Geneva, occupied by a youngish Australian couple who had seen duty in Bangkok, Istanbul, and Kuala Lumpur, appeared to be a favorite watering spot of the career foreign service types, who relaxed on broad banquettes strewn with embroidered silk pillows. Low Turkish tables carved of aromatic woods held trays of liqueurs and bowls of sweets. Sampling one platter, Drew discovered, much to his distaste, that they were chocolate-covered ants.

The hosts had farmed out their children for the evening, a wise decision, considering the amount of substance use that pervaded murky corners of the darkened rooms. In the main hall, stills of erotic sculptures from Khajuraho were projected onto the ceiling by an automatic slide carousel. The couples, dancing to a blend of eastern music and the latest American records, seemed to be inspired by the postures of the Kama Sutra.

As Drew made his way to the bar, a tall blonde woman gaily broke away from her partner and grabbed his arm. "Hello!" she cried, her British accent lending a certain élan to her words, "Do you know how to do the snatch?"

He found himself dancing with her. "It doesn't seem to matter much what you do to this music, does it?"

"I'll teach you," she laughed, pulling him up against her. "One, two, three . . . *s-n-natch!*" She caught one of his legs between her thighs and squeezed it. "There! Nothing to it. Now, it's your turn."

He should have known it was a come on.

"I'm afraid I'm not a very good dancer," he said, backing off. She shrugged, gave him a rueful glance, and danced away.

Aren't I the superior ass, though?

Damn! Why hadn't Nicole come to Geneva? Although Prem and Luís hadn't said so, he thought they suspected it was because of him. For her sake, he hoped Henry didn't.

He missed her terribly, especially in this city where everything now reminded him of her. The thought of spending two months in Africa with Anija, when it should have been Nicole, was as bleak a prospect as he could imagine.

Why had he made it an either/or ultimatum in New York? He'd been angry and hurt, his pride was wounded. He had said some foolish things, and Nicole responded in kind. He was sure she hadn't meant them, any more than he had. They could have gone on the way they were for a long time. Anything would be better than this. He had written to tell her he was sorry, that he still loved her, wanted her on any terms. She hadn't even bothered to reply.

He went to the bar and asked for a Scotch and soda. Across the room, he noticed Luís dancing with a striking, Titian-haired woman who was wearing a clinging black halter-neck jumpsuit, cut down to the waist in back. When she turned, it appeared that it was similarly low cut in front. He had never seen Luís in action. Despite his reputation as a Don Juan, until now Drew had thought it was all talk. Luís had told him once that it was important to be discreet, that only in the proper circumstances was it permissible to misbehave. Evidently these surroundings provided the proper circumstances.

Joining him at the bar for a moment, Luís ordered two champagnes. "You have never felt skin like that, Drew!"

"I'll take your word for it, Luís."

Exploring, he discovered a nook entered by stooping to pass through the low doorway. On a stand beneath the painted ceiling of a star-filled sky sat a large gilded Buddha in whose upturned hand incense was burning. One man had assumed a lotus, and was ohm-ing his mantra. Couples of varying sexual persuasion reclined on low divans, smoking reefers and gazing at the simulated Milky Way.

Hastily backing out, Drew nearly bumped into a woman,

causing her to spill her drink. "Sorry," he mumbled apologetically. This was ridiculous! He was going back to the hotel.

When he passed through the hall on his way out, the dancers were still struggling. There among them he noticed Alton Schmidt, a smooth-faced, dandyish man, attractive in a ski-instructor sort of way. Drew's former dancing partner, the blonde English woman, seemed successfully engaged in teaching Dr. Schmidt how to do the snatch.

"How did it go with Anija?" asked Luís.

"A lot of laughs," Drew replied, giving him a long look.

It was October, four months since they had seen each other. In the interim, Drew and Anija had spent two months in Ethiopia working on the smallpox program. They had presented their report to the IHTF that morning. Drew's Yugoslavian team partner had not taken well to the primitive conditions in the African desert.

Luís and Drew were having dinner at the grill in the Gare de Cornavin, Geneva's railroad station, conveniently located near their hotel. The rental agent had found a tenant for the apartment on Place de Ville three months ago.

"So, what's with Nicole?" Luís asked. "This is the seond meeting she's missed."

"You know as much as I do, Luís." Drew continued eating his onion soup.

"I don't believe the story—that she can't come to the meeting because of work. None of us would ever make it if that were the case." Drew did not respond. "You know, I consider myself your good friend, Drew. What happened between you two?"

Luís noted the pained look that crossed Drew's face. "Are you implying that's why she hasn't come to Geneva?"

"No!" Luís assured him. "Nicole's far too professional for that. I'm not sure why she's not here, but I'll bet it isn't because she can't get away from the hospital." He tasted the wine and nodded at the waiter. "I asked about you and Nicole because it's obvious something went wrong,

and you look about as down in the mouth as any man has
a right to be."

Drew sighed. "Yeah. I'm not so happy these days."
He smiled wryly at Luís. "She wouldn't marry me. It's as
simple as that."

"She's in love with you, isn't she?"

"I thought so. I guess I was wrong."

"Oh, come, Drew. There must be more to it." He
lifted his hand. "Don't tell me . . . let me guess. Nicole
insisted she must continue her work in Lima because she
would be running out on her obligations. And you, for
obvious reasons, can't move to Lima, even if you were
stupid enough to want to."

Drew regarded him with astonishment. "How did you
know? Has she spoken to you?"

Luís laughed. "No, she never said a thing. I haven't
had a word with Nicole for eight months, since New
York. It's not a very original script, you know."

"I suppose not," admitted Drew. "But when it happens to you, it seems unique. The trouble is, Luís, I
believe Nicole meant it when she said she didn't want to
marry me. And that can only mean she wasn't really in
love with me. I might as well get used to the idea."

They ate in silence, each wrapped in his own thoughts.
For all his machismo irreverence, Luís was a sentimental
man with a great sense of loyalty. To him, friendship
meant everything. Although they had met only two years
ago, the members of the Task Force had come to mean
as much to him as people he had known all his life. And
within this group, no two were more special than Drew
and Nicole. He considered them his closest friends.

You did not usually have women friends in Mexico,
even among your colleagues. Women were always females, first and foremost. If they were your mother,
sister, or wife, you revered them. The wife of a friend
was respected. Girlfriends and mistresses were sex objects. Although you might speculate about other women,
you never really got to know them, particularly if they
belonged to an acquaintance. Rare was the Mexican who
would tolerate another man paying attention to his wife,
even innocent friendly attention.

To Luís, his friendship with Nicole was a privilege.

Finding her a compelling personality, he had become
something of a Nicole watcher over the past two years.
He thought he knew her well enough by now to judge
that she was truly in love with Andrew Tower. Even if
she had quarreled with Drew, he did not believe that
would keep her from attending the Task Force meetings.
Luís was positive that the only reason she had not traveled to Geneva was because something was preventing
her—something more powerful than love or duty.

Luís knew a great deal about events in neighboring
countries. Americans and Europeans seldom took the
trouble to understand social and political currents in Latin
America, he had observed. Take his own country, Mexico, as an example. Right on their doorstep, what did
Americans know about Mexico?

How many Americans even remembered the name of
the Mexican president? Their chief concern with Mexico
was to control their common border so not too many
wetbacks would succeed in sneaking across the Rio Grande!
Wealthy Americans came to shop in the Zona Rosa, flew
to Acapulco and Cancún to watch jai alai or gamble,
listened to the romantic music of the mariachis, drank
tequila, and got sick on the salad. That was their Mexico.

Pale complexions flushed from hours of lolling in the
tropical sun, they romanticized the native horsemen who
rode bareback on the beaches in the glow of evocative,
roseate sunsets. Did they ever pause to look up at the
hills around them as they sipped their Margueritas on the
terraces of their luxe, epicurean hotels? If so, did they
wonder how long it would take until the droves of desti-
tute people who dwelled there in unspeakable poverty
descended en masse to take over by sheer numbers?

Luís owned a condominium in Acapulco. He went
there often, sport fishing on his motor launch, water-
skiing, playing tennis at his private club, swimming in his
pool. And on every single day that he was there, he
never failed to look up at those hills and acknowledge
. . . it was only a matter of time.

"What do you know about politics in Peru?" he asked
Drew.

He saw a look of concern flash in Drew's eyes. "I
know there's a leftist military junta and they're anti-
American. Why do you ask?"

"It occurred to me that Nicole's reason for not coming to the meetings may have something to do with the government—not the hospital."

"Christ! I was afraid of something like that! But why now, Luís? It's never made a difference before."

"For one thing, there was a bloodless coup in Peru at the end of August, when you were off in the Ogaden desert. No doubt that wasn't made much of in the papers you read. President Velasco was deposed and another general, Morales Bermúdez, became head of the junta. Although it could be good for the country in the end, there's more unrest in Lima right now than at any time during the past five years.

"I have nothing to go on, Drew—it's just a hunch. When things got hot in Chile and Argentina, my colleagues were prevented from attending conferences in other countries."

Drew sat back, alarmed. "Nicole mentioned in New York that the Peruvian government suspects the IHTF might be a front for the CIA. She asked me what I thought about that."

"What did you tell her?"

"I told her it was a ridiculous idea. What else would you expect me to say? It worried me at the time, but she didn't seem to take it seriously. In fact, that was one of the things we argued about. I told her she should leave Peru and she said I was acting like a Latino!"

"She didn't mean that as a compliment," Luís laughed. "I agree with you that any suspicions about the Task Force are baseless. But I know the Peruvian junta is paranoid about the CIA after the coup in Chile. It's possible that Nicole is *afraid* to come to an IHTF meeting."

"Luís, I called her after New York, when they had riots in Lima, and she said everything was fine. I admit that was a while ago, but Henry's spoken to her a couple of times lately. Wouldn't she have mentioned any fears she had?"

"Maybe she doesn't want to discuss it on the phone."

Drew slammed his fist on the table, causing several diners to glance in their direction. "What the hell! Why are we sitting here like this? I'm getting my ass down there!"

"Wait a minute . . . hold everything!" Luís shook his head. "That's not a good idea. If I'm right, and it's connected with anti-Americanism, it could be the wrong thing for Nicole if *you* went." Sitting back, Luís puffed on a Cuban cigar and scrutinized the ceiling paneled in dark rosewood.

"I think maybe *I* shall pay a visit to the Department of Maternal and Child Health at San Martín University."

Chapter 32

This was the second time Luís Ribera had visited Peru.

Years ago, when he was a schoolboy, his father had taken the family on an educational tour of South America. The elder Ribera had believed that his country was caught between the two Americas and, as fellow remnants of the Spanish conquest, Mexicans ought to know and understand their Latin confreres.

But Luís had not found much with which to identify in Peru at the time. He recalled riding a railroad high in the Andes, above the cloud level, where the train leaned over the edges of heart-stopping precipices, and a porter walked through the cars giving passengers whiffs of oxygen from a tank to counteract the effects of the high altitude. His clearest recollection was of the ruins of Machu Picchu, which had struck him even then as a sad testimonial to the transitory nature of civilizations.

Even in the fifties, Lima had been violated by runaway development. He remembered an essentially Spanish Colonial city of gracious parks and plazas, old churches and palacios with carved wooden balconies and arcades. But with new techniques in earthquake-proof architecture, modern highrises had already begun to take over the skyline, and the construction sites and *barriadas* had marred the beauty for him.

His negative impression of the Peruvian capital was much the same as he rode in from the airport, except there was more of everything. More buildings, more people . . . and more slums. Not unlike Mexico. With one notable difference.

Wherever he looked, there was the conspicuous presence of armed military police.

He knew as soon as he saw Nicole that there was

something terribly wrong. Around the emerald and gold eyes a strained aspect, and faint circles standing in relief against the pale skin. Underneath her false bravado, Luís detected an attenuated vitality.

Nicole was delighted, even euphoric, at his visit. Questions tumbled from her lips about the Task Force and the missed meetings. "Congratulations on your project, Luís. The data are superb. Have next year's field assignments been planned yet? I received a copy of the minutes . . . and the smallpox report. I felt positively *deprived* not to be able to go to Africa!" Not looking at him, she asked, "How did Anija do there?"

"We'll talk about all that later. I want to hear about *you* now, and see what you're doing here at San Martín."

She showed him through the department—the laboratories, clinics, and wards, presenting the most interesting cases. She drove him to a mobile clinic operating that day in a northern suburb, explaining apologetically that their funds had been cut back severely, but they were hopeful that the new administration of General Morales Bermúdez would reestablish support for the complete services the clinics had formerly provided.

Luís agreed to give lectures to the medical students in her classes and another, more formal talk at a faculty meeting, correctly sensing that it would enhance Nicole's position and allay any doubts some of her colleagues might harbor about the validity of her association with the IHTF.

That night, they had dinner with some of the department heads and their wives at Tambo de Oro, a fashionable restaurant with a colonial atmosphere. Seated at the opposite end of the table from Nicole, Luís had no opportunity for private conversation. Afterward, one of the professors dropped him at his hotel.

It was on his second day in Lima that Professor Jorge Alvares took Luís for a walk through the San Martín University campus and told him about Nicole's difficulties with her passport.

"I suspected it was a political problem," said Luís.

"She hasn't mentioned it? I know she plans to tell you."

"We haven't been alone. I'm dining with her at her home this evening. Perhaps she'll discuss it then. I had the impression, though, that she thought things were easing in Peru with the new administration."

"That's true," the professor agreed. "There is a mood of optimism. The curfew has been lifted, some of the exiled journalists will be returning, and there's a general lessening of restrictions. But it could change just as swiftly as it began. It's still a leftist military, and we mustn't get our hopes pinned on the improbable."

"What do you think it means for Nicole's permission to travel?"

Jorge shrugged. "Who can say? The problem, as I understand it, is that the police insist it's a matter for their political department—while the Interior Ministry wants to resolve the question in a hearing, which won't be scheduled for months. Not reassuring for a quick resolution."

"What's the reason her passport was taken?"

"I don't know. She hasn't said," Jorge answered, evasively, Luís thought.

"But she's not in any danger, is she? I mean, she won't be arrested?" At Alvares's startled expression, Luís hastened to add, "I have many friends in Chile, Professor. Some suffered during the Allende years, and others under Pinochet. You must forgive me if I'm blunt. Nicole means a great deal to me."

The bald professor slowed his steps, surprise written on his face. "Do you mean . . .?"

"Oh, no! Let me assure you, I already have a wife. Nicole and I are good friends, that's all."

"Dr. Ribera, I might have been *more* reassured if you had told me you and she were planning to marry. I worry about Nicole. But I think I can tell you honestly that life is improving for us in Lima and I believe the worst is over. Now is a time to watch and wait."

That evening, Nicole's chauffeur called for Luís at the Gran Hotel Bolivar, where he was staying. Accustomed to the sumptuous living of rich Mexicans, he was nevertheless awed by the grandeur of the Légende estate. Once inside the gates of Casa Loma, they traveled for nearly a quarter of a mile along a winding driveway before approaching the huge, sprawling replica of a colonial palacio.

Before dinner, Nicole took him on a tour of the house,

since he had indicated an interest in the beautiful antique textiles and tapestries that struck his eye in the broad gallery bordering the central patio. It was a remarkable collection, all the more so when he considered it had been amassed by a man born in France who had remained devotedly French until his dying day.

Luís's breath caught when Nicole touched a switch on the library wall. A bank of glass-enclosed display cases was flooded with soft light, which played on the most incredible collection of pre-Columbian sculptures and pottery he had ever seen.

"Where . . . *how* . . . I didn't think it was possible to find anything like this outside a museum!" he exclaimed.

"Papá began collecting early. In those days, no one cared anything about Chancay or Chimu. The *huaqueros* robbed graves with impunity,and when the Pan American Highway was extended, the workers just discarded pottery shards and stone fragments on the side of the road." She opened one case. "These are all pre-Inca. Isn't she sweet?" She handed him a tiny statuette. "It's a fertility symbol—see the rounded abdomen and breasts?"

"Amazing!" Luís handled the figure with reverence. "To think how long ago this was made."

"You know, everyone speaks of how cruel the conquistadors were, destroying the Inca culture. Of course, they were—but the Incas were just as heartless. They obliterated the history of the people they conquered and forced them to practice the Inca religion and use their language."

She replaced the figurine, her hands moving carefully from one artifact to another. "Someday, I suppose, I'll give most of this to a museum," she said, a wistfulness creeping into her voice.

"Someday?" Luís teased, with a knowing smile.

She looked away. Luís caught her hand. "Nicole, I haven't come all this way to give lectures to medical students—or even to see this magnificent collection of art. I came because I was worried about you." In a gentle voice, he added, "Drew is worried also—to put it mildly."

She looked at him with those large, brilliantly glittering green eyes in the heartbreakingly beautiful face, and he did not at all blame Drew Tower for being hopelessly in love with her.

"How is he?" she whispered.

"Miserably unhappy. That's on his good days. He wanted to come himself, but I persuaded him not to. You might say I'm a kind of emissary. I'd like to help the two of you. I wish you would talk to me."

"What is there to say, Luís? I couldn't seem to be what he wanted."

"He wants you the way you are, Nicole."

"You're wrong! We had a terrible row . . . and it's all over between us."

"Surely you can patch it up. I know he still loves you."

She did not reply, and he wondered whether this was really any of his business. But since he had begun, he might as well continue.

"He . . . uh . . . he told me you haven't answered his letters. That you didn't return his phone calls."

She kept her eyes focused on the shelves of artifacts. "There haven't been any phone calls—not for a long time."

"Well, he's been away a great deal in the past few months."

She shrugged indifferently. Shutting the glass doors to the display cases, she looked at him directly and said with finality, "It's much better this way. I really *prefer* not to hear from him. Please . . . I don't want to talk about it."

Luís felt he had said all that he could on the subject without being intrusive.

"Forgive me, Nicole. I didn't mean to meddle. It's just that I don't like to see two unhappy people who should be together separated by thousands of miles."

"Anyway, I'm not permitted to leave Peru, even for a meeting, Luís. Professor Alvares said he told you about my passport."

"Yes, but he didn't explain anything. Why has your passport been taken away?"

"I'm not sure. I surmise it's either because of the IHTF or that I associated with some Peace Corps volunteers, although they didn't give me a reason. There was a state of emergency when I returned from New York, resulting in alarmist regulations that lasted for a short time. I just had the bad luck to get caught up in it."

"And once started, it was a process that couldn't be halted?"

"Something like that."

"I suppose for now you're safe from harm, but what of the future?"

Her brow furrowed. "I don't see how they can touch me. I haven't acted against this government—not in any way!"

"Do you have any rivals? Anyone who might bear a grudge against you?"

She shook her head. "None that I know of. I suppose some people at the university could resent my trips abroad and the IHTF, but I've purposely not called attention to the work I do. They all know that a third of my time is supposed to be spent on Task Force projects."

They strolled across the illuminated courtyard where water purled in a decorative fountain. Luís admired the superb *azulejos,* the hand-fashioned ceramic tiles with the distinctive blue glaze.

Being here in Lima with Nicole was reassuring to him. Although there was visible evidence of the military government, there was certainly not the oppressive environment he had found in Santiago de Chile, or at the medical congress last year in Buenos Aires. Even the stolid Fabricio in her automobile had not unduly alarmed him. He was accustomed to that in Mexico. Some of his friends in the government were accompanied everywhere by armed guards.

Nicole would be all right for the moment. Yet he had an uneasy feeling that her situation could deteriorate. He recalled Jorge Alvares's words . . . "it could change just as swiftly as it began."

After dinner, when they were drinking coffee and liqueurs in the study, he said, "Nicole, here's the number of my private line. There is always someone there who knows where to reach me. I want you to call me if ever there is the slightest problem—even if you think it's not necessary. Will you promise?"

She took the card on which he had written a telephone number, looking at it with a contemplative yet doubtful expression.

"Please, Nicole, do humor me," he pleaded, smiling as if he were a fond uncle asking for some foolish indulgence.

She laughed gently. "Oh, all right, Luís. I promise. Although if I really needed help, I probably wouldn't be able to get to a telephone—and in any case, what could you do from Mexico?"

He remembered the cables he and a number of other scientists from around the world had once sent to Santiago when Allende was overthrown. They learned that one of their colleagues had been arrested and was being held in the soccer stadium, from which people were mysteriously disappearing, never to be seen again. Luís's friend had been lucky—the new government had released him when international pressure was applied.

But he wasn't going to tell Nicole about that. Placing his hand over hers, he said, "You'll never need it, I know. But in any case, you should have my private number. I don't give it to just anyone!" He was again the roguish, debonair sophisticate.

As he was leaving, Nicole said, "Thank you . . . for everything, Luís. Please explain to Henry about my predicament. Not too many people should know, but I owe him an explanation."

"All right. I'm sure he'll keep it confidential." He cocked his head and peered at her. "Any message for Drew?"

He saw her eyes moisten. "No message," she answered softly.

They embraced in the marble entrance foyer. Luís ran lightly down the steps to the waiting limousine. Nicole stood watching the tail lights disappear over the long slope of the driveway. Leaning her forehead against the carved panels of the massive door, she let the tears spill down her cheeks.

After Luís's visit, Nicole felt twice as alone.

She spent longer hours in the hospital and took papers home to work on each night. Thoughts of Drew would creep into her mind whenever she was unoccupied. Now she seldom slept through the night. She, who had never before had trouble sleeping. Drew used to tease her about her blameless conscience, declaring that she was like a child, deep in slumber the moment she closed her eyes.

If he *had* written, as Luís had suggested, then why had his letters not reached her? In the past, they were sometimes delayed, but eventually they had arrived. Come to think of it, she hadn't received many letters from abroad recently. Like many services, the mails were inefficient,

but it was unlikely that letters would be lost, unless . . .
was her mail being intercepted? She dismissed the thought
because she did not believe surveillance was sufficiently
well-organized in Peru to selectively confiscate mail.

Manuel had not shown his face since the terrible evening she wanted to forget, although he called occasionally. He mentioned that he had made her excuses in
Paris, at the board meetings of Légende et Cie. It was
not unusual for directors to miss meetings, and evidently
there had been no critical comment. A committee had
been formed to study a motion to go public, which had
been placed before the board by the two Swiss directors.
Manuel advised her to support the proposal, saying that
without sufficient family involvement and in the absence
of a younger CEO who would lead the firm for years to
come, there was no particular advantage to remaining a
private company. She had written to Claude Montagne to
get his views on the subject before acting.

Manuel had been making frequent trips to the States
on various missions whose nature she did not fully understand. She imagined it had to do with renegotiating bank
loans to cover the payments on Peru's immense foreign
debt—although he was vague when she questioned him.
Sensing he had been up to something mysterious before
the recent coup, she had assumed he was in the confidence of this new administration and would be asked to
join it. The Morales Bermúdez government had appointed
some civilians to the Cabinet and the Finance Ministry. It
had come as a surprise to Nicole that Manuel had not
been among the latter.

Three weeks before Christmas, a month after Luís had
left, a jubilant Lucy telephoned. "Horacio has returned
to Lima, Nicole. We're getting *married!* On New Year's
Eve. Will you be my witness?"

Nicole was astounded.

She said all the right things and was genuinely happy
for Lucy. But after hanging up, she sat alone contemplat-
ing how ironic it was that the unconventional Lucy Monaco could manage to get her life in order—if that was
how you could describe being married to a man who
admittedly was difficult, even impossible, for her to live
with. Yet, Lucy was willing to make that commitment, to

share her life with Horacio Salamanca. Because she loved him.

And she, Nicole? With whom would she share her life? No one. Obviously, Drew was determined to forget her, if he had not already. She thought Luís was being kind, trying to spare her feelings, when he had told her Drew wanted to come to Lima. There had been no word from him since Luís's visit. Who could blame him, after the things she had said in New York? Why would he want her any longer?

She cloaked herself in her unhappiness, wearing it like a hair shirt.

She thought of going to church, but it had been too many years since she had attended mass. Occasionally she sat in the little chapel where her mother used to pray. It had remained undisturbed all these years. Vera regularly ordered the maids to dust and air the unused rooms in the mansion, but there was an atmosphere of mournful neglect in Tina's suite. Nicole had never experienced its mood of dejected abandonment anywhere else, even when she visited the graves in Huaranca.

Once, she passed the synagogue where she had long ago accompanied her father to services. She entered, searching for the names of Daniel and his family among the memorial plaques. The caretaker came and guided her to the List of the Dead. There were all the names of the family Légende. The following day, she sent a contribution in remembrance of her father, addressing it to Miguel Cohen, the old man who had been her father's first Jewish friend in Peru—still alive and in his late seventies. Señor Cohen called to thank her, and she accepted his invitation to come to his home for tea one Sunday afternoon.

And so the year 1975 approached its end, with no encouraging word about her passport, and she knew without being told that she would have to miss another IHTF meeting. She tried not to let her thoughts dwell on her problems, telling herself that the worst of the waiting was over and soon her hearing would be scheduled. In the liberalized political climate, she was hopeful that the January meeting of the Task Force would be the last to convene without her.

Nicole had offered her home for Lucy's wedding to

Horacio Salamanca. The couple could not be married in a church because the groom was Jewish and Lucy, who was born Catholic, had been divorced. Since neither a priest nor a rabbi would perform the marriage ceremony, the civil wedding would take place in the registry office, and a friend of Lucy's who was a judge would conduct another, more personal ceremony in the library at Nicole's house.

The beautiful old estate was perfect for lavish entertainments, of which there had been few, even when Daniel was alive. As Christmas neared, Nicole found herself more and more caught up in a festive mood with the wedding plans. She invited Lucy to come discuss preparations with Vera and the cook but ended by making most of the decisions herself, since Lucy was singularly unconcerned with such banalities as whether to have salmon or langostino for the fish course, or how many tiers should be on the wedding cake.

On New Year's Eve, the marriage was delayed for almost an hour because one couple failed to arrive—a popular television personality and his wife, who were close friends of Horacio's. Finally, it proceeded without them.

After the exchange of vows, everyone moved out to the tiled courtyard, transformed for the champagne reception into a fairyland of tiny lights on silver and white trees. The sound of music and laughter rang along the gallery, through the rooms of the mansion, and out across the grounds of the estate.

The sixty guests, minus the missing couple, were seated for dinner at festively decorated round tables for ten in the dining room. There were more champagne and toasts and the ringing of crystal as the men tapped their glasses for the bride and groom to kiss. Nicole worried momentarily about her father's Baccarat goblets, but nothing was broken, and after all, what was the sense of having beautiful service if it remained shut up in locked cabinets?

Nicole knew few of the guests. They were all friends of the bride and groom. Lucy's and Horacio's son, Francisco, sat with them at dinner, smiling with childish delight and wonder, Nicole could imagine that for the seven-year-old this was the fulfillment of his dreams, to have the three of them become a family.

Well after midnight, the party had moved out to the terrace, where couples began dancing, their hips swaying in subtle unison to the Brazilian music of the group Nicole had hired. Suddenly Drew invaded her consciousness. *I never danced with him. There are so many things we never did together!* She could think of nothing except Drew. Why, when she wanted to force him out of her thoughts, was she unable?

The dances became faster and more pulsating. A carnival mood took over, as the musicians swung into a frenetic samba. Nicole watched Lucy dancing with Francisco, holding his hands and teaching him the steps.

A telephone call came for Horacio, and Nicole told the maid to show him into the study where the noise would not disturb him. Half an hour later, she realized she had not seen the groom return.

Searching for Salamanca, Nicole found him sitting in the study behind the desk, his head bent on his hands in an attitude of despair. She hesitated in the doorway, about to leave, when he looked up.

"Come in," he said in a ravaged voice.

"What's the matter, Horacio? Are you ill?"

Salamanca was a thin, wiry man with a high forehead and beaked nose. His skin had a marmoreal quality, more pronounced in the dimness of the study. He closed his deep, dark, intellectual eyes.

"That was Samy's brother calling. Samy's dead."

"Your friend? The TV host?"

He nodded, dazed, clearly not accustomed to the idea.

"How did he die?"

"They arrested him late this afternoon, as he left the station. He was found dead in his cell a few hours ago. The police are saying he committed suicide."

"How terrible!"

"Samy no more committed suicide, Nicole, than I would! *He was murdered by the police.*" He crossed his arms and held himself, leaning forward. "He was doing caricatures of the generals on his show. I warned him he was going too far." Rocking slowly back and forth, he shook his head in anguish. "I wondered when it would begin again. I knew it was too good to last!"

A bridegroom is supposed to be happy, Nicole thought, as she watched him struggle not to weep. She attempted to utter comforting words, but stopped mid-sentence, knowing this was not a man for platitudes.

"What about Lucy? Shall I go get her?" she asked.

That seemed to bring him out of his despondency "No, I won't spoil her wedding! Tomorrow is soon enough to tell her. Let her have this happy occasion. Who knows when there will be another?"

Horacio's words proved to be prophetic.

The new year that had begun with the ill omen of a political murder produced further detentions of journalists and tighter controls on the press. An air of hovering menace pervaded Lima. Lucy reported that Horacio was in a black mood, foreseeing insurrection and civil war.

In February, when the U.S. Secretary of State, Henry Kissinger, visited Peru, leftist students stoned the American Embassy, and the police intervened with hoses and clubs. Some of the injured were brought to San Martín Hospital. Nicole was of the opinion that it was not necessary to break bones in order to subdue unarmed youths.

Then, without any warning or explanation, in the beginning of March, the government closed the mobile clinics, informing the department that it was forbidden to hold them until further notice. Carlos, Pepe, and some of their fellow interns came to Nicole, asking her to lead a protest to the Health Ministry to convince them to reinstate the clinics. Nicole was prepared to take action, but Dr. Alvares was sharp in his response when she told him of the plan.

"Don't be crazy, Nicole! You'll get yourself and the rest of us in an imbroglio with the Health Ministry. This is no time for you to make waves."

She was forced to tell the interns that she could not endorse their protest. She knew by the look in Pepe's eyes that he was disappointed in her.

Professor Alvares later apologized for his harsh words.

"You were right," she told him. "Sometimes I act without thinking. This is so hard to accept, though."

"I know, my dear," he answered kindly. "It was the best idea for health care to come along in all my years at San Martín."

"The irony is that I recently heard the model program we developed for the clinics has been adopted by a number of other health ministries in developing nations. And here in my own country, they won't let us use it."

"Will you come with me to the Odría Pavilion this afternoon?" Lately Jorge had asked her to help with the private patients who preferred to see the professor in the elite garden annex to San Martín Hospital. "Come in my car and then I'll drop you at home," he suggested.

"All right. I'll send my driver home and meet you downstairs."

Fabricio had been driving her to work recently. At least he fulfilled a function! She had never been convinced that a bodyguard was a necessity. Nicole found Fabricio talking with the other drivers and told him he could leave for the day, after taking the Renault to her house.

Two and a half hours of listening to the complaints of women whose well-nourished, over-indulged children were difficult to manage left Nicole restless and relieved to get away from the Odría Pavilion. Jorge Alvares had an obligation to see these patients, however she suspected he did not enjoy it any more than she did.

Traffic was heavy in downtown Lima, as it always was at the end of the day. They had stopped at an intersection near the Civic Center when Nicole spotted the bulky figure of Fabricio hurrying across Paseo de la República. With idle curiosity, she followed his progress to a group of parked limousines awaiting their owners.

As Jorge's chauffeur edged the automobile forward in the slowly moving stream of cars, Nicole watched Fabricio stop to speak to one of the uniformed drivers. With cold fury, she saw the man who was her employee get into a steel gray limousine. It was an automobile that she recognized. A Bentley.

It belonged to Manuel Caldeiro-León.

Chapter 33

Nicole called Lucy. "I have *got* to get away from Lima or I will go out of my *mind!* Will you come up to Huaranca for the weekend? It's Condor Rachi. Francisco will adore it—parades and fireworks."

"*Love* to! We all need a vacation. This will be the honeymoon we haven't had."

"Some honeymoon, with you old maid pal tagging along."

"Some old maid!" Lucy gaily retorted before ringing off.

The idea of spending the holiday weekend at the hacienda had come to her suddenly, a few days after she had gone through the unpleasant business of firing Fabricio. She made up a vague excuse, not wanting to tell him the real reason. All along, she'd had a bad feeling about that bodyguard. No wonder Manuel knew her every move!

But why? Why would Manuel spy on her? Surely his jealousy would not impel him to the extreme of collecting information to be used against her. And if so, in what way? It was too much for her to fathom. Thoroughly depressed and fatigued, she felt heavy and dull and her head ached constantly.

With Pedro driving, Nicole called for Lucy, Horacio, and Francisco early on Thursday morning. Vera had packed a large hamper of cold chicken, sandwiches, fruit, and cake. They were scarcely an hour outside of Lima when Francisco decided it was time for lunch.

"You should wait to be invited to eat," Lucy gently reprimanded him.

"Oh no," objected Nicole. "I want him to feel at home. Besides, I'm starved myself."

She and Francisco shared a sandwich and got on fa-

mously together. Nicole naturally loved children, and
what a respite it was to be with a healthy, happy child
after her daily contact with her pathetic, sickly patients.
This boy was a delight—unspoiled, bright, and full of
curiosity. Initially shy with her, by the time they neared
the Callejón de Huaylas he had decided that she was
magnifica and he really must call her *Tia*.

There was an atmosphere of holiday along the way in
every hamlet they passed. Peruvians of the highlands
took their fiestas as a serious obligation to celebrate.
Among the Indian population, many of the observances
were relics of the pre-Columbian era, with an overlay of
Christianity. The festivities usually began several days in
advance of the actual feast day itself. With the religious
procession and mass conveniently out of the way while
everyone was sober, the revelry began in earnest, climax-
ing in an orgy of music, dancing, and drinking.

The Feast of San Mateo, celebrated throughout the
country, was overshadowed in the Callejón de Huaylas
by the rather bizarre fiesta Arranque del Condor, literally, the pulling apart of the condor. The high moment of
the fiesta was a pagan practice dating back to the rule of
the Inca, and later modified by the Spaniards. It con-
sisted of men mounted on horseback clubbing to death a
live condor—once worshiped by the Incas—and then tearing it apart, but not before the bravest of the horsemen
had taken the bird by its throat and bitten out its tongue.

Lucy and Horacio decided they would not be depriving
Francisco of a cultural experience if he missed that bloody
spectacle. Nicole agreed. "Papá never permitted me to
see it when I was young, although Rosa used to take me
when he wasn't around."

It had been many months since Nicole had visited Flor
del Viento. Rosa chided her for her neglect of them,
beamed when she saw Francisco, and welcomed Lucy
and Horacio with warmth. Their rooms had been readied, fragrant with bunches of mountain flowers. Rosa
delighted in cooking hearty, delicious meals, which Horacio
and Francisco, especially, consumed with gusto.

In no time at all, Francisco was playing with the children of the hacienda and learning to ride a pony. Late in
the afternoon of the second day, they drove into Huaranca
where the excited boy stood on the roof of the car to

watch the *comparsas*, costumed groups performing folk dances, and the colorful procession led by a padre and accompanied by a cacophonous brass band. With nightfall, spectacular *voladores* lit up the sky over the valley of the flamesword, after which Horacio carried a sleepy Francisco up the stairs of the manor house to bed.

"This is a child's heaven," Horacio remarked.

"It was for me," Nicole agreed.

Horacio spent hours talking to the men of the plantation, amazed at the cooperative community they owned and had run successfully for so many years.

"Your father must have been a remarkable man," he said after one of these discussions.

She smiled. "He was."

Horacio was especially interested in Daniel's Jewish background. She told him the story of her family, which he had never heard before in its entirety.

"It's amazing," he concluded. "How many landowners in Peru would have voluntarily given up what they owned?"

"Ah, but you see, he never considered that he owned it! Once when someone asked him why he had deeded the plantation to the *campesinos,* he said he had come to this country with nothing and these were the people who had taken him in. He felt he had made his fortune because of a quirk of nature, a trick of fate, and the land should no longer belong to him."

While Lucy and Horacio walked together through the beautiful valley, Nicole rode out alone over the hacienda. Gazing across the fields to the distant peak of Huascarán, her melancholy lifted. Back at the house, feeling renewed and eased of the enormous tension that had gripped her for the past year, she was determined she would return to Lima in a more positive frame of mind.

On the last afternoon, Horacio took Francisco fishing in the rushing mountain stream, while Lucy and Nicole sat in the sunny garden, talking lazily.

"You might as well know," Lucy told her, "I'm going to have a baby."

"Lucy! How wonderful. When?"

"Oh, ages yet . . . not for seven months. We thought Francisco should have a sibling, before it's too late. I'll be thirty-six soon."

"I'm so happy for both of you, Lucy. I can see how good this marriage is for you."

Her friend looked at her searchingly, "What about you, Nicole? Aren't you going to marry Drew?"

"It doesn't look that way, does it?" she said wistfully.

"Is it some kind of contest . . . are you trying to see who can hold out longer?"

"It's been almost a year since I've heard from him . . . I would say there's *no* contest."

"Why don't you call him?"

"And tell him what, Lucy? I want to marry you, but you'll have to come to Peru because they won't let me out of the country!"

"Soon, Nicole. I know we'll get the hearing. Then you can start going to the IHTF meetings again, and you'll see him."

"I'll go to the meetings, Lucy. But I doubt that Drew and I will ever get together again." She looked at her friend ruefully. "I have a feeling he may have met someone else."

Back in Lima, Nicole attacked her work with new vigor. When they had first been unable to hold the mobile clinics in the *barriadas,* she had organized the outpatient clinic in the hospital along the same principles of providing comprehensive, maternal-child care, emphasizing preventive medicine. If a mother came because her child's eyes were infected, she was offered complete immunizations for all the family, along with health education and family planning advice. To see the comprehension dawning in a mother's face that illness was not inevitable for her babies was reward enough for the extra hours the staff devoted to the augmented clinics.

Nicole wrote long reports on her work to Henry Campion, declaring that when she was able to "report in person," as she euphemistically phrased it, she would have many exciting results to share with him. Impatient at the time she had wasted, she vowed she would never again allow preoccupation with her personal problems to interfere with work.

And she succeeded. Until the night Carlos came to tell her that Pepe had been arrested.

He arrived by the back road, apologizing for climbing

over the fence. The gate had been kept padlocked, at Vera's suggestion, ever since the time Pepe had been shot and his friends had brought him to the house through the rear entrance. Few people were aware of the private lane leading to the estate, and it had occurred to Nicole to wonder how Carlos had discovered it.

"I made sure I wasn't followed," Carlos assured her. "I thought I shouldn't call, in case they're monitoring your telephone."

"Why would they be doing that?" she asked in irritation. He dipped his head, dismissing the question.

"Pepe was picked up by the police last night. He's being held at El Sexto with a bunch of graduate students from San Martín and San Marcos Universities."

"Oh, Carlos . . . why? What has he done now?" she cried in dismay.

"Nothing so terrible. He was attending a lecture on exploitation of the working class, or some such worthy subject. There's a ban on all political meetings." He rubbed his hands together, cracking the knuckles in that annoying habit of his. "Stupid fool! I *told* him he should stay away from those crazy organizations. What can he hope to accomplish by listening to that crap?"

"Is there anything I can do? Shall I get him a lawyer?"

His eyes lit up. "Would you, Nicole? That would be splendid!"

She nodded slowly. "Tomorrow morning I shall call a woman I know—Señora Monaco Salamanca. It's too late to disturb her tonight."

"I know who she is. You once brought her to a clinic. She's first rate!" He looked at her, smiling with that especially sweet, gentle expression he had. "So are you, Nicole. Why can't there be people like you in the government?"

"If you recall, Carlos, we once had an administration made up of people like me. That's not what this country wants."

"Belaúnde was weak. He was no match for the military."

"Carlos, I'm not going to sit here at this hour discussing the politics of Peru with you! I'll call Señora Monaco first thing tomorrow. Let's hope she can get Pepe out of jail."

                    *   *   *

Nicole telephoned Lucy at dawn the next day, Sunday, apologizing for wakening her so early.

"Unfortunately, these days I'm always awake at this hour," Lucy replied with self-mocking acerbity. "I am the victim of morning sickness, a most humiliating indignity for a woman of my distinction!"

When Nicole explained about Pepe, her friend said, "Nothing can be done on Sunday. It will have to wait until tomorrow. I'd better get him out quick, or else it'll be Carnaval. Then he'll be stuck for a week."

On Monday, Nicole had a faculty meeting, then grand rounds, in addition to her usual lectures and clinic. She did not pick up her messages before leaving the hospital because it was late and she had promised to attend a banquet at the Club Hebraica in honor of Miguel Cohen's seventy-fifth birthday. Cohen was recognized as the leader of the Lima Jewish community, numbering less than a thousand families.

It was not a late evening. She was home again by midnight, and Vera had waited up for her. "Señora Monaco called several times, señorita. She said you should telephone, no matter how late you return."

"I've been trying to reach you all afternoon, Nicole," Lucy told her urgently. "Pepe's not at El Sexto! I've checked every jail in Lima. I even walked through the cells, looking for him, in case he used a false name. Not a pretty sight. The police claim he wasn't arrested."

"Maybe he's at home by now, Lucy. Although, if so, Carlos should have informed me. He knew I was planning to call you."

"Did you see Carlos today at the hospital?" she asked.

"No. But that's not unusual. I had an extremely heavy schedule. I'll talk to him tomorrow."

"Call me as soon as you do," she said before hanging up.

But in the morning, when Nicole succeeded in locating Carlos in the men's surgical ward, he reported that he had not seen or heard from Pepe since Friday night when he left for the meeting, held in the Rímac neighborhood.

"How did you learn he was arrested?" she inquired.

Carlos looked around nervously. "This guy, Victor, who was at the meeting but left just before the police raid, sent me a message. I went to see him. He says he followed one group and swears Pepe was among them and that he saw him taken to El Sexto."

"Will he talk to Señora Monaco?"

"I'm not sure. I'll ask him." The sister in charge of the ward glanced curiously in their direction. "I'd better get back to work."

Nicole called Lucy to report what Carlos had told her.

"I must see that fellow, Nicole. May I come to your office this afternoon to talk to Carlos?"

Nicole agreed, and then had to again go in search of Carlos, who had left the floor and was in the OR. By the time she spoke to him, half the morning had passed. She worked through lunch, trying to catch up, but she had not finished with her patients when a messenger came to say that Lucy was waiting for her in the department.

Carlos arrived shortly after Nicole, apologizing for keeping them waiting. "I asked Victor. He doesn't want to be seen speaking to you, so I convinced him to wait for us on the corner of Avenida Emancipación and Jiron Lampa. It will be safer to talk in the car." He spoke in a low voice, as if he thought they might be overheard in the office.

"In that case, perhaps we should take my car," Nicole volunteered. "No one can see through the windows from outside."

Since the departure of Fabricio, Pedro was driving her to work. They sometimes used the Citröen limousine that had belonged to Daniel, Pedro declaring that it needed to be driven occasionally to remain in working order.

A slight, sallow young man, wearing the usual dark trousers and short-sleeved shirt of a university student, was leaning against the side of a building at the appointed street corner, reading a book and glancing up nervously whenever an automobile passed.

Carlos was sitting in the front seat with Pedro. "Pull down to the middle of the next block and let me out," he instructed the chauffeur. "Then go around the block and pick us up at this corner," he pointed to the cross street they were passing.

This was taking on the unpleasant aspects of a melodrama, Nicole reflected, and she was not enjoying it. Pedro followed Carlos's directions, driving slowly with agonizing care. He drew up just short of the corner, and the two young men quickly got into the car, sitting on the jump seats facing Nicole and Lucy.

"Take the long way out to the Costa Verde, Pedro, and continue to drive carefully," Nicole told the driver, whose inscrutable, lined face registered no reaction to the unusual proceedings. She raised the dividing glass, giving them privacy in the rear, making certain the intercom was not on.

"If we can see out the windows, why can't they see in?" Victor inquired, nodding toward pedestrians.

"It's darkened glass, designed for one-way viewing," Nicole assured him.

She sat back and listened while Lucy queried the youth, taking copious notes in a small, careful hand. Hesitant at first, he gradually relaxed and answered Lucy's questions. She had a respectful, reassuring way of addressing him, which presented no threat and put him at his ease. Her manner seemed to say: I'm on your side, I understand, I'm your friend.

Yes, he had attended the lecture . . . it wasn't a rally, there were no chants or slogans or cheers. It had been held in an ordinary meeting hall near the Rímac neighborhood development.

Yes, as far as he knew, the organizers had a permit. The reason it was held there was that political meetings are forbidden on the university campuses. He had listened for a while but found it dull. Two people, a man and a woman, talking about the *colectivos* and why they weren't changing the lives of the poor workers. He decided to leave because his sister wanted him to stay with the children so she and her husband could go to a friend's house . . . He lived with his sister, he told Lucy. He studied engineering at San Marcos University, and his sister's husband was a draftsman for an architect.

So, he said goodbye to his three friends, one of whom decided to leave with him. The two of them walked to the bus stop and waited about twenty minutes for a bus, which was a pain. While they stood there, they heard a commotion in the area, police whistles and sirens, but they couldn't tell from which direction. They paid little attention, and finally their bus came and they boarded.

A few blocks later, an open army truck passed the bus, and in the rear, he saw some students he knew who had been at the lecture. He called his friend's attention to the truck, and they discussed what they should do. They were kind of frightened—after all, in a few more minutes, it could have been them—but they also felt guilty that their friends had been arrested and they had escaped.

For a while the truck drove along the same route as their bus, sometimes falling behind the bus, sometimes ovrtaking it when the bus made a stop. Then it pulled ahead and turned off the route in the direction of the prison, so they jumped off the bus at the next stop and, scared to death, ran along the street in the shadows, tailing the truck until it turned in at the prison. At one point, the truck stopped and a street light fell on the faces of the students closest to the rear. They distinctly saw Pepe, whom they recognized from other meetings.

"Are you certain it was Pepe?" Lucy asked.

"Yes, señora. I know it was him. He was wearing a red and white printed shirt."

"That's what he had on when he left the apartment," Carlos agreed.

"You didn't actually see him enter the prison, then?" Lucy continued.

"No, but he was in the truck and it went into the yard, then the gate was closed."

"What did you do then?"

"We separated and we each went home. Then I got to thinking about Pepe, and I knew he lived with this other guy, Carlos. So, I asked a kid I know to take a note to him. I paid him, and he did it."

"And that's all?"

He nodded. "That's it. I haven't left anything out."

"What about the others you recognized?"

"I heard most of them were let go with a warning not to attend political rallies. But I haven't seen any of them."

"Can you give me some of their names?" Lucy pressed him.

He was unwilling. In such times, it was not a good idea to rat on someone, even to save a friend.

"Look," said Lucy, "all I want to do is find someone who knows whether or not Pepe was actually taken into that prison, or if he was pulled aside and sent elsewhere."

Extremely reluctant, Victor gave her two names and told her where the boys could be reached. He was clearly unhappy to be a part of this. Lucy assured him no one would ever know her source of information.

"But if there should be a trial, Victor, I would want to ask you to testify."

He looked terrified, protesting that he would never have talked to her if he thought he would have to testify in court.

"I won't insist, but I want you to give some thought to this," she told him. "Why is it you listen to anarchists and revolutionaries, but you wouldn't be willing to stand before a court of justice to help an innocent person, a friend?"

He flushed, then looked down. "Because I'm a coward," he muttered.

Lucy quickly put out her hand and touched his head. "No, you're *not* a coward, Victor. You didn't have to send word to Carlos. And no one forced you to come with us today. If it's necessary, you'll just have to decide how much of a hero you want to be."

They dropped the boys at a bus stop, then took Lucy home.

"Will you have dinner with us?" Lucy invited.

"Oh, no," Nicole said, not wishing to cause Lucy trouble.

"Then come have a drink, and we'll decide," insisted Lucy.

Horacio Salamanca was dubious when they told him what they had learned. "You say this boy, Pepe, comes from Ayacucho? Maybe he ran away, back to his family."

"Yes, but wouldn't he have sent word to Carlos? They live together. He would know his friend would be looking for him."

"They're only kids! Sometimes they don't think. I'm sure they don't have a phone. Wait a week or so, he'll show up." He fondled Lucy's head. "I don't want this pregnant lady running around prison cells all day."

"I'm sorry, Horacio," said Nicole. "It's my fault. I'm the one who asked her to take this case."

Lucy argued good-naturedly with Nicole about whether she would let her pay a fee for Pepe, while Horacio opened a bottle of red wine, and Francisco brought a board game for Nicole to play with him. Convinced to stay for dinner, Nicole called to tell Vera she would not be home, then sent Pedro out to eat at a neighborhood bistro he liked, a treat for him.

Lucy's maid had prepared a fragrant *paella Valenciana,* full of shrimps, langostinos, clams, muscles, and peppery *chorizos.* In the book-lined room that served as a place for Horacio to do his writing, the desk was pushed into a corner and a table set with a colorful cloth woven by Indians in a remote village near Cuzco. Elaborately sculpted ceramic *candeleros* from Quinua held a dozen handmade candles, which cast a flickering light on the wood-paneled ceiling of the room.

Nicole found it a most charming and heart-warming ambience. Lucy, whose ordinary demeanor was one of adroit intelligence, had a feline contentedness, appearing ever so slightly pregnant in a poncho worn over her pants and shirt, while Horacio was unusually animated for one of his scholarly, pessimistic temperament, and Francisco excited at being included in this adult dinner with Aunty Nicole. After the little boy had gone to bed, they sat in the living room, talking and sipping wine, to the accompaniment of classical guitar recordings.

Glancing at her watch, Nicole was amazed to see it was almost 1 A.M. "How did I ever stay this late?" she exclaimed. "I have to be at the hospital by seven-thirty tomorrow."

Horacio saw her to the automobile. Pedro was dozing in the front seat. "Come again, Nicole. This was good for all of us," Salamanca said, bidding her good night. As Nicole's limousine drove off, Horacio returned to the apartment building. He did not notice a black sedan pull away from the curb and, with dimmed headlights, follow the Citröen.

All the way home, Nicole was aware of the seductive luster of harmony in Lucy's and Horacio's family. Approaching the beautiful mansion, situated high on the cliffs above the Pacific, it chilled her to think of its exquisite, unused rooms.

As the wrought iron gates of Casa Loma closed, the car trailing Nicole's limousine slowed for a few seconds outside the periphery of the compound and then continued on its way, indistinguishable from the darkness of the night.

Chapter 34

The news reports from Lima alarmed Drew. For all he could learn from the Philadelphia papers, Peru might have been an island of quaint fascination somewhere in the middle of the Pacific. He had been following the events there through *The New York Times*, although even that coverage was spotty.

It appeared that the initial optimism, after the swearing-in of President Morales Bermúdez eight months ago, had worn off. This government was learning that institutions are more easily torn down than replaced. The idealistic social goals expected from land reform and redistribution of wealth under an ailing General Velasco had not materialized because of poor planning, an outflow of capital investment, and an enormous national debt created by the need to borrow from foreign banks.

The new government, with its back against the wall of default, turned to restrictive measures. The *sol* was devalued. At the same time, wages were frozen and price supports removed, resulting in tremendous inflation. When the people reacted with strikes and demonstrations, the junta resorted to the inevitable tactics of all military dictatorships. Force.

Gradually, news items filtered into the press indicating that this regime was surpassing the authoritarian methods of the Velasco administration. Censorship had been tightened and demonstrations countered by police brutality, mass arrests, and further restrictions on public assembly.

It sounded like things were heating up.

Drew called Luís in Mexico. "I'm going down there, Luís, despite what you say!"

"It's not the best idea, Drew. I've been keeping in touch with the situation through friends, and there's a

379

definite anti-American climate. You might be doing Nicole more harm than good by your presence."

"It will be a professional visit. A colleague from the IHTF going to see the department, talk to Alvares, and to Dr. Légende—that is, if she'll talk to me."

Luís chuckled. "I imagine she will. I had the feeling that time was in your favor."

"Why, you rat! What do you mean by that? You told me she said she didn't want to hear from me."

"Yes, that's what she said. But, to tell you the truth, methinks the lady protests too much!"

"Your knowledge of Shakespeare is lacking," he retorted, his pulses quickening. "I'm coming to see you . . . *on my way to Lima!*"

His excitement rose as he contemplated action. It had been *impossible,* standing by all these months, as his friends had urged. Both Luís and Henry had argued with him over and over, stalling him, telling him to wait it out. If he let the matter run its course, they insisted, Nicole's passport would be returned, and the only thing lost would be a few months.

"I know these governments, Drew," Luís had said repeatedly. "If you lean on them, they feel honor bound to dig in their heels and prove how macho they are."

Henry, an old Asia hand, had agreed. He had pretended surprise to hear that Drew and Nicole were more than platonic friends and IHTF colleagues, but it was apparent to Drew that both Campions, Henry and Beth, had long ago guessed the truth.

All three of these friends were offering him what they considered the best advice, but Drew had played it their way long enough. He had given it time—too damn much time! Now he was going to do what he should have done a year ago . . . *go there.* Find out what was happening, tell her how much he loved her and needed her, beg her to take him on any terms.

He stayed in Mexico for two days with Luís. Part of the visit was professional, but mostly it was pleasurable. Forgetting Nicole had been easier when he worked, so he had been driving himself unmercifully since their rift. Unwinding with Luís and his charming family, he felt more relaxed than he had since the times he spent with Nicole in Paris and Geneva.

On the long flight to Lima, he examined his motives. What would going to Peru accomplish? Despite what Luís had said, he had little hope of winning her back. She had virtually closed the door the last time they had spoken. But he had to know how she felt about him now. Whatever he said, he would have his final answer.

If she was in trouble, he thought he stood more of a chance of helping her than anyone else. He knew people in the U.S. State Department. In fact, he had recently learned that Clem Farquhar, a Psi U from Dartmouth who had gone on to the Fletcher School, was vice consul at the embassy in Lima.

Seen from the air at night, Lima was a great, glittering swathe of sparkling jeweled lights, sweeping along the undulating shoreline and inland to the foothills. The beauty, he soon learned, did not bear close inspection. The drive from the airport took him past the decay and ordure of sprawling slums. Behind adobe fences plastered with graffiti slogans and posters proclaiming *Revolución!*, the blighted neighborhoods stretched for miles, as congested and hopeless as any he had ever seen.

It was late when he arrived at the Bolivar, the landmark, old-world hotel that dominated the Plaza San Martín. Luís had warned him not to expect to be invited to stay at Nicole's home.

"Remember, she is an unmarried woman in Latin America. Peru is the most formal society! You must respect the customs," he had cautioned.

"Don't worry, Luís, I won't disgrace myself," he had answered laughingly.

Luís had been shocked when he realized Drew had not informed Nicole of his plans to come to Lima. "You're out of your mind! You mean you're just going to show up? What if she isn't there?"

"Where could she go, Luís? I thought that was the problem!"

"She has a house in the Andes, you know. She might have gone up there."

"Then I'll just wait for her to come back to Lima." Luís had shaken his head at Drew's obduracy.

Truthfully, he did not want to give Nicole advance notice of his arrival. She might refuse to see him. He would have to figure out a way to approach her.

The hotel room had an air of former splendor, with heavy gold damask draperies and a faded bedspread that followed the contours of a mattress that, like an ancient retainer who has served the master well, deserved to be retired. A sheet of glass protecting the desktop was cracked, and when he put his shirts in the bureau drawer, the bottom fell into the drawer below. He went into the bathroom, washed his face and hands, and stared at himself in the mirror, wondering what to do next.

Just being in the same city was enough to make him crazy to see Nicole! Maybe he should call her immediately, tonight. He dialed the number.

A maid answered. "I'm sorry, señor, she is not at home. Would you care to leave a message?"

" . . . No, thank you. I'll call again."

He went down to the English Bar, a dark alcove with dusty game trophies mounted on its paneled walls. Ordering a sandwich and a beer, he was lost in thought, oblivious of the other foreigners who sat drinking *pisco* and imported whiskey. What would happen if he took a taxi to Nicole's house—simply went there and waited for her to return? No, he couldn't do that. They probably wouldn't let him in.

Back in his room, he turned on the ancient plumbing, showered, and got into bed. The television offered a choice of reports on the production of agricultural cooperatives or old movies—and his Spanish wasn't all that good.

Drew watched the screen with blank eyes, and within an hour he had planned his strategy. Turning off the lamp, he fell asleep.

They came for Carlos at the clinic on a Friday morning.

Nicole heard the police were there and ran down to intercede before they could take him away. But they only wanted to ask some questions about Pepe. Pepe was officially listed as "missing."

Since Nicole knew the missing person, she was asked to come into Mona Ramos's office, which the police had commandeered. Although it was not as unnerving an experience as the time she had been taken to headquarters when her passport was confiscated, she was relieved when it was over.

It was then a week since Pepe had last been seen. The
police were acting immensely concerned, extremely solicitous. His father had come to Lima, all the way from
Ayacucho by bus, a short, anxious, careworn *mestizo,*
whose faintly Asiatic features had a look of perpetual
worry. Nicole wanted to help him by offering to pay his
expenses, but he was too proud to accept money.

Nicole called Lucy. "What's going on? The police came
to question Carlos and they also spoke to me—since I
intervened, like a damn fool."

"That was *dumb,* Nicole! I'm going to have to lock you
up if you don't behave," Lucy scolded.

"Has there been anything new on Pepe, Lucy?"

"Nothing. I spoke to those two students and some of
their friends. He was in the truck when it entered the
yard, but in the mêlée, they lost track of him and another
fellow. No one remembers seeing either of them in the
prison itself. Most of the boys were freed the next
morning."

"Where do you think he is?"

"I'm afraid to think. Judging by past experience, the
PIP are probably holding the two of them somewhere in
secret for interrogation."

Nicole gasped, "Oh, no!"

Under the increasingly repressive junta, the PIP were
gaining virtually unlimited powers.

"Yes, Nicole, it's probably as bad as you think. I hope
I'm wrong."

Twice more the police came to the hospital to question
Carlos and the other interns, and the second time they
wanted to see Nicole again. She thought they were putting on a rather convincing show if he was already in the
hands of the PIP.

Jorge Alvares was extremely pleased to receive a colleague of Henry Campion's, even on such short notice. It
was a double pleasure, since this was the virologist who
had worked in India with Nicole. An attractive young
man. One of those large *norteamericanos* who are surprisingly gentle, he seemed gracefully comfortable with
himself, unaware of how he dominated the room.

Alvares thought it was exquisitely sensitive of Dr. Tower
to contact *him,* as the department head and friend of

Campion's, before notifying Nicole of his visit. That was the kind of statesmanlike conduct he had long ago ceased to expect from North Americans, especially the younger ones. He understood them, of course, having spent enough years in the States to accustom himself to their hearty, cavalier manners. Discipline was not in their culture, and few of them bothered to learn or pay attention to the academic protocols.

There was no apparent purpose to Andrew Tower's unexpected visit. His primary concern seemed to be Nicole's welfare and her failure to appear at the IHTF meetings. They had a nice chat, and as the conversation progressed, Professor Alvares began to understand something.

The notion came to him slowly: This was a man whose interest in Nicole was more than professional. Absolutely. There was not a doubt in his mind. Jorge Alvares recognized the emotions on Tower's face. Anxiety . . . and love!

"Perhaps you would like to see Nicole," he suggested. He was amused at the eager flash in the young man's eyes.

"Now let me see," he fondled his mustache, dissembling. "Where would she be now?" He made a show of consulting his watch.

I must be a sadist at heart, he thought amiably, walking out to his secretary's desk. "Where is Dr. Légende?" he asked.

"In the clinic, of course, Professor," she told him, her tone clearly indicating that she thought he was losing his grip.

"Ask her to come up here immediately," he ordered crisply.

Back in his office, he shook hands with Drew. "I'm afraid I have an appointment, Dr. Tower. It was a pleasure meeting you, and I hope you'll come to Lima again."

Thanking him, Drew prepared to leave, but Alvares said, "Don't disturb yourself. Nicole will be here in a few minutes. You might as well wait for her." Taking his briefcase, he left the room.

In the hall, he lingered until he saw Nicole hurrying along the corridor. "You called for me, Professor Alvares?"

"Yes, Nicole. There is someone in my office who wants to talk to you," he said portentously.

She looked at him with apprehension. "The police?" *Oh, my God!* He smiled reassuringly. "No, my dear. It's one of Campion's Task Force . . . just passing through." He started to lead her to his office.

"Oh," she said, with obvious relief.

Her eyes searched Alvares's face. Who can it be, she wondered. *Not possibly* . . . her heart began to hammer.

Alvares smiled stepping aside and motioning for her to enter. Gently, he closed the door behind her. He sighed happily. Jorge had always had a soft spot for romance.

He was standing at the window, observing the military sentries posted in the courtyard below.

She recognized him from the back and thought that if she did not know him, she would fall in love with his profile, even before seeing his face.

He turned and they stared at each other across the room.

"I didn't know you wore glasses," he said.

"Just recently, for working. I've had headaches." She held onto the back of a chair to keep from falling.

He had not moved. "You haven't answered my letters."

"I never received them!" She began to cry.

A look of pain slashed his face as he crossed the room and swept her into his embrace, crushing her against his chest.

"They were love letters," he said, kneading her with his hands, his voice muffled against her hair. "I wanted you to know how much I love you."

Their tears mingled as he brushed her cheeks with his, his lips groping, seeking her mouth.

"Do you love me?" Gently, he touched her face, his look searching.

Cosseted in his arms, she clung to him, her breath merging with his, as she murmured *"Yes, yes, yes. . . ."*

"That's all I have to know. All in the world I care about."

"I'm so glad you're here. It's been terrible," she wept.

In the waiting area outside his office, Jorge Alvares directed others away. He sent his secretary on a long, pointless errand and, much to her surprise, spent fifteen minutes in conversation with a disgruntled laboratory technician who had been trying to see him for weeks.

"I don't have a handkerchief." Nicole let out a tremulous breath.

"Here," Drew smiled, handing his to her. "Everything will be all right, Nicole, now that I'm here."

She shook her head. "You don't understand, chéri. My country is sick, and there may not be a cure."

But the sheer joy of having Drew there was a cure for her malaise. Jorge could see it the moment they emerged from his office. Nicole was smiling and her eyes were dewy, while Tower put him in mind of a knight who has defended his lady against the dragon. If there had been any doubt about these two, there was no longer.

"Nicole, why not take Dr. Tower around the city. We can manage without you for the rest of the day," he suggested. The professor had completely forgotten that he was supposed to have rushed away to a pressing engagement.

"Where's your luggage?" Nicole asked when they were in the car.

"At my hotel."

"You are *not* staying at a hotel!"

"Luís said I would compromise you if I didn't."

"That's just macho Luís! No one in Lima knows, or cares, what I do. They have more serious things to worry about these days, unfortunately."

Nicole sat in the crowded rotunda of the Bolivar, where waiters served tea and cocktails under the elaborate glass cupola, while Drew collected his luggage and settled his account. Pedro waited with the Citröen in front of the hotel, parked amidst an assortment of vintage American automobiles—Chryslers, Pontiacs, Cadillacs with tailfins— and limousines with CD plates. As they pulled away from the curb, a black Hillman fell behind them in the line of traffic moving around the plaza.

Traffic was heavy along Arequipa. Not yet over the thrill of Drew's being there beside her, Nicole kept up a steady conversation all the way home. Then suddenly she would stop mid-sentence to stare at him, and the two of them would grin and hug each other. When they entered the gates to the estate, they grew silent. They rounded the last curve in the driveway, and Casa Loma came into view.

Drew was astounded. "This is how you live?"

She nestled closer to him. "What difference does it make?"

"None at all."

But he could not shake a certain uncomfortable awareness of the opulence with which Nicole was surrounded. Nothing in the States could match this. Would she ever be willing to give it up?

Vera, imperturbable, made up a guest room for Drew. Only later did Nicole realize it was a suite that connected to hers through a sitting room.

Oh, Vera, what an inspired romantic you are, she thought.

Later that night, Drew came to her room and they made love. Never had he been so full of need, of desire for her. She wondered fleetingly, as his lips commanded hers, how she had managed to live without him for all these long months. Each touch, each kiss, seemed to reaffirm their love and heal the wounds of separation. Whatever else happened, she knew that she could only find happiness with him. And it was clear that his love was as deep as hers.

"I can't make it without you, darling," he told her. "I *must* be with you, even if it means staying in Lima."

"You don't have to do that, Drew. But they won't let me leave."

"Don't worry," he promised. "I'll get you out."

"There's a conflict of interest," said Lucy. "If I'm successful in helping Nicole leave Peru, I'll lose my best friend!"

They were having dinner at the Salamanca apartment with Lucy and Horacio, who had immediately warmed to Drew when Nicole had invited them to her home to meet him. Nicole was pleased that the couple who had become her closest friends in Lima got along so well with Drew.

Halfway through the evening, Francisco, who was sitting on the floor at Drew's feet, announced, "My mother's going to have a baby!"

"Yes, I can see that," Drew smiled.

"Are you and Aunty Nicole going to have a baby?"

Drew grinned, while Nicole's cheeks colored.

"Francisco, that's the kind of question you shouldn't ask someone," admonished Horacio.

"Why not?"

"He's right! Why not?" Drew laughed. He ruffled the boy's hair with his big hand. "The answer to that is, yes, I hope so."

"Good!" he exclaimed. "When?"

"Really, Franco . . . that's too personal," said Lucy.

"I just thought if they have their baby *soon*, then it can play with *our* baby," he explained.

"That's the best reason I can think of," Drew replied, hugging him.

When dinner was over and Francisco had left them, Lucy brought out law books and mimeographed briefs of legislation governing passports and immigration. Hunched over in concentration, she and Drew launched into a technical discussion of the regulations governing Peruvian citizens who wish to emigrate to the United States.

It was clear that Drew had spent considerable time familiarizing himself with the various avenues and loopholes they should explore. Nicole was filled with admiration, love . . . and a deep sense of shame that she had ever thought he had abandoned her. She would never again doubt his devotion.

"I have a friend at the U.S. Embassy," he told Lucy. "Do you think I should ask him if there's a way Nicole can enter the States without her passport . . . let's say if . . . Nicole and I were married."

They were all four silent, the three others glancing at Nicole, who was looking down. She lifted her head, and Drew was afraid to see her face, but she smiled at him with shining eyes.

"No, I wouldn't advise that, Drew," said Lucy in her most lawyerlike manner. "Obtaining U.S. citizenship for a marital partner is not an automatic or speedy process. As for a visa, the embassy can only grant one on a valid passport. In any case, it wouldn't be wise to indicate that Nicole is planning to leave Peru. In fact, you shouldn't even mention the possibility of marriage or emigration to your friend at the embassy or anyone else just now. Nicole's situation is very delicate. It could go against her case."

"Well, isn't there some loophole, Lucy? Some other way we can try?"

"I've explored *all* the possibilities, including a French passport," she told him, explaining that France recognizes *jus sanguinis,* the rule of blood relationship, and thus, as the daughter of a French citizen, Nicole had dual citizenship. "The problem is not getting her into the States, Drew . . . It's getting her out of Peru!"

It was Lucy's opinion that the moment Nicole tried to exit Peru, by any means other than with the permission of its government, it would be considered an illegal act—just the sort of move they were waiting for her to make.

"It's outrageous, denying her the right to leave Peru! They're as bad as the Soviets."

"Wait a minute," Horacio cried, "the U.S. has denied passports to its citizens. And they prevent foreigners from entering the States if they don't like their politics!"

Drew did not think it was a reasonable comparison but decided it was not the time for a political disagreement. "I'm worried about her staying here," he said. "Is she in any danger?"

"I don't believe so," Lucy answered.

The government had nothing on Nicole yet, she told them. They hoped she would make a mistake. The best thing she could do was to stay quiet, out of trouble, and not lose her cool. Eventually, they would give up. The main thing was to keep it a non-police matter, within the jurisdiction of the Interior Ministry.

"Thus far, she hasn't committed a crime. There's no illegal act on the books. So if they're trying to get evidence against her, it would be playing into their hands to try something circuitous."

But *why*, Drew asked, was the government trying to "get" Nicole?

Lucy explained it this way . . .

Because the government investigators believed Nicole was aiding the smoldering ultra-left insurrection—not as a political activist, but as a sympathizer and leader of social reform—they wanted to control her freedom of movement. The junta, in its present instability, feared an attempt to overthrow the government might succeed. They even suspected the existence of a shadow government, which conceivably would appoint Nicole to a position in the Health Ministry if it came to power.

"But, that's ridiculous! I'm not even a member of a political party, much less a communist," Nicole objected.

That doesn't matter, Lucy told her. They knew of her professional contacts with student activists, and they believed she was in sympathy with the dissident movement. That was the real reason why they put an end to the mobile clinics, because they thought they were aiding subversives.

Then, Drew asked, surprised, Lucy did not think it was Nicole's connection to the IHTF and the government's fear that it was a front for the CIA that had caused them to take away her passport?

That was a pretext, said Lucy, an excuse to keep her under suspicion. In the absence of other evidence, they would use it to prevent her from leaving the country. But the real danger was this other . . . their belief that Nicole supports the guerrilla movement.

"All they lack is something concrete with which to charge her," said Lucy. The point was—and she could not emphasize it more strongly—they *must* be patient and give the legal process a chance before trying anything that would put Nicole in jeopardy.

They sat silently, sobered by what Lucy had revealed.

"Do you mind," Drew finally said, "if I ask how you obtained this information?"

Lucy smiled cryptically. "These are things that are known to me."

Drew was trying not to be paranoid, but he found the idea of a military government oppressive. Lima seemed to him like a city-state, a garrison, cut off from the rest of the country.

If a Peruvian were to walk past the Russian Consulate in New York, he reminded himself, it would be thick with patrolmen and he might conclude that he was in a police state. But those were the navy blue uniformed city cops, and they did not stand at attention with loaded rifles. Since he had come to Peru, he had even seen soldiers in battle dress walking along the road, carrying machine guns. Nicole told him they were *sinchis*, special troops trained to fight guerrillas. They did not look friendly.

He was not certain when he had first noticed the black automobile. He thought the atmosphere of *revolución* probably had him imagining things. But by the end of his third day in Lima, he knew it was not his imagination. *They were being followed.*

Whenever he was in Nicole's limousine, if he idly turned his head, he would see another vehicle behind them—although initially he could not be sure if it was always the same one.

What he wondered was, were they following Nicole or him?

They had accepted an invitation from the Farquhars. His old college friend at the embassy had been more welcoming than Drew had expected. He could see how impressed Clem was when he asked whether he could bring Nicole.

"Légende," he said, awe and admiration in his tone. "That's quite a name in this country."

The Farquhars' curiosity had been apparent throughout the evening, but neither Drew nor Nicole gave them any insight into their connection.

It was on the way home from the American dinner party that Drew, bending to brush Nicole's forehead with his lips, caught sight of the dim headlights on their tail.

"Do you happen to have a mirror in your purse?" he asked.

She looked at him questioningly. "I think so . . . why?"

"Please find it and give it to me . . . and then I'll tell you."

There was a small, double-sided hand mirror with rounded edges, which she removed from a pocket in the lining of her beige reptile Hermès bag, handing it to Drew.

"Look here," he said, holding the mirror between them and shading it with his hand so it would not reflect light. "That car has been following us all day and all evening . . . and as far as I can tell, ever since I arrived."

"Oh, Drew, that's . . . that's not possible," she protested, but he could tell she believed him.

"Have you ever thought you were under surveillance?"

"Yes, but not like this. . . ." And she told him briefly about Fabricio and how she had finally gotten rid of him.

"Let's see what happens when we reach your home."

Just as Drew had expected, the car fell back, its lights extinguished, when they approached the gates to Casa Loma.

"Is there some way we can watch without being seen?" Drew asked.

Nicole pushed a button for the intercom. "Pedro, pull into the parking area behind the gatehouse and turn off the headlights, please. Quickly!"

The driver did as he was told, and Drew and Nicole were out of the limousine before he could move. "Wait here," Nicole instructed him, "and make no noise."

The guard had secured the iron gate and was returning to the gatehouse. He stopped when he saw them come around the building. Nicole remained in the shadows, saying, "Pretend you don't see us. Stand in front near the gate for a minute. Then go inside and stay there until I come."

Grasping Drew's arm, she led the way behind a shrub to a small door in the tall stone wall. Unobserved, they could stand there peering through the iron gate and have a full view of the boulevard. They heard a door close as the gatekeeper returned to the house.

The night was hushed and starlit, and the perfume of oleander and orange blossom filled Drew's nostrils. He folded his arms around Nicole, standing behind her and pressing her against him as they listened.

In a few minutes, a compact black sedan without lights slowly rolled along the road past the locked gates, past the inconspicuous door where Nicole and Drew stood watching. When it reached the corner of the road nearest the end of the property, its lights went on as it turned in the direction of Avenida Santa Cruz, toward Lima.

Chapter 35

Drew was right, Nicole. Your tails are the PIP."

"Señora Monaco, you are a woman of many resources!"

They were rapidly learning that Lucy had contacts who could supply her with all sorts of information. Such as the identities of undercover investigative agents.

They had given her the numbers on the license plates of the black Hillman. It had not taken Lucy long to verify that Nicole was under surveillance, and by whom.

For several days they confused the PIP by taking a different car each morning. At first it seemed to work, but soon their tails caught on and followed the first vehicle to leave the grounds.

Worse, Drew realized what they were doing. "We're giving them a complete inventory of all the automobiles you own, *with* license plates, if they don't have that information already."

"You're right. We should save one for when I make my great escape."

"What do you do, run a rental service?" Drew joshed when he saw the fleet of vehicles in the garage.

"Funny!" she replied. "Cars were Papá's indulgence. These are all years old, except for the Volvo, which was assembled in Peru. You don't junk foreign cars in this country—not while they're in good operating order."

Among the automobiles, in addition to two Citröens and the Renault, were the Jaguar-E that Daniel had loved to drive, a Volvo station wagon, and on blocks—a ghostly reminder of her father's enthusiasm for classics— the Rolls Royce Silver Cloud that had been a vanity purchase in the 1950s and, except for Tina's funeral cortege, had never traveled more than the eight miles to downtown Lima.

The reality of being followed was too grim for amusement. By the end of the week, Drew was getting edgy. "Why don't we just stay holed up at home for a few days? Maybe that will bore them so much they'll go away."

Nicole was pondering something. "We'll do better than that," she announced with a satisfied smile. "They'll think we're here, but we'll be the ones to go away!"

"What do you mean?"

"You'll see. Pack your casual clothes and take a warm jacket and sweater. Then go to sleep. We have to be up before dawn tomorrow morning."

Nicole drove the Renault, having asked Pedro to be sure it was in good condition for a road trip, with a full tank of gasoline. She swore him and Vera to secrecy. No one else, except Lucy, knew their destination. In fact, none of the other staff at Casa Loma realized they were gone, because they left by the back entrance before daylight.

By the time the sun rose over the Andes, they were well on their way to Huaranca, heading north on the Panamericana, the vagrant artery that runs for two thousand miles along the coast of Peru, part of the system that links all of the Americas from the United States to the south of Chile.

As soon as they reached a point beyond the Lima area, the highway deteriorated to an uneven asphalt surface. The barren coastal desert was sparsely populated with drab, dusty *mestizo* towns, each with a Petroperu station and a *contról*—a checkpoint of the Guardia Civil, where travelers were supposed to stop and log in with the police. In this way, road travel was well monitored. Nicole explained that at times of national emergency, *un estado del sitio*, it would be necessary to have a *salvoconducto*, a safe-conduct pass, from her local police prefecture in order to move from one district to another.

"That's more often than you might imagine," she told him lightly. "We've had *estados del sitio* quite regularly of late."

Today she was taking chances.

At each center along the way, she avoided the *contról*

by either passing it by, if it was on a side street, or taking to the back roads, if it was on the main highway.

"There's nothing they can really do," she shrugged. "They're not going to chase us."

After an hour Drew took the wheel to give Nicole a rest, since she told him it would be better for her to drive through the sierra. At widely separated intervals, the arid beige gave way to tentacles of lush, tropical greenery that snaked inland along narrow river valleys. Near Paramonga, Nicole directed him eastward toward the mountains, over a road that followed the Fortaleza River.

Drew was impressed with the extensive irrigation system, which Nicole told him had its beginnings in civilizations that predated the Incas. They passed cotton fields and orchards shimmering in the hot sun on the terraced hills of the valley. For a considerable distance they drove through a sugar co-op, formerly a plantation that had belonged to one family.

They stopped for gas at a collection of flat buildings where, on the adobe walls, they saw faded slogans from the beginning of Velasco's revolution: "Chino, el pueblo está contigo!" ("Chino, the people are with you!") *Chino*, Nicole told him, was an inoffensive nickname for a Peruvian whose appearance is Indian, whereas to call someone *indio* was an insult in this land of the Incas.

"I can see I'm better off not trying to speak Spanish," Drew laughed. "I probably use the wrong expressions all the time."

"It *is* different from country to country."

Soon the cultivated valley had become a rocky canyon, and the outlying desert gave way to craggy hills with little vegetation other than cactus and brush. The only moisture here was from the mist of low-hanging cloud layers that occasionally formed at night.

"Let's have something to eat," Nicole suggested. "We're getting close to the mountains, and once we're on that road, we won't be able to stop."

They ate the sandwiches Vera had packed and finished the thermos of strong coffee, thick with sugar and milk.

Wearing a heavy cardigan, Nicole slid behind the steering wheel. "Better put a sweater on," she said. "It gets chilly."

The road inclined steadily as they entered the gorge

and began the ascent to the pass. Nicole maneuvered the car with skill. Soon they were twisting in hairpin turns so sharp they could not see beyond the next curve. Drew looked down hundreds of feet to the valley floor, where the river ran white.

"What happens if we meet someone coming down?" he asked at a particularly tight spot, where the road was barely wide enough for one vehicle.

"This is an 'up' day," she answered, explaining that the direction for traveling the convoluted road alternated on odd and even days of the month. Soon, however, they came to a halt behind two trucks, deadlocked nose to nose, the drivers arguing about who was going to give way.

"*Carajo!*" shouted one, waving his fist in the air.

"*Sincojones!*" responded the other, although he was in the wrong.

Finally, one backed up slightly to a wider section of the road, and they scraped by with less than an inch to spare, while Nicole and Drew held their breath, expecting to see the outer truck go hurtling into the abyss. When the impasse had been successfully negotiated, the drivers left the cabs of their trucks to embrace each other and cross themselves at their good fortune.

Nicole and Drew laughed together. "Let's just hope they don't decide to break out the *chicha*," she said merrily. Turning to Drew, she leaned over to kiss him. "This was a wonderful idea. I feel great."

"You just get us over this road . . . and I'll feel even greater!"

The sky had grown dark and threatening, the air became thinner and cold. Nicole turned on the heater, but the Renault had not been made for freezing temperatures. At thirteen thousand feet they were nearing the crest. Nicole glanced at Drew, who had put his head back against the seat and closed his eyes.

"Headache?" she asked.

"Umm-hmm . . . how did you know?"

"It's *soroche*—altitude sickness. Takes a while to get used to this. I'm sorry I don't have any oxygen. We'll be over the pass soon, and then you'll feel better."

"Doesn't it bother you?"

"Not too much. I haven't been coming up here regularly, so I feel a little short of breath."

They were silent until they reached the pass, where large snowflakes thickened the air. Driving slowly and carefully, Nicole headed down the serpentine road to the Callejón de Huaylas.

The rapid change of climate and landscape, according to altitude and rainfall, was for Drew the most vivid aspect of the journey. From the parched rocky desert to the oasis of the agricultural river valley, to the barren, forbidding crags at the summit of the Cordillera Negra, there had been an ascent from sea level to fourteen thousand feet and a drop in temperature of seventy degrees. When they reached the Callejón, there again everything was green, for this was the end of the rainy season in the Andes.

"No one can ever find this road unless they know it's here," Nicole remarked when she turned abruptly onto a still narrower, unpaved trail that led through a gorge carved by a rushing glacial stream.

They drove over a suspension bridge that Drew decided had been constructed by mountaineers equipped with sky hooks. The road became smoother, sharply descending, bending back on itself in loop after loop. Nicole told him her father had given the funds to pave the road and modernize the bridge, enabling vehicles to reach the valley for the first time in 1950.

Drew's ears were popping at the rapid loss of altitude, and he soon shed his sweater as the air became warmer. Nicole turned right where the road forked, and they soon were at the bottom of a canyon so deep and narrow that, looking up, the walls appeared to meet at the top.

At the end, the mountains actually came together in a natural tunnel through which they passed. When they emerged, Drew beheld the gently sloping bowl-shaped valley spread before him in mottled shades of silvery green and emerald splashed with golds and pinks and reds, where the sunlight played on stands of eucalyptus and palm trees and fields of maize. In the middle distance lay the village of Huaranca, with its russet tiled roofs and pink adobe houses, nestled amongst frangapani, bougainvillea, and tropical fruit trees.

*   *   *

Later, Rosa would tell Nicole she knew immediately, as soon as they got out of the car and walked across the courtyard to the broad veranda. . . .

"It was ordained by the gods, *cariñita mia.* He was chosen for you as your destiny. The moment I saw you, I said to myself: *This is the man. How perfect they are together . . . una flor del viento!*"

But Nicole didn't know that when she first brought Drew into the house at the hacienda. She found she was nervous, afraid Rosa might not approve of her gringo.

"Rosa is all the family I have, chéri," she had told Drew when they were driving, so he would understand how important this was. It thrilled her to see him bend to kiss Rosa, the way a son-in-law would in Peru, and greet Tómas with a warm *abrazo.* He won them over from the beginning.

It amused Nicole that Drew was self-conscious about sharing her room.

"In the sierra, marriage often comes after the birth of a child, and not always then," she told him. "They call trial marriage *watanakuy,* which means 'a year together.' I think it's a rather sensible custom, don't you?"

"Yes, but I feel strange with Rosa and Tomás here."

"Don't worry, chéri. They did the same thing."

There was time to talk, more time than they'd ever had before. Time to share confidences and to learn what had happened to each of them during their estrangement.

"Tell me about Africa."

"My work didn't go well at all. We have to come up with a more stable medium for antibodies. The smallpox program there is very different from India, by the way. You would have been interested in that."

"If you only knew how miserable I felt when I heard Anija was going with you. I've never been so jealous in all my life."

He gave her a slow, lazy smile. "You really had something to be jealous about!"

She hit him playfully. "You *know* that isn't what I meant!"

"I was rather hoping it was." He grabbed her, and for some minutes they didn't think about Africa or smallpox.

When he let her go, he said, "I'm not wedded to

Philadelphia, or Penn, you know. We can get jobs together, maybe overseas."

"Why didn't you tell me that *before,* when we were in New York?"

"You never gave me a chance. And then, I was so damn mad, I didn't want to!" How often in the past year Drew had castigated himself for his stubborn pride and his "dominant male" expectations—they had almost caused him to lose Nicole forever.

One day became another, a blend of sights and sounds and unimaginable beauty, of fragrances he had never smelled and vistas undreamed. The plantation seemed a remote and unreal utopia, although of course they knew it wasn't, and their troubles would be awaiting them when they returned to Lima. But Drew followed Nicole across the hacienda, listening to the amazing history of her family and how her father had come to this hidden valley, where he found his wife and made his fortune and eased the lives of the *campesinos* who lived there.

More than ever they understood how unlikely it was that they two had met and loved. Having found each other again after an unhappy year of separation, they became even closer, sharing personal revelations.

One day they climbed down into a ravine.

"This is where my grandfather died," she said. "I've always been afraid to come here since then. When I was a child, I used to think an *apu* lived here and would claim me next. This place has remained one of my demons. . . . I can face it now with you."

Looking straight up into a faultless blue sky, they saw the creviced rocks massed above them in chiaroscuro, while at the bottom, the narrow darkness was ruptured by the white, frothing violence of the river. On the brink of the canyon, silvery-green leaves of young eucalyptus swayed in the breeze, catching the reflections of an unfiltered sun.

Drew decided it was time to tell her his secret. "I saw my mother living all those years without a husband," he began. "I never fully understood why until last year in India, when I learned something about myself."

She watched his face, rapt, as he spoke of what Ranjit Kar had revealed to him, her eyes filling when he described the touching scene with his father recently, when he had finally told Arthur that he knew the truth.

"We are so much alike," she whispered, drawing him into her arms.

Their hunger for each other was insatiable.

Each night, after eating one of Rosa's hearty mountain stews served with a crusty sourdough corn bread, they would sit in the main hall in front of a roaring fire of eucalyptus logs, hardly able to hide their eagerness to be alone. Soon Nicole would say good night and go upstairs, and Drew would stay a while longer conversing with Tomás.

At last he would come to their room where she awaited him, wrapped in a soft woolen robe against the chill of the Andean night. In the hearth a fire was lighted, and on the balcony they could look up at a sky so filled with constellations that their own place in the universe seemed insignificant.

Trying to push away the pain of the grief-filled months without her, Drew filled his senses with her, drinking in the richness of her beauty and the aroma of her skin and hair. The way she responded to him unreservedly made him forget that there was any other place, any life but this. Once, he was moved almost to tears, and she touched his face as if it were an icon, then bent to kiss away the saltiness from his lashes.

He marveled at the long, elegant lines of her body, outlined in the glow from the embers of the fire. Her hair was loose, rippling over her shoulders in a shimmer of midnight silk, and her emerald eyes, almost black in the darkness, shone under the delicate arch of her brows. She hovered over him, kneeling, taking the length of her hair and sweeping it slowly down, its satin caressing his neck and chest and trunk and the most intimate folds of his body. He seized handfuls of the silken mantle, holding it to his face, breathing in her scent, luxuriating in the exotic, spicy rapture of her.

Nicole took him to the hacienda's small cemetery, where her family graves were clustered. The wind stirred a field of wild roses and yellow amancay, carrying the fresh scent of humus and minty herbs, while darting green

birds called soaring threnodies. He noticed when Nicole
added some stones to a cairn in the graveyard, and he
walked off to give her room for private memories. But
she called him back, and they stood before her parents'
headstones in silence, while Drew reached the absolute
conviction of what they must do.

They rode out to the perimeter of the plantation, dismounting where terraced fields rose up the slopes of the
mountain. Tethering their horses, Nicole reached for
Drew's hand, leading him through a passage where a
stream bed intersected with the main cut.

"Come," she said, "there's something I want you to
see."

Climbing up broad, step-like rocks toward a place where
the valley opened, they stopped at the portal of a great
natural amphitheater. On the far side was an expanse of
brilliant flowers, tier after tier, shading from a soft delicate pink, to lush rose, to a flaming blaze of deep crimson. A rivulet tumbled down in a succession of waterfalls
to join the brook below. Entranced, Drew caught his
breath, clasping Nicole to his side. Above them, the sky
was that deep, unreal blue of the sierra, and beyond rose
the Cordillera Blanca in dazzling magnificence, its diamond whiteness, against the indigo dome of the Inca
heaven, blinding in the midday sun.

Drew seized her hand, running toward the meadow.
"What are they, Nicole? I've never seen anything like
them!"

"Those are my wind flowers," she laughed breath-
lessly, as she kept pace with him. "These are the root-
stock for the plantation. All the seeds for the flamesword
plants come from here."

They had reached the boundary of the sea of flowers,
and Drew could tell it was not a field at all, not in the
usual sense. The surface was rough and uneven, a series
of ledges, full of rocks and crags, which gradually sloped
upward until they became part of the sheer cliffs at the
base of the mountains.

"It's not cultivated!"

Nicole nodded delightedly. "Yes! That's the idea, chéri.
These plants grow here naturally. No one knows exactly
how they got here, but this is the only valley in the
Cordillera where they grow, Some say they're a cross

between a cactus and an aloe plant, brought by the conquistadors from the Canary Islands. But I believe they've always been here."

Nicole sat on the ground, and Drew sank down beside her. She told him the legend of the Inca princess and her Spanish knight, a tale that Rosa used to whisper to her when the nights were dark and the winds swept down from Huascarán. Her features became animated as she spoke, and Drew thought her the most exquisite woman he had ever seen, with her heartshaped face framed by the cloud of blue-black hair, and the incredible eyes, heavy-lashed and jade green in the golden sunlight.

When she had finished, they were silent, watching the stretch of riotous color. Nicole was aware of the strength of Drew at her side, feeling nothing could harm her in his presence. His hair fell in a careless wave over his brow, free now of the lines that had marked it when she had first known him. In Peru, where most men were small, his stature, his long, powerful frame and broad shoulders, made him seem almost Olympian.

He turned and smiled up at her, and she felt a quickening inside. "I used to cry when I was a little girl and my father brought me to see the wind flowers."

Drew sat up and took her hand. "Why did you cry?"

"Because they only lasted for a short while, and then they were gone, blown away by the wind. What a spectacular sight it was when the air was filled with flying flowers! Later, when the seedlings from the previous year were harvested and planted, it was a wonderful time. There was a *minga*—a get-together of all the workers in the valley to help with the crop—and my father would host a celebration for everyone. I remember how exciting it was, with singing and dancing and the women wearing their best dresses. The men all got drunk on *chicha*. At night, there were bonfires for the *pachamanca* which is like a barbecue. It was the happiest time for the *campesinos*, because they were well paid and if the crop was especially good, my father gave them a bonus. Of course, he always found some reason to give them something extra."

She gazed off in the distance. "I always loved the time of the wind flowers. That's how the hacienda got its name. Flor del Viento."

"Flower of the wind . . . I like that," Drew murmured.

Nicole lay back in the grass.

"It has come to mean more than that, the way the *runa* say it. It's hard to explain. . . . It's as if they believe the smallest effort will eventually have a significant result. Whenever something unexpected happens, something good that comes from out of nowhere, they say it's a *flor del viento*. I suppose they must think that way. Their existence is so harsh, so limited. They have to feel that what they do is important, that their lives will have meaning."

Drew was staring down at her as she spoke. She smiled when her eyes met his, but he wasn't smiling. He was gazing at her, intently serious.

"Marry me, Nicole! Marry me *now* . . . so that *my* life will have meaning."

Chapter 36

Drew was conscious of Nicole kneeling at his side, her face half hidden by the white lace mantilla.

The interior of the church was beautiful, with a carved Churrigueresque altar, which Rosa said Daniel Légende had given in memory of Nicole's mother. Multitudes of candles glimmered in the knave and in alcoves dedicated to saints conveniently reminiscent of the old Indian gods, who were identified with the important phenomena of life, such as agriculture, rainfall, earthquakes, or fertility. An aureate luster illuminated the creamy stucco walls of the sanctuary. By comparison to the intimate warmth of this adobe chapel, Drew remembered the Irish churches of his youth as cold and forbidding, doing nothing to draw him in. In those days he had been seeking.

A carapace of joy encased him. He listened uncomprehendingly to the droning voice of the padre, speaking in a lisping mixture of Spanish and Quechua.

Nicole was the most magnificent bride imaginable, in the mantilla and dress that had been her mother's and grandmother's. They had lain all these years in a huge carved storage chest, protected in a linen bag to keep them from yellowing with age. The front hem of the bridal gown stopped above Nicole's ankles, while the back formed a short train. It had touched the floor and trailed behind when Tina had worn it, Rosa reminisced, remembering that wedding from her girlhood.

Drew stared at the figure of the crucified Christ, a sad, suffering Jesus with light hair and blue eyes. Who, he wondered, in these mountains populated with the descendants of copper-skinned natives and Mediterranean conquerors, had decided that Jesus was a gringo?

Rosa was happily weeping, and even Lucy looked suitably misty-eyed. He and Nicole had considered whether to invite the Salamancas to come all the way to Huaranca for the wedding. Nicole decided that Lucy would never forgive her if they didn't, even though as Nicole's lawyer she might disapprove of their choosing this particular time to get married.

"It's crazy, but it's wonderful!" Lucy had greeted their news. She and Horacio had driven to Huaranca in seven hours, putting their lives in the hands of the gods, according to Lucy, who tended to become superstitious with her advancing pregnancy.

Tomás had called on the local mayor, who arranged with the priest to marry them without the usual public notices. Everyone had known and loved Nicole's father—and those old enough to remember Don Juan Carlos, her grandfather—so no favor was too difficult to ask. Drew congratulated himself on his inspired decision to be married in Huaranca.

In a haze, he slipped the gold filigree ring he had found in the Callejón on Nicole's finger, then bowed his head with her for the benediction. The padre made the sign of the cross and smiled at them, indicating they should rise. Drew turned to Nicole, who was comforting a sobbing Rosa, then realized that the nuptial kiss was not part of the marriage ceremony in this church.

When they reached the massive, wooden, iron-banded doors of the house, Drew paused. "Do you mind if I introduce an old American custom into this wedding, darling?" He swept Nicole into his arms and carried her over the threshold, kissing her lingeringly before setting her down, while everyone from the hacienda cheered and Lucy and Horacio applauded.

Nicole was flushed and radiant as she took the seat of honor next to Drew in the main hall, while all the *campesinos* filed in to bring them candies and fruit to symbolize the sweetness of life and the fecundity of marriage.

The women, under Rosa's direction, had prepared a wedding feast, with *aka picchu, anticuchos, cau-cau, chiriuchu,* and a dozen different sweet pastries, in addition to an elaborate coconut wedding cake.

Horacio had managed to bring three bottles of real champagne, procured from a friend at the French embassy. "I told him it was for a wedding, but I didn't tell him *whose* wedding!"

Nicole suggested Tomás serve *pisco* to all the workers and their wives, but he insisted they would prefer *chicha* or *trago*, the strong spirits brewed in the sierra.

The fiesta continued in the courtyard, with music and dancing and much consuming of food and spirits, while the wedding party celebrated more sedately inside. Rosa lingered to serve them; Tomás drifted back and forth between the two celebrations, becoming increasingly more joyous and uninhibited with each reappearance.

Horacio toasted the bride and groom, proving himself as clever and eloquent as his controversial articles in the restricted press. Their laughter reverberated against the beamed ceilings of the ancient manor house, where dozens of tallows flared in the great hanging candelabra. As Drew surveyed those gathered around the heavy trestle table, its surface smooth with the soft patina of time, he was profoundly stirred by the tableau of their wedding dinner at Flor del Viento.

Nicole studied Drew's strong features in the candlelight. She thought he could have been a Castillian warrior except for the softness in his eyes. He turned to her, his lips parted in a smile. "I want to say it once . . . only one time. Because I can't believe it."

"What, chéri?"

"*Mrs. Tower.*"

Laughing, she threw her arms around him, kissing his neck. "Oh, Drew! What have you let yourself in for?" she murmured, nestling against him.

He held her closer. "Heaven . . . I expect."

Much later that night, they retired to their room, where the bed was covered with a silky *cobija* woven of natural alpaca and vicuña hair, a wedding gift from Rosa and Tómas.

Nicole removed the lace mantilla with the ivory comb, laying them carefully on a chest. Drew came up behind her to unfasten the dozens of small buttons of the bridal gown, bending to kiss her nape beneath the coil of her chignon. She arched her neck, her eyes closing with ecstatic happiness.

Suddenly, they were interrupted by an enormous, strident cacophony in the courtyard below their balcony.

"Good lord," exclaimed Drew. "What's that racket?"

Nicole began to laugh. "Oh, no! They're doing a charivari!" She took his hand, pulling him toward the door to the galleria. "We have to go out. They'll tease us unmercifully if we don't."

"But what is it?"

"It's a mock serenade—for the married couple. I didn't think they would have the nerve. They must be crazy drunk!"

Cheers for the bride and groom rang out when they appeared on the balcony, the bolder of the younger men calling encouragement to Drew in Quechua words that Nicole didn't know but nevertheless understood. The musicians below broke into a traditional Andean melody, somewhat in unison and relatively harmonious. Across the courtyard on their balcony, Lucy and Horacio waved and did a little dance to the music.

At last, the musicians let them go inside, but it wasn't long before there was another blast of dissonance beneath their window.

"Oh, no," groaned Drew.

"We don't have to go this time," murmured Nicole. "I think we've been good sports."

Soon the revelers gave up and wandered away.

As a half moon rose over the snowy peaks of the cordillera, pale luminescent clouds descended like spectral *apus,* catching the pure, silvery light and drifting down among the hills to the field of the wind flowers. Soon the valley was silent, and in a black sky the stars lit a path beyond the universe.

Chapter 37

On the drive back through the Callejón, they were delayed by crowds of celebrants preparing for one of the many feast days of the harvest season. In each town, they crept along the highway as good-natured drunks threw water and flowers at their car. Finally, they reached the pass and headed down the twisting course toward the coastal valley.

Lucy and Horacio had departed for Lima the day after the wedding, following another round of discussions about the best way to get Nicole out of Peru. Drew was all for going directly to the American Embassy and requesting assistance, but once more Lucy argued against this and finally succeeded in convincing him that it would not achieve the desired result.

Drew told them it would look bad for Peru, as well as the IHTF, if Nicole did not attend the smallpox evaluation meeting in Geneva in nine weeks.

"If you arrange for her to receive the invitation directly from the WHO, I'll get the hearing moved up," Lucy asserted.

"Are you sure it wouldn't be better to ask whether she can leave now with me, since we *are* married?"

"Of course, I'm not certain, Drew. It would be a gamble. But if it doesn't work, then we've ruined any opportunity we might have for her exit permit. I'm groping in the dark. This government is under duress, and there's no telling how they'll react."

He was considering Lucy's advice. The Salamancas had left with the final decision still unreached.

Rosa behaved strangely when she bid them farewell. "There will be a *pachakuti*," she said, using the Quechua word for a cataclysm. "I fear I may not see you again in this life."

408

"Don't say that, Rosa," protested Nicole. "You *know* it's just silly superstition. I'll see you soon, I promise."

But Rosa had stared after them fatalistically when they drove away, a phantom vision in her eyes, as if she perceived what they were unable to. It had unnerved Drew and frightened Nicole. "I hate to say it, chéri, but Rosa seems to have a way of knowing things. She has always had premonitions."

"Well, *I* have a premonition that everything's going to be fine!" To put any credence in Rosa's auguries was ridiculous. Trained scientists did not believe in mysticism.

It was dusk when they reached Miraflores. Nicole drove along the shore and up the cliffs to the private road leading to Casa Loma. High, thick hedges screened the rear entrance to the estate. Drew unlocked the gate, securing it again after Nicole had driven through.

On an impulse, she said, "Keep that key, Drew. I have another one in my purse. You might want to come in this way when you're alone."

Drew slipped the key into his pocket. It wasn't the time to tell her he would have no use for it, that he had come to a decision. He would be leaving Peru within a few days.

Nicole was unprepared to see Manuel.

He had arrived at the house without warning, Vera told her, having called repeatedly, demanding to know where her mistress was. Vera was almost in tears.

"Thank God you're here, Señorita Nicole! I didn't know what to say to him." She looked unhappily in Drew's direction.

"It's all right, Vera. I'll take care of it." Glancing at Drew, she said, "You'd better come with me."

Manuel started toward her, his arms spread and a look of relief on his face. But then he noticed Drew standing in the doorway of the study, and a cold mask settled over him.

Nicole introduced them. Manuel shook hands and bowed correctly. *"A sus órdenes, señor,"* he said, with icy formality.

"Dr. Tower has come to visit the department," explained Nicole, avoiding Manuel's eyes. "We are colleagues on the IHTF."

"Of course," Manuel answered, with a dismissive nod.

Heatedly, he spoke to Nicole in Spanish, too rapidly for Drew to follow. "I've been trying to reach you for *days*—almost a week, in fact. Why haven't you returned my calls?"

"I'm sorry, Manuel. I took some time off. I'm afraid I haven't paid much attention to messages."

"I was *worried* about you! If you hadn't fired that bodyguard, Fabricio . . ."

She cut him off impatiently, "Was it something important?"

"Yes! Unless you no longer consider the future of the company your father founded to be important." He was so agitated he barely bothered to be polite.

"Let's sit down," she suggested soothingly, speaking in English. "Why don't we save the business until later, Manuel? Would you care for a sherry?"

When she had poured an aperitif for each of them, she said, "Dr. Campion sent Andrew to see if there isn't some way I can go to an important meeting in Geneva."

"Yes," Drew added. "We've all been concerned about Nicole's absences. There's a smallpox meeting in July at the World Health Organization, and we're—that is, the people there are hoping Nicole will attend."

"When is your hearing?" Manuel addressed Nicole.

"It wasn't supposed to be until August, but Lucy says she'll get it moved up."

Manuel continued to direct his words to Nicole, virtually ignoring Drew, who presently left the room, saying he had to make a telephone call.

"Why is that man here in your home?"

Nicole regarded Manuel with surprise. "Why shouldn't he be here? We're friends as well as colleagues."

"I know what kind of friends you are! I saw you together in Paris."

She fought to control her shock. "What was there to see? Am I not permitted to have houseguests?"

He scrutinized her, hope invading him. Was it possible he was wrong about them? He, too, had been a guest in her house, and nothing had happened between them. He wanted so much to believe it.

Before Manuel could answer, Vera was at the door of the room, announcing Señora Monaco. Lucy made her pregnant entrance, accompanied by Drew. She exchanged an affectionate kiss with Manuel.

"I'll wager it's twins," he joked, indicating Lucy's expanding girth. Nicole could tell he was flattered that Lucy treated him familiarly, while indicating only a slight acquaintance with the visiting American.

"Will you have a drink, Lucy?"

"Just water. No more alcohol until this child is born!" She joined Nicole at the bar and whispered. "What have you told Manuel?"

"Nothing!" She poured mineral water over ice and handed it to Lucy.

"Well, counselor, what can we do to get Nicole permission to go to Geneva?" Manuel called over his shoulder.

"I'm hoping the invitation from the WHO will be enough," Lucy answered. "Who do you know in the ministry?"

Nicole was grateful to her friend, who kept the conversation going. Lucy spoke mainly to Manuel, as a colleague, sensing the tension between the two men.

Manuel said decisively, "I think it would be in Nicole's best interest for Dr. Tower to return to the United States and arrange for an invitation to be sent from Geneva, independently of the IHTF."

Nicole could see a frown forming on Drew's features. She tried to catch his eye to warn him to keep his cool. He and Manuel were like stags pawing the earth, prepared to lock antlers.

So much was clear to her now that Manuel had revealed he had seen her with Drew in Paris. Had it been accidental, or had he been spying on them? She wished she knew. It would clarify many contradictions about Manuel if she learned the answer to that question.

Fortunately, Lucy was still diverting Manuel with legal talk. It was clear to Nicole that Drew thought him pompous and resented his intrusions. If the circumstances were not so serious, it would be amusing.

Promising to use his influence when the invitation from the WHO arrived, Manuel rose. "May I see you alone for a few minutes?" he asked Nicole.

They went into the library.

"I was in Paris last week. The board approved the Swiss proposal to take the company public. Claude had your proxy and he finally went along when he saw that everyone else wanted it. He'll remain as CEO for now, but I can see it won't be for long. The Swiss will ease him out."

Her brow wrinkled in concern. "But why would they do that? He's been doing a wonderful job."

"The Swiss pharmaceutical operation wants to take over the parent company, Nicole. They've made no secret of their intentions." He sat back and looked thoughtfully at the ceiling. "Actually, they're being rather decent about it, and I think it will be better for the company in the long run."

"That's not what my father would have wanted, Manuel."

"Your father isn't here, little one," he answered gently. "That's why it will be the best thing. A proprietary company needs a strong hand at the helm, and there's no one who can fill Daniel's place. Claude has been fine for the interim, but he's losing his zest."

Manuel explained that Nicole would receive a large block of stock in Légende et Cie and its subsidiaries, while her interests would be protected in whatever future developments transpired. If she wanted a place on the board of the reorganized company, it was hers.

"Isn't that rather unrealistic, Manuel, considering that I can't even go to Paris?" she asked bitterly.

He put his hand over hers. "If only you would marry me, *querida*, you would no longer have these problems. They wouldn't dare touch you if you were my wife."

Her head was down. "I can't do that, Manuel," she said in a low voice.

"You'll never forgive me for that awful night," he exploded, rising and pacing back and forth.

"You're wrong, Manuel! I've forgotten all about that. You were drunk—anyone can do something foolish when he's had too much to drink." She was afraid he would become maudlin again, the way he had been on that occasion. "Besides, you really didn't behave as badly as you seem to think. Now, come on, let's both of us forget it ever happened."

Manuel soon left, pleading another appointment. Nicole saw him to the door, feeling some guilt for causing him pain, yet still not trusting him. She thought how in each person there is something that reveals vulnerability.

With Manuel it was in the hollows of his face. Tonight he had a tense and tragic air. As they stood in the hall, she noticed how a muscle in his left cheek quivered.

When Nicole returned to the study, she invited Lucy to stay and have dinner with them.

"Caldeiro is right, Nicole. Drew *should* leave Peru," said Lucy. "I think Manuel is jealous, but I trust his judgment."

On the point of telling them her suspicions about Manuel and the bodyguard he had hired for her, Nicole caught herself. *It isn't wise to accuse him when I don't have proof,* she thought. *Lucy will think I'm imagining things, and it will only add to Drew's worries.*

She had been made love to like this before, long ago . . . with the same intensity, the same hushed reverence. As if he wanted to imbed it in his consciousness forever. As if it were for the last time! *Oh God, no! Not now, not when we can spend the rest of our lives together.*

With slow, savoring gentleness Drew caressed her, loving her in ways that only he had done, to bring them both to exalted fulfillment. He was so skilled and knowing and sure a lover, and yet their love remained as new and thrilling for him as it was for her. When he covered her with the long stretch of his body in all its male beauty, she felt him moving deep inside her. Looking into his eyes, she saw fear as well as passion. Again and again he took her, until he finally slept, his head pillowed on the spreading mass of her hair.

At last she fell into a dreamless sleep, awakening with a start at dawn, alarmed when she felt the emptiness beside her. She sprang out of bed. Drew was shaving in the bathroom of his connecting suite, having already showered. It was painful for her to see his suitcase lying open on a bench at the foot of the undisturbed bed.

Pedro drove them to the airport. Drew suggested they not use the rear exit, reserving it for a possible emergency. They left through the front gate and were followed by an old gray Dodge.

"Trying to fool us by switching cars," remarked Nicole. "They must think we're pretty dumb." She took Drew's hand. "I've become used to having you around. It's going to be lonely."

"I'll only write if there's something important," Drew told her. "Clem said I can send a letter in the embassy pouch." He ran his hand up and down her arm. "I'll call once a week just to hear your voice and know you're all right. We won't be able to talk about specific details. If anything goes wrong, Lucy will know how to reach me."

She nodded, feeling weepy. The day before, they had discovered her telephone was being tapped.

Lucy had phoned about a trivial matter, and just as they hung up, Nicole thought of something else she wanted to say. Calling Lucy's name, she realized they were disconnected—yet, there was no dial tone. Instead, she heard the sound of a magnetic tape winding, the same electronic vibration she had heard at the Task Force meetings when she sat near the secretary who recorded the proceedings.

Hanging up, Nicole told Drew. He lifted the receiver, began to dial a number, then broke the connection and continued to listen. There was the distinct sound of a tape recorder engaging. Quietly he replaced the receive.

"We'd better warn Lucy, darling. No more open discussions on the telephone. I don't know why we didn't think about that. How long do you suppose this has been going on?"

"I've never noticed that sound before."

They questioned Vera, who later reported that the gateman had observed some men working on the telephone lines next to the estate three days earlier, the same day that Nicole and Drew had returned from Huaranca.

"That's probably when it began," said Drew. "Not too much harm done." But she could tell he was disturbed.

When Lucy and Horacio had come to say goodbye last night, she overheard Horacio say to Drew, "That's PIP all right. They're the only ones who can do wire taps."

Drew, as well as the Salamancas, insisted she promise not to make any attempt to foil the PIP. "Just go to work normally each day and never try to shake your tails," Lucy cautioned. "Don't do *anything* that could cast the slightest suspicion on you, Nicole. We're too close to the end to take risks."

And now it was time for Drew to leave. He had checked in at the counter and come back to sit in the car with her. They took it for granted that inside the airport someone would be watching. It was best to say goodbye here, behind the darkened glass of the Citröen. Pedro stood outside smoking a cigarette, trying not to look conspicuous.

"This isn't good for his nerves, poor old soul," laughed Nicole.

"I'm rather sorry you fired that guard Manuel hired for you. Pedro looks like a strong wind would blow him over."

She had explained about Fabricio to Drew, but not all of it. He resented Manuel's possessive treatment of her as it was.

"Why would I need a guard when I have the police tracking me, chéri?"

"You need protection from *them*," he replied. "I don't trust them any more than I would a common thief. Remember what Horacio said—stay in crowded, public areas when you go out."

She could see that he was even more apprehensive than he had let on. Lucy's husband had told him that friends of his had been picked up and held incommunicado without being charged or permitted to get in touch with a lawyer.

"Don't worry, Drew. I shall be very careful. I've got too much at stake now—*we* have so much to look forward to." She twisted the gold filigree ring, which she had removed to her other hand, although it did not necessarily look like a wedding band.

Drew raised the hand to his lips, then took her in his arms. *"Au revoir, mon amour . . . je t'aime toujours."* His embrace had a desperation to it. She closed her eyes, wanting to capture the memory of his mouth on hers.

As soon as she lost sight of him going through the entrance to the departure area, she asked Pedro to take her to the hospital. Turning back, she could see a commotion in front of the terminal. A short, squat man in dark trousers and polyester shirt came running out of the building toward a black Hillman that was forced to stop for him.

"Drive slowly, Pedro. Give them a chance to catch up," she told the chauffeur.

The day seemed interminably long. Nicole found it difficult to keep her mind on her patients. There were many messages and a pile of letters and reports that had accumulated on her desk during her two-week absence. The department secretary told her that Mona Ramos had inquired about her several times.

"What did you tell her?" Nicole asked, an uneasiness coming over her.

"The truth. I said I didn't know where you were, and I finally referred her to Professor Alvares," the woman responded.

The secretary liked Dr. Légende, who had always been especially pleasant to her. The thought had even crossed her mind that there might be some connection between Nicole's unannounced leave and the sudden appearance in Professor Alvares's office of that handsome gringo. She would never have suggested such a thing to anyone, especially Señorita Ramos, whom she did not like. There was something devious about that woman, even though she was so pious. Praying did not necessarily make someone a good person.

In the afternoon, Nicole found Jorge Alvares in his office. "I was wondering whether you were ever coming back," he said with good humor.

"I hope you received my message. I thought it was better to leave it at your home."

"Yes, my dear. That was sensible." He leaned back in his swivel chair. "I hope you're feeling better after your bout of influenza."

For a minute she stared at him. "Oh—yes, I'm quite all right," she answered.

"Come, let's go over to the laboratory." She followed him to the elevator. When they were crossing the campus, Alvares said, "How was Dr. Tower's visit?"

Nicole blushed. "I feel I owe you an explanation, Professor Alvares. Andrew and I—well, we're more than just friends."

Jorge's eyes twinkled knowingly. "I rather suspected as much. He looked like a man in love to me."

Nicole laughed. "You were right!" She hesitated only for an instant. "We were married while he was here. The wedding took place in the little church in Huaranca where my parents were wed."

"My dear Nicole—I am so very happy to hear this wonderful news. Felicitations!"

"Thank you. But you mustn't tell anyone. The resolution of the judgment order for my passport is coming up." She explained about the invitation to the WHO meeting on smallpox eradication. "If it were known I had married an American, it might go against me."

Alvares sobered, nodding. "Yes. No one must know you are married. But I'm glad you told me."

"How could I not tell *you?* You've been so good to me. Besides, if it weren't for you recommending me for the IHTF, I would never have met Andrew."

They sat on a bench in the garden while the professor described his visit from Nurse Ramos. Alvares did not understand her motives or the circuitous way she had gone about questioning him.

"She asked me whether you had left Lima."

"How odd. Why do you suppose she would ask a question like that?"

"I have no idea. I told her you had the flu and I had suggested you take some time off for a rest. I'm not at all sure she believed me." He grinned. "I more or less suggested that what goes on in my department is none of her business."

Whatever Ramos's motive, Nicole was certain it was not idle curiosity. She had endeavored in vain to maintain a reasonable civility between herself and the nurse. They almost never exchanged words nowadays. Nicole remembered with a pang that it was Pepe who had most recently encountered the head nurse's wrath, shortly before the mobile clinics had been halted by the government.

"There has been no trace of Pepe?" she asked the professor, realizing she would have heard from Lucy if there were any news.

He shook his head sadly, "None. Nor of the student from San Marcos. I understand word is circulating that they were both ultra-left subversives."

"Who says that? It's not *true!*" she cried vehemently. "Besides, what if it were? Does that make it right that the police can just let them *disappear?* They're not terrorists. Pepe wouldn't harm anyone!"

Jorge smiled gently. "Nicole, you must take care not to become too righteously indignant. Words uttered in this unguarded fashion could be your downfall."

* * *

The big house seemed desolate without Drew. She
wandered from room to room, wherever he had been,
sitting in this chair or that sofa, touching the table where
his hand had rested. She, who had vowed never to become dependent on any man ever again, now craved the
presence of one man, now lived only for his love.

She found a letter on her desk that night, the first night
without him:

My darling Nicole,
   I can't sleep. I would like to wake you and make
love one more time, but you look so peaceful lying
there. I watch you and think how beautiful you are
and how much I adore you. You are all that I want
or need to be completely happy. When this last
separation is over, I'll be content to spend the rest
of my life just loving you.
   Although I'm terrified, I can't make myself believe
you're in any real danger. I don't *want* to believe it!
Yet, I realize that every day there are people in
Peru who are being arrested without having done
anything wrong. For an American, it's a sobering
thought. I take my freedom too lightly, as if nothing
could jeopardize it.
   I told you the letters I had written to you—the
ones you never received—were love letters. I've never
sent letters like that to anyone before. I'm not the
most eloquent person, but they expressed the depths
of my love for you, in a most personal way. The idea
that someone else may have read them, someone
who is your enemy, fills me with anger. . . .
   . . . If my life were over tomorrow, darling, it would
have been wonderful because I met you, and we fell
in love. Whatever fate brought us to each other, I'm
grateful for it, and am counting on it to reunite us. I
believe Rosa, that this is a *flor del viento!* We *are*
destined to spend all eternity together.

                              With endless love,
                                         Drew

When she closed her eyes she was unable to fall asleep,
for her mind was filled with foreboding. My armor has

been removed. I knew this. I knew love made you vulnerable. If I didn't love him so much, if I didn't want to live for him and be free to go to him, I wouldn't be feeling this terror.

She lay in bed, aching for Drew, remembering the security of his body next to hers. Often, at moments of special closeness, he spoke to her in French, the French of a child. It was stirring and oddly comforting, the intimacy that only happens in bed, between two people who love each other. When the long silk of her hair enveloped him, he would sometimes grasp it, growling, *"C'est magique, mes cheveux si noirs. . . ."* or *"Jamais casse la magie. Ne les coupe jamais!"* And at times when she gasped with pleasure, breathing incoherent phrases, he would demand, *"Ça tu plait . . . dite moi, Ça tu plait!"*

What if I never hear his voice again? she asked the nameless demons. *He's my husband! What if we never see each other for the rest of our lives?*

As if to give substance to Nicole's blackest fears, one night at the end of May, Lucy came to her home with dreadful tidings.

"Pepe is dead."

"Dead! What happened?" The room seemed to be spinning. She caught hold of a chair and sat down.

"Are you all right?" asked Lucy.

She nodded, whispering, "Tell me."

"He has been positively identified. His body was washed up on the beach near Bocanegra. It was badly decomposed, but there were signs of torture." Lucy closed her eyes and leaned her head back. "The police are protesting ignorance, as usual. But this time I think they really weren't responsible. The PIP probably had them at El Frontón and disposed of their bodies when they were finished."

"Them . . . ?"

"The other fellow is almost certainly dead, too. Or soon will be, if he's still being held. The one from San Marcos."

Tears started in Nicole's eyes. "They were *boys*, Lucy. Pepe was only twenty-three years old! He had his whole life ahead of him." She swallowed, trying to control herself. "Do you know about him? He came from a peasant family who had left the land. His father is a carpenter who believed education would lift his children to the middle class. Pepe was smart and he worked hard. He was a living example of what this junta says it's trying to bring about!"

"Well, there you are, Nicole. Now you really understand what's happening in Peru, with this government. And why I say that you must be careful."

"I never doubted you, Lucy. When I saw that girl they brought into the hospital, it was clear to me what was going on. I just haven't wanted to admit it was this bad, even to myself."

At San Martín, everyone was in a state of disbelief. Pepe dead! How was such a thing possible? He was one of the favorites. They all loved him. Remember how he used to kid around, cheering us up? He always had a joke for any situation. Remember, in the clinic, how the children were crazy about him? He could get them to take medicine and shots when no one else could. *Dios!* Pepe dead. . . .

Even those who approved of the Morales Bermúdez government were shocked and saddened.

Carlos came to Nicole's office the next evening. He had lost his restlessness. He sat immobile, his face expressionless. "It's over, Nicole."

"What do you mean? What's over?"

He tossed his straight black hair back from his forehead with an exaggerated theatricality. "Youth, joy, dreams—whatever it was that kept us laughing." He looked down and his shoulders shook. "I had to identify him!" He put his face in his hands and wept.

Carlos lifted his head. Tears streamed down his cheeks, and he did not bother to wipe them away. "I loved him," he cried. "I loved him like my little brother. I should have kept him from going to that meeting! I didn't want him to go—I could have stopped him!"

"You couldn't have prevented this, Carlocito—he was destined to go," she heard herself saying. "If it hadn't been that time, it would have been the next. Or the next. Pepe was going to keep on trying to change things for all of his life. He would never have stopped."

Carlos continued to weep. She sat there silently, letting him purge himself of his tears. He was right when he said it was over. When would they ever laugh again together with the joyful abandon of youth?

She knew what he would say before he formed the words.

"I've come to tell you goodbye, Nicole."

She bit her lower lip. "Where will you go?"

"Back to Ayacucho. I'm a doctor now. I'll do what Pepe and I always dreamed of doing, bringing health care to the *runa* there. Maybe in that way I can make some part of what he believed come true."

"I'll really miss you, Carlos. I always hoped we would reorganize the mobile clinics someday and you'd be in charge of them."

"That's what I'll try to do in the highlands, Nicole. Will that be a reasonable substitute?"

"A more valuable one, I expect. At least in Lima the people can get to a hospital." She regarded his kind, plain *mestizo* face with affection. "When will you leave?"

"Day after tomorrow. I must pack up our things, mine and Pepe's. His family will want his clothes and books."

"I'll come with my station wagon and help you take everything to the train," she said.

"No, Nicole, you shouldn't do that. But thanks."

"I insist. This is something I *must* do, Carlos!"

Two days later, she went with Pedro to Carlos's apartment. The chauffeur's face was a study in inscrutability when they loaded the valises and cartons of books into the Volvo.

Carlos was silent as they drove along Jiron Lampa to the Rímac River. They waited on the platform until the train came steaming into the station.

Carlos was half a head shorter as he looked up at her. Smiling his sweet, newly confident smile, he said, "I'm going to tell you something you were never supposed to know." He lowered his eyes and laughed. "I was in love with you—so was Pepe. We used to lie in bed at night before falling asleep and talk about what it would be like if you loved one of us."

Nicole's lips parted in surprise. "I—I never suspected."

"No, I'm sure you didn't! I just wanted you to know, suddenly. Are you offended?"

"Of course I'm not offended. I'm flattered."

He took her hand. "There's no way for me to thank you, Nicole."

"Just be my friend," she answered. "Let me hear from you, Carlos. I want to know what happens."

Again, the smile. "If something happens, you'll know."

At the last minute, she pressed a heavy envelope into his hand. "Don't read it until you're on the train." She was barely able to hold back tears.

"All right."

He embraced her quickly and swung up into the slowly moving train. Nicole waved until the last car had disappeared from view.

Pedro held the back door of the station wagon for her. Before entering, she turned her head and stared directly into the eyes of the man behind the wheel of a black Hillman.

Chapter 38

Now was a time of waiting. The invitation arrived from the World Health Organization. It came in the form of a cable addressed to Nicole at San Martín University Hospital, followed by a copy of the letter of notification sent to the Ministry of Health. The health ministry of a country was asked to approve such invitations. In any but unusual circumstances, this was a matter of courtesy.

Lucy had succeeded in getting a special passport hearing scheduled for the first week in July. That was playing it rather close, but if the court ruled in her favor, it would not matter. Of course, if the decision went against her, there would be no time for an appeal.

Each Friday night, Drew called. She was happy and excited at the sound of his voice, but the talks were frustrating because of their inability to speak freely. Once she telephoned him from the Salamanca apartment but would never repeat it because they refused to accept money from her to pay for the call.

Nicole spent many evenings with Lucy and Horacio at their flat. She enjoyed the homey warmth in Lucy's family. The simple provincial dishes served with domestic wine or beer, the strains of classical music in the background, were a welcome change from the formality that had always prevailed at Casa Loma. Horacio and Francisco played games on the living room floor while Nicole chatted with Lucy, who lounged on the sofa with her feet elevated, as ordered by her obstetrician.

Some of these evenings were work sessions. Lucy would sit with a pad of lined paper, taking notes, while she queried Nicole on all matters related to her personal affairs. Gradually, this process developed into an accounting of what would become of Nicole's vast wealth when she left the country permanently. The bulk of the Légende holdings were in France, Switzerland, and to a lesser degree, the United States, Lucy discovered in their conversations. That was fortunate, she told Nicole, since the government would not permit large amounts of money to leave Peru.

Nicole wrote a will. In a tactful, businesslike manner, Lucy forced her to specify what she wanted done with Casa Loma, its furnishings, her father's collection of ancient and modern art—even the automobiles.

"Sell the Rolls, I guess—and give Pedro his choice of the others. He can use it for a taxi."

One week Lucy spent many hours making a complete inventory of everything on the estate. "I realize all this is sensible and necessary," said Nicole. Nevertheless, it was unnerving.

Lucy had her execute an affidavit of *jus sanquinis*, attesting to her right to French citizenship on the basis of her father's nationality.

"This is what the Americans call 'covering all bases,' Nicole. In an emergency, I want you to be able to claim citizenship of some country other than Peru."

"Not the United States?"

"We still can't take a chance. That's a more complicated process and it would be hard to keep confidentiality. You're already French by right."

Nicole signed papers giving Lucy the power of attorney, rejecting her suggestion that Manuel be designated as an alternate.

"It can't be Drew, Nicole. It has to be someone who lives in Peru. Why not Manuel?"

In answer to Lucy's quizzical expression, she said, "Manuel has been an executor of Papá's estate, and a self-appointed guardian to me for a long time, Lucy. It's probably just in my mind, but I sometimes feel as if he's a surrogate father. If you must name an alternate, make it Jorge Alvares."

At work, Nicole had formed the habit of dropping into Jorge's office for coffee each afternoon. Generally they talked medicine, about health services for the poor, exercising care when others were within earshot, for they both felt it wasn't quite safe to speak freely in the office. Their conversations ranged on the philosophical. They were more intimate than in the past, indicating they had become professional equals rather than professor and junior faculty.

One day they were discussing family planning and abortion. They agreed that these were integral components of maternal and child health care. Deaths from botched illegal abortions were an everyday occurrence in the hospitals of Lima, a reality that the government and the church hierarchy refused to acknowledge.

Nicole reminded Jorge it was over this issue that she and Mona Ramos had had their first confrontation. "Remember? It was a patient who almost hemorrhaged to death after an abortion."

"Yes, and if you recall, I warned you *then* that she was a vindictive woman!"

Jorge Alvares had reached a showdown with Nurse Ramos after Pepe's death. Learning that the administrator had been using her duplicate key to his department's clinic supply room and was in the habit of regularly checking its inventory, he had marched unceremoniously into her office one afternoon, demanding she hand over the key.

"From this moment, the Department of Maternal and Child Health is off limits to you, señorita," he had told her in a voice of controlled fury. "You are never to enter my department again. Is that clear?"

"You have no right to give me such an order," she had answered, her voice rising in anger.

"I have that right. If you care to question it, you may go to the director." When she did not reply, he added, "It would be my suggestion that you remove yourself from this hospital altogether and spend the remainder of your days in your precious prayers—for the redemption of your soul!"

Leaving the nurse's office, Jorge had been shaking with suppressed rage. He had heard from his secretary that it was common knowledge among the staff at the outpatient clinic that the head nurse had been receiving regular visits from an agent of the feared Peruvian Investigative Police. What she had told him, whether Pepe's name had ever been mentioned, he would never know. But Jorge Alvares did not believe in coincidences.

In the campus garden, Alvares related to Nicole what

had occurred between him and the administrator. "I wish I had spoken up long ago. Perhaps I could have prevented—"

"No one could have prevented it," she said, for the second time.

"I have never been a political activist, Nicole," he mused, "but I've spent the last thirty years staging my private revolution here at San Martín. When I began as a young man, they wouldn't take care of a patient in the clinic unless she could pay."

Nicole would miss the gentle humanitarian Alvares. She treasured these conversational interludes with him. Without saying so, each was coming to the realization that soon their association would end, if everything went the way they hoped it would. As anxious as she was for the day when she could join Drew, Nicole was greatly saddened at the thought of leaving Lima.

A happy letter from Carlos arrived at the department in the third week of June:

Dear Nicole,

If only you could have witnessed the scene on my arrival! To see me with my baggages, trying to convince the driver of a junkheap *camión* to take all of it was worth the price of a ticket! He protested, but he didn't realize he was dealing with the intrepid *médico* from San Martín, who has used all of his persuasive powers in overcoming resistance. If you can sweet talk a kid from the *barriada* into letting you give him a shot, a *camionero* is a pushover!

So I made my way home to my parents, who were appropriately tearful at the joyous return of the prodigal. And then, the next day, I had to go out to the town near Wari where Pepe's family lives—so small it's not even on the provincial map. I won't describe that experience, or I'll be in tears. Their sorrow will never be assuaged. The gratitude they showed for your gift was so sincere and touching, Nicole. Enclosed is a letter dictated to me by Pepe's father. He is a proud man, but I persuaded him to take the money and use it for what you intended, the education of his younger children.

You are not only big-hearted, but you're a crafty

one, telling me not to open your "letter" until I was on the train! As soon as I settled myself, I opened the envelope. That was the most money I've ever seen at one time in all my life, and I lived in fear of being robbed before I reached my destination. I immediately went into the lavatory and secreted it inside my socks. As a result, I have blisters on both feet! There I was, miles from my destination, with this fortune in ten thousand *sol* notes in my shoes. I didn't sleep a wink, thinking of how to safely get to Ayacucho without my feet being cut off by bandits.

The first thing I did was open a bank account. The next thing I will do is buy a landrover and outfit it as a mobile clinic. I think I even have a partner. A terrific guy I met who studied surgery in Santiago de Chile during the Allende years. Not only that—he has a beautiful sister, whom I saw for the first time last night! When she isn't home on leave, she teaches school in Huanta.

You see! I promised you would know if something happened. I have a feeling there will be more—good things, for a change!

Thank you, thank you, thank you—from the bottom of my heart. Believe, I'm your friend,

Carlos

She was still smiling when Jorge Alvares came to her office that afternoon after the clinic. "Am I disturbing you?"

"No, I was just finishing up some reports. Is it already time for coffee?" She glanced at her watch.

"It's early. I thought you should know—there's been some news from the Health Ministry."

"Yes?"

She had that same eager look of expectation that had captivated him eight years ago, the first day they met, when she had come to his department as an intern from Paris. Her freshness, her enthusiasm had not dimmed. Nor had her hopes. In the wide-spaced green eyes, the warm smile, the open shining intelligence and honesty of her beautiful face, the professor saw no indication that she had lost faith in fair play or the goodwill of others.

"They cabled Geneva, Nicole. I'm afraid it's not good

news. They accepted the invitation of the WHO on behalf of the brother-in-law of the deputy minister. A physician with a private practice who has never seen a case
of smallpox, has never attended an international medical
meeting, and doesn't know the first thing about epidemiology."

She did not react, but he saw the light go out in her
eyes, and it cut deep into him in that private place
reserved for the cherishing of those we love.

"I see," she whispered.

He cleared his throat. "My real worry is what this
means for your future. It simply could be the typical
nepotism that we have to contend with in Peru. Or it may
be more." Jorge lowered his head and rubbed his forehead. "I think you had better inform Señora Monaco."

Nicole took a deep breath. "Yes, Lucy should know
about this immediately. . . . Perhaps it won't influence
the hearing. They may not even have heard about this."

"I wouldn't be too sure, my dear."

She dialed the attorney's office, but Lucy had left for
the day. There was no answer at the apartment. She
couldn't call from her house, with the wire tapped! "I
shall have to stop there on my way home."

Jorge returned to his office and sat heavily in his chair.
He had a vise-like headache and a tightness across the
back of his neck.

"Damn! The one time I need him, Caldeiro is out of
touch." Lucy stalked into the living room of her flat. Or
would have stalked, if she had not been top-heavy.

"Where is he?" Nicole wasn't at all convinced that
Manuel would be of any help, but she was in a desperate
situation. Now that the WHO meeting was out of reach,
Lucy feared the hearing would be delayed or canceled.

"I could have caught him, if that stupid secretary of his
weren't so officious! I finally called Elena Quesada, and
she told me he'd just left her house half an hour ago, and
she doesn't know where to reach him."

"Who is Elena Quesada?" asked Nicole.

Giving her a peculiar sidelong glance, Lucy said, "His
girlfriend, of course."

"Oh." Nicole attempted unsuccessfully to hide her
surprise.

"You mean you didn't know? I thought everyone in Lima knew about them."

"I guess no one bothered to tell *me!*" She began to laugh and could not stop.

"I'm glad you're amused at a time like this," grouched Lucy. "Do you mind telling me what's so funny?"

"It's just that I've been so afraid of how Manuel will react to the news of my marriage to Drew when I finally tell him. I thought it would break his heart. How stupid of me!"

"Not stupid at all, dear. What he has with Elena is not necessarily love. As I told you once before, your naiveté is sometimes astonishing." She settled carefully on the sofa, kicking off her shoes. "Whew! Being pregnant at my age is no joke."

They gazed disconsolately at each other.

"I could pretend I'm not worried, Nicole, but you would see through me. This is bad . . . very bad."

Lucy didn't have to tell her that. It would not be surprising if the next move was a quiet request for her resignation from the International Health Task Force.

Nicole refused Lucy's invitation for dinner. "I'd better go home. Vera expects me, and Drew might call tonight. He may have heard about the Health Ministry's reply."

"*Do* call him from here, Nicole, so you can explain everything to him. I'll even let you pay the bill."

"No . . . I need time to collect myself. Besides, I'm not sure where to reach him. He was supposed to visit his parents this week. His father hasn't been well."

"Is the PIP still on your tail?" Lucy asked, looking around when she walked Nicole to the car.

"Most of the time, not always. I think even *they* are getting bored with this." She kissed Lucy's cheek. "You ought to get more rest. You're looking peaked."

Lucy waved as they drove off. As soon as she had reentered the building, a battered gray Dodge that had been parked on the opposite side of the street swung around in pursuit of the Citröen.

Vera was perturbed that her mistress tasted so little of the dinner. What was the point of having a cook, she asked. "I can prepare your meals, señorita Nicole. There's so little to do, as it is."

Vera had let the two maids go when Nicole was away in Huaranca. She claimed she only needed occasional help in the house. Pedro and the gardener had wives who were only too happy to earn extra income by assisting her.

Nicole preferred this arrangement. It made them a tight little community within the compound.

After dinner, she sat in the study staring at the fire, her coffee growing cold. She was weighted down with depression. If only Drew would telephone! Just speaking to him would help. *Should I place a call to him,* she wondered. If she did, the police would know. It took all of her willpower not to lift the receiver.

"Would you like me to shampoo your hair tonight, señorita?" Vera interrupted her thoughts.

Nicole hesitated. She found Vera's way of brushing her hair and massaging the scalp before a shampoo a most relaxing and soothing indulgence.

"Come," said the maid, "you're very tired tonight. You work too hard. I'll do your hair, and then you can get in bed and have a nice restful sleep."

Vera fussed over Nicole, obviously concerned at her melancholy. She rubbed Renouveau Légende into her scalp, kneading it with the dexterity of a professional masseuse. Then she brushed and brushed the long strands until they gleamed. She kept up a steady chatter, not requiring any answer on Nicole's part.

"Next time, I'll trim the ends a little, señorita. Just a touch, where they're raggedy." Nicole leaned back in the reclining chair, closing her eyes. She could feel the tension easing in her neck and scalp. "What wonderful hair." said Vera, for the thousandth time, feeling the weight of it. "A joy to work with."

Vera was a professionally trained personal maid. She was especially accomplished at hair dressing and would have done well in a salon. Nicole seriously doubted that anyone could really *enjoy* being a servant, yet Vera took pride in her work.

She probably thinks I'm feeling low because I'm lovelorn! Nicole had not told the housekeeper about her marriage. Lucy thought Vera was too easily rattled and might blurt it out to the wrong person.

By the time her hair was dry and arranged in a single

French braid, Nicole was feeling pleasantly drowsy. "That was wonderful, Vera—better than a sleeping pill. Thank you."

Vera smiled happily. "I'll see you in the morning, señorita. Have a good rest."

Nicole tried to read but in a few minutes turned out the lamp and fell immediately into a deep slumber, drifting into a wonderful dream. She clung to sleep, not wanting to let go of the pleasurable warmth, the sunny happiness that embraced her. It seemed composed of her father and Drew together . . . and childhood at the hacienda. . . . Her mother was there in a white gown and the lace bridal mantilla, and her baby brother, André—except he was a man and the people were calling him Erik. The air was filled with flying flowers, their fragrance overwhelming . . . and in the distance the church bells were pealing while her grandfather rode through the mass of flowers on Flame, galloping . . . galloping . . . closer and closer . . . the thunder of Flame's hooves beating, beating, beating across the floor of the valley . . . descending on Flor del Viento!

What was that?

She was sitting up in bed in the darkness, her heart hammering in her chest, her entire body drenched in a cold clamminess, the pounding of hooves still alive in her mind.

She had heard a scream, high and shrill . . . was it part of her dream? It had been so *real!*

Straining her ears, Nicole listened for the sound, but the house was quiet. If she left the bed, she was afraid she would never fall back to sleep. Reaching for another pillow, she placed it behind her, lying back. She closed her eyes, trying to summon a state of relaxation.

She had almost dropped off when her body jerked. There had been a noise, a thud, as if a heavy object had fallen. This time there was no doubt.

She sensed immediately there was an intruder in the house. Lima was plagued with robberies these days. The city was full of migrants from the country in search of jobs, of which there were none.

Creeping from the bed, she reached in the dark for her robe and slippers. She started for the door to her room but instead turned toward the sitting room that connected to the guest room—Drew's room. From there, she silently entered the back hall, crossing to the opposite wing. By standing in an alcove at the end of the corridor, she would be able to observe the broad stairway and the main hall without being discovered. If a burglar was in the house, the best thing would be to let him take some valuables and leave. She had no weapon, but even if she did, to confront him would be taking a foolish risk.

Suddenly she heard a commotion below, at the foot of the stairs. "The bitch bit me," a man cursed, and a woman screamed for help.

It was Vera! She cried out in pain and screamed again, while the sound of men shouting and running up the stairs reverberated through the mansion. The immense chandelier burst into light, illuminating the entire staircase and the main hall.

Six men wearing street clothes and black masks over their faces were in the lower hall and on the stairway. Vera was lying on the floor, sobbing, her hands protecting the top of her head.

Nicole stepped out of the shadows. "Leave her alone!" she shouted hoarsely.

One of the men in the hall below wheeled and pointed a gun at Vera's head, while another froze on the landing, aiming his automatic pistol at Nicole.

"What do you want?"

Nicole was amazed at her own calm and the strength of her voice. Somewhere in the back of her mind, she thought that all her training in emergency clinics had prepared her for this moment.

She noticed, as an incidental observation, how the masked heads of the others turned to the man holding the gun on Vera. "You will come with us, señorita, or the woman dies," he said, in the accent of a *cholo*.

"Who are you?"

"Never mind who we are. Get down here!" He hit Vera with the flat of his hand. The woman cried out, cringing.

"Don't hurt her again! I'll come."

"No-oo!" wailed Vera.

"Silence," shouted the leader, knocking the barrel of the weapon against the side of Vera's head.

"Stop it!" cried Nicole. "I told you I would go with you."

"Come down, then."

Her mind was working frantically. "Only after I get dressed!"

He started to object, then said, "Very well, do it quickly." With a motion of his head he signaled the man on the top landing to follow her.

At the door of her room, Nicole stopped, "Give me five minutes. Don't worry, I won't try anything."

"I have to watch you," he said with an unconvincing leer. Despite the mask, she could tell he was just a boy of around eighteen, and he appeared nervous.

She shrugged indifferently, opening the door and turning on the lights. He looked around the luxurious bedroom with curiosity. Spotting the telephone on a table, he walked over to it and yanked at the cord, ripping it out of the wall.

"That was not necessary," she said icily. "I'm hardly going to call for help with a gun pointing at me." He had read her mind, unfortunately. She had planned to try to call Lucy. To tell her what? Who were they? They could be kidnappers or terrorists . . . or the PIP. "Who are you people? The police?"

"That—that's no business of yours," the boy replied. Some of his insolence had dissipated.

"I think I have a right to know. Am I being arrested?"

"We have our orders, señorita. Please get dressed."

He was speaking respectfully now. He must be fairly new at this. Was he with the PIP? Probably. But, he could be a young recruit for the counterinsurgency unit of the civil police. She *had* to get word to Lucy. If only she had some indication of who these men were and where they were taking her.

"I'll be ready in a minute. You may sit down, if you wish."

Before he understood what was happening, she had gone into her dressing room and shut the door, locking it. He rattled the doorknob and called angrily, "Hey! You can't do that. Open this door."

"Don't worry, captain, I'm just going in the bathroom. I'll be right out." She was counting on her elevation of his rank to achieve the desired effect. Evidently it had, for he quieted and made no further attempt to break into the room.

Quickly she slipped into some khaki pants she kept for riding at the hacienda. She rummaged through the drawers of the dressing table looking for something on which to write a note. Finding nothing, she searched desperately in the shelves of a cupboard, and spied a large pocketbook, one that she sometimes carried for traveling. Inside was a memo pad and ball point pen. Furiously she scribbled and folded the sheet of paper several times into a small rectangle which fit into the palm of her hand.

Maybe she could manage to slip the note to Vera as she left. No, that was taking too much of a chance. She had to leave it here, somewhere in a place where the maid was certain to find it.

"Come on, come on!" shouted the PIP—if he was a PIP.

"All right! I'm coming." She opened the door. "I need my glasses. I can't see well without them."

Crossing to the bed, she pretended to feel around a book that was opened face-down next to the pillows, slipping the folded note underneath.

"Oh, here they are!" She picked up the glasses from the night table, putting them on. "Let's go, captain."

"Hey," he muttered, embarrassed. "I'm not a captain—just a private."

"You act like an officer," she told him lightly. So. At least she knew they were official. PIP or civil police?

Wasn't it amusing how all men, no matter who they were, responded to flattery? *Am I crazy,* she thought wryly. *I may be on my way to my death!*

Downstairs, the intruders had been ransacking the desks and book shelves in the study and library. Vera was wringing her hands and weeping. Nicole noticed she had a large contusion on the side of her face.

"You better put some ice on that," Nicole told her gently. "I'm sorry they hurt you, Vera."

"Oh, Señorita Nicole," Vera wailed, "what will they do with you?"

Glancing at the masked man who seemed to be in charge, she said, "If I knew who they were, perhaps I could answer your question. Don't worry about me, Vera.

Since you're awake, you might as well make up the beds and clean the house as usual."

Vera looked offended. "Señorita, you *know* I won't neglect my duties." In her night clothes, the maid was crying uncontrollably as they led Nicole away, a pistol at her back.

The last thing she saw before a black hood was placed over her head was the leader of the intruders pocketing a sterling silver paperweight that had belonged to Daniel Légende. She was taken by the arms, more roughly than necessary, she thought, and pushed into the back seat of an automobile between two men whose hands wandered at will over her body.

"Not yet!" snapped the *cholo* from the front seat. "There's plenty of time for that."

Her sense of calm control deserted her, replaced with a numbing terror. That voice! She had heard it before. . . .

It was the voice of the man who had questioned her on the day her passport had been taken away. He was the captain whom she had last seen at police headquarters.

Chapter 39

How long had she been in this place? She had lost track of time. It seemed like weeks. Certainly it was more than a day.

They had moved her twice. Why? To confuse her, or to keep others from knowing where she was being held?

She had never been in such physical misery in all her life. She had not been fed or given water, and her hands were tied behind her back. The hood had not been removed since she was taken from her home. She felt as if she were suffocating. There were small air holes, but it was stifling, and lint got into her nose and throat, causing her to cough.

Five or six times, someone had come in and permitted her to use a bucket as a latrine. It was horrible and humiliating, but it had ceased to matter to her.

As a doctor, she was accustomed to dealing with bodies in an impersonal manner. When she performed surgery it was necessary to be objective, not to permit herself to become emotionally involved with the patient, as she did in the clinic. It was the only way she was able to work on surgical cases. In the pathology lab, performing autopsies, she had schooled herself to regard a cadaver as a series of anatomical parts.

That was how she now thought of herself. That was going to be her salvation, not to let them force her into feeling shame, robbing her of her self-respect. She vowed she would not become craven or psychologically dependent on her captors.

Thus far, they had not physically abused her—tortured or raped her.

Depriving her of food and drink, keeping the hood over her head, and making her perform the acts of urination and defecation in the presence of male guards, all these tactics were designed to break her spirit, she was certain. Although she abhorred the indignities and felt faint with hunger and thirst, these were not the worst of what went on in this place.

She had heard the screams of other prisoners, men and women, and even some who sounded like they were not yet out of childhood. Sometimes loud music was played to cover the screams, but usually they did not bother. She had heard beatings and whippings, and tortures involving tubs of water in which the prisoner was half drowned. And most recently, she had tried not to listen to the repeated raping of a mother and her young daughter nearby. The cries of both were pathetic, and the sadism of their tormentors without limit.

Why had they left her untouched, she wondered. Was it to soften her up, to make the eventual torture even worse because of the suspense, the anticipation? Or were they afraid to mark her with abuse, realizing she had influential friends?

There was no way of knowing. Perhaps they were waiting for sufficient time to pass, to be certain it was safe to begin on her, that her whereabouts remained undetected. Or were they perhaps saving her for something special, some particularly horrible diabolic invention?

She heard Lucy's voice that long-ago night when they had sat at the dinner table at Casa Loma, in that other life that was beginning to seem unreal. Her father had been in New York, seeing the doctors at Columbia University, although she had not known it then, and she had invited the lawyer to dinner because she liked her. They had spoken about Lucy's sideline of aiding dissidents who had run afoul of the police.

"I have to hurry whenever one of them is arrested," she had said in her husky, languid voice. "They would be tortured otherwise. The police are afraid to touch them after a lawyer shows up. That's why they don't want witnesses when they take them in."

They didn't want witnesses! What had happened to Vera after they had taken Nicole from the house? There were at least two other men besides those in the car with her. They must have had a second car. Had the others murdered Vera in order to silence her?

Her mind was beginning to work against her. She must not give in to this!

Think of Drew, hang on to that reality. By now, he must have heard she was gone. If Vera was still alive and had found her note—even if she had not—she would certainly have thought of calling Lucy, and Lucy would inform Drew.

She couldn't stop herself from thinking—*what if Vera is dead, or tied up and not found for days?* But Pedro would have come to drive me to work in the morning. . . .

What if they had killed *everyone* at Casa Loma? They could have! She had heard rumors of entire families and small communities in the Andes wiped out by counter-insurgency forces. She had never believed those stories. But they *did* kill people! Pepe. The young woman from San Marcos University . . ..

This was counterproductive! She must stay calm, try to sleep while she could, conserve her energy, and pray that Lucy or someone would get to her before she died in this place.

"We meet again, Señorita Légende. The pleasure is all mine." It was the voice of the captain!

The hood was yanked off her head. She closed her eyes, stabbed with blinding pain from the light. She could not put her hands to her face, for they were tied to the back of the hard wooden chair.

She had been asleep when they dragged her from the cot by her arms, taking her through a long corridor and down a flight of stairs. There had been moans of suffering from cells along the way.

"I trust you've been comfortable, señorita." He turned the lamp so the bright light wasn't shining directly into her eyes. "You see, we aren't heartless."

"I want to call my lawyer," she said.

He smiled as if she had uttered an inanity. "Not this time, señorita. Things have changed since the occasion of our previous meeting."

Her eyes were becoming adjusted to the light. She noticed he was not wearing a uniform. Her glance swept him from head to foot. "By changed I gather you mean you're now an undercover agent."

"Correct, señorita," he smiled broadly. "You are as intelligent and alert as they say!"

"Do they say that?" she answered sarcastically, then was seized with a fit of coughing. Her thirst was enormous, the dryness in her throat making it difficult to speak.

"Would you like some water?" the captain asked.

"Yes, please."

She watched him pour water slowly from a pitcher. *He's going to taunt me with it. He'll hold it to my lip and not let me drink. I must prepare myself for that.*

But he let her drink her fill, then poured more and let her drink again.

"Better? Good. Now let us get down to business."

"Captain, why will you not permit me to call my lawyer? If I'm arrested, I have the right to be charged and represented by counsel."

"Señorita Légende, you seem not to understand your situation." He spoke softly, in an exceedingly polite manner, his *cholo* accent all but indiscernible. "You are in a special detention center of the antiterrorist unit of the state security police. No one else knows you're here. No one here, other than myself, knows who you are. I don't *have* to charge you, because you have not been arrested. And if you haven't been arrested, there is no case for a lawyer."

This is what happens to people when they "disappear," she realized. No one knows where they have been taken. They can be questioned, tortured, imprisoned for months. Or killed. And there's nothing anyone can do about it.

What could she do? *Stall,* she thought. Stall, and pray that Vera had contacted Lucy and somehow Lucy would find out where she was being held. Lucy, with her contacts, her eyes and ears that kept her informed of the secret goings-on within the police and the government ministries.

"What is it you want with me?" she asked, her voice defeated.

"Just the answers to a few very simple questions." He sat on the edge of a table that had restraining straps attached to it. "Tell me whatever you know about the terrorist organizations you support."

She gaped at him. "I support no terrorist organizations! I don't even *know* any terrorists."

"Of course. Perhaps I'm not putting it properly, señorita. Where have you taken the medicines you've been stealing from San Martín Hospital?"

"I *haven't*—that's the most outrageous fabrication! Why do you think I've taken medicines?"

"We know you've been diverting medical supplies to guerrilla organizations, señorita. You have been doing this for the past two or three years, first from the mobile clinics—and since they were closed, from your department's clinic."

"That's not true!" Her mind was in turmoil. Where did they ever get such insane ideas?

"You made a recent trip to your villa in Huaranca. Is that where you've taken the medicines? Do you keep a storehouse there?"

"No!"

"In any case, we'll soon find out. We don't need you to tell us."

Despite her own terror, she was seized with concern for Rosa and Tómas. "What will you do? Please—you won't hurt the people there, will you? They're innocent! They haven't done anything wrong." Was this Rosa's *pachakuti?*

"If they have nothing to hide, then of course they won't be hurt."

"As I won't be?"

"That, señorita, is another matter."

The captain stood up and approached her. He reached forward and grasped her blouse by the neckline, wrenching it with both hands so that the buttons flew off, scattering across the floor like pebbles.

"You must believe that I don't wish to harm you, Dr. Légende. But I *will* learn what I want to know."

Now it begins, she thought. Her heartbeat quickened and became irregular. *I won't be able to hold up under a beating! They can force me to say anything they want, whether or not it's true.* She pictured again the body she had seen in the Emergencia the girl who had been interrogated. Her head whirled and the gorge rose in her throat.

*   *   *

Luís Ribera was awakened by the insistent ringing of the telephone. He glanced at the digital clock . . . six A.M. Who would be calling him on his private line at this hour? Only his good friends had this number.

When he answered, there was static and the high decibel singing of electric signals that always prompted visions of air waves moving with the speed of sound along thousands of miles of international telephone cable.

A Spanish-speaking operator announced Lima was calling. So it wasn't from the States. The connection was made, but all he heard were some incomprehensible words and the sound of a woman hysterically weeping.

"Señor . . . Señor Doctor Ribera! La señorita Lé . . . Lé . . . gende . . . pobrecita! Por favor, señor . . . qué lástima! Ay, señor . . . !"

"What, *what?* Who *is* this?" He tried to speak above the woman's sobs. It wasn't a wrong number—she knew him by name. Obviously she was in a dire situation. What was she saying? He couldn't understand.

"Please, señora, you *must* calm down. Speak slowly, and tell me who this is and what you want," Luís kept his voice loud and deliberate.

Finally, he succeeded in getting the woman, who it seemed was a household employee of Nicole Légende's— the head maid whom he had met when he visited the house in Lima—to explain why she was calling him so early on a Thursday morning, the first day of July.

What she told him filled him with alarm. Nearly overcome with dread, Luís listened as the woman haltingly related, with many promptings from him, the story of the middle-of-the-night intrusion at Casa Loma. Realizing this was the materialization of his worst fears, he knew that giving in to panic was not going to help Nicole. His mind raced as he tried to think how to deal with this crisis.

"Now listen—who else knows about this?"

She gave him Lucy Monaco's name and telephone number. "They cut the telephone wires at Casa Loma, señor. I came to an exchange to call you. Señorita Nicole left a note behind. She said I was to call you at the number listed in her personal book—that you would know what to do." Vera was calmer now. She sounded old and frightened.

"Yes, Vera. You did the right thing. I know exactly what must be done." After assuring her that he would take action, he said goodbye.

Immediately he placed a call to Drew Tower in Philadelphia. Drew had been noncommittal about his trip to Lima when they had met three weeks ago at the Task Force meeting. Luís's curiosity had been enormous, but he respected his friend's privacy. Drew would tell what he wanted him to know, in his own good time.

Luís waited while the phone in Drew's apartment rang thirty times. There was no answer.

Lucy Monaco came close to losing her equilibrium this time.

She had handled dozens of cases where clients had been arrested, detained, and horribly abused. She had made it through Horacio's imprisonment and exile with her sanity preserved. She had even survived without panic her own brief detention several years ago when there had been a sweep by the PIP of lawyers who had criticized the government.

This morning it had taken all of Horacio's strength and rational persuasion to keep her from going to pieces and becoming of no use to Nicole.

After receiving Vera's call, she had succumbed briefly to tears, and then, fortified by a steaming cup of bitter black coffee prepared by her husband, she set to work. By dawn, she had managed to wake every leading member of the Lima Bar Association (those who were not themselves in detention), as well as the few judiciary whom she could still count among her friends.

At six-thirty, she screwed up her courage and dialed Señora Quesada's residence, only to be informed by a sleepy-sounding Elena that Manuel was not there. Receiving no answer at his home telephone, she had naturally assumed . . . *Oh Lucy, what a fool you can be at times!*

She was on her second cup of coffee, and about to call Jorge Alvares, when her phone rang. It was a Dr. Ribera from Mexico City, who said he was Nicole's colleague from the International Health Task Force.

"Has Nicole been arrested, Señora Monaco?"

"I assume she has, señor. It sounds like the Investigative Police, who are plainclothes, vicious, and operate extra-judicially."

"Does that mean she will be held without legal guarantees?" he asked.

"Yes, Dr. Ribera. That is exactly what it means."

"What can be done?"

"As soon as the office of the Ministry of Justice is open, I will enter a plea of habeas corpus. They will then refer it to the police, who will investigate the matter, then deny that she was ever detained. And so the courts will throw out the plea. By that time, Nicole could be incarcerated somewhere far away from Lima—for example, at El Sepa, our fine maximum-security penal colony in the Amazon jungle, so inaccessible that it's reached only by military aircraft! Or . . . or worse," she finished lamely, sarcasm failing her.

She could detect he was struggling to remain unemotional on the other end of the wire. "Would it do any good, señora, for me—for her many friends abroad, to send cables? I know of at least one instance when it saved a man's life—in Chile."

Lucy's spirits lifted. "Yes! What an excellent idea! *Do* send cables, the more the better."

"I've been trying to reach a special friend of hers, Andrew Tower," he told her. "He seems to be away, but I'll track him down through his department at the University of Pennsylvania."

"I know Drew. Nicole said last night that he was visiting his parents," Lucy told him.

"Is that so?" Luís murmured. "Then, uh, they've been in touch recently?"

"Yes, Dr. Ribera . . . you might say they've been in touch."

Luís assured her he would not cease trying to reach Drew until he was successful, and he promised to see that the Peruvian government was deluged with cablegrams from the international scientific community.

Within hours, a steady stream of telegraphic pleas for the release of Nicole Légende, M.D., who was believed to be in the custody of the Policias Investigaciones del Peru, was being directed to the President of Peru, the Minister of the Interior, the Minister of External Affairs, the head of the National Justice Council, and to the

Peruvian ambassadors in dozens of capitals around the globe.

He had tufts of hair growing out of his ears. She had not noticed that before. She tried to concentrate on his ears, but her head kept dropping forward. He raised it by lifting her chin with the leather crop he held in his hand. He kept slapping the crop into the palm of his other hand.

"I have been patient, Señorita Légende, very patient. But I am becoming weary of this conversation."

They had finally taken her back to her cubicle . . . when? Yesterday? A few hours ago? This time she had seen the broken prisoners in other cells along the way. The sight of them had horrified her.

When she said she was hungry, they gave her an evil-smelling mess in a metal bowl. She tried to eat it, but her stomach rebelled and she regurgitated the few spoonfuls she had forced herself to swallow. She lay on the cot, carefully nursing her bruises, drawing up her knees to ease the intestinal cramps, and after a while fell into fitful sleep. Again, they awakened her and brought her to the room where the captain was waiting.

By now she was past the point of hunger, but she had a burning thirst. "Water, please."

"Not just yet. First you will give me some names. We know all the medical students and interns—we don't need you for those. But they aren't important. What we want from you are the names of the leaders, the ones who recruited you."

"I've told you again and again, I don't know what you're talking about!"

"I think you do, señorita." He shifted restlessly, tapping her shoulder with the crop.

"Please, I'm so tired . . . can't I rest? I'm too tired to think."

He punched her face hard, with his fist. She cried out and groaned, feeling the pain in her cheekbone and lower lip, which immediately began to swell.

"Maybe that will wake you up!" He walked behind her to the door and opened it.

A second man entered the room. He was large and burly, with massive arms. In his right hand he carried a rubber truncheon and from his belt dangled a metal device fashioned to fit over his hand. After briefly examining a long instrument attached to an electric cord, he seated himself against the wall and stared at Nicole. Trying not to look at him, she concentrated instead on the captain.

Looking toward the bored, heavy-set man who lounged with his chair tilted against the wall, the captain nodded. The man stood up, took a pail from under a sink, and doused her with cold, dirty water. The shock of it brought her out of her stupor. She began to shiver uncontrollably.

"Now, señorita," said the captain. "You see this man?" He pointed with his chin in the way of the *runa*. "You know, he has studied in a school. For weeks and weeks, he has studied diligently how to inflict pain on people. He is a specialist in his work, and like all specialists, he is anxious to practice his expertise. . . ."

Lucy's voice was saying, *Those thugs enjoy their work!*

". . . Now, I am going to ask him to leave the room for a short time. And I am going to give you one last opportunity to tell me what I want to know, before I turn you over to him. I assure you, señorita, if I do that . . . you will never again look or feel the same."

Her eyes smarted with tears. How long would it take her to break, she wondered. It was only a matter of time before she was worn down. Weakened with hunger and lack of sleep, her face swollen and body bruised from the captain's blows, her arms and hands numb from being tied for so many hours, she was cowed with terror. She would succumb to the pain of torture.

Tell him *what?* She *had* no information for them. There *was* no guerrilla network she was supporting! She hadn't stolen medical supplies for an underground army! She hadn't sheltered terrorists in her home! She wasn't traveling abroad to receive funds for subversive activities against the government, using the IHTF as a front for her real purposes! All these things, the captain had insisted over and over, she was guilty of doing.

"Why won't you believe me?" she suddenly shouted. "Don't you think I would've told you by now if I knew anything? Cowards, that's what you are! All of you, with your guns and cudgels. You're too weak to change things by working hard, too stupid to confront ideas! *You* are

the real enemies of my country—it's people like you and
the junta who have ruined freedom in Peru and destroyed our nation's credibility in the world!''

She saw the smoldering coals of his eyes spark into
hate-filled conflagration. He seized a knife from the table, rage blinding him as he rushed at her. She cringed
and dropped her head forward, closing her eyes and
hunching her shoulders.

He's going to kill me! Please, let him do it quickly, she
prayed, to whatever god would listen.

He gripped her braid, pulling up on it sharply, so that
she cried out in pain. She scrunched herself lower into
her shoulders, waiting for the knife to penetrate. There
was a hacking noise and a sawing at the nape of her neck,
and suddenly her head snapped up, with the lighter-than-
air release of a parachute opening after a free fall.

Startled, her eyelids flew open. The captain stood before her, his face brindled. In his left hand he held a whip
. . . a long braided whip of human hair. It caught the
beam of the overhead light in shimmering coruscation.

"Work," he screamed. "Look who's talking about hard
work! Your father's fortune was made on the backs of
the peasants of his colonial hacienda. I'll 'hard work'
you!'' With every word he lashed her across the face with
the rope of her hair, back and forth, back and forth, until
the braid became unraveled and trailed limp in his hand.

Eyes locked, they stared at each other. His chest was
heaving with his breath, and tears ran down Nicole's
cheeks.

"I warned you," he snarled, walking to the door without looking at her again.

Nothing happened immediately. Behind her, the door
remained partly open. She heard voices, lowered to almost a whisper. A frantic conversation was taking place
between the captain and someone else. The captain's
voice was raised in protest as he argued.

She sat waiting, her head lowered in despair. In the
windowless stonewalled room, she was chilled from her
wet clothes. The nightmare of what was happening to her
could still astound her. How long, she wondered, did it
take to accept the situation of being held prisoner? Would
she live through this? Others had, so perhaps she could.

The door sprang back, hitting the wall. Hands on hips,

the captain appeared in front of her. He was accompanied by a young police guard.

The guard untied her hands, which dropped heavily at her sides, lacking sensation. Released, her shirt and brassiere fell around her waist. She tried to cover herself, but her hands would not obey.

"Here," the captain said roughly, pulling the shirt up around her. "Get up.

She staggered as she rose. The guard supported her by the arm. "Where am I going?" she asked, confused, faintness overcoming her.

"You'll find out." He smiled cruelly. "We haven't seen the last of each other, Señorita Légende—you can be sure of that."

She lost consciousness as another hood was placed over her head. The guard was joined by a second, and the two carried her sagging body out of the building. They put her in the back of a *tanqueta*, a military personnel carrier, which drove along the periphery of Lima to the Lurigancho prison, situated in the desert. Inside the van, they removed the hood.

Nicole regained consciousness before they reached their destination. As she was taken through a side door and escorted down a hallway, she noticed that someone had tied the tails of her shirt together in front, in an effort to make her more presentable.

They stopped before an unmarked door. One of the guards leaned in front of her, turned the knob, and thrust her into the room. A gray-haired commander of the Guardia Civil turned to confront her.

At his side stood Manuel Caldeiro-León.

Chapter 40

Clem Farquhar had not understood the purpose of Drew Tower's call yesterday morning. An operator repeatedly interrupted their conversation, asking whether they had concluded, and finally cut them off. That was one of the last telephone calls to get through to the embassy after the state of emergency had been declared.

The only sense he could make out of what Drew said was that Clem should contact Señora Monaco, which he had. The controversial woman lawyer came to see him at the embassy, and thus he learned that Nicole Légende had probably been arrested by the Peruvian Investigative Police.

That appeared to be the reason why Drew was coming to Lima. There was no time for Clem to notify Lucy Monaco after the telex from Washington arrived late in the afternoon, informing him that Dr. Tower was on his way, "as requested by the vice consul."

It seemed a heroic gesture for Drew to be making on behalf of a professional colleague.

Hell of a time for him to be coming to Lima, though, in the middle of an *estado del sitio!* The state of emerency had been called only this morning, so everything was in confusion. Some airlines weren't being permitted to land at Chavez. He hoped Drew was on the AeroPeru flight— damn thing was four hours late. He had to intercept him at the airport, or else he'd be stuck at the Crillon or the Richmond, wherever they were taking foreign passengers. Then Clem wouldn't be able to get to him until tomorrow moming after curfew.

"Wait here at the car," he instructed his driver. He didn't want the man wandering off to gossip with the other chauffeurs. Once he got hold of Drew they would have to hurry. It was almost time for curfew, and diplomatic immunity was tricky in times of emergencies. Sometimes the police or military shot first and asked questions later.

The plane had landed, they told him. He made his way to the customs, showing his diplomatic passport and the telex. They saluted and let him pass.

Christ, it was crowded! You'd think these tourists were coming to see the show. Genuine state of emergency, folks. Step right this way.

Gads—an awful lot of firepower around here. Look at the bastards! It made him nervous. This country could blow at any time, just like Chile.

It wouldn't take the CIA to start a counterrevolution here. The people of Lima were fed up with shortages and inflation, strikes and unemployment, with police harassment and crime in the streets. And the rest of the country was like a cauldron of simmering revolt. Lima was a feudal city-state, completely cut off from the sierra and the Amazon, with little knowledge or understanding of the people there.

President Morales Bermúdez had declared this emergency because of public demonstrations and riots against his announced tax and price increases. The police had reportedly arrested hundreds of civilians. There was enormous unrest in Lima, with constant rumors of a palace revolt by some of the President's ministers and military advisors.

This government was going to go under—you could bet on it. It was a question of when and how and what would replace it—the hard-line Marxist left, another wishy-washy moderate like Belaúnde, or a new military junta with fascist leanings. In any case, the Americans would probably be blamed when it fell apart.

Wait'll Drew gets a load of all these fucking riot troops! He'll wish he'd stayed in Philadelphia!

Clem searched the lines of people winding through the passport control. Not spotting his tall American friend, he sought the commanding officer of the airport police. He didn't want Tower slipping by and getting on that bus.

Drew had never seen so many armed military guards in an airport. Or anywhere else, for that matter. They stood

with machine guns in front of them, looking like they'd
love an excuse to fire them.

What did this state of emergency mean for Nicole?

He'd almost gone crazy when Luís told him she had
been arrested. He felt so powerless. Luís had reached
him in Wilkes-Barre. Unable to get a confirmed plane
reservation to Lima, unable to contact Lucy Monaco, in
desperation he had called Clem Farquhar at the embassy.
Miraculously, the call had gone through—but the connection was poor and they'd been cut off before he had a
chance to explain about Nicole. When he signaled the
overseas operator, he had received the chilling information that she could not reconnect him because Peru had
declared a state of emergency and was under martial law.

Drew had immediately driven back to Philadelphia to
pick up his passport—grateful that his Peruvian visa was
still valid—and flown to Miami. The connections to Lima
were overbooked. He was put on stand-by and had been
lucky to get a seat.

He had come to Lima despite all the advice against it
from the people in Washington. He was determined to
get her freed if he had to go to the President of Peru. He
would create an international incident if he had to. To
hell with those creeps at the State Department. Caution?
While they were tiptoeing around in their pinstripes urg-
ing him to wait, she could be killed!

All passengers disembarking at Lima would be required to board military buses at the airport and proceed
directly to downtown hotels, they were told. A strict
curfew was imposed and travel within the country cur-
tailed until further notice.

Shit! He might not be able to see Clem or Lucy tonight, by the time they got the fucking buses loaded and
transported all these people with their luggage. *Damn!*
What would he do? He didn't have a hotel reservation.
Luís said the phone lines at Casa Loma had been cut, so
he couldn't call ahead. He would just have to go there, if
he could manage to by-pass the bus and get a taxi. He
had a key to the back gate. That was luck. If no one was
in the house, he would figure a way to get in.

The tension was beginning to get to him. He had been
traveling for days—ever since leaving Philadelphia to visit
his parents in Wilkes-Barre. Arthur was going to be all

right, which was a relief. At least that was one worry off his mind. The arterial surgery performed at Penn had gone well, and with luck, his father could live another ten years—well into his eighties.

This line was unbelievably slow-moving. The thought occurred to him: What if the police had learned he was coming and were waiting for him? That was ridiculous. They didn't want him, they didn't even know about him, or that he was married to Nicole. Or did they? By now, they might have found out . . . He noticed that passengers were periodically being taken out of line and led away. For what? Security checks? Frisking? Maybe he wasn't paranoid, after all.

All during the flight he had fought to keep from giving in to panic, to prevent himself from picturing Nicole in the hands of the police. *My darling, my darling, don't let them hurt you,* he prayed over and over. He imagined her terror, what it must be like for her to be kept in a prison cell.

Luís told him Nicole had been abducted by armed men who forced their way into the main house in the middle of the night, after overcoming the guard in the gatehouse and cutting the telephone wires. They had taken her at gunpoint to an unknown destination. That was all the information Luís had.

I should never have left her here. They were wrong—all of them. I should have found a way to get her out when she was still free. *I may never see her again.* The thought sank in for the first time. *I really may never see her again.*

At last he reached the counter and handed his passport and landing card to the officer. The man examined his documents carefully, checking against a much-thumbed sheaf of papers secured with a clamp.

He looked up and pushed a buzzer on the side of the counter, asking Drew to step aside. What the hell was this all about? A policeman came to the counter, exchanged a few words with the official, and took the passport, motioning for Drew to follow him. *Christ! This is all I need now.*

He saw the soldiers, swaggering and insolent, in total control of the airport throng. This wasn't a screenplay with props and extras—this was reality. Who was he kidding about creating an international incident? Going to the President. What a joke! They could squash him like an insect. Who would prevent it?

I may never see Nicole again. . . .

Drew followed the policeman through a pair of frosted glass doors. They were in the customs area.

"Señor Tower?" asked a uniformed immigration officer.

"Yes."

The man pointed to his right, and Drew turned to see Clem Farquhar loping toward him across the enclosure.

"Hiya, babe!" Clem slapped him across the back and gave him a gringo version of the *abrazo*. Before Drew could ask any questions, Clem started fast-talking, "Got any checked baggage? No? Good, then we can get right over to the embassy. We're late. *Muchas gracias, comandante, muy amable.*"

"No importa," the officer responded, touching the visor of his hat.

Clem grasped Drew's elbow and propelled him through the customs toward the outer lobby.

"What the hell . . .?"

"Just keep walking. Try to look like you do this all the time." He glanced with disapproval at Drew's casual attire, a cord jacket and blue buttondown shirt without a tie. "I told them you were an American doctor, a big *especialista* coming to see my wife on a consultation. I'm surprised they fell for it, the way you're dressed."

"Well, at least they won't confuse me with the spooks."

In the car, Clem steered him away from any serious topic of conversation, with a cautionary nod in the direction of the driver. Along the highway, they passed convoys of military vehicles, many of them loaded with soldiers. Occasionally a building still bore the stenciled outline of Tupaq Amaru, one of a dynasty of Incan martyrs, whom Velasco had adopted as a symbol of his socialist reforms. As they approached Lima proper, at regular intervals military command posts had been established.

"They don't fool around, do they?" Drew murmured sotto voce.

"That's for sure."

In the darkness, the floodlit white limestone buildings of the city center, with their ornate Moorish balconies, seemed a frivolous touch behind the armored vehicles and helmeted troops in combat boots.

"Have you talked to Lucy Monaco? Is there any news of Nicole?" Drew asked the minute they were inside the doors of the embassy.

"Yes, Mrs. Monaco came to see me." Clem told him everything Lucy had explained about habeas corpus and the various efforts she was mounting on Nicole's behalf.

Impatient with talk, Drew interrupted. "Do they know where Nicole is? Has anyone made any efforts to see her?"

"Calm down, buddy," Clem urged him good-naturedly. "She's not in any of the Lima prisons. Monaco seems to have certain connections among the inmates. She says she hasn't been able to find out where they've taken Nicole, but she does know it was the PIP—the Investigative Police—and she thinks she's being held in one of their secret detention centers. That's bad news. Now that there's a state of emergency, they can hold someone incommunicado up to fifteen days without officially charging them or allowing them to contact a lawyer."

"*Fifteen days!*" he was seized with panic. "She'll be dead by then! I've got to find her, Clem. I've got to get her out of there!"

Clem was sitting behind the desk. "Yeah?" He leaned forward on his elbow, his hand squeezing his lower lip, his forehead raised in skepticism. "Who do you think you are, Drew?"

"I'm her husband."

Clem had purposely taken an embassy car. He drove slowly through the darkened streets. It was after eleven and he didn't want any armed patrols firing at them for breaking curfew.

This was the first time in his three years in this post that he had been involved in anything approaching a cloak-and-dagger incident. It might make a good story someday, if everything worked out all right.

Drew married to the daughter of Daniel Légende. Was that unbelievable?

Clem remembered when he had taken up his new assignment in Peru at the beginning of '73. One of his first and lasting impressions of the continuing importance of wealth in Lima society, even in the era of the socialist

junta, was the prominence given by the various media to
Légende's illness and subsequent death.

Légende had always been a name he'd known, the way
he knew Chanel or Lancôme. It was only when he came
to Lima that he had learned of the French company's
Peruvian connection.

"There's not much more I can do to help you, buddy,"
he told Drew as they headed toward Miraflores. "I wish
there were. I can only issue a visa on a valid passport,
Peruvian or other. It takes time to apply for citizenship
on the basis of marital relationship."

Clem's hands were tied by regulations and he didn't
have enough clout to push something through and answer
for it later. He was almost ready for reassignment, so he
didn't mind taking some risks. But there was no way he
could grant Nicole a U.S. passport. He wouldn't tell
Drew, but if the Peruvian government considered that
this arrest established a criminal record, it would compli-
cate matters even further.

They passed half a dozen checkpoints along the way
but were stopped only twice. Clem showed his diplomatic
ID, explaining that Drew was a visiting physician who
had come to see an American taken seriously ill. The
soldiers glanced at Drew's passport and waved them on.
Drew noticed one young private cross himself. Someone
must be pretty sick if a gringo doctor comes all the way
to Lima in the middle of an *estado del sitio*, driving
through the city after curfew in order to tend to him.

As Clem talked, Drew's mind was elsewhere. His eyes
held a penetrating, fearful hurt. He had a flash of remembrance of what it was like to hold a death watch at
the bedside of the one he loved. Momentarily, there was
a hospital smell and the scent of roses in his nostrils. He
closed his eyes, thinking he would be sick.

Where was she? What was being done to her? His
longing for her to be safe, his need to hold her close and
protect her from harm, were so overpowering they took
his breath away. Tears stung his eyes as he contemplated
a life without her. She couldn't be dead! She was so
much a part of him that if she were dead, surely he would
know it. Something within him would also have died.

He turned his head and realized they were nearing the
garden suburbs. "Take the shore road," he directed Clem.

"I have a key to the back entrance. The police may be keeping a watch on the front gate."

In the dark, it was difficult to find the unmarked lane leading to Casa Loma. They made two wrong turns and had to go back. Clem was remarkably patient, but Drew could tell he was edgy. About to give up and tell him to drive to the main gate, he caught sight of a large boulder he remembered as a landmark.

"Here it is, Clem. I'm certain I'm right this time."

The unpaved alley came to a dead end. In front of them was the bank of hedges screening the entrance.

Drew turned to Clem. "I'll go alone from here. Wait a couple of minutes, and if I don't come out, it means someone has let me in."

"Are you sure I shouldn't come with you? What if the police are there?"

"Lucy would have mentioned it to you or Luís if they were. I'll be okay."

"I'll come over tomorrow morning. You have my home number if you need me." He put out his hand. "Good luck, Drew."

"Thanks, Clem . . . for everything."

Carrying his bag by the shoulder strap, he stepped behind the first clump of hedges. It was black as Hades under the trees, without moonlight. The unpleasant damp of the winter mist was a surprise to him. It had been dry and balmy when he was in Lima seven weeks ago. Was it only seven weeks? It seemed an eternity.

He felt his way along the hedges until he came to the sharp turn, then walked with his hand out in front of him like a blind man. The hedge ended and he could see the outline of the high wall and the dim reflection of lights from the back court of the house.

Good. Lights meant there was someone there, probably Vera. He hoped she would not be alarmed by the ringing of the bell at this hour. Of course, this wasn't late for Peru. It was just past dinner hour in Latin countries.

He felt for the key in his pocket. Luckily, he had a small pocket flashlight. It had been a stocking gift from one of the family last Christmas. He put down his bag and shined the beam of the light on the gate, searching for the lock.

There it was. He remembered it was a little hard to

turn. His hand was trembling as he inserted the key. It hit the edge and missed, falling on the ground with a ping.

Goddamit! Get a grip on yourself, Tower. You're losing it.

He shined the flashlight on the ground to the right, where he had heard the key land. It wasn't a strong light. He stooped, holding it close to the earth and slowly rotating it. If he couldn't find the key, he would climb over the gate.

The light caught the sheen of metal. There it was!

He picked up the key, being extremely careful this time to place it securely in the lock. There was resistance for an instant, then the lock released as he jiggled it.

The gate swung open with a grating sound. He moved his bag to the inside and closed the gate again, locking it.

He realized he was in a cold sweat. Shivering slightly, he returned the key to his pocket and bent to pick up his carry-on bag.

As he straightened up, he was jammed painfully in the neck by a cold metal object.

"Don't move, or you're dead," said a voice in Spanish.

Chapter 41

When Nicole entered that room and saw Manuel standing next to the commandant of the Lurigancho prison, it was as if the final piece of a puzzle had fallen into place. It was almost a relief, to know at last.

He registered no emotion when she was thrust before him. She swayed, feeling faint again. It was the warden who stepped forward to support her, putting her in a chair.

Her ears were ringing and there were bright spots before her eyes. As if they were suspended above her, she heard what they said.

"Is this the woman, señor?" the commandant asked Manuel.

"Yes, *comandante*, this is the woman," he answered tonelessly.

"Very well. Please sign here that she has been given over to your custody."

Nicole heard the scraping of a pen. Someone took her arm firmly, lifting her from the chair. Her body was like a limp bundle. Ungentle hands supported her, almost carrying her from the room.

In a daze, she allowed herself to be taken from the building to a yard where the battered gray Dodge was waiting. Sodium lamps illuminated the area.

It did not surprise her when Fabricio sprang out of the automobile and held open the rear door. His stocky figure swam before her eyes. Turning her head, she looked up into Manuel's austere face. It was odd how she noticed insignificant details, like the twitching of the muscle in the hollow of his left cheek.

He put her into the gray car, seating himself beside her. Fabricio shut the door and took the wheel, driving out of the prison yard without a word, knowing without being told where to go.

Her head drooped, too heavy for the stem of her neck. She tried to lift it, but she had no strength. "It was *you,*" she whispered, her voice ragged, hardly able to force the words out. "All along . . . it was you."

She heard a torn, strangled, animal moan and managed to move her eyes in his direction. He shook his head from side to side, his ruined face streaked with tears, his mouth working.

Pulling her against his chest, he laid his sorrowing cheek against her shorn head. *"My God! I let this happen to you. I promised . . . I promised I would take care of you. I let this happen."*

Her eyes were not focusing when they reached the gates of Casa Loma. They carried her into the house, up the stairs to her room, and laid her on the bed. They dimmed the light because it pained her eyes.

Strong arms were around her and someone patiently spooned warm milk with sugar and salty broth into her mouth. She drank and drank with insatiable greediness as the cup was put to her trembling lips. Keeping her eyes closed, she lay back on soft pillows, shivering and breathing shallowly because of the pain in her chest and ribs.

She was vaguely aware that Vera was there, and later Lucy and Jorge Alvares. And that she had made a terrible, an unforgivable mistake . . . but she could not remember what it was.

Gentle fingers probed her face and chest. There was the burning stab of an injection. And that was the last of her awareness.

Nicole came awake slowly, lured by a sense of deliverance.

The aroma of coffee was like ambrosia. Vera had wheeled in a table with soft foods—stewed apples, poached chicken, rice, milk toast, blanc mange, and the ubiquitous coffee.

She stretched in the bed, wincing with each separate aching part of her body. Raising her hands, she contemplated burn marks where the ropes had bound her wrists. Memories entrenched on her reverie as she realized why she was in bed and all that had happened.

"Vera. . . ."

"Oh, señorita!" Vera came to the bed and embraced

her. "I'm so thankful you're alive. I have made many novenas for your safe return." Tears of happiness shone in the woman's eyes.

"Thank you, Vera. I—I'm really here. I don't even know what day it is."

"It's Saturday—and you've slept half the day away," said a voice from the doorway.

Nicole turned to see Lucy leaning against the door-jamb, a huge smile on her face.

"Lucy! I'm so glad to see you."

"*You're* glad to see *me!* I haven't been anywhere." She came to the bed and hugged Nicole gingerly, then turned to the table of food and helped Vera wheel it to the bedside. "I've been waiting all morning for you to wake up."

Lucy drew up a chair while Vera prepared a plate for Nicole. They watched approvingly as she devoured the food. She swallowed, thinking it was the most delicious meal she had ever tasted. With every mouthful, strength flowed into her, seeping through her veins.

While she ate, Lucy questioned her. Nicole repeated the outrageous accusations of the PIP captain.

Lucy told her she had learned that the government was preparing a case against her, intending to charge Nicole with forming a band of three or more to support terrorism by acquiring and storing medical supplies for subversive organizations. They were collecting testimony and trying to get witnesses. Although it had been obvious all along that Nicole was under suspicion, the critical danger of her situation had become apparent only during the few days since she had been abducted by the PIP.

"It's not arrest when they don't charge you," stated Lucy emphatically. "It's kidnapping, and in civilized societies it's illegal. I'd give anything to prosecute the bastards who took you away."

"You'd never get a judgment order," Nicole answered quietly. "After what I saw and heard, I know that justice in Peru is a pretense, a charade."

"When you're ready, I want to hear," Lucy said gently. "But only if you want to talk about it."

Nicole regarded her for a moment. "I don't mind telling you everything—or anyone else, for that matter. I was lucky, Lucy. Much luckier than some of the others

who were in that place. It was far from pleasant, but I
wasn't raped or tortured. What you see is what they
did—the hair, the face, a few body bruises."

"You *have* got a fat lip and a shiner," grinned Lucy,
obviously relieved.

Vera had returned for the food cart and was listening
fearfully, her hands twisting her serving apron. She burst
into tears.

"Why, Vera! What is it? I'm all right, I told you."

"Your *hair*, Señorita Nicole! Your beautiful, beautiful
hair."

For once, Nicole had no choice but to lie back and let
others take charge. She dozed, periodically waking to eat
the frequent light meals Vera brought on a tray. Lucy
was making the decisions and Vera was caring for her
like a nurse for a child. They told her that while she
slept, tranquilized by the powerful sedative Jorge Alvares
had administered, he had examined her for broken bones
and lacerations. Vera had sponged her body and applied
compresses to her battered face, hence some of the swelling had receded, although the welts and bruises remained.

By evening she was ready to leave her bed.

"A bath, Vera! I've been *dreaming* of a bath. I bet I
have lice." Vera recoiled in horror. Soon she had prepared the tub and shampooed the butchered hair.

"You always wanted to cut my hair," teased Nicole,
holding up the uneven ends. "Now's your chance."

An hour later, she appeared in a dressing gown, her
hair softly waved around her face.

"Very becoming," approved Lucy. "It's a whole new
you."

"In more ways than one," answered Nicole significantly.

As soon as Vera closed the door, leaving them alone,
Lucy said, "I must talk to you, Nicole. I got a call
through to Luís Ribera this afternoon. He told me Drew
is coming to Lima."

"Oh Lucy!" She hardly dared to believe it. "That's all
I've been thinking of. When?"

"Dr. Ribera didn't know. It's a bit of a problem. While
you've been kept in detention, we've had a state of
emergency. The airports are closed, and there's a strict
curfew. Drew's already left home, but it will take him
days to reach Lima."

"Drew will find a way. I hope he doesn't take any chances, though. If only he knew I'm all right."

"He'll be that much more relieved when he gets here."

"Lucy, I have to ask you about Manuel. He . . . he came for me, didn't he?"

"Yes. At great personal risk, too. I called him. He knows everyone, and he managed to find out who had you. I can't imagine what he had to do to get you out. Sold his soul, I bet. You knew he was a leader of the secret democratic opposition, didn't you?"

Nicole gasped. "No! I didn't know."

"Well, evidently everyone may know soon, because there's been a shakeup in the government and some of the ministers involved have had to flee the country. If Manuel's part in it is revealed, he'll have to get out too—or go to jail."

Nicole couldn't believe what Lucy went on to tell her about Manuel's efforts to mount a campaign for a constitutional assembly and elections. She remembered Manuel's stock reply, his voice full of boredom and lassitude whenever she went on one of her rampages about the social injustices in Peru.

"You know I'm not a political man, Nicole," he would drawl. "I try to steer away from all that."

Manuel a leader of the opposition? Her offense was even worse than she had imagined.

"There's something awful I have to confess, Lucy. I don't know how to begin to tell you."

Lucy gave her a long steady look. "Just tell me. That's the best way."

She explained her suspicions about Manuel to Lucy, who sat listening, incredulous.

"I'm so ashamed. He knows what I thought, too. I *told* him. That's the last thing I remember saying before I became a zombie. I doubt that he'll ever want to see me again."

Lucy shook her head, laughing. "Not likely, love. He's sitting downstairs waiting for you to appear."

"Manuel? Here in the house?"

"Absolutely. He says he won't let you stay here without a man ever again."

"Oh, no! What will I say to him?"

"I think it's time you made a clean breast of it, don't you?"

*   *   *

She found Manuel in the study exactly where she expected him to be. Even before she entered the room, she could picture him sitting in the leather club chair near the desk, where her father had liked to read. Manuel's dreams of marrying her had always been an amalgam of love and a wish to fill Daniel's place. He may not have understood it himself, Nicole thought, but she felt it was the basis of his devotion for her.

The hurt in his gray eyes was almost more than she could bear. She went to his side and knelt there, taking his hands in hers. He looked down at her, attempting to smile.

"Are you feeling better?" he asked.

She nodded. "Oh, Manuel . . . I'm so sorry," she whispered. "I've done you such an injustice. How can you ever forgive me?"

He touched her hair gently. "There's nothing to forgive, little one."

"But there is! Lucy told me about you, about what you're trying to do to help bring back democracy in Peru. I was so wrong about you. How could I ever have doubted your sincerity, your goodness?"

"I set up a smoke screen to protect myself—and you. What you didn't know you couldn't reveal."

"I should have realized you couldn't betray me. It was just that—you always seemed to know everything about me—and then one day I saw Fabricio getting in your car after he'd left me. It seemed so sinister, and I came to my own conclusion."

He laughed softly. "You weren't entirely wrong, Nicole. Fabricio was reporting to me. I had him watching you and telling me where you went for a long time, even before I sent him to be your bodyguard. I couldn't very well follow you myself, but I was worried about you because I heard you had aroused suspicion within the state security police, and I feared you were in danger."

"And now you're in danger. Lucy says you may have to leave the country."

"Possibly. Oddly enough, I haven't done anything illegal. But my advocacy for a new constitution has made me not too popular lately. The police would like to prove there's a conspiracy. A few of my friends have been arrested. In the process, I fear someone may have talked in order to save himself. In any case, it wouldn't hurt for me to take a vacation for awhile."

"I used to have hope for Peru, Manuel. After my experience of the past few days, I'm very pessimistic about the future."

"I still have hope," he said. "Compared to some other Latin governments, the junta has a fairly good record on human rights. But whenever you put guns in the hands of bullies, you're going to have abuses. Who else would take those police jobs except thugs—people who would be outside the law if they weren't in charge of enforcing it?"

"But the military is in power. How can you have hope?"

"They won't be forever. And when they're gone. . . . We're not a poor country, Nicole. Yes, there's poverty, terrible poverty. But Peru is rich in natural resources—copper, oil, forests, water power . . . and manpower.

"We're not overburdened with a huge military-industrial complex like the U.S. and Soviets. What we lack is a strong economy and a leadership committed to education and internal development. Our governments have been so busy trying to shore up their hold that too late they realized the sheer mass of the poor and the workers would overwhelm them. They sold out to foreign interests, no matter what the cost. Now we're paying the price.

"We've had an endlessly repeated cycle of political and economic failures, and it will go on until we have an *elected democratic government,* with a free hand to do what's best for all the people."

This was a new Manuel. Nicole had never seen him so fired with zeal. It sent a prideful thrill coursing through her.

"In a way, the generals have done us a favor," he said. "They've restructured Peru's economy forever. If we don't fall into the hands of the communists, I believe we'll make it. That's why I've been working to bring back a democratically elected administration—with free enterprise and safeguards to make sure we won't have the extremes of wealth and power we've always had in the past. But we must do this without violence."

Manuel clapped his hands together and laughed. "I
didn't mean to get off on a political lecture. I'm sorry."

"I love hearing you say those things, Manuel. You've
always treated me like a precocious child, you know. I
never suspected your true sympathies."

The lines of his cheeks softened and he looked at her
fondly. "Would it have made a difference in your feelings
if you had known, do you suppose?"

She shook her head. "No," she said regretfully.

"No," he repeated in a tone of finality. "I'm making
plans to take you out of Peru, Nicole. As soon as possible. I've got to get you away before they come to arrest
you. By tomorrow, if you're strong enough, we should
leave."

She looked at him aghast. "But I *can't!*"

"What do you mean, you can't? You must. I can't save
you again if they arrest you. The minister who interceded
stepped down today—he's run away himself!"

"I understand. But I can't leave until . . . until Drew
gets here. He's on his way."

He was very still. "Drew? Do you mean Andrew
Tower?"

"Yes."

"Nicole! We are talking about your life. What can this
man possibly mean to you, that you would risk everything by waiting here for him?"

She had to say it, she had to tell him! "He's my
husband, Manuel. We were married when he was here
. . . at Huaranca."

She saw his cheeks draw in as he struggled to control
his reaction. His eyelids blinked rapidly and he took a
sharp breath.

"I didn't realize . . ." He looked away.

"I would have told you, if I'd known everything, if I
had understood about you. I was afraid to. Lucy said the
hearing might go against me if they knew I'd been married to an American, and . . ."

"Yes. Yes, of course. You did the right thing." He
rose from the chair and put his hands in his pockets.
Taking a deep breath, he said, "Well. Then you must
wait for him. I shall wait here with you."

He walked out of the room.

*   *   *

Manuel paced the length of the library, noticing how his feet fit within the squares of the paneled Persian carpet. The dim spotlights shone on the glass cases filled with pre-Columbian artifacts whose faces seemed to stare back at him, timeless and patient, unaffected by the upheavals of the passing centuries.

What did he feel? After the first shock . . . nothing. It was strange. There was almost a release. He was free now. *Free of her!* For the first time in eight years, he would be able to act independently, without wondering how it would affect Nicole.

He had made a vow to Daniel, and he had endeavored to fulfill that commitment. There would be one last obligation to discharge. And then he would be truly and completely . . . *free*.

Lucy was about to leave. There was only an hour before curfew. "Horacio must wonder what's happened to me," she told Nicole. "I've been out of touch all day."

The telephone line had not yet been repaired, thus the house was cut off.

"I'll have Pedro drive you home," said Nicole. Just then the doorbell chimed. "I wonder who that can be at this hour."

They reached the front hall as Vera fearfully opened the door. It was Jorge Alvares.

"Professor Alvares!"

"Ah, Nicole, I'm so pleased to see you walking around," he said, looking distracted.

She thanked him for taking care of her, assuring him she was feeling fine. Why was he here, she wondered. It was so close to the curfew. "Won't you come sit down?" She led the way through the gallery.

"Is Manuel Caldeiro still here?" he asked abruptly.

"I believe so. Vera, where is Señor Caldeiro?" she called, shrugging her shoulders at Lucy behind Jorge's back.

"Here is Señor Caldeiro," announced a purposeful Manuel, emerging from the library.

"Ah, Manuel," Jorge looked greatly relieved. "May I have a word with you?"

"Of course, come in here." The two men went into the library and closed the door.

"You're going to be stuck here, Lucy," said Nicole. "It's almost ten o'clock."

"If you think I'm going to leave now, you're wrong! What do you suppose he's telling Manuel?"

"I don't know. I've never seen Dr. Alvares act in such a peculiar fashion. He's usually so polite, so correct."

"Well, I guess I'm just going to have to spend the night. Can Pedro go somewhere nearby and telephone Horacio so he knows I'm all right?"

"Of course."

The two women sat waiting in the study. Once the library door opened and Manuel rushed out shouting for Fabricio, who was in the kitchen with Pedro and Vera. Manuel took him and Pedro into the back courtyard and stood speaking for a few minutes, then came back in the house alone, returning to the study.

Nicole looked at Lucy speculatively. "Don't you just love mysteries?"

Vera came to ask about dinner for everyone. "Perhaps you'd better prepare a buffet, Vera, and set it up in the breakfast room. Then each of us can take something when it's convenient."

Manuel came into the study with Alvares. The two men looked grave.

Without preamble, Manuel said, "There's an informer at San Martín, Nicole. You must leave Peru by tomorrow, without fail. Professor Alvares will tell you about it."

Unable to believe what she was hearing, Nicole listened to Jorge Alvares's words.

"You have many friends, Nicole. Today they have come to me, to warn me on your behalf. You have been denounced by Mona Ramos. She has come forward and agreed to testify that she has witnessed you and two interns taking medicines and surgical equipment from the hospital. She accuses you, on numerous occasions late at night and early in the morning, of loading these supplies into a van that was driven away by strangers."

In this room, she thought, *my father sat and talked of the generals and warned that good ideas in the hands of bad men could result in evil. I'm glad he didn't live to hear these things.*

"Nicole . . . ?" Jorge prompted.

She sighed. "Who would believe her?"

"There are those who want to believe it, who will use any excuse to proclaim martial law and a license to make all-out war on subversives," Manuel answered.

"Then what's the use of resisting?" she asked, rising and heading toward the door.

"Nicole!" It was Lucy. "You must listen to them. You can't stay in Lima, you can't stay in Peru!"

"I'm not leaving until Drew arrives. If he comes for me and the police are here, he might do something reckless and get arrested. I can't take that chance." She turned and looked at Jorge. "I'm sorry to cause you distress. You're very kind to come warn me. I'm tired and I'm going to bed now."

They watched helplessly as she walked through the gallery to the front hall.

Jorge struck his head with his hands. "What shall we do? They'll arrest her. It may be only a matter of a day until they come for her!"

"I won't let that happen," said Manuel. "I'll take her away tomorrow, even if I have to use force."

"Shall I go talk to her?" asked Lucy.

"No, let her sleep. She'll need to be rested."

"I must get home," said Jorge.

"But it's after the curfew."

"I have a safe-conduct. I'm a physician and I paid a house call. Would you like me to drop you?" he asked Lucy.

"No, thanks. I'll stay. I may have to get some last minute instructions from Nicole, if we can convince her to go."

"What if they come tonight?" Jorge asked Manuel before taking his leave.

"My men are guarding the estate. They're well armed . . . and they'll shoot to kill."

Chapter 42

Not for years had she been overcome with one of these premonitions. Rosa had them often, seeing the end of the world in every earth tremor or rockfall that came thundering into the valley.

As a child, Nicole remembered believing that she had a personal spirit, an *apu*, that walked with her. If by some unfortunate circumstance they became separated, it would mean disaster.

Tonight, Nicole's spirit was not prepared to desert Casa Loma. She had the most intense intuitive feeling that if she went away from here without Drew, it would result in tragedy. She was resolved that nothing any of them said would convince her to go without him.

Lying awake, she knew that she would have to resist them.

"What time is it?" Lucy asked Manuel.

"Almost midnight. Would you like some more coffee?"

"No thanks. I won't be able to sleep."

She wouldn't sleep anyway, wondering whether a squad of military police might invade the compound that night. It wasn't likely, she thought. The ministries did not move that quickly. If only they did, Nicole's passport hearing would have been resolved long ago, before this dreadful turn of events.

They kept up a desultory conversation. Guest rooms had been prepared for them upstairs, but Manuel intended to remain on guard all night. Their plates contained food from the platters Vera had set out in the small dining room, but neither of them was hungry.

"You were at their wedding?" Manuel asked.

"Yes. She was the most beautiful bride I've ever seen. It was as if that church, everything there, was especially blessed. There was a *presence . . .*" Lucy stopped, seeing how he lowered his eyes and drew in his cheeks. "I'm sorry."

He looked up and smiled. "Don't be. I'll get over it, and God willing, she'll be happy." He lit a cigarette after asking if she minded. "Tell me, is he a good man?"

"Yes, Manuel," she said seriously. "He's extraordinary. You may not want to hear that, but I think you should know."

"You're wrong, Lucy. That's *exactly* what I wanted to hear."

Lucy admired Manuel. He was brave and honorable. But he was finding it difficult to accept what was happening to him, to adjust to his loss of influence. Manuel was playing a high stakes game, and he did not like to lose. To him and Nicole, both children of privilege, their fall from the pinnacle was a terrible blow.

For Lucy it was different. For years she had known the terror of friends and clients whose lives were under constant threat from the police. The jails of Lima, the excesses of the security police, were familiar to her. She lived with the constant fear that Horacio would break out of his self-imposed censorship, causing his deportation or disappearance. He restrained himself for her sake and for their children—Francisco and the unborn baby. But for how long?

"When will you leave?" she asked Manuel.

"Before dawn. The moment the curfew is lifted."

"Nicole won't go without Drew."

"She won't have a choice, Lucy. It's all arranged."

"I'm going to miss her," she sighed.

"Yes." He looked off for a moment. "So shall I," he said, almost to himself.

Lucy's head lifted abruptly. "What was that? I thought I heard something . . ."

Manuel put out his hand to quiet her. He sat very still, listening through the silence.

Suddenly there was a loud report, like a gunshot, followed by a commotion in the rear of the house. They heard shouts and then Vera in the kitchen, speaking in an agitated voice.

"Get in the library behind the sofa and stay there," commanded Manuel. He ran from the room.

Manuel moved stealthily along the wall of the darkened pantry, wishing he had a weapon. Obviously something had gone wrong. There was no doubt the noise they had heard was the firing of a gun. He peered through the crack of the partially open door into the kitchen.

Vera was standing transfixed in the doorway leading to the back entry. Hands at her mouth, she babbled in a patois of Quechua and street Spanish, forgetting her lady's maid parlance.

"*Ay Dios! Chino*, what have you done? *Madre!* Look at him! Bring him in."

Manuel saw Andrew Tower, dazed and disheveled, stumble into the kitchen. His tan slacks were blackened, and one sleeve of his soiled cord jacket hung torn from the shoulder. Fabricio, whose face was scratched and bloody, held the barrel of an automatic at his back.

"Good God . . . *Tower!* What happened?" Manuel stepped from behind the door. "It's all right, Fabricio. Let him go."

"What happened? This gorilla threatened to blow my head off with that thing! He damn near succeeded, too."

Greatly offended, Fabricio laid the gun aside. "Señor!" he said reprovingly. He wiped his face gingerly with a handkerchief, looking at the blood.

"*Lo siento*," Drew apologized.

"We owe *you* an apology," said Manuel. "The house is surrounded by my men. I didn't expect you to come unannounced at this hour."

"Where is she?" he demanded of Manuel.

"Don't worry, she's here. She's all right."

Drew's eyes closed in relief. He moved toward the door.

Manuel grasped his arm. "Come in here first. We've got to talk." He led the way to the study.

Drew immediately began to ply him with questions. Manuel interrupted. "There's time for all that later." He put out his hand. "First, let me say I know about your marriage. My congratulations."

Drew shook hands warily. He had no reason to trust Manuel Caldeiro.

"We have an urgent situation on our hands," Manuel began. Briefly he explained to Drew what Jorge Alvares had reported about the nurse who had denounced Nicole. "There's no point in saying she has no proof, Andrew. It's a very serious matter. The police want to win this case and they would probably succeed. We must get Nicole out of Peru immediately. I have a plan. . . ."

Manuel spoke with the authority of a man in charge. Drew sat forward, following every word.

"I won't tell you it isn't dangerous," Manuel concluded, when he had described the arrangements. "There are great risks. But it's the only way."

Drew studied the long aquiline features, a *criollo* face, sensitive and cultured. "I believe you."

Manuel exhaled and smiled. Impetuously, he grasped Drew around the shoulders.

"And now," he said, with a gallant toss of his head, "your wife is waiting. Go to her!"

All was still in the upper hall. The thick carpets silenced his footsteps. There were the clean, domestic odors of cedar, lavender, and lemon oil, and the promise of restful comfort in the softly lit bedrooms that stood open and readied, their carved bedsteads mounded with plump downy pillows. The peace of these surroundings was a beguiling deception.

Quietly, he opened the door to Nicole's suite. She had left a lamp burning low in a far corner. His heart contracted when he thought of the terror that had invaded this room in the night.

Bending over the bed, he lifted the hand that lay limp on the comforter. As he pressed his lips to the dark red rope burns, sadness welled within him, and anger. His hands reached out to hover over the bruised face. What hellish wrath could compel someone to do this? What was the monstrous nature of a man who could bear to inflict such pain, to mar her beauty?

Her eyes opened, shining and unsurprised. "You're here," she whispered. "I *knew* you'd come in time." She reached out for him.

His heart was shaking. He held her in his arms, filled with impossible love. Softly, so he wouldn't hurt her, he began to touch and kiss her brow and cheeks and the damaged lips, examining each mark, feeling the pain of the blows that had caused them.

I could kill! I could take the lives of those who did this to her! He could not believe himself. He, who did not accept violence, ached to get his hands on her tormentors. He thought he had known himself, but his rage boiled and frightened him.

"How could they do this to you?" he asked over and over, his voice trembling. "What else did they do?"

"Nothing, darling. Nothing more. I'm fine, really," she assured him. "You must believe me." She stroked his forehead and cheeks and rubbed her fingers over his lips and chin, trying to erase the angry tensing of the muscles.

For a long time they held each other, not saying anything, feeling the healing solace of being together.

Drew's hand idly stroked her hair. "He cut it off," Nicole said sadly. "Your magic . . . it's gone."

Looking deep into her eyes, he shook his head. "The magic is us."

They were grateful for the *garua*. The winter mist that obscured the sunlight and blanketed the coastal region in the early hours provided protection for them.

They had slipped through the back gate of Casa Loma an hour before the curfew ended, because Manuel wanted to be on the road to the mountains by the time morning came. It was Sunday, and he feared the lack of commercial traffic would make it easier for the police to track them.

They drove along the Pacific, then cut inland south of Chorrillos, skirting Lima and avoiding the main roads. The landscape was dismal, dry desert with clusters of *pueblos jóvenes* inhabited by workers employed by the foreign companies whose plants were enclosed within fenced, guarded compounds along the fringe of urban sprawl.

Near Vitarte they picked up the old road along the Rímac River, diverting whenever they approached a *contról*. In this circuitous fashion, it took twice as long to reach Chosica. Fabricio was driving the same antiquated gray Dodge, however its motor was in better condition than the exterior would indicate. Winding through the brown foothills, they left the highway and came to a small secluded villa.

"Where are we?" asked Nicole, when the automobile halted inside a walled enclosure next to a military vehicle.

"This is the house of a friend of mine," Manuel answered hesitantly.

The moment the handsome, full-figured woman appeared at the door, Nicole knew this was Elena Quesada. Nicole saw warmth, curiosity, and fear in the large Goya eyes, as Elena extended both hands in welcome. With her finger, she traced the purple contusions on Nicole's face. "I have something for that. It will heal quickly," she said in a mellifluous voice.

She adores him, Nicole thought as she watched Manuel greet Elena. His eyes met hers briefly, with a reserved tenderness.

"Come refresh yourselves before the journey," she invited them.

"For only a few minutes," answered Manuel. "We have a long way to go."

A maid served fruit, coffee, and rolls to them, while Elena applied an herbal poultice to Nicole's bruises. "Keep this on all day," she instructed. She gave Nicole more of the preparation in a jar.

"Thank you, Elena. What is it?"

"I don't know the secret. I get it from the Indians."

Manuel hurried them, saying they were driving into the mountains and he wanted to reach the divide before nightfall.

At the door the two women embraced. Nicole thanked her and Elena smiled at her and responded, "Good luck. I know you'll come back someday."

As she walked down the steep, curving steps to the cobblestoned courtyard, Nicole heard Manuel's voice above saying goodbye to Elena. She glanced up in time to see the woman clasp her arms around his neck, her eyes closed, heartbreak on her lovely Maja face. "God keep you," she told him in an anguished voice. Then she quickly turned and went into the house.

It was a long journey. They had switched to the army jeep, which was better suited to the sierra winter. They drove all day, stopping twice for Fabricio to pour gasoline into the tank. Nicole leaned against Drew's shoulder, eyes closed, trying to ignore the aching of her head and the pain in her joints each time they were jarred by the rough surface of the road.

She could not believe that she was really leaving Peru. The final two hours at Casa Loma had been traumatic. She had sat with Lucy, raising last-minute questions about her affairs. Lucy reminded her that everything had been inventoried, that this was the day they had planned for, but somehow Nicole had never envisioned it like this. She had never thought of running away. She had pictured herself, in possession of her Peruvian passport, leaving in an orderly fashion, thinking it would be an extended trip abroad, not a flight for refuge.

"If I have a buyer for Casa Loma, I'll let you know immediately," Lucy said. She thought it likely that one of the embassies would want to purchase the estate, perhaps with the furnishings.

"I'll see what I can arrange about shipping the items you want, and I'll contact the museums about the antiques and art that can't leave the country." Nicole had nodded, willing to let Lucy make those decisions.

When they were almost ready to leave, Lucy handed her a traveling case. "Vera has packed your jewels, Nicole." Nicole protested that of all things to think of, that seemed frivolous. "No it isn't!" Lucy answered sharply. "They won't let many things go, and you should have your jewelry—the things that belonged to your mother, and your father's gifts to you."

She held up a large manila envelope before slipping it into the case. "In here are notarized copies of your birth certificate and your marriage certificate. And your new French passport."

Nicole's mouth fell open. "French passport! How did you manage to get it?"

"It wasn't too difficult. You'll need a passport to get into the United States. If you remember, you filled out the papers a while ago. When you were arrested, I figured you'd have to get out fast. I know someone at the French consulate who owes me a favor."

Lucy and her contacts!

"I wanted to be here when your baby was born," Nicole said, putting her arms around Lucy, tears starting. "Oh, Lucy, when will we see each other again? I've never had such a dear friend."

"We'll always be friends. Before you know it, I'll bring the entire family up for a long visit," she had answered with a game smile, pushing Nicole toward Drew.

Vera cried when they said goodbye. She would stay on, along with Pedro, as well as the gardener and the gatekeeper, to care for the property until it was sold.

Before they drove away, Lucy's final words had been, "I'm wracking my legal brain to figure out a way to get a judgment against Mona Ramos for defamation of character!"

As they approached the divide, Drew wrapped a blanket around her. It was freezing at sixteen thousand feet, driving over the pass. Each of them, except Fabricio, sniffed from the small tank of oxygen in the jeep, experiencing the high altitude headache and dizziness of *soroche*. By the time they reached the *puna* the rugged plateau barren of trees, it was completely dark and it was snowing.

Before Cerro de Pasco, they turned onto a treacherous, unpaved road and came at last to a cluster of deserted buildings that had once been the site of a silver mine. This was the end of their journey.

Nicole was in that twilight distance between sleep and wakefulness. She was weighted with dread, afraid of what she would encounter, yet knowing she must emerge. Before she opened her eyes, she heard the sound of men speaking in low, conspiratorial tones.

"I think you should be the one to tell her, Manuel."

It was Drew's voice, and with the fresh realization that he was here with her, she stirred and came awake eagerly, throwing off the sleep-induced depression.

They were in a shack that had been the office for the mining operation. A kerosene lamp threw large shadows against the planked walls. It was so cold that she could see the vapor of her breath. Manuel and Drew were seated at a table near the iron stove, drinking coffee. They were wearing heavy jackets and held the steaming cups to warm their hands. Manuel chain-smoked, using the metal lid from a jar as an ash tray. The thin air was fetid with smoke.

They noticed she was awake. She stretched and sat up

on the cot, throwing back the blankets and straightening her rumpled clothing.

"You slept for almost three hours." Drew smiled at her, constrained by Manuel's presence. They were unaccustomed to acting like husband and wife in front of other people.

"Have some coffee, Nicole," said Manuel, his eyes avoiding hers. "There are some sandwiches left."

What's bothering him, she wondered. "I'm not hungry, Manuel. I'll just have coffee."

"You should eat something. It will be a long day."

"Maybe later." Actually, she couldn't have eaten anything because her stomach was fluttering. Shivering and drawing her jacket around her, she took the mug of coffee, stirring sugar into the strong brew. "What time is it?"

"It's almost four. It should be light enough in another hour. The pilot must be able to take visual sightings because he flies in the valleys between the mountains—to avoid radar."

"Well," she said, "we're halfway there."

The men did not respond. Were they as nervous as she? They were behaving oddly; they seemed so quiet. Why? They probably had not slept, and of course, they were worried. The flight would be dangerous and there was the constant possibility they would be forced down and apprehended enroute or at the border.

But there was something more, something they were not telling her.

"Has anything gone wrong?" she asked.

"No. Everything's proceeding as planned," Manuel answered.

Drew stood up. "I'll be back," he said, and walked outside.

She smiled at Manuel. "He's edgy. I can understand that. Until a few days ago he was drinking coffee in his lab on Spruce Street."

Manuel nodded. "Soon it will be over and you'll be there on Spruce Street with him."

"Have you talked with Drew about your plans, Manuel? Not that you need his help—you know so many people in the States. But you'll want to do something to occupy yourself until it's safe for you to come back to Peru."

The door opened and the young mechanic said, "Raoul says he will be ready in twenty minutes, señor. Their bags are on board, and the truck is waiting as you requested. I put your things in the rear compartment."

Manuel thanked him.

Nicole spun around as the mechanic left. "What truck, Manuel? What is he talking about, putting your things in a truck?" Her heart began to thud.

Manuel came to her and took her face between his hands. "I'm not going with you, little one. We must say goodbye now, Nicole."

"*No!* You *must* come with us. We won't go without you."

Manuel shook his head, eyes blinking. "I have to stay here, *querida.* There's work for me to do. Peru won't always be like this."

"But not now. You could be arrested, put in jail," she protested.

"First they'll have to find me! I think I shall disappear for a brief period, until this latest emergency blows over."

He laughed, his teeth flashing in the light of the flickering lamp, and she felt the warmth and generosity of his spirit. She noted the lines that had formed in his face, at the corners of his eyes, and across the forehead. The gray hair at his temples was even more pronounced. When had that happened? These past few years had aged him. Her heart ached with compassion and guilt. *Manuel.* Her friend, her protector.

"I don't want to leave you, Manuel. You . . . you . . ." But she couldn't go on.

"I never thought I'd see you shed tears for me, Nicole," he said gently. With his thumb he brushed them away. He kissed her forehead. "Thank you for the joy of knowing you. Be happy, little one. You have a man worthy of you."

Drew opened the door and came into the shack. He glanced from one to the other. "You've told her?" Manuel nodded.

Nicole went to Drew's side. "Can't you convince him to join us?" she pleaded.

"I've been trying for hours, darling. I thought you might have more influence."

Manuel put his hand on Drew's shoulder. "My only reason for leaving Peru was to take Nicole to safety. I promised my friend Daniel that I would take care of his daughter. I entrust you with her now." He clasped Drew in an *abrazo*. "Come, it's time to go."

The outline of jagged peaks stood against the paling sky when they emerged from the abandoned mine office. A twin-motor Piper Navajo had been moved from a shed and waited on the snowy tarmac, guarded by two sentries. Off to the side were parked an army truck and the jeep.

Nicole spoke to Fabricio, telling him goodbye and apologizing once again for the way she had doubted him, dismissing him in anger. "You couldn't have known, señora, and that means I did my job well," he replied. "Go with God."

The pilot approached Manuel. "I think we must leave without delay. It's just the right timing to pass into Ecuador when the border patrol is having siesta." He grinned, displaying even white teeth. He was deferential to Manuel, despite his cocky aviator's air.

"Good. I want to know the minute they're across, Raoul."

"Yes sir. Señor, señora—if you will come now."

Under the wing, Nicole put her arms around Manuel. He held her against his chest with fierce emotion. "Goodbye, my sweet Nicole. God be with you." She buried her face on his shoulder. Gently he disengaged her arms and put her into the plane.

Drew grasped Manuel's hand. "How can we ever thank you, Manuel?"

"You already have, my friend. Watch over her with care. She may not seem to need anyone, but you know her."

Manuel stood on the edge of the improvised runway as the small plane sped past and became airborne. Nicole leaned her forehead against the window pane, watching him wave, until his figure was blurred by her tears.

She felt the comfort of Drew's arm around her. "Do you think we'll ever see him again?" she asked.

"I hope so, darling—I hope so."
"It's my country, Drew. *My country!*"

As the rising sun burst over the Cordillera Blanca, the shadow of the plane fell on the canyon where Daniel Légende had been found thirty-seven years before, by the *campesinos* from Huaranca.

EPILOGUE

*Flowers of
the Wind*

In the summer of 1978, Carlos entered his home in the high sierra to discover the cruelly mutilated bodies of his wife and infant daughter. A villager told him that government counterinsurgency soldiers had destroyed his clinic and committed the atrocities.

After burying his family, Carlos was beyond grief or despondency. He wanted revenge.

For weeks he wandered in the mountains, seeking to make contact with one of the elusive bands of guerrillas who hide in the Andes planning the revolution. One morning he awoke surrounded by a circle of armed men. They led him blindfolded through impossible terrain to the hideout of their commander. When they removed the blindfold, Carlos was standing in a hut in the presence of a gray-haired man.

The man was Maestro Gordo.

In September 1978, Nicole and Drew moved from Philadelphia to New York where Drew became an associate professor at the Rockefeller University and Nicole was appointed Director of Medical Affairs for UNICEF, the United Nations Children's Fund.

Vera came from Lima to live with them in their townhouse on Beekman Place to help care for their children, Danielle and John.

In December 1979 in Geneva—two years after Ali Maow Maalin, a cook from Somali, became the last person on earth to contract smallpox by natural means—the Final Report of the Global Commission for the Certification of Smallpox Eradication was issued by the World Health Organization. Target Zero had been reached.

The world was free of smallpox.

*   *   *

In May 1980 Peru, for a second time, elected Fernando Belaúnde Terry President of the new constitutional democracy. Manuel Caldeiro-León was named to a post high in the Ministry of Finance.

In February 1981, as he was leaving the Odría Pavilion of San Martín University Hospital where he had visited his wife Elena and their newborn son, Manuel was gunned down by terrorists.

Also killed in the resulting crossfire were his bodyguard Fabricio and one of the assassins, later identified as Carlos.

The following April, in the valley of the flamesword, the hacienda received some visitors.

On a bright morning, a man and woman emerged from the manor house. The man carried a small sturdy boy on his shoulders and in her arms the woman held another boy, an infant. Between them skipped a raven-haired girl of unusual beauty, her limbs beginning to elongate in graceful lines.

They walked across the sunlit fields of the hacienda toward a fenced-in garden where rows of simple headstones cluster in comforting proximity. The woman pointed to the names on the gravestones, and the children placed flowers in front of each marker. Then the woman stooped to gather some stones, adding them to a scree that stands beneath a manzanita. With a last glance over her shoulder, she joined the man and children who were walking hand-in-hand toward the place where the valley narrows.

When they reached the ravine, they climbed an embankment until they came through the passage to a broad meadow, which was a spectacle of deep crimson.

The man and woman seated themselves on a rock, holding the baby between them, while the boy and girl ran in circles in the tall grass until they dropped laughing into the soft greenness and lay there dreaming.

Suddenly the girl sat up, lifting her head. She kept very still as the others watched. The woman turned to the man and he smiled reassuringly, placing his arm around her shoulders.

There was a stirring from the surrounding hills.

Silently, the first scarlet blossoms of the flameswords

were lifted from their stalks by the gentle wind. Aimlessly they floated, like restless birds. Then, caught by a stronger gust, they were carried across the meadow to the bottom of the valley, where they fell to earth in the loamy soil of Flor del Viento.